forgive us our Trespasses

M.L. STEINBRUNN

Catherine!

Thank you for the support, congratulations on winning; I hope you enjoy the book!

M.L.Steinbrunn —xoxo—

Contents

Dedication

For my husband and children. You have been my moon and stars who have guided me on this fantastic journey.

For my mother. She was both a mother and a father to our little family and I'm so grateful for the courage she had to take on that daunting task. I am a better mother today because of her powerful example. She was my inspiration for Vivian, and she will always be my compass.

Prologue

1990

"Please, Daddy, don't go. Your favorite show is on tonight; we could pop popcorn and all watch together."

Pushing his blonde shaggy hair out of his face, my father puts his overnight bag on the floor and crouches down beside me. "Oh, Princess, I can't tonight. I have to get everything ready for the grand opening tomorrow, but I promise we will have some special time once the new store opens."

"Okay, but I get to pick the show."

"Deal," he says, pulling me into his lap and then standing with me. "After school tomorrow your momma is bringing you to the new store for the party. When it's all over, we will come home and veg out with snacks and Disney movies. Amanda and Charlotte can help build the fort."

"No way, Manda's too little; she always pulls down the blankets."

"Well, we'll figure out some job for her." He kisses my cheek, scratching me with his stubble, making me giggle and I pull away. "Love you, Princess. You have a good day at school tomorrow, and I'll see you tomorrow evening."

He puts me down on my feet and steps away to give my sisters and my mom a kiss before stepping out the door.

I'm restless the rest of the evening, picking out the best blankets and selecting a variety of movies that we could all agree upon for father/daughter night. My dress for the grand opening is already laid out, as are my school clothes for the next day. So, I toss and turn, hoping the sun will come up and the day can begin.

My dad is not home often, so these special nights are few and far between. But he always keeps his promises, always. We live just outside Colorado Springs in a relatively small suburb. My mom has been trying to convince my dad to move to her hometown, which is even smaller, but my dad insists that we need to stay in the city for work. She is a secretary at one of the doctor's offices downtown, and my dad owns a hardware store on the northern end of the city. He has always worked long hours, but when he decided to open up a second location, we have seen him even less.

I'm awake before my mom comes into my room to get me up for school. I quickly get dressed, grab a muffin from the counter, and am waiting on everyone else to load into the car. I'm only five, but I'm fairly independent, to my parents' dismay. Besides, if I step out of line, Charlotte usually corrals us back in. She's only three years older, but thinks she can tell us all what to do.

My day at school is nothing spectacular. We put letters together to make single syllable words, recess, lunch, and I'm not sure what kind of meat was on my tray, so I've blocked out that part, story time and tissue paper craft- time. I'm now holding my rainbow paper picture when Mrs. Adler pulls into the front of the school to pick Charlotte, Amanda, and me up.

Mrs. Adler lives next door and watched all of us when we were little. Since she stays home, she and my mom made a deal to have her take us home each day and watch us for an hour or so until my mom gets off work.

"Hi, Mrs. Adler," we all shout as we wave and climb into her Buick. The poor car has seen better days; there's rust on the outside, and there's duct tape holding the upholstery together on the bench seat in the back. When she backs up, she has to hold the rear view mirror to see because it fell off the windshield ages ago.

"Hello, girls," she says as we buckle in. Instead of asking us about our day or my picture, something she always does, she just stares straight ahead, not giving us a second glance. She is one of the most cheerful people we know, so I just figure one of her boys must have gotten in trouble again; they always seem to be grounded.

"I made a picture today, Mrs. Adler," I say, trying to make her forget about her naughty sons.

"That's great, sweetheart," she responds, still looking ahead at the road in front of her, her voice lacking enthusiasm. I'm definitely going to have to sic Charlotte on the boys when we get home.

It's a short ride, and soon we are pulling into her driveway. I jump out, gathering my backpack and picture.

"Can we play with the boys before we have to get ready for the party, or are they in too much trouble?" I ask, putting my arms through the handles of my backpack.

Mrs. Adler wipes away a tear that slips down her cheek; those boys must be in BIG trouble. "No, Vivian today is not a good day for you guys to come and play. Your momma came home early and needs you girls to go on home."

I step around the car and hand her my picture, "I was going to give this to my daddy tonight at the party, but I think you need it more. I hope it cheers you up." I quickly turn and jog to follow behind Charlotte, who has Amanda in her grasp and is halfway across our front lawn already.

There are cars lining the street, and I have to maneuver around more vehicles in the driveway to reach the front door. "I thought the party was going to be at the new store. Why did everyone come to our house instead?" I ask Charlotte.

"The party is supposed to be at the store; I don't know why we have company," she answers turning the handle to the front door.

As soon as we pass through the doorway, I quickly realize that there will be no party. Our house is filled with people, some hugging, some crying, many I don't know, but none of them look like they are here to celebrate.

Just as I get my backpack off to hang on the front hook, my mom appears through the crowd. The sea of bodies parts for her as she walks toward us. She's wearing the same navy blue dress that she left for work in this morning, but it's not as crisp. The tension of the day is apparent with wrinkles stretching all across the front. Her face is pale and her eyes are fiery red. I've only seen my mother cry a few times, but it was enough to remember what the aftermath looked like, and I can tell she's been crying.

"Come with me, girls," she says quietly, picking up Amanda and placing her on her hip before grabbing my hand. Charlotte trails behind us until we reach my parents' bedroom.

The room is dark, but instead of turning on the main light, she clicks on the bedside lamp, leaving a soft glow in its wake. "Please, sit down on the bed girls, I need to tell you something very important," she says before turning to close the door behind us and moving to sit on the bed with us.

I'm feeling anxious and worried, not understanding what's going on. Something bad has happened, but I don't know what. The scenarios are swirling around in my mind. Did they cancel the party? Did Daddy have to close the store? A boy in my class said that his parents were getting a divorce; maybe that's what my mother needs to tell us. Never in all the situations in my head did I ever come up with the actual truth.

My mother takes a steadying breath and gathers our hands in hers, lightly stroking the knuckles of each of our hands. "Your daddy was very excited about opening the new store today. Last night, he went back to the store to make sure everything was just perfect for the grand opening."

"We know; why aren't we getting ready to go to the party? Why is everyone here? Did the party move?" Charlotte asks.

Tears build in my mother's eyes, but she fights to keep them at bay. "Baby, there isn't going to be a party anymore. Last night, when your daddy was at the store, someone came in and hurt him very badly."

"Is he okay?" I ask.

"No, Viv. No one knew that he was hurt; there was no one there to help him." She pauses, just looking at us for what feels like an eternity. "He died girls." The sob that she's been holding back breaks free, and she begins to fight to breathe through her tears.

"He's not coming back?" Amanda asks as she begins to cry.

"No, baby, he's not."

"NO!" I shout, startling everyone. "He promised that we would build our princess fort tonight after the party. Daddy always keeps his promises. He is not in Heaven; he's coming home tonight," I insist.

My mother pulls me close to her. "I'm sorry, Vivian, but he's not coming home, sweetheart. It's just going to be us girls from now on."

"Who did this?" Charlotte demands. She has been quiet up until this point, not even shedding a tear. I see more anger than grief in her expression.

My mother sighs; her patience is clearly wearing. Normally the epitome of understanding, the emotional strain of the situation has frayed my mother's nerves. "Don't worry about that, Charlotte.

The police know who the man is that hurt your daddy; they are looking for him now. When they find him, he will be going to jail for a long time."

"Do we know him?" she asks again.

"Charlotte, it doesn't matter; he can't hurt us any more than he already has. There are some things you guys don't need to know about."

"Somebody took our daddy away from us; I want to know who did it," I add in.

My mother stands quickly, nearly bouncing Amanda from the bed. I can almost see how my words cause this woman to finally snap.

"He's gone, Vivian Grace, and he's not ever coming back!" she shouts. "You want to know who killed him, like that will bring him back. Raymond Michaels strangled your father, and knowing that will never make one bit of difference of whether he walks through that door again or not. Raymond was a friend of your father's; he worked for him, we trusted him, and look where that trust got him!"

I put my head down, listening to her switch gears from weeping to hollering her rant. "Does that make you feel any better about not having a daddy anymore, Vivian?"

"No," I whisper.

She finally collects her bearings, realizing the damage being done with her outburst of emotions. "I'm sorry, Vivian, but I don't know what to say," she sighs. "He was our friend, and he took your daddy from us. I don't know why this happened, but I do know that sometimes people make bad choices- choices that you can't take back. This was one of those mistakes."

"I'm sorry that I yelled, Viv. I'm just scared and sad." She gathers me in her arms and squeezes me tightly. "I won't let anyone ever hurt you guys; you are my everything now. We will figure this out together, okay?"

I bury my face into her neck and nod, the gravity of the situation crashing down on my little body. My daddy is never coming back, and someone he loved took him away. Listening to my mother and sisters' cries, my emotions come to a halt and I begin to feel numb.

It is in this moment that I become the master of emotional avoidance. I vow never to get too close to people, to love people, because opening yourself up to others creates weakness. That weakness is what gets you hurt. I decide to build the fort my daddy promised me, but this one would be a citadel around my heart. When times get rough, and my fight or flight kicks in, I will fly. The day my father died is the day that I grew wings.

VIVIAN

"Holy crap, Viv! Could you have brought any more stuff with you? I swear I'll be hunch-backed by the time we finish moving you into the dorms. Are you trafficking small children in these duffel bags?"

Aw yes, Amanda, my younger and colorful sister. I'm sure if I were sneaking college boys in those duffel bags, we wouldn't have heard a peep from her. "Come on, Manda, we are almost there. Besides, this is the only load," I reason.

"Yeah, and then I get to help carry whatever doesn't fit back to the truck; I can hardly contain my excitement," she hisses.

Manual labor has never been her forte, but somehow my sister always manages to find some handsome and, of course, hopeful young man to complete any task she felt beneath her. Amanda could get guys to do pretty much anything. The reason: my sister is gorgeous. Long, tan legs, wavy blonde hair that she does nothing with—yet it looks like something professionally done—and everything else is toned and perfect. She is serious model caliber. I know it, guys know it, but worst of all, *she* knows it, and uses it to her fullest advantage. This weekend she can't put her skills to use, hence the attitude. While she and I have always been relatively close, I'm sure her conscripted moving duties did nothing to help our relationship.

"Enough, girls," my mother says in that quiet but stern tone that you know means you are embarrassing her in public, and repercussions will surely match her strife. The silence and glares that ensue could freeze the wheels on the elevator that was transporting me to my new independent college life.

I worked hard to get accepted into Colorado State University; it is one of the best teaching schools in Colorado, so it is the place I absolutely want to be. It's an added bonus that it is on the other side of the state from my teeny tiny hometown. No more cows or chickens. Goodbye to small-town gossip; hello to streetlights and classrooms full of boys I'm not related to. To say I am looking forward to college is putting it mildly. I don't even care if my roommates are a gang of sluts, the guys on my floor are douche nozzles, or my professors can give Professor Snape a run for his money. My excitement to have the freedom that college would provide has me bubbling. I'm sure the stupid toothy grin I am sporting does nothing to hide it either.

As the elevator doors slide open, we are greeted with a dorm floor bursting at the seams. The hallways are jam-packed with freshmen and their families, everyone lugging huge bags. The massive amount of people in such a small space is causing a serious increase in room temperature, and the body-funk that is permeating through the dorm has my stomach turning inside out. *Great, I'm going to throw up in front of all my new housing buddies.* With the constant bumping of strangers, incessantly saying, "excuse me", and tight smiles that say, "I'm sorry for whacking you in the head with my bag," we slowly weave our way through.

"Thank you, sweet baby Jesus. There is your door," Amanda announces. Yes, thank you. I swear that if I have to hear Amanda for one more minute, I am going to trip her and let the herd around me trample her.

My door flies open and I'm surprised to see that I'm the first of the roommates to move in. My dorm is not your typical room; it really resembles an apartment more than a dorm room. There is a small living room and kitchenette, a hallway with two bedrooms to the right, and a bathroom to the left. Yes, my actual bedroom is smaller than my closet back home and I'll have to share it, hopefully with someone that won't want to smother me in my sleep, but it's mine, and I already feel different. I feel grown up, independent, and I'm excited that I'll finally get to be just me. No one's little shadow, no more sisterly beauty comparisons, no more reputations to protect, secrets to keep, no more rumors or pretending. *Yes, college and I are going to get along great.*

I throw my bags on to the ground in front of my bed, Amanda, of course, flings herself on the couch like she gets to live here, and my mom gets busy making my bed. I can see Amanda is no longer going to be of any use to me, so I quickly get to work unpacking and organizing my cramped little cubicle of a room.

The knock and hesitant "hello" breaks my feverish work, but the boisterous screech that follows forces my attention to the door. Stumbling through is the cutest slight of a girl with short blonde curls, blue eyes, and a death glare directed at her mother, who from the looks of it, pushed her into the room.

"Dammit, Jen, these people out here are going to stage a revolt; get through the door." The pixy's mother comes to an abrupt standstill when she notices us in the room, and her eyes go wide. Amanda, once again, joins the land of the living and we follow the woman's gaze directed at my mother.

"Evelyn," she gasps, "I haven't seen you since the trial; it's been so long." I see my mother begin to tear up, and the lady rushes to her and pulls her into a strong embrace. Pixy and I look at each other like we are lost in translation, with no answers for one another, just waiting on our mothers to clue us in.

"I'm fine, thank you, Kim. Yes, it has been a long time. Thirteen years this fall," my mother says, stepping away from the bear hug she is engulfed in. "Vivian, this is Kim; she worked with your father. Jen, it's good to see you again, sweetheart. The two of you used to play together when you were little. You were getting ready to go to the same preschool before we moved."

And there it is. I look at Jen, and I see the exact moment when it clicks for her; she knows all about my family. I have to give her credit though; she recovers quickly. "Thank you, Mrs. Donavan. It's good to see you all as well."

My past, my father's death, my constant pity-party has followed me to college...*great*. I came here to get away from this exact scenario. When we moved to my mother's hometown after my father was murdered, the uncomfortable feeling of having an entire town know what happened was suffocating. All I wanted to do was turn eighteen, go to college, and start over. I couldn't keep seeing the sad stares and watching people try to tiptoe around my lack-of-a-father situation. Now here it is again, looking me straight in the face.

My face feels warm and my ears are burning. This predicament has me completely turned inside out and completely let down, embarrassed that Jen and I will have to not only know each other, but live together.

But then, Jen gives me a huge smile and takes my hand in hers, shaking it fiercely. "My mom kind of stole my thunder. So I'd like to start over. I'm Jen! Please tell me that you have cute shoes, because the closets look pint-sized and sharing is going to be a must. I don't care what size you are; I will squeeze my feet into whatever you have."

Relief floods my face, and my laugh spills over my lips. "I'm Vivian. And you can borrow whatever you like, as long as you have awesome handbags that I can steal."

"Don't you worry, Jen; I carried the entire Macy's shoe department up here in duffel bags. You guys will be fashionably well-equipped," Amanda chimes in.

The tension that was choking me is completely gone, and we all get to work unpacking and finishing up. Jen and I decide to share the same room; the other two roommates haven't shown up yet, and since we already get along, it would be better to be safe than sorry.

Within the hour, everything is done, and I am itching to get my mom and little sister out. Jen and her mom go out to pick up a few things from Target for our room, and the others have not shown up, so it's the perfect time to say our goodbyes. I know what's coming; my mother won't be able to contain the waterworks, but in no way do I regret my decision to come here.

No longer able to contain herself, Mom belts out, "Baby girl, if you miss home, you can always transfer back and go to the community college for the spring semester."

"I'll be fine, Mom. I'll call every week, and I promise to drive home often." I pull her into a hug and whisper into her ear, "You know I'll miss you, and I love you, but I need to do this...for me. Please be okay with this."

"I am, Viv. I'll just miss you so damn much," she says as a tear escapes her eye. She wipes it away quickly; she's trying to be strong for me, but her eyes are betraying her.

Amanda finally looks up from her phone that she has been on all afternoon, texting her flavor of the month, no doubt. "Hey, what am I, the leftover kid?" she complains.

"I'm glad that you can finally admit that, Manda. I was starting to feel guilty about being Mom's favorite," I shoot back in a teasing tone.

Amanda crinkles her nose in insult, and rises from the couch that she has not moved from in hours. Her idea of helping has been to bark orders from her throne to all of us peons. Now that she is a senior in high school, apparently her coolness-level is off the charts. "*Ha ha ha,* Viv, that is just *so* funny. Besides, you and I both know that that coveted role belongs to Charlotte."

"That is absolutely not true, Amanda Marie! I love all my girls just the same, and you know that," my mother's clipped tone lets us know the teasing is officially over. Her nerves are shot, and her emotions are written all over her face. She certainly doesn't want to be having this conversation, joking or otherwise.

Yes, Charlotte, my older sister. She went the route my mother wishes I would. She's three years older and went to a community college locally to get her Registered Nurse License. She graduates at the end of this year, and plans to stay there and work at the local hospital…well, until she gets married at least. Her dream is to get married, have kids, and be a stay-at-home mom. While I think that is great, Charlotte has more potential than any of us, is smarter than any of us, has more talented than any of us, and yet she doesn't want to do anything with it. I really love her, but when I see her, all I can think is wasted talent. I don't want that to be me.

After my father died, she took on a pseudo-parent role in the household. While Amanda is the free-spirited sister, Charlotte is the mother hen, and well, I'm just trying to be normal, whatever that is.

My mom's voice breaks into my whirling thoughts, "Okay, it's getting late, and it's a long way home; we better get on the road Amanda."

I give my mom and Amanda one last hug and say my good-byes, promising a trip home as soon as possible. It's a promise that I hope I really don't have to keep. When they finally leave, I let out a heavy sigh and relax onto my perfectly made bed. *This is my new home. Good, bad, or ugly, this is my new life, and I've never wanted anything more.*

Classes don't start for another three days, so I'm not too worried that only one more of our roommates has moved in by Friday evening. We were told that kids would be moving in all weekend; I just insisted that I be there on the actual day that they let us in—yeah… I'm that girl.

Jen and I clicked with Carly the minute she walked through the door Friday morning. Uber-nice is putting it lightly, but she is not at all fake. Ditzy, yes, but not in a let's-save-mankind-and-drown-her kind of way. She has gorgeous light brown hair that is paper straight, and sapphire blue eyes. She has curves for days, which I'm sure attracts lots of male attention, but I get the feeling she is a tad self-conscious.

Jen's never said another word about my dad, and I'm totally okay with that. I came here to get away from the old me, the me who was swallowed up by her father's death. I don't know if Jen is uncomfortable with my past; or she just doesn't judge me for it. Either way, I am thankful for her and the fresh start.

Our Three Musketeers status is cemented pretty quickly. Once Carly is settled in, we go exploring, checking out the neighbors who we could find, the bookstore, and the dining hall—which, by the way, has the best and largest waffles known to man. I can feel myself drooling, and I can already feel my curves expanding at the sight of those huge disks of breakfast perfection; if I'm not careful, the 'freshman fifteen' would turn into the 'freshman thirty'. I am on the short side…*who am I kidding?*…I'm a hobbit with shoes. So needless to say, any pound gained is definitely a pound seen. There is nowhere to hide it. Not to say I'm husky or big-boned or whatever the new politically correct term is, I'm just average. I'm not gorgeous like Amanda, I'm not super-tiny like Jen, nor am I full-figured. I am more the athletic build; I rock the 3Bs: b-cup and a bubble butt. Yep, I'm average, which means I'm not noticeable. I'm not beautiful, but not ugly, just average, and that's okay by me.

"I say we stay in tonight, hang out, and then tomorrow meet some people on campus after waffle time; hopefully my roommate will be here by then," Carly says, hanging over the end of the couch, her long hair sweeping across the floor, as she, no doubt, is trying to digest the massive subs we just inhaled for dinner.

I could not agree with her more, especially about the waffles. "Good idea, I don't think I could even move at this point. Let's just put PJs on and watch movies, or play a board game or something."

Slowly we all gather ourselves off the floor and couch to get ready for our chick-flick-o-Rama evening.

We each take our turns in the bathroom, scrubbing the remains of the day off our faces and changing into our pajamas. In my most comfortable yoga pants and tank top, my long auburn hair piled high on top of my head, and wrapped in my favorite fleece blanket, I make it back out to the living area. We all come armed with our movie selections, *Girls Just Want to Have Fun*, *Sixteen Candles*, and *Pride and Prejudice*.

We get settled and start the first movie; of course, we all love a little Mr. Darcy time.

"I don't know; I think if I had the choice, I would want the Jane and Mr. Bingley love story," Carly says, shoveling a handful of popcorn into her mouth. Jen turns to her wide-eyed, mouth open and just stares at Carly.

"WHAT!" Jen screeches once she gathers her voice. "Mr. Darcy is soooo worth swooning over. I would chop off my left arm just to have the chance to have a guy say those things to me."

"Why can't it just be a quiet, comfortable relationship? Jane and Mr. Bingley were smitten, just not over the top." Both look to me to settle the argument. *Good call, guys. Yeah, ask me, the girl who has never been in love, the girl who hates what love can do to a person.* I'm not sure if I'm even capable of that emotion; I'm too afraid of losing my heart to ever take the risk.

Dodging the question, I get up to refill my soda and start another bag of popcorn for the next movie. When I get back, they are still waiting for my answer. *Well shit...think, think, think. Act like a girl; what is the girly, touchy feeling thing to say? SHIT!*

Out of desperation, I finally blurt out the first thing that comes to mind. "Carly, while Jane and Charles were absolutely adorable, and it was evident that they cared for one another, I think what Jen is saying is that they lacked the fire that Mr. Darcy and Elizabeth obviously had. I guess there is no right answer. They each had two different kinds of love; the real question is, what kind of love do you want?"

Jen's glazed-over look tells me immediately that I'm either half-crazy, or it went totally over her head. Yep, the girl with no heart strikes again.

"Okay, so I have no idea what in the world you just said, but what I do know is that if you aren't in my Lit class this semester, I'm *so* transferring to yours. You can definitely help with my literary impairment. I could never come up with something like that, and I have a feeling that my GPA will need every little bit of help it can get."

"Oh, my God, I am not cheating for you!" I shout, hitting her with a pillow.

"Hey, I didn't say cheat," she says, grabbing the pillow from my hands and resting it behind her head. "But a little assistance never hurt anything. I swear you're like a walking, talking style guide; it would be a shame to not put that brain to use to help others."

I can't help but chuckle at her very thorough defense of what I consider bending, if not breaking, the rules. Despite my resistance, I know that I will probably help her out. Damn, I'll probably end up writing some of her papers myself. I shake my head, "You are going to get me in so much trouble this year; I can already tell."

"I surely hope so; this is college. We are supposed to have fun!"

"Just don't get me arrested." I have never been in any real trouble before, but I'm sure that phone call home would not go well. Knowing my mom, she'd let me sit in the cell all night to think about what I did, just like when I would get sent to my room as a kid for picking on Amanda. Then after letting me sweat it out, she'd drive up here and drag me home.

"Anyway, so Carly, are you scared you got matched with a dud for a roommate? We can always make a special bed on the floor in our room if she turns out to be completely terrifying," I tease.

"Just for that, you can't come dancing tomorrow night. I'll invite all my new *nice* friends to The Suite. It should be packed because it's the last Saturday before school; I thought we could all go."

"Oh, come on, I'm just teasing. I'm sure she won't be too bad; you know, maybe she'll be like a Tarantino gun slinger or something."

"It would be nice if we get along, but really, as long as she sticks to her side of the room and doesn't borrow weird things like underwear or anything, I think we'll be good."

"Seriously? Underwear, Carly?" I ask skeptically. I'm not sure I would be okay even *looking* at their underwear, let alone stealing it and then wearing it. That ranks up there with crazy lint-stealing guy who keeps girls' dryer lint from the Laundromat in his pocket and smells it all day. I'm not sure he exists, but my mom sure warned me of such creatures when she explained college basement Laundromat safety on the drive here.

"Well, you never know! My sister said that her roommate in college had no concept of personal space. She borrowed her B.O.B., and my sister found it under the girl's pillow!"

"Oh, my God! That is absolutely nasty!" Jen shouts with a body shiver to help enunciate her complete disdain. I smile, but I am clearly lost in the conversation.

"What is a B.O.B.?" I ask casually. Jen looks at me like I'm insane and have escaped the state hospital.

"You have got to be kidding me. It's every girl's trusty companion; you never leave home without it," Jen defends.

"You mean, like Chapstick or your Visa card?" Carly jokes, earning a dirty look from Jen, who apparently takes this particular topic seriously. I hide the bottom half of my face in my pillow to cover my growing smirk that would put me in the hot seat like Carly.

"A B.O.B. is a battery operated boyfriend, also known as a vibrator." Jen sits up straight like she is going to lecture us on something of grave importance. And from the sounds of it, she finds vibrators to be of the utmost significance. I haven't lived in a cave my entire life. I have heard of pleasuring yourself; I've even tried it a time or two. When I had sex for the first time, I figured one or both of us were doing it totally wrong, and I'd needed to figure it out ASAP; yeah, it was him. In a town the size of mine, I didn't want rumors of my abilities–good or bad–floating around. I initially had sex to see what the fuss was about, and as it turned out, there shouldn't be such a fuss. I have never used a vibrator, but as I tune in and out of Jen's lecture, I'm starting to think maybe

16

she has a point; I've been missing out. Lit education for a little sex education doesn't seem like a bad tradeoff. I zone back in for the last bit of her rambling to catch probably the most significant piece to her oration.

"They have been saving girls from romantic dry spells since the late 1800s, and in the last decade orgasm engineers have managed to perfect the design of those wondrous little mechanical love sticks. No girl should go without. Don't worry, Vivian, we will fix you up beautifully."

I nod and smile instead of verbally responding. All words have truly escaped me. What does one even say in response? 'My favorite color is purple, so make sure it's a big ole lavender thing.' Yeah, I think not.

Feeling proud of herself, Jen snuggles back into her blanket and pillow to finish our girls' night. We start *Girls Just Want to Have Fun,* but none of us makes it through; we all fall asleep. Carly is on the couch, and Jen and I sprawl out across the floor.

Brooks

"Dude, the room is so far; why does the room have to be so far?" Will slurs as he stumbles into the dorm elevator.

"Shut up, Will. We are almost there," I say, holding him up against the wall of the elevator as the doors close. "I swear if you throw up in this elevator, I will leave you in it."

My roommate Will and I thoroughly enjoyed our Friday night. I've decided college is definitely the place for me. We started at a few dance clubs on College Avenue, but it didn't take long to realize that Will has about as much rhythm as a three-legged dog, so his wingman status was demoted. We left and made our rounds at the house parties off campus, and from there, our night took off. The alcohol flowed, and no one cared that we were underage. Will was hilarious, which brought invites to more parties, and my looks brought the ladies. I know my strengths, and a pretty face happens to be one of them, so of course I play it up. It's helped to get many girls in the past, and I look to increase those numbers here.

We both had our fair share of drinks; I'm feeling the dizzy fuzzy feeling that lets me know I've reached my limit, but Will, on the other hand, is apparently having trouble handling his liquor. Helping his drunk ass is no easy feat; the boy is large—not tuba player in the band large either—I mean linebacker, rugby player large. I can hold my own, but Will...well...he's scary. We got to know each other pretty quickly though, and he is just a big teddy bear. He really is just an all-around nice guy, the kind that all the girls would love to bring home to their mothers, and the kind that their fathers' wouldn't threaten and/or kill.

Will's definitely not like me. Maybe one day I'll care about actually being with a girl long enough to want to know her last name, let alone meet her parents, but that time is not right now. I'm interested in one thing—pussy—any way I can get it. After tonight, I realize there is certainly an abundance of it for the taking, and Will is the perfect guy to help reel them in.

The ding of the elevator signals our stop and the doors open, giving me a brief moment to muster my strength to carry Will down the hall to our room. We live on a co-ed floor, which is evident from all of the fluffy door decorations and white boards saying 'I heart whoever' on them. Having beautiful girls around all of the time is fantastic for collecting images for the spank bank, but I know better than to shit where I eat, so the girls on this floor are off limits. I may be a man-whore, but I'm not stupid. There is nothing worse than a crazy obsessed woman, who knows where you live.

We stagger to our door, barely making it without falling. Thankfully, it's unlocked, and we walk right in. It's pitch black, so I drag Will as best as I can down the tiny hallway to our bedroom. The dorms are small, but I was adamant that I get the apartment-style dorm; we have more people in the rooms, but we get a living room and our own bathroom. There was just no way I was going to share some tiny living space with some other guy when I wanted to 'entertain'.

The door is already open, so with every bit of strength I have left, I heave Will onto his bed on his side of the room. Completely out of breath from lugging Goliath the fifty feet to our room and still feeling my buzz, I slip off my shoes and crawl into bed. I let the spin of the room and thoughts of young naive co-eds ready to experiment lull me to sleep. Yeah, this year is going to be epic.

BROOKS

"Ahhhh!"

"Oh, my God, call security!"

"Shhh, we can take care of them ourselves."

The high-pitched screams and threats of ball removal rouse me from my blissful sex dream. I moan, but the shrills continue, only making the throbbing in my head worse, and forcing whatever I drank last night to rise to the base of my esophagus, ready to spew out at any moment. I'm totally hung-over, and whoever left the television on will die.

"Turn it off," I hear Will grumble. "My head feels like it's going to pop off."

His words are met with more screams, prompting me to open my eyes. Staring right back at me, no more than an inch from mine, are the most beautiful eyes I've ever seen. They are this funky combination of hazel, brown, and green; it's like they just can't make up their mind. I've never seen anything like them, and they instantly pull me in.

"Carly, you were wrong; he's absolutely alive," she says, backing away from me. I lurch backwards on the bed to gain control of my surroundings. I take a look around to see pink plastered everywhere, except for the purple zebra-print blankets that Will is rolled up in–a far cry from our simple blue and grey comforters in our room.

I scan the room, taking note of each angry face until I land on the girl with the eyes. Now that I get the full picture of her, the eyes are no longer what I notice; it's her complete package. She is absolutely gorgeous. She has chestnut hair but it looks like there are streams of fiery red tones woven throughout. I swear the girl is a walking contradiction, like her features couldn't make up their mind, so she was blessed with a little of everything. It's piled on top of her head, and she doesn't give two shits about it, or that she has no make-up on. Really, neither do I; she is a stunning creature just the way she is.

I know I'm in the wrong room for sure; I just hope to Christ that I didn't fuck any of them. And if I haven't, then hopefully this isn't my floor so that I can have a go at Red. I can feel myself just staring at her, but she looks away, like I'm making her feel uncomfortable. Considering the circumstances, I can understand her discomfort, but still, I usually get at least a small flirtatious smile back from the opposite sex. She's giving me nothing, zilch, nada; I'm gum under her shoe that she stepped in and fucked up her morning.

"Okay, assholes, fun's over," the petite curly-haired blonde demands, shaking the mattress of the bed with her foot. Oh, yeah, this is the ball-buster of the crew; she has that air about her. At all costs, I try to avoid those, but it never fails, the ones I want are always hidden behind the female-muscle of the gang. And this little waif is Red's muscle. If I want any chance in hell, I need to smooth things over with this feisty little thing.

"Up, boys. You passed out in the wrong room; time to go," the curvy brunette intercedes, trying to mediate the awkward situation. If Red wasn't in the picture, her curves would absolutely be on my radar, but they pale in comparison to who is standing next to her.

"I apologize, ladies. It was very late when we got home last night," I say, trying to mend the strained introductions. "I was so worried about getting my friend Will to bed, that I didn't check the room number, and it was so dark in the dorm, I didn't notice the décor."

The girls look to Will to back up my story—*nope, they don't trust me*. I take no offense; I get that a lot. Will gives them a pathetic wave and smile, embarrassed by the situation. I just hope that he hasn't pissed their bed, which would take this to a whole new level. "We really are sorry, girls; this was an honest mistake. I don't even remember getting home. Are we at least on the ninth floor?" he asks.

His soft, easy tone lifts a weight off the girls, and I can see that we—well, at least, *he*—have been forgiven. The teddy bear strikes again; I knew I liked him for a reason.

"You're in room 913," Red pipes up, and I zero in on her. The sound of her voice is like a melody that I could never get tired of. It's dripping with sweetness, and I want nothing more than to see if I can make it turn raspy.

I think for a minute about my home court rule and how willing I am to break it, but looking at Red once more, I bounce off the bed and stand before her. "Well, it looks like we are next door neighbors," I tell her, leaning in close enough that I can catch a glimpse of her eyes again. "I guess we will get to know each other pretty well after all." I whisper the last bit, tucking a piece of renegade hair behind her ear. I'm trying my damnedest to let her know that I'm more than interested, but she looks away from me and takes a step back like I'm shit on a shovel. *I like a challenge, but fuck, throw me a bone, woman.*

Will comes up behind me and slaps my back; I can hear his low rumble of a chuckle at my obvious rejection. "Looks like you're barking up the wrong tree, Brooks. You may need to walk away while you still can."

"I'd listen to the Hulk there, buddy. My girl Vivian is country, and you just never know what those country folks will do," miniature bitchy girl says, crossing her arms across her chest like it's some kind of threat. *Yeah, okay, totally frightened,* I think sarcastically.

I disregard everything that cunt-o-licious has to say, except for the one nugget of crucial information–Vivian, she told me Red's name. It fits her perfectly. Vivian looks strong and warm, and I want to curl around her, feel every inch of her. The rest of it, well, it's an empty threat. Country or not, Vivian could never hurt anyone, I know her kind; she's as rare as they come. She's not the type to cause hurt; she's the type that gets hurt.

"Let us make it up to you," I say, giving Vivian some space, but maintaining as much eye contact as she will allow, which isn't much. "Let us walk you to the dining hall for breakfast, or let us take you girls out tonight. Since we're neighbors and all, we might as well get to know each other. You never know when it will be handy to have guys right next door." Yes, there is a double meaning in that, but from the eye rolls I receive from the mean one, and smiles from the other two, not everyone catches the hidden meaning.

"Thank you, but we have a girls' day planned, and then we are going to Suite 152 to dance tonight," Curves says. "I can't imagine that you guys would like to dance, so maybe we can hang out some other time."

"Fair enough," Will agrees. The boy hates to dance, which is good since he barely has enough coordination to walk, but she left the door open for another invitation. Fuck, he needs some lessons in conversing with the opposite sex. At least he finishes introductions; I have to give him that. "This is my roommate Brooks, and I'm Will."

"Nice to meet you," Curves smiles. "I'm Carly; this is Jen," she points to the short callous one. "And you met Vivian. We are still waiting on our fourth roommate to show up; her name is Campbell, but that's all we know."

"Well, it's great to meet you all, even under such weird circumstances. We really are sorry if we scared you," I say. "It would be great to hang out sometime; come over whenever you want." I direct the last line towards Vivian, but she doesn't even give me a second glance, which I'm not going to lie, hurts a little. I want her to notice me like the other girls do. I usually have to bat them away, and this girl couldn't care less.

Will pushes me along, and we head toward their front door. We aren't even completely in the hallway before Jen slams the door behind us. *So glad I met her; she is one awesome gal.* They may not have accepted our invitation right now, but I have every intention of being a thorn in their sides until I find an angle to get to Vivian. In one single meeting, it has become my mission of the semester to have this girl any way I can get her.

VIVIAN

Since Saturday morning, I have tried to avoid our new neighbors, but I swear Brooks is stalking me. I go to the vending machines in the front lobby, he's there. I go to the basement laundry to wash my favorite jeans for dancing, and he's there. I'm now sitting in my first class of the semester, English Composition, and guess who walks through the door? Yup, Brooks.

I know guys like him; Amanda is constantly dating boys who treat girls the way I'm sure he does. Who am I kidding? Amanda is Brooks' female equivalent. They use people to get what they want, and then leave them heartbroken and clueless when their usefulness has expired. Brooks is no mystery; his goal is to sleep with anything and everything. He sees me as a number, a notch on his bedpost, and when he's completed his challenge, he would throw me away like I was nothing. Well, he has targeted the wrong girl. No matter how unbelievably gorgeous he is. I can use images of him to take care of myself after Jen takes me to get my new special purple friend. I don't need to experience the real thing, not if it means risking myself in the process.

Waves of students file into the classroom and I slouch down in my seat, looking down at my notebook, hoping that Brooks won't see me and will walk right by. No such luck. He slides into the seat across the row and leans across the aisle to get my attention. I peer at him from the corner of my eye, hoping that maybe if I pay him no attention he'll go away.

"Hey, Red," he says, giving me his best smoldering grin.

I try to remain unaffected, but I *am* a girl after all. This is a guy whose looks demand attention. He walks into a room and everyone, girls and guys alike, takes notice. I never thought I would consider a man as beautiful, but Brooks truly is. His jet-black hair is just messy enough that it makes me want to run my fingers through it. His cerulean blue eyes are like never-ending pools that are perpetually inviting me to dive into them. Once I let my eyes roam though, it's easy to notice the amazing physique that he has under his dark jeans and blue button-up shirt that somehow enhances the color of his eyes. It takes every bit of willpower not to melt like every other girl that passes his desk. The difference is those girls think he might fall in love with them and they would live happily ever after. I imagine that this semester many will find out the hard way that he has no interest in such emotional attachments. I know what I am to him, and I respectfully decline the opportunity, no matter how cute he is.

"Hello, Brooks, it's nice to see you again," I say pleasantly. I figure maybe if I try to be his friend, it will stop his pursuits, and this crush I have will slowly fade. When he moves his chair closer to mine, I realize that may not be the best plan of defense.

"You know, I'm not really great at writing papers; I could always use a study partner," he says, whispering the last part of the sentence. His hushed voice causes my body to shake from the inside out until I feel every inch of my skin vibrate. I never react to guys this way; in fact, I typically try to stay clear of them as much as possible, and guys like Brooks, I need to avoid like the plague.

"I'm sure you'll manage just fine," I tell him, moving my desk away from his. Overhearing our conversation, the brunette behind him interrupts.

"Well if she won't help, I would be more than happy to help in any way that I can," she purrs, leaning forward to touch his shoulder. Oh, yeah, I'm sure she would give him a hand—more like she'd offer some vagina to go with that Shakespeare. Her well-endowed chest pouring out of her tiny shirt and the overdone make-up she has plastered all over her face provides a pretty clear picture of the kind of help she would like to provide.

Brooks turns around to address her, and when I see him smile, I have to hold myself back from jumping across the aisle and stabbing her with my pencil. This pang of jealousy is something new, and it's not a good color on me. Besides, I only have a mechanical pencil; it wouldn't leave enough of a mark. I need to remember to start bringing good ole number twos to class.

Before he can answer, the professor, Dr. Vauldin, walks in and immediately begins passing out the course syllabus and discussing class expectations. For an entire fifty minutes I keep my eyes forward, desperately trying to forget about whatever flirting extravaganza may or may not be going on behind me. I know the best thing for me will be to see Brooks with someone else, that it will help me get over whatever this is, but *holy shit*, the idea of it makes me angry.

The instant Dr. Vauldin ends his long-winded, mind-numbingly boring tirade on the importance of correct grammar in all compositions; I spring out of my seat in an attempt to ditch Brooks and his little tag-along. Walking through the doors and hitting the fresh air, I feel like I can finally breathe again. It's like his presence sucks all of the air out of the room, and I'm left to survive on whatever he leaves behind. I need to get away from him.

I don't make it far down the hallway before he catches me, landing his arm across my shoulders. "Wait up, Red; you didn't need to run off. I can walk you to your next class; I have an hour before my next one starts." It makes my stomach flip-flop, and my defense mechanisms kick in to high gear. I shoot him a look of disdain and he removes his arm, immediately placing his hands at his sides. I feel the loss as soon as he takes it away, and I have to remind myself that it's better to not get involved with someone like him.

"Thanks, but I have a break, too. I was going to go back to my dorm and see if Campbell has finally showed up." I see Will and Jen just outside the exit of the lecture building, so I move quickly to try to get to them; they can serve as my Brooks buffer. Even though he took his hand away, he's still walking very closely.

Just before we reach the exit, another class lets out and a crowd of people rush into the hallway, forcing us to stop. "So, Vauldin's class is going to be rough to get through," I mutter, trying to make friendly small talk; running from him isn't exactly working.

"Seriously, if you weren't in there, I would strongly consider dropping the class." The Brooks charm is back in full force. I stare at him, considering my options. Do I go for it and go on a date with him? Maybe he's not as bad as I've made him out to be. Do I put him in his place so that he'll leave me alone for good? Or do I avoid the situation by dropping the class myself, maybe even transferring dorms? Because that is totally sane and logical, and I'm sure my mom would understand. Luckily, I don't have to make the choice.

"Brooks! I was hoping to run into you today," exclaims a decent-looking blonde with legs for days. She snakes her arms around Brooks' waist, and rests her head on his shoulder like she's

27

staking her claim of him. She looks at me and I see the competition in her eyes; she's threatened by me and wants me to know that she is going to win. I brace myself for what's going to come next, because in girl-world, this type of fight usually isn't pretty. Brooks, on the other hand, looks embarrassed and unsure of how to proceed. Yup, that karma is a bitch, isn't it, buddy.

"Sondra, what a surprise," he mutters with a half-smile. It looks like he's starting to sweat a bit, and I almost want to laugh. Here I thought maybe I could bend my rules and see past his arrogance, but thankfully, fate stepped in just in time to show me his true Douche McGee status. I almost feel sorry for him; the scenario is not ideal: previous weekend make-out buddy shows up while in progress of hitting on new make-out buddy target.

"Saturday was wonderful; we are going to have to do it again sometime. I had no idea guys could be so dexterous with their fingers, and what you did with your tongue...I'm pretty sure is illegal in several states." Her statements are directed at both of us—an invitation for him, and a warning to back off for me. I feel my face scrunch in disgust that I'm privy to this conversation, but then sympathy I had for Brooks is now nonexistent. "Thank goodness I'm so flexible, or we never would have been able to fit in that club bathroom."

My eyes widen and I choke on my own saliva. The Skank-o-meter blares in my head, and I look to Brooks to confirm that not only is she a slut-puppy, but that he may in fact have gonorrhea from his bathroom tryst. With guilt written all over his face, he evades my eyes and looks down at the floor, which gives me all the confirmation I need to stay away from him.

"There's no need to say anything, Brooks; she didn't say anything that would surprise me. But something that I guess would shock you is I'm not that type of girl who'll blow someone in a public bathroom, nor am I into one-night-stands. So, whatever you thought you were going to get from me isn't going to happen," I try to make my voice as commanding as possible. I take him off-guard and he stares at me like I've beaten his dog or something. "Besides," I say, pointing to Legs, "it looks like you have more than enough volunteers to fill up your punch card."

I turn on my heel, leaving Brooks with his bathroom Barbie behind. I walk the remaining distance to the courtyard where Will and Jen are. I'm hoping they will help clear my mind of the guy I actually wanted, who proved he is exactly what I shouldn't.

BROOKS

When Sondra found me in the hallway and said those things in front of Vivian, I wanted the tiles of the floor to split in half and swallow me whole. Not because I fucked some girl in the bathroom of a night club—shit, I'm proud of myself for remembering her name–no, what embarrassed me is that Vivian heard it. For the last month, I've showed up to English Comp class excited to see her, and she always smiles politely and gives me a little wave hi, but then ignores me.

The girls have adopted Will as their official fifth roommate; I, on the other hand, am probably just tolerated because I'm with him. Our other bedroom was left open, so Will and I are the only ones in our dorm; I can't exactly complain about that. Four guys living together…I can't imagine it always being pleasant. At least there will always be toilet paper in the suite. I've heard stories of guys having to wipe their asses with notebook paper because their roommate can't manage to replace the roll. No, thank you. However, it would be nice to have some other testosterone around.

Will has turned into an excellent wing-man, but he has hooked up with very few girls himself. Considering that, and the amount of time he spends with our neighbors, I was worried I was going to have to do some detective work and figure out if he had a vagina. When he joined the intramural rugby team, he put my mind at ease a bit. I've been to a few games, and *fuck,* those guys are crazy! No vaginas allowed, for sure. I usually tag along and go to the games to watch, and when I see Will after the game with Vivian, I can barely contain myself. There isn't anything going on between them, but it still pisses me off to no end that she thinks so little of me, and yet so freely spends time with him. When I see her hanging out with Will, watching movies and eating in the dining hall together, my jealousy spikes, and I swear I could spit nails. When I first met Red, I was merely interested in fucking her, but the more I've been around her, she has somehow found her way under my skin. I've used half of the female population on campus to try to exorcise her from my body, erase her from my mind, but then I see her, and she wiggles right back in.

Every day after our class together, I come back to the dorms hoping that she'll invite me to hang out like she does Will. It has yet to happen. I don't dare invite myself over without Will. Bulldog Jen would not take too kindly to that, and I have become quite fond of my balls; I'd like to keep them. I swear those girls think Will walks on water, while I am the green goopy scum under a rock. I have yet to meet their elusive fourth roommate, Campbell, but I'm sure word of mouth has given her a pretty similar opinion of me. Really though, they can all kiss my ass; I have nothing to apologize for, and the only person's opinion that I even care about is Vivian's.

Once again, I make the lonely pathetic trek from Comp class to the dorms, and I'm met with disappointment. Today, Vivian didn't even come back to the dorm. Instead of Red at their door like I was hoping, it's a dark-haired Goth chic, which I can only assume is Campbell. At first appearances, I can't imagine that she fits in well with the other girls. She is completely and utterly punk rock, with her short choppy hair, tattered jeans, Nirvana tee-shirt, and purple Converses. We are a month into school and Jen hasn't done any fashion magic on her, so I would say that she's a pretty independent strong-willed girl who won't get pushed around. I haven't even talked to her, and from that assessment alone, I like her.

Her eyes slide to mine as she starts to push the key into the lock. Her notice of me catches me off-guard, and I fumble with my keys trying to avoid the awkwardness of being caught staring. She smiles for the tiniest of milliseconds, but it gives me just enough of a reprieve from feeling like the king pricks of the ninth floor. "Are you going to stand out in the hallway all day, or would you like to come over, Brooks?" she says, directing her attention back to the lock.

Shit, she already knows my name, which can be no big deal, or the most likely option, my reputation precedes me and she already hates me like the other girls do. My brain pounds with the possibilities of why she would invite me over. Running my fingers through my hair, pulling the ends to snap myself out of the mental clusterfuck I have rolling around in my head, I take a deep breath and put my keys back into my pocket. "Campbell, right? Are you sure it's alright that I come over?"

She laughs and opens the door. "Jen's not here; you're safe for now," she says, walking through the threshold, leaving me in the hallway to make up my mind. "What the hell," I say under my breath and follow her into the living room, taking a seat on their couch. My leg won't stop bouncing, and I try to calm down by wringing my hands together. It feels so weird being here without Will, my safety net.

After placing her backpack on the long wooden desk that runs the length of the living room where the girls have lined their computers, she walks down toward the bedrooms without saying another word. I look around like I'm being set up on some kind of sick and twisted joke. Kneeling down on my hands and knees, I lift the bottom of the giant purple sheet that they have used to cover the tacky brown couch to see if anyone is hiding underneath, but the only thing I come up with is a black high heel.

"You know, if you really want to play dress-up, I'm sure Jen would call a truce long enough to give you a tour of her closet," I hear Campbell say behind me, halting my movements. My ass is still straight up in the air while my head is half-under their couch.

"Um, sorry, I dropped something and it rolled underneath, and I found this under there." I stand, dusting myself off and handing her the shoe, hoping that she believes my little fib.

She accepts it, but throws it back under the couch, and turns to head toward their kitchenette. "Would you like a soda?" she says, opening their tiny fridge.

I have no idea what is happening, but I'm pretty sure that in the last five minutes, she has broken about a million girl code rules. My opinion of her has skyrocketed from admiration, to where I might have her name tattooed on my ass. When I don't answer her right away, she grabs a soda for me, shoves it into my chest, and walks past me. The pop of her soda lid brings me back to the present, and I sit back on the couch across the room from the recliner where Campbell is slouching with both legs hanging off the sides. She looks completely comfortable with me being here; she's not flirting, not nervous…it's like she's just one of the guys.

"Don't you think someone is going to miss their shoe?" I ask, opening my Coke and taking a drink. The tension in my shoulders eases as she begins to talk, and I realize this is what it's like to have a friend that's a girl. She is being nice for no other reason than to be nice to me, and the newness of this feeling, this situation, has me buzzing.

"Of course Jen misses her shoe," she laughs. "She is constantly losing her things because she leaves her shit everywhere. We all know that those are her favorite heels and we know exactly where it's at. We have a bet going how long it will take her to find it."

Exuding comfort and approachability she speaks to me with such ease that all of the anxiety from being in this dorm room, and any fear of what she may or may not think of me, vanishes. I melt into the cushions, allowing myself to feel the fabric, taking in the lavender scent of the room, and hearing light rock music softly playing in the back bedroom. No wonder Will spends a lot of time here; the only thing that would make this scenario ideal would be if Vivian was sitting here with me and I had my arms wrapped around her.

"Well that's seven shades of fucked up; I thought you guys were all friends?"

"We are, but the princess needs to clean up after herself. That shoe has been there since the first night they went dancing. I found it while cleaning up two weeks later, and that's when Vivian came up with the bet." She smirks like she's been privy to the plot of a lifetime, which is endearing considering it's just a damn shoe. I hear Red's name and I sit up straighter on the couch; fuck, even her name winds me up. My stomach feels like curtains of hair being twisted around a round wire brush.

"You know she actually does like you, right?" Campbell says, setting her soda down on the brown coffee table between us. It looks just like ours, shit. The covering has been peeled away in patches, exposing the particleboard underneath, but the girls have done a decent job of masking it with random placemats and a huge wooden bowl filled with pine cones in the center.

Swinging my leg up on my knee and leaning into a throw pillow, I settle into a conversation I'm not sure I want to have. The idea that Vivian might actually like me, has my heart racing, but I try to remain cool and collected, logical. "Yeah, I don't think it would matter who exactly you're talking about; all three of your roommates like me about as much as a nurse likes laxative day at the nursing home."

"Okay, Jen would probably put you in that category, and Carly is the peacemaker that would like you if everyone else did. But Vivian–she's different. She hates you because she likes you."

"That makes absolutely no sense at all," I say incredulously, putting my foot back down on the floor and leaning my forearms onto my knees. Here I thought she was on the guy level and could give it to me straight, and then she pulls a bipolar move and warps into girl mode. I don't speak girl, I'm not a symbolist, and I don't read hieroglyphics. *Girls, don't let the pirate movies fool you; we can't do treasure maps and clues. If you want us to understand something, you have to spell it out with very few adjectives, and even fewer multisyllabic words.*

"It makes perfect sense; you just don't know why it makes sense." Campbell slides her legs off the side of the recliner and squares her shoulders at me. Everything relaxed and nonchalant, which had comforted me about this situation five minutes ago has been erased. She scrunches her nose, and the scowl lines between her brows deepen. "Look, we all know that you like her. But they all think that you want a piece of ass and then you'd be on your way."

"Is that what you think, too?" I snap back, matching her posture. I feel the sweat on my palms, nervous from this unexpected turn in conversation. My defenses are up, but I try to disguise it by wiping it away on my pant legs.

Noticing my sudden discomfort, she backs off a tad and reclines back into her chair. "Is that the truth?" she sighs.

I hang my head, collecting my thoughts and gathering my composure. I don't know who this chick is, but for some reason, I don't want to lie to her. Whether she can help me get Vivian or not, I just want to tell her the truth. This whole cocky, arrogant thing I have going on is all for show. I'm a messed up piece of nothing underneath, and with a glance, she sees right down to my deep, dark shit layer.

"When I first saw her, I thought she was the most beautiful girl I had ever seen. Yes, I wanted to fuck her, and if I was going to get to screw her on more than one occasion because of our living situation, then I thought even better. But then I was around her more, and even though I still don't know anything about her–damn it if I don't want to, even if it means I never sleep with her."

Every word I tell her is true. Vivian has captivated me in ways I didn't think was possible, and it's no longer about having my hands on her body, although that would be ideal. I want her more than I've ever wanted anything. Considering where I stand with her, I would be honored just to have her acknowledge me.

Campbell crosses her arms across her chest; her eyes narrow on me, sizing me up, looking for any wavering on my part. "If that's true, then you need to stop being such a fucking douche and show them that you're not the womanizer that they think you are," she finally says. "You don't think Vivian hears about all the girls you've slept with? All you're doing is confirming for her that her original assessment of you is right."

"Except, Campbell, I'm no different than any other guy," I explain, holding my hands up in defense. "Those girls don't like me because of something that all other guys do; I am just more successful at the game." I lean back again, waiting for her to explode after my last statement.

She uncrosses her arms and moves to the edge of her chair. "That's my point, fuck-stick. It doesn't take a rocket scientist to see that Vivian is terrified to get close to someone; she thinks that they will leave her. When she talks about you, she says that she thinks that you would use her and then be done with her. This game you're talking about, well, she's afraid to play because, when it comes to you, she knows she'll lose."

"And this is why she stays away from me and never interferes when Jen rations out handfuls of shit in my direction?" My fingers find their way into my hair again. Images of all of the one-night-stands I've had over the last month and what Vivian's reaction would have been after hearing about them invades my mind. The pain of tugging on my dark strands helps to ease my torment of hurting her, but I still consider coiling the purple couch cover around my neck and putting myself out of my misery. All this time I just thought she hated me. If I, for even a second, thought that she liked me, I never would have slept with a single one of those girls.

"All that easy pussy isn't looking so hot now, is it?" she asks, standing and walking into the kitchenette. She returns quickly with a small trashcan and a towel. "Looks like you might need this. Jen is a messy roommate, but I'm pretty sure she would notice puke on the carpet." I harshly take the towel from her, and then she sets the trashcan on the ground next to the coffee table before returning to her chair. An ear-to-ear grin is plastered across her face. If she was a guy, I would punch her for enjoying my moment of dejection. I have no intention of throwing up, but fuck if my stomach doesn't feel like I swallowed an entire bottle of rubber cement.

"I appreciate you having me over and dropping this wonderful karmic bomb on me, but what am I supposed to do now?" I use the dishtowel to wipe the remaining sweat from my forehead and the back of my neck. "She's not going to just decide I'm this amazingly decent guy overnight. Shit, right now you wouldn't be able to convince *me* of that."

Campbell polishes off the rest of her soda and crushes the can, tossing it in the trashcan like an NBA player. It would have only been more impressive if it were a beer she'd slammed. "Well, I can only go by what I've heard," she says, and then produces an almost hissing noise as she scrunches her face, baring all of her teeth. Just as I suspected, she's only heard negative things about me. I roll my eyes and motion for her to continue.

"Well, first I would say to stop thinking with your dick." I only nod, because I knew that one was coming. If I have a real chance to be with her, I don't want any other girls. "I don't know how, but you need to figure out a way to show her that you would value her for her, and not only what is in her pants. She needs to know that you're the type of guy that can stay put and fight for what he wants."

"Fuck, okay, I can do that. You know, if you had been around a little bit more, this month could have worked out a little differently. I really could have used someone on my side; Jen can be scary."

"Yeah, well, I'm not around much; I have friends who live in a house off-campus. I'm helping them start up and promote their band. Actually, they are having a concert next weekend downtown; you'll have to come with us." She rises quickly and heads toward the door, effectively ending our conversation now that it was heading in her direction. I stand as well, throw the towel in the trashcan, and follow her to the door. I guess bonding time is over. When I hear the doorknob rattle, I understand why.

Jen and Vivian waltz through the door, but both abruptly stop when they notice me. Vivian's eyes lock with mine, and that ball of rubber cement that had been rolling around in my stomach melts, but then she diverts them to the floor. The rubber ball returns.

"What the fuck is he doing here?" I hear, pulling my attention from Red to the bundle of aggression issues that I lovingly call Jen.

The witty zinger for her is ready to burst out of my mouth, but Campbell defends me immediately. "I finally met him in the hall after class, and invited him over. And actually, you owe him a thank you."

Jen and I both look at Campbell's two heads that she has apparently sprouted, but she continues on. "He found something important to you that you have been looking for."

Vivian's gaze flies up from the floor and the heat of her glare that is bouncing off Campbell is warming my face. I catch Campbell's hint that I need Jen to disengage in her quest to destroy me, but I'm conflicted. I'm not sure how fucking up a month-long bet would help me win favor with Vivian.

Campbell's look passes over me to Red, shooting her own play-along-and-give-the-guy-a-break look, and I see Vivian ease up out of the corner of my eye. That's all the green light that I need. "Um, yeah, Jen, are you missing a black heel?"

Her lips purse, she hooks her hands around the shoulder straps of her backpack, and taps her fingers on the cloth. It might just kill her that I was the one who found her shoe, and now I want to tell her just for the satisfaction of seeing her swallow down a little bit of that self-righteous shit she so freely dishes out.

I pack away the douche bag comments and smirk that I so desperately want to give her, and go with the advice and opportunity that Campbell is offering. "Yeah, um, I dropped my keys and accidentally kicked them under the couch. When I looked under it to get them, I saw a shoe. Campbell said you were looking for it. I'm glad it turned up; she said they are your favorites."

I don't give her a chance to respond; watching her nostrils flare is enough vindication for me. I move past them all, giving Vivian a smile as I pass. Once I safely make it into the hallway, I turn around, and as politely as possible, thank Campbell for having me over.

"It was great to meet you; you're definitely not what I expected. Don't forget about the concert next weekend, I'll drop off details when I have them," Campbell says with a smile, triumph written all over her face. Jen, on the other hand, hasn't thawed, but I'm hoping that I at least made a dent in the ice queen.

"Thanks, Cam, I would appreciate that. Let me know if you need any help spreading the word. I can hang flyers or something." Yeah, the last bit would be a pain in the ass, but when I see Red smile, I would sign up to hang a thousand posters, or wear one of the stupid fucking flashboards on the main street just to have her smile at me again.

She nods and begins to close the door. Once I hear the lock click, I let out the air I was holding in and relax into the door, resting my forehead on the cool wooden veneer. I take a second to collect myself before heading to my room. I'm going to ditch the rest of my classes for the day and figure out a way to get into Vivian's good graces. Hopefully, Will gets home soon so I can drill him on all things Vivian. I need to get into the female mind and figure out what girls want.

Vivian

I was a little pissed at first when Campbell let Brooks ruin our little roommate bet. But after experiencing the new Brooks this week, I now consider it a small price to pay for his dedouchefication. This entire week he has done things to be helpful and has shown me that he can care about something other than getting laid. Will even told me that he hasn't been out drinking or on a date since he had his Campbell intervention.

I don't know what she did or said, but the results have been impressive. A few different days this week, when I got back from class, there were poems or different kinds of red flowers either taped to our white board, or stuck in our mailbox in the commons area. He and Will hung up and passed out flyers for Campbell's concert. He even helped Carly study for her algebra test—the guy freaking knows math. I, however, have to use a calculator to figure out a twenty percent tip on a ten-dollar ticket. He has been a completely different person; the problem is, I don't know which version is the one I should believe in. This change in him, though, actually has me excited to spend a little time with him tonight at the concert. The overabundance of pretty girls in one place will be a true test of whether this transformation is only skin deep or not.

I frantically look at the time on my phone and then shove my style guide and notebook into my backpack. When I see how late I am for class, I let out a long groan and grab my keys. Jen took over the bathroom this morning, so I look a little less than stellar today. I just love being late for class, especially when I have to walk in with yoga pants, a sweatshirt, and my hair in a ponytail. At least after a half-hour of pounding on the bathroom door, I was finally able to get in long enough to brush my teeth.

I consider her one of my closest friends, but you can certainly tell that she has lived a spoiled, privileged life, one that didn't require her to think of mundane things like picking up after yourself or sharing a bathroom. Our parents knew each other when we were little, but her father moved onto bigger and better things, starting with being elected into the state Senate. The result: she is fiercely loyal and a great friend, but she could use some help in the roommate department.

I rush through the door, throwing my bag over my shoulder when I notice Brooks leaning on the cinder block wall in between our doors. "I was starting to wonder if you were going to ditch class today," he says, pushing off the wall and reaching for the straps of my bag. I allow him to take it off, and we both head toward the elevator. "Jen hogged the bathroom this morning. You didn't have to wait for me," I tell him, unable to hide my surprise that he didn't take off without me.

He laughs and pushes the button for the lobby. "I know I didn't have to wait for you; I wanted to. We have walked together every day this week, why would I ditch you today? I was going to give you a few more minutes, then I was going to come knocking. I was just hoping that you didn't leave early."

I pull my eyebrows together, offended that he would think I would stand someone up. "I wouldn't do that," I say, reaching to take my backpack back. He swings it away from me, not allowing me to have it.

"I didn't say that I thought you would; I just hoped that I didn't miss my chance to walk with you."

I cool down, letting the last part of his statement sink in. "Sorry," I mutter, leaning against the back wall, waiting for the doors to open. I close my eyes and allow my nose to enjoy the intoxicating scent of his cologne. It's a mixture of sandalwood and apples; you can't help but want to get close and smell him, but I'm pretty sure that would be frowned upon in most social settings.

"It's okay; I get it. You think that is something I would do, and you don't want to be put in the same category. I don't blame you; I haven't exactly shown you otherwise." He then turns away from me and looks up at the lights indicating the descending floors. Dammit, that is precisely what I thought, but hearing it out loud makes me feel like the biggest bitch imaginable. I don't have anything to say that would help me to regurgitate my foot, and I see no point in trying to lie to him just to make him feel better. So when the doors open, I do the only thing that I think will help; I bump his shoulder with mine, propelling him slightly forward, and when he looks at me for an explanation, I smile and jerk my head in the direction of our lecture building. When he smirks and moves out of the elevator, I know that I've been forgiven.

By the time we reach the courtyard outside of our dorms, we have less than ten minutes to get to our class that is a fifteen-minute walk away. We start with a speed walk, but our pace soon turns into an all-out run to get there on time. I suddenly don't feel so bad about the yoga pants and sneakers. I consider myself in relatively decent shape, but when we reach the lecture hall entrance, I am sucking in air. My ribs feel like there are ninjas combating the forces of evil with swords on them, and my lungs refuse to adequately take in oxygen. I lean down, resting my hands on my knees and try to catch my breath. I look up at Brooks, whose appearance is pristine. There are no signs of fatigue, lack of breath…his damn collared-shirt isn't even wrinkled, the bastard.

He grabs my arms and gently pulls me down the hall, encouraging my feet to continue moving, even though they feel like they have been dried in cement. We make it to the lecture hall with a minute to spare, and I finally pull myself together enough so that I can at least sneak into the back of the room and hide behind my notebook for most of the hour.

Brooks opens the door for me, and I'm met with only two available seats, one in the front row and one about halfway back. I typically don't give a crap where I sit; but considering my appearance today, and our professor's tendency to call on students in the front row, I absolutely care today. "Go ahead and take the seat in the back, Vivian," Brooks whispers, handing me my backpack. "I'll take my turn in the hot seat." He winks and nudges me to the back of the row and then slides into his seat. I wiggle through the sea of chairs and dodge the awkward glances. I can read their minds, *What is this mess doing with that package of male perfection?'* Class today is turning into a major self-esteem booster.

Dr. Vauldin glides into the room, throws his brief case on the lectern, and scans the room, no doubt searching for his victims of the day. His class is the most wretched thing to have to sit through—boring as hell and it is a struggle to stay awake. So, he punishes us all by randomly calling on students to answer questions. There's no such thing as a raised hand in this room; everyone is eligible to be his prey.

"Alright, guys, we won't be here the entire fifty minutes today," Vauldin announces in a low monotone voice. Hushed "thank fucks" and "yeses" reverberate through the room. I remain still and silent, not wanting to attract attention to myself. I remember Jurassic Park; T-Rex couldn't see you if you didn't move, and I'm hoping this dinosaur falls into the same classification as old Rex.

"You there, in the Bronco sweatshirt," he says, pointing in my direction. I point to myself and he nods, "Yeah, you, please come pass these assignment sheets out." Nope, not T-Rex, he must be one of those damn Velociraptors.

Like the sacrifice of the Lottery Rose, I sluggishly begin to move out of my chair. Here I thought I was going to just hide myself this morning and could get ready for the day during my break between classes; now I'm being called to the front of the class to my own social suicide.

"Sir, I can pass them out," Brooks shouts, bouncing out of his seat. He snatches the papers from Vauldin and begins passing them out before our professor can respond. Vauldin shrugs and continues on with his explanation of the assignment. I sink back into my chair, feeling something that I never thought I would for Brooks Ryan–grateful.

Professor Vauldin quickly clarifies the requirements for our task, and we are released. Everyone files out, but I wait until they are all gone to leave. I don't consider myself a vain person, but my mother taught me well enough to know how to be presentable in public, and I am not anywhere close to those standards. Brooks is waiting for me in the hallway, and I relax at the sight of him.

"Thank you for doing that in there; I really do appreciate it," I tell him, setting my bag down and adjusting my ponytail holder.

"It was no big deal, really. It's been a rough morning for you, and I said I was taking my turn in the hot seat. I'm pretty sure that includes passing out papers." He bends down and takes my bag like before. It's a small gesture, but it pulls at my heart a little. I can't picture Brooks even holding the bathroom door open for Sondra Slut McFunbags, but here he is carrying my backpack all over campus.

"Well, anyway, thank you. Right now I just want to go back and take a long hot shower, and wash this morning off of me." We step outside and begin the fifteen-minute walk back. I'm half-tempted to run again, just so that as few people as possible will see me in the condition I'm in, but the memory of rib ninjas is too fresh.

"So, who are you going to write about for the paper?" Brooks asks about five minutes into the walk. The prompt is to write about someone that has impacted our lives so drastically that we are different people because of them, or the things they've done. I get that the assignment is meant to be a self-reflection on the type of people we have become and why–hell if I don't want to do it though. My father's death and how my mother has handled it all of these years, I know has been the root of a lot of my issues. I'm not so blind as to not see that. However, that doesn't mean that I'm excited to tell the raptor all about it in a stupid three-page paper.

"I don't know; I guess I'll have to think about it a little bit," I shrug.

Brooks is silent for a moment, staring at the ground as we walk. The arrogant shell that he's usually encapsulated in seems cracked, if even for a moment. "Yeah, me too," he says, still examining the sidewalk. He's lying. He has issues, too and probably because of the same people in his life.

"Fuck," he sighs under his breath, just loud enough that I hear. When he finally looks up, his pace slows for a second, and then he starts walking at warp speed. I have to almost run to keep up. I follow his gaze to a girl walking towards us. I figure it would be safe to assume it's another previous conquest. Her perfectly coordinated outfit, heels clicking against the cement, and her gorgeous flat-ironed blonde hair scream money. She notices us approaching and she straightens her back, flashing us a fake smile that would give Miss America a run for her money.

She blocks our path, demanding that we stop. Now that I'm close enough, I see the icebergs in her ears that I guarantee are not Target knockoffs, and the white gold 'S' necklace around her neck confirms that she's wealthy. The necklace also tells me that she's in the Sigma Sorority. Jen had the opportunity to rush the sorority because she is a legacy; her mother was a Sigma. She refused to join though; she said they are rich and mean.

"Brooks, it's been a few weeks; where have you been hiding?" she asks, not bothering to even acknowledge my presence. I'm common folk in yoga pants, not worthy of her time. Jen was right, rich bitches.

"Around." His tone is clipped and uninterested. He refuses to give her the attention that she is seeking, and I am more than thankful. "Um, Amber, this is my friend Vivian. Vivian, this is Amber Jennings. Our fathers know each other from business transactions."

I try to remember my manners and hold out my hand to shake hers, but she gives me the once over like I might give her some kind of contagious infection and rolls her eyes. "Anyway, we need to get together again sometime; we have some unfinished business to attend to," she says, directing her attention back to Brooks, leaving me with my arm outstretched. I snap it back to my side in an attempt to save at least a little dignity.

"Yeah, well, we are late for our next class. See you around." Brooks puts his arm around me and pushes past her. Her expression is a mixture of horror and disgust, and I absolutely take it personally.

"I'm sorry she was like that to you," Brooks says, dropping his arm from my shoulder when we are a safe distance from Amber, the sorority twat-waffle.

"What do you mean? She was a delight," I sarcastically retort. He laughs, but then regains a serious posture.

"No, really, she's a bitch. I only know her because of my stepdad. We kissed once and she thinks that it means we're going to have a relationship. I'm sure her father would love that; it would be a business merger of sorts. But I have no interest in her, and my family already knows I have no intention of taking over the business."

"So what do you want to do then? Aren't your parents disappointed about that?" I ask the question, but immediately regret it; it's personal and intrusive. I never appreciate personal questions like that, and I feel like Brooks is similar in that regard. "I'm sorry; you don't have to answer that. I'm being a little nosy."

Brooks abruptly stops and I look around, preparing myself for another brat pack bombardment. When I see no one near us, I look at him, waiting for an explanation. "Vivian, I understand that you don't know me very well, and I don't know a lot about you, but I hope to change that. No, I don't share a lot with many people, but you're not just anyone to me. Never apologize for asking me something, okay?"

My shock causes all words to lodge in my throat, and I simply nod. No one has ever said anything like that. I've never gotten close enough to anyone to have any honest personal conversations. My roommates and Will probably know me the best, and even they haven't ever heard everything about me.

He nods back and grabs my hand. Though he doesn't lace our fingers together like I'm expecting—like a boyfriend would do with a girlfriend—he holds my hand like a friend would. I look down at our conjoined hands, letting the tingling feeling in my fingers shoot up my arm until I feel those tingles in my stomach. "Come on, let's get you back so you can clean up," he says, squeezing my hand.

Brooks drops me off at my door and promises to stop by later before the concert. I quickly shower before my next class, and go through the rest of my day with thoughts of Brooks, my reflective paper, and a phone call home I would need to make to complete it. All of it is plaguing me. It will take a good amount of guts to call my mother to have the discussion about my father that is long overdue, and it will take even more fun activities, and possibly alcohol, to revive myself afterward.

BROOKS

This has been the best fucking day ever; well, besides the brief encounter with the she-devil Amber Jennings. Vivian seems to be opening up more to me, and I even held her hand. I know, big fucking deal; I'm not fourteen, and this isn't junior high. But with Vivian, I'll take what I can get, and to hold her hand felt so damn good. I've spent extra time this evening picking out the right outfit and making sure my hair is just right. Shit, I might need to worry less about Will and check my own vag-status.

I'm running the last bit of gel through my hair when I hear a soft knock at the front door. I swiftly wash my hands and dry them on my shower towel to answer the door. When the door swings open, all of the light and fluffy feelings I had two minutes ago evaporate, and my heart drops in to my stomach.

"I'm sorry, is Will here?" Vivian sniffles and attempts to hide her smeared mascara and rosy cheeks. Her efforts are fruitless; she is a total wreck. I scowl, thinking someone has hurt her and that she needs Will to beat someone's ass. I peer into the hallway, looking for the culprit, only to find it empty. "What happened? Whose ass do Will and I need to kick?"

"No one." She tries to laugh through her tears. "I just needed to talk to someone, and the girls are already gone."

My jealousy and rage spike. I contain myself out of respect for her obvious fragile state, but I'm pissed that she came here looking for him, and didn't bother to think of me. "He's not here; he left early to help Campbell set up." My tone sounds surprisingly calm, considering how my insides are vibrating from my disappointment.

"Oh, that's right; I knew that. Sorry to bother you." Her eyes build with tears, and she looks down to avoid me seeing them. She turns to walk back to her room, and I stow away any of my damaged pride, realizing I don't want her to leave. "Wait, Red," I say, reaching for her elbow. "I know I don't compare to Will, but I would really like it if you came in. If you feel like talking, great; if not, that's okay, too. We can watch a movie or something to help you get your mind off of whatever is going on."

"What about the show? You look like you are all ready to go; I don't want to ruin your evening."

"Vivian, for being one of the smartest people in our little group, you sure can be clueless sometimes," I tell her. "The only reason I was going tonight was to hang out with you, and if you're not going, then I have no interest in being there."

She pauses, evaluating either my offer or how I feel about her. Frankly, I don't give a shit, as long as I can convince her to come over. I begin to fidget with my shirt, worried that she might actually decide it would be better to go home and be alone than spend the evening with me.

Just when I don't think I can take another second of indecision, she walks past me into my room. I exhale and give myself a second to figure out what to do next. I didn't really think about what would come next; I was too worried about getting her to stay. I've never had a girl here. This is my safe zone, and she's not here in a hook-up capacity, which makes this even more foreign to me.

I walk back into the living room, expecting to see her on my couch having a complete emotional breakdown. Thankfully, she's in the bathroom, which gives me a few more minutes to collect myself. I grab two glasses and a bottle of tequila and set them on the coffee table. I then review our collection of DVDs and pull out a few of our girliest movies. I end up with only one, Dumb and Dumber. I figure at least it's a comedy, and it will make her laugh if nothing else.

I hear her blow her nose, followed by the bathroom doorknob turning. I hustle to the couch and take a seat, hoping that I appear relaxed without looking overzealous. I pour us each a drink when I see her just standing in the hallway unsure of what to do next. I stand, taking it to her. "It looked like you could maybe use this," I say, placing the glass in her hand.

She offers a tight-lipped smile and takes a small sip of the liquor. Instantly she begins to choke, and her eyes tear up from the burn. I pat her on her back, but she waves me away. "I'm alright," she chokes out. I grab her a bottle of water from the fridge and she guzzles the cool liquid to ease her throat.

"Come on. I picked out a movie; find a spot and get cozy." I direct her to the couch and head to the DVD player to get the movie started. Our couch is not covered like theirs, and I notice the look she gives it before she sits down. "I never bring girls here, if that's what you're thinking," I tell her before continuing my work on the film preparation.

"No...well yeah, sorry," she stutters as she sits down. I want to be offended, but I laugh instead; she smiles back, letting me know that her anxiety is slowly fading. "I always sit in the recliner when I'm over here with Will. I guess I just assumed that the couch has seen a lot of action. I'm sorry, that really is kind of shitty of me to think."

I push play and return to the couch, sitting on the opposite side, not wanting to seem presumptuous. "No, it's fine; I would think it would be a safe assumption. But really, you're the first girl I've ever invited to my dorm room. Now I can't confirm the amount of upholstery cleaning that occurs between years; who knows the history of this bad boy?" I say, patting a cushion. When I really evaluate what I could be rubbing my hand over, I pull it away with a look of disgust that matches Vivian's. "Maybe a couch cover isn't such a bad idea. I'm never out here; when I'm home, I usually watch movies in my room."

"Is it a hygienically safer place? And do you promise to keep your hands to yourself if we watch the movie in your room?" she asks skeptically. I don't blame her. I wouldn't feel confident being alone in a bedroom with me either if I was a girl. I would usually show off my best moves and lay the charm on thick, but right now, I have no desire to go that route with her. Scratch that—desire, yes, but my conscience wouldn't allow it.

"I promise this is an evening on friendly terms only. I wouldn't sleep with you tonight, even if you begged." I stand, gathering the glasses and alcohol and hand them to her. She grips onto the bottle and waits for me to eject the movie. She then tentatively follows me to my room, and I close the door behind us. "Go ahead and sit anywhere," I tell her, taking everything from her and sitting it on the minuscule desk in the corner of the room. Without having a roommate, I was able to rearrange a bit to make my room a little more comfortable and spacious. That included taking down the extra bed and replacing it with a chair and small desk.

She takes off her shoes and crawls up onto my bed. I try to ignore that she is, in fact, sitting on my bed, because this fabulous idea of mine is proving to test every molecule of willpower I have. I quickly think of every non-sexual thing I can think of to calm my hormones: grandmas, Will in a bathing suit...Jen—yup, that does it.

I kick my shoes off into the compact closet and apprehensively approach my bed. "It's okay, Brooks; you can sit on the bed with me," she says as she flattens her hand on the duvet, signaling me to sit beside her. I don't hesitate, practically bounding onto the bed.

We both settle back against the headboard, but I make sure to keep my hands to myself. I remain diligent for the entire film. I don't pay attention to most of the movie; I'm enjoying just watching her lose her sadness in the comedy. I unwind to the sound of her laughter. Occasionally I feel her head on my shoulder, and I remain as still as possible so that she won't realize our contact and move. Her touch leaves a streak of fire across my skin, and when she takes it away, my body feels the loss, yearning for her warmth once again.

When the movie ends, we both stretch and look to one another for the next step in this unforeseen evening of ours. "Are you feeling a little better?" I ask tentatively.

She rests her hand on mine. "Yes, thank you for being here, Brooks."

I brush a piece of her hair behind her ear, similar to the way I did the day we met, but this time she doesn't take her eyes from mine, nor does she shrink away. "I'm hoping that one day you'll see that I'll always be here."

We sit in silence for a moment, neither of us taking the offensive. I refuse to take advantage of this situation and push her towards being physical; she would only regret it, and all the progress I've made would be lost. Making the decision for us, I pull away from her. "So, what would you like to do now? I can get another movie, we can talk about what was bothering you, or I think Will may even have some playing cards somewhere."

"I think I'd like to talk about why I came over here," she says. "First, I'm going to need a few drinks. Why don't you get some water, and I'll pour a few more shots?"

My eyes narrow. "Are you sure? You don't seem like much of a drinker; I don't want you to get sick or anything."

"You're right; I'm really not. I think two would be my limit."

I laugh, shaking my head, and move towards the hallway to get the waters. When I return, the shots are poured, and Vivian is sitting on my bed once again. I place the waters on my desk and take my shot from her. I quickly throw it back, wishing I had some kind of chaser for it. I wasn't really prepared for company; I was lucky to even have the alcohol. Vivian does the same with her drink and hands me her glass.

"Let that one settle and you can have another in a little while," I tell her, setting the glasses on the desk alongside the waters and climbing back onto the bed. "Okay, now tell me what's going on. It was horrible seeing you cry earlier."

Vivian pulls her knees to her chest, and hooks her hands together around them. I want her to open up to me, not hide within herself, so I grab her hands and pull them away from her legs. I lie down, pulling her with me so that we are facing each other. We each tuck an arm under our heads and let our bodies acclimate to our closeness.

"You're not at all what you were like the entire first month of school; what's up with the change?" she asks.

"I'm not the same," I answer. "I wanted to be with you, but you never gave me the time of day. I finally realized that how I was acting was pushing you away. I may not be the best guy in the world, but I could never intentionally hurt you, Red. I just wish you didn't hate me so much." My eyes divert to the duvet that I've been picking at, embarrassed that I admitted that all to her.

"I never hated you, Brooks." My eyes fly to hers.

"You don't need to lie to make me feel better; I know that you detested me."

She sits straight up and places her hand under my chin, forcing me to look up at her.

"I need you to understand something, Brooks. I never hated you, ever. I liked you from the minute I found you in my bed, but I didn't trust myself around you, so I avoided you. You overwhelm me, and it terrifies my very being to think of what would happen if I gave in to you. I saw how you were with other girls, and I wouldn't walk away unscathed and in one piece like them. You would break me."

I sit up and wrap my legs around her, pulling her to me. "I wouldn't break you, Vivian. I want to be the guy that mends the piece of you that is already cracked. All I want is the chance to have that honor, no matter how difficult the job might be."

She tries to turn away from me, but I lightly palm her cheek and bring her gaze back to mine. "What fractured you, Red?" She shakes her head and then leans into my hand, closing her eyes to absorb my touch. "I'm not ready yet," she whispers with her eyes still closed.

I pull her face to mine and rest my cheek against hers; her scent of lavender and vanilla envelopes me, and I want nothing more than to drown in her. "Is it the same thing that upset you tonight?" I whisper in her ear. She doesn't move away from me; instead, I feel her nod and wrap her hands in my shirt. "Would you like to know what damaged me?" I ask, and she nods again.

I turn into her, delicately kiss her cheek, and then run my nose along her creamy skin until I reach her forehead, planting another feather-light peck. I then pull away, take her hands away from my shirt, and lace my fingers with hers. Feeling my absence, she gradually opens her eyes.

"I've never met my real father. He took off before I was born. Then when I was two, my mom got married and had a whole new family with my stepdad. He adopted me, but really, it was more for appearances than anything. Recently my dad started writing to me, wanting to meet. I just don't know if I even want to know him. I've always been someone's afterthought; no one has ever picked me for me. The attention that I get from girls, it makes me feel wanted; for once I have the control to choose, instead of always being last pick."

"Brooks, you're not my last pick. That control you seek means you have the power to crush me. You and I are not all that different."

"I don't believe that; you're so much better than I am. You're good and pure and loyal, all the things that I pretend like I am. But I'm a fraud; all of this tough shit and arrogance is all just a show."

"You're not a fraud; you're just trying to survive. I get that." She takes a deep breath, pulls her hands from mine, and shakes them out. "Okay, here it goes. When I was little, my father was killed. The man who was responsible went to prison. After it happened, my mother packed my sisters and me up and moved us back to her tiny hometown, trying to forget that it ever happened. To this day, she refuses to talk about what happened. I've heard rumors about it, and the things my father was into that possibly got him killed, but she refuses to talk about it. She has gone overboard trying to shelter us, keeping us from the outside world. It took a lot to even get her to let me come to school here."

I entwine our fingers again, attempting to show her my support. Hearing that her father was murdered and that he was possibly into some kind of trouble before his death certainly surprises me, but I pass no judgment. "Is that why you were crying?"

She nods. "I called home to ask one more time about my dad. I thought maybe I would use it for my English paper. I mean, I wasn't sure I wanted to throw all that drama out there for Vauldin to read, but I at least wanted the option. I thought maybe writing it down would be therapeutic for me."

"You know, there would be case files that are public record if you really wanted to know the story. If you wanted to find out, I would go with you." I'm not just offering to be nice, or because of the moment. Being this close to her, feeling her, she has bewitched me, and I would go to the ends of the Earth for her.

"You would do that?" she says in disbelief.

"I would do anything you needed to see that smile." I bring our tangled hands to my mouth and kiss her wrist. "Thank you for trusting me with that story," I say as I take our hands away and tuck them into my chest.

"I'm sorry about your dad," she responds, the words so hushed I can barely hear her. I smile lightly and then direct her body down to the bed. Resting our heads on my pillow, I loop my arm around her waist and tenderly tug her body backwards until her back is snugly against my chest. I curl around her tiny frame and nestle my face in her soft auburn hair. I wiggle in closer and kiss her neck. "Please stay here tonight. We don't have to do anything but lie here. I just want to hold you and wake up with you in my arms in the morning. I'm not ready to let you leave yet."

Vivian turns in my arms, letting me see her beautifully muddled eyes. "I don't want to leave either. Your arms around me are the only things that have felt right in a long time."

I allow my fingers to explore her fiery locks, her exposed cheek, and then her neck, cupping my hand around the base and pulling her lips to mine. I'm never nervous with girls, but I feel Vivian shiver in my arms and it sends chills down my body. My stomach is fluttering with anxiousness, but I know I can't let this go any further than this for now.

I deepen the kiss, allowing us to briefly lose ourselves in the moment. She tastes like drops of Heaven, and I try to drink in every ounce of her. It feels wrong to slow things down; we should be mangled together, enjoying every inch of each other, but if I want this to be something real, I know I need to back off for tonight. Sensing my hesitation, Vivian moves her head away briefly and returns only to leave a long lingering peck on my lips. I've never had sensual. I've never had emotional. It's always been just fucking and getting off with other girls. This is entirely different. I feel more turned on with her one kiss than I ever had fucking some random girl. I could spend a lifetime discovering her mouth.

I kiss her forehead once more, and she snuggles into my chest. I gradually hear her breathing even out, and relish the feeling of her asleep in my arms. I hold on tight, afraid that I'll wake up and it will all have been a dream. I struggle to stay awake, not wanting our night to really end, but eventually I give in to the pull of exhaustion.

When I wake the next morning, I realize that our bodies have not moved. Vivian is still nestled tight to my body, and I just relax onto my pillow to watch her sleep. I study every feature, committing them all to memory in case last night was all I ever get with her. It isn't long before she stirs, and her eyes leisurely open. That's when her most amazing feature is revealed. Staring back at me are the most brilliant green eyes. Her eyes have always been a mixture of colors, never pledging allegiance to any one shade, until now. Now I'm sucked into a field of clovers. If mornings are the only time that they are like this, then I want to make it my mission to wake up next to her for the rest of my life. I want to be stingy and never share my emerald orbs.

"What's wrong?" she asks when she notices that I'm just staring at her. She tenses in my arms, and I squeeze her tighter, trying to ease that tension.

"Nothing, Viv, everything is perfect. This has been perfect. Please tell me it doesn't end when you leave this morning." I rest my head on the top of hers, bracing myself for the possibility of disappointment.

"I don't want this to end either. Can you handle what that means though?" She's questioning my fidelity, and I understand.

But she needs to know that there is no other girl that would ever compare to her, I don't need to look any farther than what is in my arms right now.

"I'm not going anywhere, Viv. I promise. It's just you and me."

Not caring about our morning breath that could probably choke a donkey, she scoots up and kisses me, and then whispers the only word I needed to hear. "Okay."

BROOKS

November has officially brought the change of seasons. The first snow hasn't arrived yet, but we have all been anticipating it. While December 21st marks the first real day of winter, in Colorado, winter weather begins when it wants. I've barely noticed though; the only thing that has my attention is Vivian. She fills every minute of my day; if I'm not with her, then I'm thinking about her. I have to force myself to pay attention in class, but I don't mind the distraction; my time with her has been the best month and a half of my life.

With Campbell's help, the girls have gradually accepted me. Even Jen has called a truce, which is maybe the cause for the change in weather–hell froze over. Will, on the other hand, has been somewhat standoffish about mine and Vivian's relationship. I think he misses their friendship, and seeing me with her seems to make him uncomfortable. I've suggested setting him up on a few dates, but he has refused each time.

Vivian is in class all morning today, and then we are supposed to be meeting everyone for lunch in the dining hall. I'm using the time to try to work on my final English paper. Our reflective essay for Vauldin is due in three weeks, and neither Vivian nor I have written a single word. We both feel stuck.

The letters from my father have continued to arrive, and he keeps asking me to visit him. Vivian has encouraged me to see him; she even offered to go along, but I can't decide if I'm ready to see him. My mother has refused to ever talk about him, and there are so many unanswered questions. I suppose maybe that's why Vivian and I relate to each other so well. We fill each other's voids that our parents left behind. She is taking the first step though. Next week, before our Thanksgiving break, we are driving to Colorado Springs together to read the court documents and investigative reports surrounding her dad's case. I'm so proud of her for facing her past. I'm not that brave; to be honest, when it comes to my real dad, I'm a coward.

My computer screen is still blank when Will walks through the door, throwing his backpack on the couch and falling into the recliner. He doesn't turn on the television or pull out his books; he just sits, silently staring at me, fidgeting with his hands. "Dude, what's going on?" I ask him, turning in my chair to fully face him. "I'm fresh out of Xanax, and you're way too damn big to have to resuscitate if you keel over from a panic attack." I thought that was rather funny, but he merely cracks a small smile. The usual Will would have some witty retort that would put me in my place, but he says nothing.

"Okay, let's hear it. Something has crawled up your ass and I can tell that you're dying to extract it."

"Fuck," he mumbles as he rubs his hands over his face. He finally steadies himself, placing his hands on his knees. "I need you to tell me that you love her. I need you to tell me that you are not going to make her fall for you and then break her heart. You need to promise me that you are not the guy that I first met when we moved in here."

"What the fuck, man!" I say sternly, squaring off my shoulders. "I haven't even told *her* that I love her, and you want me to tell you? I had always questioned whether or not you actually have a vagina, and you're pretty close to confirming my suspicions of Team Pink. Guys don't talk about this shit, Will."

He stands and begins pacing the room. "Dammit, Brooks, you're my friend, and if the two of you are happy, then I'll back off. I just want to make sure that you treat her the way she deserves. I know you two are sleeping together, and I don't want to see her hurt when you get bored and move on."

"Fuck you, Will," I growl and stand. "If you were my friend, you would think more of me than that. You know what I think? I think you're jealous. You want a relationship like she and I have, and it fucking eats you up."

Will stops, his nostrils flare, and I notice his hands shaking; for a second I'm afraid for my life. "I don't want just some girl!" he explodes. "I want Vivian!" When he realizes what he's confessed, he crumbles into his chair again, leaving me shocked and standing alone.

"W-what?" I stutter. "You want to date Vivian?" I don't know how to comprehend what he's telling me. I've entered a soap opera, and I'm the main character in a love triangle. I've seen these stories; men like me always lose to the Wills of the story. He's the funny guy, the one that would always do the right thing, even at his own expense. I wouldn't want to compete against someone like him. The difference between the two of us: I may have the appearances that draw the girls in, but he has the personality that keeps them coming back.

"I don't want to date her, Brooks; I'm in love with her." Will is hiding his face in his hands, so his words are muffled, but I can still understand every damn word and it makes my stomach hurt to the point of throwing up. I feel the bile rise, and it burns the back of my throat. *What the fuck is happening?*

"What do you plan to do about it?" I ask him, taking my seat once again. I grip onto the edge of my chair, partly restraining myself, and partly holding myself together. I fully expect him to say that I'm going to have to compete with him for her, and it's a fight I'm not sure I would win.

"Nothing, Brooks. I may have those feelings for her, and if I had the chance I would worship the ground that she walks on, but she doesn't want me. She's in love with you." I loosen my grip on the chair and feel the indentations on my fingers that it leaves behind. "But I need to know that I'm doing the right thing by bowing out. I want you to say that you'll treat her right."

I take in all that he's expecting of me, to reflect on my feelings for Vivian. "I promise, Will. I'm not perfect, and I know that I'll have my fuck-ups, but I promise I'll do my best to protect her. I know it's hard for you to believe it, but I do love her. Believe me, it surprises the hell out of me because I didn't even think I was capable of that emotion, but I do."

Will doesn't respond at first; it feels like a lifetime before he finally rises and holds out his hand for me. I meet him in the middle of the room and stretch my arm to meet his hand to shake. "That's what I needed to know," he says, shaking my hand. Then he drops back and gives some space between the two of us. "But if you hurt her, I swear to everything that is holy, I will crush you; I don't care who your daddy is. I will end you. Do we have an understanding?"

"Will, if I fuck this up, I would want to beat my own ass."

Satisfied with my answer, he nods and begins to walk past me to the front door. There is still another half an hour before the dining hall opens for lunch, and I assumed before this conversation that we would have gone together. "Hey, are you still going to meet up with the girls for lunch?" I ask. He stops and stills his hand that was twisting the doorknob. "No, I don't really feel like it," he says, refusing to look at me. "I'm going to meet up with Seth and Aaron from the rugby team. Just tell the girls something came up, please."

Without looking for confirmation, he opens the door, moves through it, and slams it behind him. I don't know if I lost my friend or not, but either way, I hope I can uphold my promise. I want nothing more than to protect her.

VIVIAN

All four of us girls have been eating in the cafeteria for at least fifteen minutes before either of the guys shows up. When Brooks walks through the door and I see his scowl and disheveled hair, I know he is stressed or upset about something. Anytime Brooks is over thinking something, his hands automatically find his hair, and he gently tugs on it until he can calm himself. He bypasses the food line and takes a seat at our table next to me. I frown at him as he sits, but he looks at me and shakes his head, waving me off. Whatever it is, it's not open for discussion right now.

Shifting his emotions, he flings his arm across the back of my chair and kisses the side of my head. "Sorry I'm late, Red," he whispers.

"No worries," I tell him, trying to ease his tension. "I thought you and Will were coming together."

He moves his hand away at the mention of Will's name, making the buzzers go off in my head. Something happened between the two of them. "He forgot that he was supposed to meet a few of the rugby guys, but he said he'd be around later." I give him a look that says that I don't buy that load of shit for one minute, but he quickly changes the subject. "So what did I miss, ladies?" he asks, and the girls jump right into our previous conversation like they never skipped a beat.

"We were just deciding who Campbell is going home with for Thanksgiving," Jen answers. "I want her to be my buffer from my parents, but Carly thinks that it's not okay to subject her to that and wants her to come home with her." Campbell aged out of foster care just after she graduated from high school, and while her last foster home was actually decent to her, she doesn't feel comfortable going to their house for the holidays. I told her that if she didn't mind crazy, she could come home with me, but I don't think anyone should be subjected to the guilt trips and mood swings of my mother. I don't even want to go home, and if the dorms weren't closing, I wouldn't be.

Whenever I feel sorry for myself, I look at Campbell and tell myself to suck it up. How she is even functioning with the life she's had is beyond me. Her parents died when she was little, and she had no living family members that were able to take her in. Her parents had named guardians for her in their wills, and even set up a multi-million dollar trust to care for her thinking they had all of their bases covered. But when the guardians found out that she would only inherit the money in small increments after milestones in her adult life, like high school and college graduation, with the remainder being paid out when she turns 30 or gets married, whichever comes first, they handed her over to the state. They didn't want her unless they were going to profit from it. She has since bounced around from foster home to foster home for the last ten years. Campbell is one tough girl; I wish I were half as resilient as she is.

"Why don't you draw straws or something; winner gets their pick of Christmas or Thanksgiving," Brooks suggests, stealing a French fry from my plate and swirling it around in the leftover ketchup.

"You guys, seriously, I really appreciate this," Campbell interrupts. "It feels good that you all would even invite me, but I don't want you to feel like you have to have me. I have enough money that I could stay in a hotel and do some work with the band. I could probably even stay with them, or go over there on Thanksgiving."

"Over my fucking dead body," Brooks snaps. He states it so sternly and sharply that we all immediately direct our attention to him. Carly's eyes look as though they may pop out of her head. Sometimes I wonder how she even stands being our friend. She never cusses or says anything mean about anyone, and then there is Jen, who can't complete a sentence without an f-bomb and a crude sexual reference included in it.

"What I mean is, we are your family, and a person spends holidays with family. I don't care who you choose to go home with—you can even come to my house—but you will NOT spend it alone. That is unacceptable."

"Okay," she mutters, stunned by Brooks' outburst. "I guess I'll go home with Carly for Thanksgiving, and Jen for Christmas; the break is longer and she might be in more of a need of a safety net."

Brooks looks around the table for objections and finds none. He then wipes his hands on his napkin and stands to leave. "Sorry I was late, but I need to get going to my next class. I'm supposed to stop by the library first to get a book that we are supposed to have for the final." He bends down and kisses me on the cheek, then leaves before anyone can try to convince him to stay.

"What in the hell was that?" Jen asks the group as soon as Brooks is out of earshot. "He acted weird the entire time he was here." She was right, and I couldn't argue otherwise, but I didn't want to talk about it. No one has a chance to answer though. Amber fucking Jennings and two of her little friends, more rich sorority sisters no doubt, stroll up to our table.

"Well, Jennifer, I didn't know you were doing charity work, or are you just taking a break from money to see how the other half lives?" I look to Jen, who is wringing her napkin between her hands. I wasn't surprised that she would have something rotten and snooty to say to us, but I am most certainly surprised that she and Jen know each other.

"You know I like you about as much as you like me, so what could you possibly want?" She doesn't even bother to look at Amber. This is a rich girl standoff, and I have no idea how to proceed. Back home, there would have been a brief fight in a pasture, you would shake hands, and it would be done. These girls play a whole different game, and I want no part of it. It's sneaky and conniving, where everyone pretends to be your friend, but then stabs you in the back just to elevate their social status.

"I just didn't know you liked the company of white trash, and I thought that you would have informed Brooks that he could do so much better than this." She points to me like I'm only an object to discuss and not a person with feelings. "We both know our parents have been planning our ending up together since we were little; I would think you would have a little more loyalty to your social ranking."

I turn to Jen, ready to invite her old best buddy outside to settle our little disagreement country style. But she shakes her head, silencing me. I follow her instructions; she knows more about this girl than I do, and if Jen tells me to shut the fuck up, then I will.

Jen takes a deep breath, pushes back her chair, and stands to meet her nemesis head on. "The thing about trash, Amber, is that it comes in all shapes and sizes. It's something you are, and money can't change that. Right now, the only piece of shit I see is packaged in a Sigma shirt and heels. Now, I suggest that you get the fuck out of my face before I take you outside and show you just how loyal I am."

"Wow, how classy; don't you think you've disgraced your family enough?" Amber's words are harsh, but they lack confidence as she takes a step back, fearful of what results they may provoke.

Jen falters a bit; whatever issue Amber is referencing, strikes a nerve with Jen. She recovers quickly though. "You want to talk about social ranking, Amber? Well, who do you think controls those city permits and tax credits for your dad's business?"

Amber's face loses all color and she stumbles over her words. "You wouldn't."

"No matter what I've done, it would only take one phone call, and my father could make your family's empire crumble."

When she fails to return a response, Jen pushes in her chair and steps around a dumbfounded Amber. "Come on, girls. It's time for class. Amber here is going to take care of our trays." We quickly jump out of our chairs and move to catch up to Jen as she exits the dining hall. It feels good to walk away winning the fight, but with girls like Amber, they don't walk away and let it lie. I know she's already plotting her revenge; I just hope I'm not part of the collateral damage.

10

VIVIAN

Today is the day I've been waiting most of my life for. I'm going to find out what happened to my dad. Brooks promised to drive me to the courthouse and go through everything with me, but I'm nervous. I'm worried about what we'll find out, and that he'll look at me differently if we find out something really bad. I've always worried that I would be judged for what my dad was involved in, and I don't know if I could handle Brooks pushing me away because of it.

The light is peeking through his old dusty curtains that I'm sure had been hanging in the dorm since the school opened. I put my hand over my eyes to shield the unwanted wake up call, hoping for just a few more minutes of sleep before I have to peel myself from this delicious guy and get ready to go to Colorado Springs. He quickly reaches for my wrist and gently holds it down to the pillow behind me.

"Please don't cover your eyes; this is my favorite part of the day." A small smile creeps across his face, and I realize that he has been awake for a while.

Feeling a little embarrassed as to what he might have seen—who knows if I snore, or talk, or *oh, God,* what if I fart in my sleep? My face begins to heat up, and I try to turn my head away. He places his hand on my cheek and slowly turns me to him. "You don't know how beautiful you are, do you?"

I'm no longer slightly embarrassed; I'm totally uncomfortable, shifting to try and scoot away. I have never had a guy really compliment me, and I really don't take them well. He doesn't let me go anywhere though, wrapping his arm around me and pulling me so close I could feel his heartbeat pounding in his chest. He lets out a little sigh and briefly closes his eyes.

"You don't understand, Viv. What we have, how I feel about you, it's like nothing I've ever had. You are the most beautiful thing in my world. I can tell that you don't hear things like that often, and you know what? I'm thankful for that."

I raise my eyebrow in confusion; I'm not quite sure if he was saying that he is glad other guys don't find me attractive, but it sounds like one heck of a backwards compliment. His lips curl around his teeth like he's trying his damnedest to hold in his laugh, and then he lets out the loudest chuckle. Shit, this asshole is laughing at me. I panic and try to get off the bed.

As I struggle to untangle from his arms to get away from him, the smile on his face quickly vanishes. He grabs my hands and rolls on top of me, settling his hips against mine. His eyes are searching mine, seriousness oozing from him. "This is coming out wrong. What I mean is that I'm glad that you haven't heard a lot of those nice things from other guys...not because I don't think that you are the most gorgeous girl that I have ever met, but because I want it to be me that you hear those things from. I want to be the only one that puts that amazing smile on your face. I want to be the one that holds you every night, to make you feel good," he leans his head down and kisses my lips before resting his forehead against mine. "You're my clover, Viv," he whispers.

I relax in his grip, but the lump in my throat begins to desperately attempt to claw its way out. "Your what?" I squeak out.

"My clover," he repeats. His eyes are closed, and I can tell he is gathering the strength to tell me whatever is rolling around in his head. He releases my hands and settles himself on his forearms, caging me in and nuzzling into my neck. I bring my arms around him, and lightly stroke his tight back muscles, urging him to talk to me or kiss me...something.

Finally, he slides off me and rolls us both so that we are lying on our sides, face-to-face. He sweeps a piece of my long chestnut hair out of my face and tucks it behind my ear, before slowly moving in to kiss me in the same spot. A shiver runs down my body; the action is reminiscent of our first night in his bedroom, when we did nothing but kiss and sleep in each other's arms. I want to pull him back on top of me and let him devour me, but instead, I let him take this where he needs it to go. He is struggling with the words that I know we both feel. Right now, I'm fine with him showing me his feelings with his body; I don't need the words. I know that I am his—he doesn't need to say it; I feel it. In this moment, we belong to each other.

"Do you know why mornings are my favorite time of day?" he asks, rubbing his thumb along my bottom lip. I shake my head and kiss the tip of his thumb, adding a little nibble for good measure. He lets out a deep moan, but continues.

"Your eyes are never the same color; they are usually different variations of brown. I can always tell your mood by the shade. But in the mornings, they are something completely different. When you first wake up, they are green. This vivid emerald green that is so enchanting and so stunning that they just pull me in, and I feel like I can lose myself in them. Your eyes are like four-leaf clovers, Viv, and when I wake up next to you, knowing that I'll be the only one to get to see them like that..." He pauses, searching for the right words. "Viv, I just feel so damn lucky that it's just me that gets to see that piece of you."

His words leave me speechless. What does one say to something so raw? He is showing me emotion that he has never shown anyone before, emotion that I have never even felt before. I have never said 'I love you' to anyone before; I know I feel it for Brooks, but God, it's scary to admit. He has somehow possessed my soul; I have fallen so hard that my heart would shatter if he decided I wasn't what he wanted anymore. I don't know if I could survive him, but I want to.

I smile, but the tears that I have been struggling to hold back begin to slide down my face. He wipes them away with his thumbs and rolls on top of me, stretching his body to cover mine. He looks into my eyes and then at my lips, like he's asking for my permission. When our eyes meet again, he crashes his mouth to mine. Our kiss is deep and urgent, like we might never get this moment back and we want to savor every second.

Brooks slows us down to catch our breath. "God, I love you, Viv," he says against my lips with a long exhale. "Don't ever fucking leave me, Clover; I don't think I could live without my green mornings."

And just like that, he calms my anxiety. He slowly lifts my shirt and begins kissing down my body, exploring every inch with his delicious lips. All I can think about is how he won't hurt me; he is as scared as I am, but found the guts to tell me anyways. He laid it all out there for me; can I really let him think I didn't feel the same? My brain is whispering. *Yes, you can. Men leave; protect your heart.* But my heart is shouting, *tell him, or you will lose him!* My heart wins the battle.

Pulling him up to meet my face, I kiss his swollen lips, and then push him over so that I can straddle his strong legs. He grips onto my hips and I can feel his excitement, his need for me. I grind into him, and he hisses between his gritted teeth. I lean down and place feather kisses along his cheekbones and over his eyes. Slightly pulling back, I sigh, "I love you too, Brooks, but please don't break me."

Brooks sits up, looking into my eyes, and he cups my face. "I promise, Clover, I'll worship every part of you that you're willing to give me. Let me love you." He kisses my cheek, dusting down my jaw line, and onto my collarbone, his soft hands caressing my back.

I let out a slight whimper at his touch. "Brooks," is all I manage to get out between my heated breaths. He stops and looks up to me, "Tell me what you need." I brush the backs of my knuckles along his cheekbone and tell him as confidently as I can, "Show me."

Grinning ear to ear, he cradles my head in his hands, smoothing my hair. "I'll spend every day for the rest of my life showing you, Red." He takes control, gently pushing me back to the bed, sliding my pajama pants down, and pulling my top off. He takes my puckered nipple into his mouth, and I gasp from the overwhelming sensation.

He licks his way from one breast to the other, giving each its fair share of attention before finding my lips again. I weave his hair through my fingers, and when he takes my bottom lip between his teeth and bites down, I pull his hair and moan from the mixture of pleasure and pain.

He grabs my hands and pins them above my head with one hand, whispering in my ear, "I want us to fall together." He slowly rocks into me, but I buck my hips, encouraging him to move faster, harder. Meeting my demands, he withdraws almost entirely out of me, only to slam into me once again. I'm panting so hard I can barely catch my breath. "Oh, God, I'm there Brooks. Crash with me," the words tumble out of my mouth on a ragged exhale. I've finally figured out what the fuss is all about.

Brooks picks up the pace and I match him thrust for thrust, creating our own symphonic rhythm until we both plummet over the edge of bliss. His whole body goes rigid, he grumbles through his teeth, and then collapses onto me, burying his face into my neck, both of us struggling to calm our breathing. "Fuck, I love you, Clover," he sighs into my hair. "This heart is forever yours, Viv."

"Forever," I respond before my body relaxes and the exhaustion pulls me under. "You're my forever, Brooks."

By the time we finally pull ourselves from his bed and load up in the car for the long drive south, all of the tranquility of the early morning has vanished. Brooks does his best to distract me along the way by turning on an all 80s and 90s radio station and encouraging me to rock out along with him. We play car games like I spy; he even tried out ridiculous knock-knock jokes. For the most part, his efforts were a success. Well that is until he pulled in front of the courthouse.

"You ready?" Brooks asks, putting the car into park. He caresses my knee and smiles, trying to ease my apprehension.

"No, but I'm going in anyways." I squeeze his hand and open the car door to get out. It's mid-afternoon, so I know that we have a limited amount of time to go through things. Brooks turns off the car and climbs out as well. Walking around the front of the car, he grabs my hand when he reaches me and leads me into the building. It's so dreamlike; the courthouse looks like nothing special, just a plain brick building that could be replicated in any city in America, but inside it might hold all of the answers I've ever searched for.

Brooks opens the front doors for me and a security officer instructs us to remove our valuables to go through the metal detector. The seriousness of my surroundings punches me in the gut, and I mechanically move through the machine, following all of his directives. Once through security, we find the directory to locate the public records office.

"Second floor, Viv. This way," Brooks says, pointing to the wide staircase at the end of the hallway off the front lobby area. He cords our fingers together, and we climb the stairs; each footstep matches the pounding of my heart, and it feels like it might beat out of my chest. "Don't worry; no matter what it says, I'm still here," Brooks declares when we reach the top of the stairs and see the sign for the office we came in search of.

The woman at the receptionist desk barely looks up from her computer screen when we enter the office. Her bright red hair has been drastically teased into some sort of beehive on top of her head, and the pencils sticking out of it would make one think that she is a busy little bee. Her actions speak otherwise. The solitaire game she is absorbed in apparently requires complete concentration. I actually have to ring the bell on the counter to pull her eyes away long enough to give us any information.

"We are here to look at the records pertaining to an old murder case," I announce.

"Do you have the case number?" she asks, clearly unhappy that her game has been disturbed.

"No, ma'am. I only have the name," I tell her.

"Sorry, can't help you without a case number." She abruptly turns her chair and resumes her clicking of the mouse, moving and shifting cards to various rows to line up the matching suits. I look over at Brooks, who only shrugs. I take a deep breath; I refuse to leave this building without seeing the files I came for. I look at the nameplate on her desk, and then ring the bell continuously until she gives me her full attention.

"Yessss?" she draws out. "I told you I couldn't help you unless you have a case number."

"I heard you, Merna is it? The thing is; that's not true. I spoke to your supervisor, Mr. Simmons, earlier this week. In fact he was going to pull the case aside for me for when I arrived today. He informed me that I would not need a case number, only a name. So, if you could either get him, or pull my files, I would greatly appreciate it."

She huffs and stands from her chair. "Follow me." She leads us to a small conference room and gestures for us to take a seat at the table. "I'll be right back with the files. What was the name on the case?"

"Greg Donovan was the victim in the case. I am his daughter, Vivian." She leaves, closing the door behind her, leaving Brooks and me behind to wait on the files that could change everything.

"Wow, look at you getting all sassy with that lady," he says, pulling a chair out for me.

"She was so unprofessional, and I wasn't about to leave just because she didn't want to get off her ass and do her job. That was ridiculous."

Brooks laughs and takes a seat across the table from me. Within minutes, Merna returns with a cardboard box with the name Donovan written in black marker along the side. She places it on the table and immediately exits without saying anything. Whoever said public servants aren't helpful, apparently never met Merna.

I hear the click of the door, letting me know that we are alone with the box, but I can't find the courage to take the last step to remove the lid. I remain frozen in my seat, staring at the words on the box. Every piece of information that my mother refused to talk about is in there, and now that I have the power to know all of it, I'm terrified of what that information could be. I think about my father's promise to build a fort, and how hard he worked to provide for us, but now a few words on a page could change everything I ever thought about him.

"Vivian, do you still want to look at it?" I hear Brooks ask, yanking me from my zone-out, and I shake my head to bring myself back to the moment. "Yes, I just need a minute to collect myself. Things might never be the same once I open that box. I can't undo it once it's done."

"It probably won't, but at least you'll have the satisfaction of facing it—that you aren't scared anymore to face this terrible thing that happened to your family."

I push my chair away from the table and move toward the box at the end of the table, and Brooks follows. Grabbing the lid on both sides, I slowly lift it until the contents inside reveal themselves. I expected a disarray of random papers and photos, but instead, everything is neatly wrapped and tied together in a manila folder. I pick up the folder, and Brooks takes the box off the table, placing it on the floor beside us.

"I'm right here, Red. Untie it and we can find out together; you aren't alone," Brooks says, rubbing my back.

His words encourage me to keep going, to unlock my past. I untie the thread and open the folder. I split the stack of papers in half and give some to Brooks. "We don't have a lot of time. You go through this stack, and I'll go through the other, and we can swap information as we go."

"Anything you need, Viv." Brooks takes the papers from my hand and walks back to his seat. We each lay out our individual piles and separately begin rummaging through the stacks. Brooks holds up crime scene photos and mug shot line-ups. "How did you say he died?" he asks, examining each picture closely.

"He was strangled by a guy that worked for him, but that's all I know," I tell him, scanning through the investigator reports. "It looks like the guy had a previous record for all kinds of offenses, but my dad hired him anyways."

"Really? Were they violent crimes?" he asks.

"No, looks like mainly drugs, fraud, burglary, theft…things like that." I drop the report and sift through the other pages, the coroner's report, and the grand jury indictment until I find the plea bargain affidavit.

"This case was pled out, Brooks," I announce, stand, and move to his side of the table. I lay the paper in front of him and begin to point out the important pieces of information. "I thought that this was a complete trial, but it says they stopped the trial midway through, and that he accepted a plea bargain in exchange for a lesser charge. Why would the state do something like that?"

"I don't know. Maybe the defense found something that would have looked bad in court, or maybe the state would rather have him in jail than risk him being acquitted," he explains.

"But I can't find anything that discusses any of that. There's nothing about private investigators uncovering unpleasant information about my dad. Did you find anything?" I ask.

"I don't have anything; my entire pile is all pictures of the scene. I couldn't even find the name of the suspect. What was included in the plea deal? Did he get off pretty lightly?"

"I didn't need to look for his name; it's one I would never forget. My mother screamed it at me the day my dad died, and it's been burned into my mind ever since. His name is Raymond Michaels," I say, looking down at the plea deal. "It looks like he pled down from murder one to second degree murder, and was sent to a maximum security prison outside Limon. What's crazy though is he was looking at life, but the plea knocked it down to 25 years."

I look to Brooks for his opinion, and I take a step back when I notice that all the color has drained from his face. "Brooks, are you okay? Are you feeling all right?" I reach for his cheek to feel if he's warm. He looks like death, and it's come on so suddenly, he has me worried.

"S-so, he c-could be out in l-like ten y-years?" he stutters through almost every word, like he's choking on them. "He could be walking around like it never happened."

"I know. It makes me sick to think one day I could run into him on the street and never even know that he was the one who changed my whole life." I look more closely at him and see beads of sweat along his hairline. "Really, Brooks, are you sure you're feeling okay? You don't look good."

He wipes his forehead with his palm and pushes away from the table. "I'm fine; I'm just going to run to the restroom really quick." He stands and heads for the door. Not waiting for my response, he opens the door and rushes out, swiftly closing it behind him.

I shuffle through the last bit of the file, and then put it back together, loading it into the box. I at least found out the basics, but all of the incriminating information that was a part of the rumors growing up is vacant from any of the reports. After I put everything together, I sit at the table and patiently wait for Brooks to come back. The time slowly passes, and after thirty minutes, he still hasn't returned.

Merna pokes her head into the room, announcing that they are closing up for the weekend. "Thank you. I'm all done. Have you seen the guy that came with me?" I ask her.

"When he came out, he asked where the restroom was, but I haven't seen him since. I figured he snuck back in when I was in the back doing some filing." Yeah, filing, I'm sure that's what you were doing.

"Okay, thank you." I stand and follow her out of the office, and she directs me towards the restrooms she sent him to. I knock on the men's room and call out Brooks' name. Nothing. I knock louder, concerned that maybe he passed out in there and is lying unconscious. I'm preparing to barge into the bathroom, when Brooks finally opens the door.

"Oh, shit, you scared the crap out of me. I thought you were passed out in there or something. Are you okay; are you sick?" I ask, reaching for him. He dodges my hand though, and scowls.

"I'm sorry you were worried. I'm not feeling well. Were you able to find out everything you needed?" He moves past me into the hallway and gets a drink from the water fountain across the hall.

"Yeah, I'm all set to go; besides, the solitaire queen said they are closing for the weekend.

"Okay," he says, leaning over the water fountain. He then continues down the hallway, past security and to the car.

"Do you want me to drive back?" I offer. He still looks so bad; I want him to be able to rest if he needs to, and it's a long drive back.

"That would be great." He hands me the keys and climbs into the passenger seat.

We drive the entire way home in silence, and it feels horrible. I let the events of the day replay in my head, trying to figure out what would have suddenly made him ill, and I draw a blank. He was fine all day, until he saw the case...until it dawned on him that my dad's killer will someday be on the streets, and if we're still together, it would be his problem, as well as mine. I understand that the situation is a lot to take in, and he said he was ready for it and would be there for me, but this feels like rejection. By the time we make it back to the University, I've counted seven words that Brooks has said to me, which only feeds into my mounting anxiety.

We're both already packed for the holiday weekend, so neither of us needs to go back up to the dorms. The plan was to say goodbye in the parking lot, and we would each make the drive to our homes. I'm expecting at least a small, memorable goodbye. But as soon as I park, I know it's not coming.

"I have to go back in for some things. I guess I'll see you when you get back," he says when I hand him his keys. He then steps out of the car and takes off in the direction of our dorm–no 'I love you', no 'drive careful', no hug, and no kiss. Nothing. I hold my emotions in until I reach my car. I slide into the driver's seat, turn on the ignition, and let my tears of rejection pour down.

11

VIVIAN

"Are you and Brooks coming to the concert tonight?" Cam asks on our way back from our final class for the day. After Thanksgiving, she started working with another band, and their first performance is supposed to be tonight. We are all planning on going. Well, almost all of us.

"I plan on going, but Brooks said he needs to finish his paper for Vauldin tonight. Finals are next week, and I'm not even sure if he's started on it." Campbell glowers at my answer. He has been MIA for most of our group outings. He has been distant and weird, but he refuses to say that anything is wrong.

"What in the hell is going on with him? He's been different since we got back from Thanksgiving. Are you guys fighting or something?" Apparently I'm not the only one that has noticed the change in him.

My throat constricts, and I feel the tears building. I try to suppress it all, cramming my emotions back down and swallowing down the lump, but when Campbell puts her arm around me, the tears begin to fall. "It's because of my dad," I choke out. "He went with me to look at the case file, and it freaked him out. He pretended to get sick while we were there and took off. Then over break, I never once heard from him. I called once to check on him, and he never called back. Now, since we got back, it feels like he's just going through the motions. It's like he's just waiting for me to get pissed and break it off with him so he doesn't have to be the bad guy."

"Oh, Viv. I don't understand this any more than you do. Before the break, the only time I can think of when he was off was when he was late for lunch. You know, the day of the Amber fight? Do you think maybe he's doing drugs or something? I mean, his behavior is completely one-eighty."

"What?" I shout. "No, I don't think he would ever do that. I really think it is because of my past. It makes me feel like such shit, Cam. I mean, he told me he loved me that morning, and by that afternoon, I was old news, a pity case that wasn't worth his time." I wipe my renegade tears as my anger begins to take over. We approach the front door to the dorms, and I don't want anyone to see me crying. I try to wipe the running make-up from under my eyes while Campbell holds the doors open for me. I look at her to give the mascara approval. She tilts her head and waves me on, which tells me we need to hurry to our room; I look like questionable shit.

"I don't know what his motives are, or what's he's expecting from you," she adds, pushing the elevator button. "But you can't keep doing whatever this is. You need to talk to him, and if he can't give you the answers you need, well, then maybe it's time that you take a break from each other. We leave for Christmas vacation next week. You cannot spend an entire month worried about this shit; you would just torture yourself."

The doors open and we both step onboard. Cam pushes the button for our floor while I step to the left and lean against the side wall. "You're right; I'll try and talk to him tonight when I get back from the concert."

The door opens and Brooks is standing there, waiting to ride it down. When he sees me and my mess of a face, his eyes widen and he immediately steps towards me. "What happened? What's wrong, Viv?"

I move out of the elevator towards Brooks, but my eyes don't meet his; instead, I look to Cam for support. She waves me on and heads towards our room, but I have no intention of having this conversation in the hallway, or right now for that matter. "I don't know what's going on with you, Brooks, but I'd really like to talk about it. Now is not a good time; I realize that you're headed somewhere, and I'm upset and a mess. But tonight, after the concert, I plan to come over so we can talk. All right?"

"Okay," he sighs as he steps around me to hit the button for the elevator that has since left him. "No matter how this conversation goes, though; I need you to know I never lied when I said I love you. I need you to believe that, Red." The tears invade my eyes again, and my ability to speak is constrained, so I nod. "I'll see you later then." He walks onto the elevator and leaves me standing alone and confused once again.

I dressed up for the concert, thinking it would be a nice touch for opening night. Jen forced me to wear stilettos, which sucked big hairy balls at a punk rock concert. I spent the entire time thinking about what I was going to say to Brooks when I went over to his room. But now, as I ride the elevator up to our room, the time has come for our big talk and I still have no idea what I'm going to say. I follow everyone into our room, Will included, drop off my purse, and head next door. I don't bother changing, or even taking off the death shoes; I want to get next door and figure out whatever the hell is going on.

Other than that first night, I've never considered knocking, but with how things have been the last few weeks, I feel compelled to be invited in, as opposed to just walking into his dorm. I reach my fist up to tap on the door, but before my knuckles can hit the wood, it swings open. Shock spreads across my face. When I see the figure standing before me, I take what might be the hardest breath I've ever had to take. I was expecting to see Brooks, open arms or not; that's who was supposed to be behind that door. Instead, a tousled version of Amber, with smeared make-up and tangled hair is there, with a smug expression that only Jen could wipe off.

"Oh, hello. Veronica, is it?" she says, straightening her shirt. "I think you might be a little early."

I try to make my mouth move to correct her, to yell at her, anything, but I just stand there like a victim of the situation. No matter how hard I try, I can't get sound past my lips.

She giggles at me. "He's in the shower right now, but don't worry, I'm sure he can see you soon. But I can't imagine why; he got more than he could handle this evening," she adds. I am in complete disbelief at what I'm hearing, what I'm witnessing. When I still say nothing, she huffs and tries to move around me. Just before she gets past me, she leans in close and whispers, "You had to know revenge was coming; trash like you never wins."

I allow her to walk a step or two before all of my fury bubbles to the surface, and I detonate. "Amber," I spit out, turning to face her once again. I shake with rage as I step towards her; the heartache that settled into my stomach transforms into a giant ball of confidence and wrath. I ball my fist, and when she turns around, I push all of my weight forward, swinging as hard as I possibly can in the direction of her face. I'm not exactly aiming at any one spot; anywhere on her pretty little face is sufficient. My knuckles land on her nose; I can feel the bones crunch under the force of my hand. She flies backwards and stumbles to the floor with a squeal; blood begins to flow from her nose.

I move over her, and she flinches. "I'm glad you feel good about what you did this evening; it made it all the easier for me to show you how we take out the trash in the country, even rich, city trash," I state simply before turning on my heel to walk to my room.

When I turn around, my roommates and Will are standing in my doorway watching my confrontation. Their mouths are hanging open, and their eyes are as wide as saucers. Well, except for Jen, she's smiling, almost gloating. "I don't want to talk about it right now," I tell them as I push through the group to get to my room. I'm humiliated and hurt; talking to anyone about what happened would only make this despair worse.

My body collapses onto my bed, and the gravity of the situation slaps me in the face. The pain of my pulsing bloody hand is nothing compared to the pain in my devastated heart. He promised not to break me and he did it anyway. I can barely suck in breaths between my cries. I bury my face in my pillow to muffle the sound because I don't want to draw any more attention to myself than I already have. I'm mad at myself for letting my guard down and believing that Brooks could be different. He is a liar and a cheater. I make a promise to myself that I won't make the same mistake twice.

BROOKS

I hear the argument in the hallway and wait. I knew it would happen, just not like this. I thought of every possible way to end this, but this was the only way I could think of that would make it permanent. I listen until silence returns to the floor and begin my walk to Vivian's room. I tried to prepare myself for the yelling, the crying, for all of the scenarios of her reaction when I set this up, but it still tore my heart out to do it.

I don't get very far. Instead of Vivian, Will is waiting for me. On some level, I was expecting that, too.

"You have lost your fucking mind if you think I'm going to let you knock on this door," Will growls at me. His arms are crossed over his chest, and his scowl is so deep, it looks like his eyebrows are touching. He looks intimidating as fuck, and if I didn't need this to happen, I would consider running for my life. "I don't care what strings your dad has to pull; I want you out of our room by the time we get back from break. Vivian shouldn't have to see your sorry ass, and frankly, I don't think I could stomach seeing you either."

"I don't need to talk to her, Will. She is never going to give me another chance, and I don't want one. I came to talk to you." His arms fall to his sides, and the ridge between his eyes flattens out as his eyebrows begin to climb into his hairline. I've been dreading this discussion because it would tear my heart from my body, but for once, I need to do the right thing. "Also, I already have new living arrangements; none of you guys will ever have to see me again."

"Brooks, I came out here to kick your ass; what the fuck is going on here?" he asks me, and I ignore him. I need to get through this speech, and if a deviate, I may lose my nerve.

"Just listen, please," I tell him. "I need you to promise that you will take care of her and that you'll love her with your every breath every day, because it's something I couldn't do. I know that eventually she will love you, but I need to know that she will have everything that she deserves. If you can promise to do that, then you win, Will; you're the better man."

I stand back and let him think about what I'm saying. "Can I speak now?" he asks and I gesture for him to continue. "We need to get something straight. What you did tonight was beyond fucked up, especially because I'm getting the sense that you did it on purpose for the sole reason of chasing Vivian away. I don't know why, and I really don't give a damn. All that matters to me is that girl in there, who is heartbroken. You don't need to ask how I would treat her, or if I can promise to love her. I don't care if it takes every day of the rest of my life to put her shattered heart back together; I would be grateful just to have the chance. And I certainly wouldn't throw it away for whatever dumbass reason that you have going on. I am completely and madly in love with her, and no slutty sorority girl in a tight skirt would change that. I'm not you, Brooks. I will always be the better man, and I don't need you to say it for me to know it."

When he finishes speaking, he walks back into the girls' room and slams the door behind him, leaving me alone in the floor commons area. Every one of his words is true, but it doesn't make them sting any less. They shred whatever bits of my heart I have left, and I stand there a wilted man. This was the right thing to do, and it hurts like hell. I only hope that the pain deadens over time, because now, it's all I have—a forever without my Clover.

12

2012

VIVIAN

"Babe, have you seen Cricket's shoes? We've looked everywhere and can't find them," Will shouts from Emma's room. I finish brushing my hair into a messy bun, and head out the bathroom door to retrieve the missing shoes. They are at the front door, of course, along with all of the other shoes. I'm not sure why we still have to go through this daily scavenger hunt, when the shoes–surprise, surprise–never move unless the kids' feet are in them.

I swing down, pick up her sparkly pink shoes, and travel toward the contagious laughter coming from her room. Leaning into the doorframe, I cradle her shoes and watch as Will rolls around on the ground with our daughter. She tries to get away from his grip, but he finds a leg or an arm and pulls her back into his continuous tickles. I'm glad I hadn't fixed her hair yet, as the carpet static has taken hold and her hair is sticking up in all directions; her curls are now a giant ball of fuzz on top of her head. It warms my heart to see them like this, and a smile creeps across my face as I silently eavesdrop on them.

"Bombs away," Blake screams, barreling past me and jumping on Will's back. With the distraction, Emma is able to slip free from Will's grasp and jumps on his back. Both kids are shouting, "Get Daddy, get Daddy!" I only laugh because I know the next move in the usual tickle game of theirs. Will reaches back and plucks them off one-by-one and pins them to the ground; he then alternates between the two, tickling them mercilessly. They both become breathless and beg for mercy, and that's my cue to intervene.

"Okay, Daddy, I think you won," I chuckle, stepping into the room. All three have collapsed onto the ground on their backs, recovering from their near-hyperventilation. I dangle Emma's shoes over their heads, "Come on, guys. If we don't hurry, we're going to be late for the game."

"See, guys? Nothing is actually lost unless Momma doesn't know where it's at," Will says. Oh what a true statement that is. I love this man, but man, he is constantly losing things. *All is lost, the world is ending, because Will has lost his keys, or wallet, or favorite Bronco hat...again.* Usually it's sitting in plain sight. There is no magic GPS app imbedded under my skin, but I'll certainly let them all continue to believe in my super-human tracking powers.

Will reaches up to take the shoes, but instead of taking hold of them, he grabs my wrists and begins to pull me down to the ground. "Mommy's turn; get her!"

I gasp in surprise and am thrown off balance enough that I tumble to the floor. Blake and Emma immediately begin wiggling their miniature fingers against my sides and under my arms. I join in the fun and laugh, but it's not until Will begins to attack my knees that I lose complete control. My hands fly to his, trying to push away from his strong grip and scream through laughs, pleading for him to release me.

"What do you think, guys? Have we tortured her enough?" he asks the kids.

"Yes," I yelp. "Momma's done. Will, please," I add with a giggle.

"All right, I think she paid the toll. Let's get up and finish getting ready." The kids jump up immediately, and Will slowly stands, holding a hand out to help me up. I lay flat for a minute in silent protest before taking his offer.

Once I'm standing again, I reach up to feel my disheveled hair. It had been a stylish messy up-do; now it's closer to the rat's-nest messy end of the spectrum. "Will, look at this mess. We need to be leaving, and now I have to go re-fix my hair," I whine.

"Hush, woman, there could be an actual bird nesting in there and you'd still be gorgeous," he says, pointing to my hair. "Now, grab your bag and let's go soccer it up." He slaps my ass hard enough to make me squeal, and then waltzes out of the bedroom grinning.

"Load up, crew!" I hear him yell from the hallway, as I stand in place, rubbing my injured butt-cheek. His playfulness was always something I adored about him, but sometimes, I swear it feels like I'm raising three kids instead of two.

After a quick hair intervention for Emma and myself, as well as a round of, 'Hun, have you seen the car keys?' we all make it to the SUV. Armed with our chairs, cooler, sparkly shoes, and shin guards, we pull away from our comfortable little farm house, and out onto the dirt driveway to head to the next town over for Blake's peewee soccer game.

I knew that when Will and I moved back to my hometown after we got married, life would slow down. I've experienced both ways of living, and rural life is drastically different from in the city. Trips to the nearest grocery store are planned events. Attending your kids' sporting events always means travelling more than thirty minutes to another town. Everyone knows everyone, and is always interested in the latest gossip; thus, you never go on said grocery trip in your sweatpants, because you WILL run into someone you know or are related to. The thing is I never appreciated those things growing up; I saw it all as an inconvenience. Now that we have children though, I value our little cocoon; it's small, and it's safe.

The kids in the back seat are busy singing the newest songs that they've been taught at preschool—ones that I've learned to tune out after hearing them for the millionth time. What is cute one minute can quickly feel like nails on a chalkboard, and turning up the car stereo encourages them to belt out their tunes even louder. So Will and I have mastered the skill of tuning out while in the car. It's a fine art.

I stare out the window, into the never-ending corn and alfalfa fields, most of which have already been harvested. The corn that is still in the ground will be used for cow feed, and many farmers have begun readying their acreage for late planting. The rows of fields are almost hypnotic.

These are the times when I let my mind travel to places it shouldn't…Brooks. I know that I absolutely love Will; he pieced me back together when I thought I was broken beyond repair. He loved me until I was ready to love myself again. But every now and then, Brooks will infiltrate the security that Will and I built together. He and I were a lifetime ago, and as much as I wish I didn't, I still have this space in my heart for him. As much as I love Will, Brooks is someone I could never forget.

85

I feel Will's large hand wrap around my thigh; he gently squeezes, pulling me from my thoughts. "What's going on in that head of yours, love? You worried about the kids staying at Charlotte's house tonight?" he asks with a gentle smile.

"No, the kids will be fine. I'm just thinking about the lesson plans and grading I need to get done tomorrow for school on Monday." I'm completely lying through my teeth, but I'm positive that he wouldn't want to hear, nor would he understand the truthful version. I don't regret for one second my life with Will; he and the kids have become my life. But there are times that Brooks creeps in, and I think about what life would have been like with him. I don't know what was going on with him, why he cheated, but I never got a chance to find out. No sooner did our relationship end, he left school and I never heard from him again. It left a void in me that Will eventually fixed.

A crooked grin spreads across his face, "Well, I promise you'll want to sleep in before you get started on school stuff tomorrow. I have plenty planned to keep you awake tonight. We haven't been on a date night in months, and I'm not going to waste a single second of it."

I reach my hand up to the back of Will's neck and begin lightly scratching the base of his hairline with my fingernails. It's one of his favorite things, and his eyes close briefly to enjoy the sensation. "I'm ready for whatever you've got, Mr. Matthews," I coo into his ear as I lean across the seat console.

He takes his hand off my thigh and grips the steering wheel tightly; a low throaty groan escapes his mouth. I pat his neck and return to my seat with a huge grin on my face; yup, we both can be playful. "You are a wicked woman, Mrs. Matthews," he says, attempting to adjust himself. "You'll pay for that later," he adds with a wink.

"I'm counting on it," I tell him, reaching across the seat to feel his excitement, which only makes his condition worse. He quickly removes my hand and places it on my own thigh. "As much I love where this is headed, we are almost there, and I don't want to be the creepy dad at the game who can't stand and cheer for his son because his zipper is about to break."

I laugh and hold my hands up in surrender, "Sorry, take a second and get it under control; I need you to carry all of the stuff to the field."

Will glances at me from the corner of his eye, "I'm glad you find me useful. I am here to serve," he jokes.

As soon as he pulls into the parking lot and puts the car into park, both kids unbuckle and begin to demand that we open their doors. Thank goodness for child lock, or on multiple occasions we would have had two small children running wild in between cars before we could even get our seatbelts off.

Will hits the button for the back hatch, and we pile out to let the munchkins loose and gather our soccer tailgating supplies. We make our way to the field to set up our cheering site along the sideline. Charlotte and her husband, Elton, are already there, along with my mother.

"Gram!" Emma shouts, breaking away from my hand and running to Mom, hopping into her lap. "I get to stay at Aunt Charlotte's tonight. Daddy said he's sending me with candy to share with everyone."

Charlotte and my mom both shoot deadly glares our way, but Will completely ignores them, leaving me to respond. "He was only kidding; if we send them with anything, it will be highly-nutritious snacks that will only further their growth and improve their percentile range at their next well-child check-up." Sensing my sarcasm, they both roll their eyes.

"Well, isn't that thoughtful of your daddy, but we have plenty of snacks at our house you can have," Charlotte says in her most condescending tone.

We move our chairs just a tad out of range of them, so that we can actually enjoy the game. I love my family, but I want to watch Blake play soccer, not listen to my mom and Charlotte gossip and carry-on about everyone in our little town, judge mine and Will's parenting skills, or lecture me for the hundredth time that I needed to stay home with my children instead of pretending like I'm some kind of career woman. Yup, the circle of love is suffocating.

Will and I sit down in our matching CSU lawn chairs, and he finally takes notice of my family. He enjoys them as much as I do. "Hey, guys! Happy Saturday," he says in an overly-pleasant voice. "Are you still good for tonight, Charlotte?"

"Of course, we are happy to have them. Do you need me to make a list of things to send with them? I would hate for you to forget to pack their toothbrushes or socks or something."

"I think we'll manage, Char," I intercede. "We've had them for a few years now, and we've *somehow* been able to keep them breathing, clothed, and most surprisingly, we've never lost them at Wal-Mart, so I think we can handle some overnight bag responsibilities."

"I'm just trying to help. I know with your busy schedules, things can get overlooked," Charlotte says, unpacking a juice box from her cooler and opening it for Emma.

"Thank you, Aunt Char," Em politely says, taking the juice and snuggling into my mom.

"You're very welcome, dear; I brought plenty of extras just in case you guys forgot your cooler."

I can feel the anger begin to roll off Will. I look in his direction to try to ease the tension, but judging from his narrowed eyes and white knuckles melding into the armrest of his chair, I should just be glad he is off duty and not carrying a weapon.

"I'm sorry," I mouth to him, but he just shakes his head and directs his attention to the field where the opening kickoff is getting lined up. He claps and yells for Blake, then leans forward to rest his forearms on his knees. I know that my family is a strain on us. They are intrusive, domineering, and condescending. When I left for college, I never in a million years thought I would come back. But life interfered, and when Will and I got pregnant with Blake, we felt it was the best option at the time. We have discussed many times the idea of moving away and beginning somewhere that we could create our own home. That's all it's ever been, though, just talk. Charlotte or my mother will piss one or both of us off, and we'll say it's time to pull out the map and pick a new town. I'm not sure we could ever follow through, though. Our jobs tie us to this town; I love mine, and I'm too afraid of Will being a police officer in a bigger city. I could never risk losing him.

I reach over and massage his back muscles that are as hard as rock from the tension that my family has created on what was supposed to be a fun day. It's my own silent apology, and when he shakes my knee with his hand, I know all is forgiven. It's our silent code, and I'm so thankful for this man that so willingly and easily gives that to me.

The game is only an hour long, but we end up standing and cheering for the majority of it. Blake scores two goals, and I think I may have sprained my ankle jumping up and down with excitement from it. I definitely lost my voice from yelling. Yes, we are those parents. I'm sure our kids will die of embarrassment at some point in their life, but dammit, I want them to know that we will always show up, and we will always be in their corner cheering them on, whether they are riding the bench or are the star player.

"Dad, you see me kick the ball all the way across the field?" Blake screams, running to us after the game, jumping into Will's arms once he finally reaches us.

"I sure did, little man! You were awesome out there," Will tells him before placing him back on the ground and rubbing his hand over Blake's shaggy hair, making it fall into his eyes. "I think the coach needed to have two defenders on you."

"I think we are going to win the championship this year. We are way better than last year; I don't think we scored a goal…ever." Blake begins to focus on unwrapping his post-game snack, and his words begin to fade off as his straw to his juice box proves difficult to master.

"You guys have improved a ton, Blake," I say, taking his juice, fixing the straw for him, and handing it back. "Maybe you and Dad can practice a little tomorrow when you get back from Aunt Charlotte's."

He abandons his snack, giving me his full attention when he learns of his evening plans. "Not Aunt Charlotte's house," he whines. "It's boring there. We can never do anything; no one is allowed to get dirty, and her food is nasty."

I bend down to speak at his eye level, and to keep my sister from hearing our conversation. "Blake, honey, you rarely stay at Aunt Charlotte's. I think it's going to be fun. I think she rented movies, and her food isn't nasty, it's just healthy, and there's nothing wrong with staying clean, big guy. It's just for one night; I swear you'll live."

"Have you ever had tofu?" he asks, folding his arms across his chest. I shake my head because God knows I wouldn't go anywhere near that stuff. I'm surprised he even knows the word. "Well, if I choke to death on her tofu lasagna, then you'll wish you hadn't said that."

I curl my lips over my teeth, trying not to laugh at my little boy's convincing argument. I too would choke to death if I had to clear my plate of tofu anything. Once I feel as though I can speak without laughing, which would only make matters worse, and by extension ending our chance at a date night, I decide bartering is the best plan of action. "Okay, Blake, I agree tofu is gross. But if you pretend that it won't kill you and encourage Em to eat hers as well, and if you follow all of Aunt Char's rules tonight, I will make homemade pizza for you tomorrow night for dinner." Homemade deep-dish pizza is his favorite, and is very time-consuming, so it's not made often. I'm driving a hard bargain for him.

He actually takes a few seconds to consider his options for renegotiation. He scratches his chin, just like Will does when he's in deep thought, and for a split second I think I may have lost the battle. But then he sticks out his hand like he's an adult man instead of my little five-year-old and shakes my hand. "Deal, but I get to pick all the toppings."

"Deal," I say, shaking his tiny little hand.

13

VIVIAN

"How did you get Blake to agree to go to Charlotte's?" Will asks before shoveling his cheeseburger and handful of fries into his mouth. Our small town doesn't exactly have elegant date night options, so we are enjoying a comfortable burger, fries, and some milkshakes at our favorite local diner. The place is pretty old school, but it's a jewel of the town. Customers use phones at the table to order their meal over a loud speaker that everyone in the restaurant can hear, and the aroma of fried food wafts through the air and attacks your nostrils the moment you step out of your car in the parking lot. It's fantastic.

Then, instead of dancing or drinks at an upscale club—because those two don't exist here unless you consider peanuts on the floor and curtains for bathroom doors classy—we are going to park at one of the last drive-in theaters in the state, and enjoy a not-so-new film. The drive-in usually receives movies about a month after the city theaters have played them, and there are only two shows a night, but it's something.

I smile into my chocolate milkshake, recounting the wheeling and dealing of my negotiating five-year-old. "I have to make homemade pizza tomorrow, and he gets to choose all of the toppings. I may have to send you to the store tomorrow to pick up the things we need."

"So pineapple, huh?" he says, swirling a long fry in his dollop of ketchup and ranch. There is so much on the fry that it bends with the weight of ketchup, and when he flops it into his mouth, a bit is left behind in the corner of his mouth. I reach across to wipe it off and lick the remains off my finger, earning myself a smirk from my husband.

"Would you expect anything less from him?" I laugh before taking a huge bite of my own burger. Juices and toppings spill out of it onto my paper-covered basket. The cheeseburgers here are the best in town, and we are here early enough that the crowds of high school kids that flood in after the Saturday volleyball and football games haven't showed up yet. We pretty much have the place to ourselves.

The quiet is nice.

"How much school work do you have to get done tomorrow, love? Are there any grading things that I can help with, you know, multiple-choice type stuff?" Every week, Will always offers to help, and I have yet to take him up on it. I just appreciate that he's willing to help. I love my job. I really do, but there isn't a weekend that I don't take grading or planning home, and I always feel bad that it takes time away from my family. Will understands that; it's one of the reasons why we spend some much time at home, instead of going to all the town activities. Between tons of grading, and Will's work schedule, we don't have a lot of time together, so we tend to be stingy with the time we do have.

"Thank you, hun, but if you just keep the kids occupied for a few hours, I should be able to get it all done. I had to cover a few classes last week, so I wasn't able to get my grading done during my planning hour. It shouldn't take too long, though."

"No problem, I can do that. How has school been? Any kids I need to make an appearance at school for? You know, show up at school in my uniform and scare them in to behaving for you." He flexes his biceps to emphasize his ability to intimidate high school kids. I choke on the fry in my mouth and immediately latch on to my milkshake straw to wash down the food particle stuck in my throat.

"Oh, my God, that was hilarious! I think I can handle it, but thanks," I say once the cold cream of the shake relaxes my throat and I'm able to speak again.

"Okay, do you at least have any new funny stories to share; you know I love hearing about the stupid things your kids do and say. I still think you need to keep a journal and then publish all the stories. You could make a ton of money; we would never have to work again."

"True, the things they say are funny; I'm pretty sure parents would die if they knew some of the things their kids do. But I'm also pretty sure if I published those things, I wouldn't have a choice about working in education again, because I would be fired."

"Fiiine," he says, drawing out the word as if surrendering, "you can just tell me then." I love that Will and I can laugh together.

There have never been major sparks of passion, or heat like I
experienced with Brooks; we have something different. We have a
friendship that grew into something more. We can always make
each other laugh; we are a team–a secure, solid foundation that will
last because neither of us would ever hurt the other. Over the
years, I've thought about the relationship I had with Brooks, and
what I have now with Will, and I really think I would rather have
the friend that loves me and won't hurt me, than the passionate
lover whose adoration would eventually burn me. Every time I
question my marriage to Will, I think about the hurt Brooks
caused, and I know I'm where I'm supposed to be.

I giggle and then stuff my face with another massive amount of
cheeseburger in an attempt to stall. I jog my memory to think of a
story he hasn't heard and would like. Washing it down with shake,
I remember a few that I can share. "I have two for you; one is from
a junior high kid, and the other is from my college literature class.
Which would you like first?"

"Either, I don't care." He shoves the final piece of his burger
into his mouth, and settles back in his seat with his strawberry
shake to be entertained by the momentary stupidity of today's
youth.

"So, my eighth graders were doing some cross-curriculum
work with their social studies content, and I found some stories
about the Revolutionary War that they were learning about. They
were at the end of the unit, by the way, and already knew what the
purpose of the war was. So we were talking about the fighting style
of the Revolutionaries, and how it helped them against the bigger
stronger English military. One of my top students is listening
intently and is on the edge of her chair, when she raises her hand.
Of course I call on her, and she asks, "So who won?""

Will's mouth drops open in disbelief. "She asked who won the
Revolutionary War?"

I nod my head. "Yup, the whole class had the same reaction
you did. Looks of complete confusion filled the classroom because
of her question. I tried to walk her through it, because I knew that
she knew the answer; she just spoke without thinking."

"Did she finally catch on?" He laughs.

"Oh, yeah, but I had to ask her if there was a queen of the
United States first. She looked at me like I was crazy, and then it
finally clicked. She was so embarrassed, especially when the entire

class laughed. She laughed too, and begged that I not tell her mother or older brother about her brain fart."

"Did you tell them?"

"Of course, it was my funny of the day. I told everyone at the teacher lunch table. Those stories are some of the highlights of our day sometimes."

"Your job makes me sad sometimes," he adds, grabbing a napkin and rolling it quickly between his hands to wipe the grease off his fingers. I ball up my own napkin and throw it at him, feigning offense. "Oh, come on, Viv, that story was kind of pathetic, and if that was the highlight of your day, you may need to check your fun gauge."

"Fine, how about this one," I say, grabbing our trash and taking it to the nearest trashcan. Will holds the door open for me, and then leads me to the car by placing his hand lightly on the small of my back.

"We were reading stories about early colonization and exploration, preparing for our unit about The Crucible," I say, climbing into the front seat. I wait for Will to get in as well before continuing. He starts the car and pulls out in the direction of the drive-in. Once he's on the main road, his right hand automatically finds his usual spot on my knee and begins caressing it, letting me know he's ready for the rest of the story.

"So, anyway," I continue, "I was talking about how some early colonizers struggled because they were more interested in finding resources and profitable goods like gold than settling the area and devoting time to establishing agricultural products to eat. I tell them that finding gold wasn't very helpful in the winter months, because you can't eat gold."

Will glances over at me, his expression clearly telling me that he doesn't find my story funny. "I'm not finished," I snip.

"Then one of my students lets out the loudest, nastiest farts I've heard in a long time; seriously, thank goodness for the ventilation system or we would have all suffocated. Then he says before I can chastise him, "'Mrs. Mathews, that's probably what it would sound like if they ate gold.' I told him that he was probably right, because it would cause a bowel obstruction, and the only thing that would escape would be gas."

I start to giggle, but when I look at Will, he doesn't even smile; instead, he gives me his best pity look. "Fine, tell me one of your funny stories; you cops are probably just as boring as us teachers."

"I can at least beat those stories, babe; those were not funny. I think you're losing your touch," he laughs, pulling into the drive-in and paying the attendant for our car speaker. We had been waiting a long time to see 21 Jump Street. Will loves cop comedies, and well, I like Channing Tatum, so it was a win-win this evening. He pulls in backwards, into our spot, and we jump out to make a cozy nook in the back of the SUV. I packed blankets and pillows so we could lie in the back and watch the movie. I continue to situate our area as Will begins his apparently hilarious story that will blow mine out of the water.

"You want funny; how about this?" He smirks like he already knows he's won. I should hit him with a pillow to take him down a notch. Instead, I continue to make our movie-watching bungalow. "A few weeks ago, you remember when I stopped by on my lunch break to eat with you guys, and I had to storm out of the house for that pursuit? Everyone on shift was called out to chase the suspect who had attempted to rob a local convenience store."

I stop laying out the blankets and grab a pillow out of Will's hands. "I've heard this story; there was absolutely nothing funny about it. I'm pretty sure I win," I gloat, fluffing the pillow.

"Back up there, cowgirl. I never told you the whole story; Rob made me promise not to tell anyone, but I'm making an exception."

This time, I do hit him with the pillow. "You chose to keep a secret from your wife at the request of your shift partner? I'm pretty sure you broke a marriage vow or something."

"Simmer, Viv, when you hear the story, you'll understand. He doesn't want anyone knowing this, let alone someone that sees him often and can regularly judge him."

I motion for him to continue, pretending like I'm sore at him. He and I both know that I'm really not though. There are plenty of things that he keeps from me about his job. It makes him uncomfortable to tell me about some of the dangerous situations he finds himself in, and he doesn't want me to worry, so he decompresses with Rob at times instead of me. I know this about his job, and the emotional support that he needs to do it, so I'm okay with it. Will grabs the pillow from me and throws it into the back of the car. He then picks me up and rubs his lips against the spot behind my ear. "I would never break one of our vows, love," he whispers. "You know I always put you first," he adds before kissing my neck.

I reach my arms around his neck; my feet are still dangling above the ground, but Will's strength has no problem holding me up, so there is no need to hold onto him tightly. I look into his eyes, feeling the love that radiates from him. "I know, Will; you would never hurt me. You have spent every second of our life together trying to make me feel safe. I love you, and am so thankful for you."

Will searches my eyes before landing a lingering kiss on my forehead. "Thank you, Viv. I need to hear that sometimes." I let go of his neck and run my fingers through his golden hair, causing his eyes to close. I pull myself up and delicately kiss his moist lips. He growls in response, and I know that if we weren't in public he would take this much further.

He slowly pulls away and flings me into the back of the SUV. I land relatively softly but the surprise of it causes me to squeal. He hops into the back to join me, and slides closer to put his arm around me. "So, the winning story of the night–where was I?" he says smugly, and I bump his shoulder with mine, making him grin. He grabs my hand and tangles our fingers together before beginning his story.

"So, we all take off in the direction of the pursuit in progress. Rob and I are the first ones to arrive at the truck stop on the edge of town where the suspect has abandoned his car. We take off on a foot chase, and I'm able to catch up to him and tackle him just outside the front entrance."

I nod, knowing this part of the story already. The whole town heard the story; it was a very big deal. There are never robberies or pursuits in our sleepy little town, so when your husband runs after and captures the person responsible for the first town burglary in probably a hundred years, of course I heard about it.

"A small crowd had gathered outside to see what was going on; most of them were truckers passing through town, no one local. Rob was right behind me to offer back up. He was having trouble keeping up; he has gained some weight since his wife left." He leans in to whisper the last part, as if it is a secret that Rob has struggled since he and his wife separated. He has spent a great deal of time at our house since it happened, and when the final divorce papers were delivered a few months ago, he completely fell off the wagon, eating anything he could get his hands on as a way to cope. Since the pursuit though, he has been doing better. He has been going to the gym with Will; he's lost the weight, and he looks like the same-old, muscular, handsome Rob we are used to, so I'm unsure of what that has to do with humor of the story.

"As soon as I have the suspect on the ground, Rob bent down to place the handcuffs on him and pull him up, so that I could get up and collect myself. But when he bent down, his pants split down the middle, and all of those truckers saw his boxers underneath. What's worse–his boxers had the words 'love machine' written all over them in hot pink writing."

As much as I know that I shouldn't, I burst into laughter, picturing Hot Rob–a nickname given to him by my single teacher friends–pretty much mooning half of the trucking fleet of America parked at our local truck stop. Will balls his fist and covers his mouth to hide his own smirk.

"To make matters even worse, all of his extra uniforms were at the cleaners, so he had to sit in one of the bathroom stalls while I bought a sewing kit at the truck stop and stitched up his pants enough to get him through the day."

The last bit of the story, knowing how pathetic my husband's sewing skills are, has my stomach hurting from laughing so hard. Of course his story is funnier; they always are. Will's ability to make me laugh has always been one of the things that I loved about him. Since the moment we met, we've always tried to one-up each other's funny stories; you would think that by now I would know I'm never going to win this game we play.

I wipe the tears from my eyes and grab all of our snacks from the cooler we packed; we are parents and have jobs in public service–of course we are lunch sack people. The concession stand is not in our future. I throw him a package of Skittles and crawl back to my spot next to him. "Okay, I concede. You win like usual." I square my shoulders and point my finger into his chest, determined to seem as serious as possible. "Just don't get used to it; I'm determined to find a better story, Matthews, and knock you off that high horse of yours."

He grabs my finger and kisses the pad of it. "I'll be ready for whatever you'd like to dish out."

We both snuggle down into the blankets to watch the film in relaxed silence. While the days here can be beautiful, October evenings tend to be cold, so we bundle around each other tightly. We haven't had our first snow yet, but the chill in the air can definitely cool your bones. I settle into the crook of Will's shoulder, and he wraps both of his strong arms around me. I can feel his breath in my hair and the rise of his chest with every laugh; it makes me feel safe. He makes me feel safe, and it's a feeling I didn't have for a long time. I thought men only hurt you, and Brooks proved that assumption right, but Will made it okay to love again. He pieced my wounded heart back together again, and for that I will always care for this man.

By the time we return home, we are both exhausted. Long gone are the days of late night partying, sleeping in until noon, and afternoon power-naps. Now, if we don't fall asleep on the couch before ten, we are having a good day. Maybe we are boring; maybe we are past the point of comfortable and into the realm of fuddy-duddy, but it works for us.

We each finish brushing our teeth, and I'm putting on my most comfy pajamas when I feel Will come up behind me. "We have the house to ourselves; I don't think these are going to be necessary," he murmurs in my ear, taking my pajama shirt from my grasp and tossing it onto the hardwood floor.

Instead of turning around, I reach my hands back to find a naked Will in my palms. His excitement rubs against my back as he walks me to our bed. The duvet has been pulled down to the foot of the bed, and when he softly pushes me down onto the mattress, the crisp coolness of the sheets sends a jolt across my chest and stomach that awakens my senses. Will leans over me, his forearms on either side of my head, and I can feel the slightest bit of his weight pressing me into the bed.

Will works in silence as he swipes my hair away from my neck, kissing along my neck and across each shoulder blade. I can feel every kiss, every lick, and when he blows lightly on my damp skin, I shudder, and goose bumps spread across my body. "So soft...your skin is always so soft, and you smell good enough to eat."

He wraps his strong arm around my waist and hauls us both up to the middle of the mattress. He turns me over and covers my body with his own. I stretch out underneath him and wrap my legs around his muscular torso. Will gently leans down, letting our lips meet delicately at first, but then his kiss becomes harsh and demanding. His hands explore every inch of my skin, while his mouth devours mine. I run my fingers into his hair, slightly tugging it, and hook my ankles together just between the indentations above his ass, pulling him toward me to encourage him further.

It took a long time for the two of us to connect sexually as a couple; the chemistry we have now wasn't something that came naturally, but over the years, we have become very in-tune with each other's needs. He completely understands what I'm demanding and begins to rock into me, deepening our kiss with each blow.

As our breathing becomes more ragged, Will breaks our kiss and buries his head into my neck; his warm breath against my skin sends my desire spiraling out of control. "Almost there, Viv," Will pants as he quickens his pace. I don't answer with anything that resembles verbal communication. I barely manage a hyperventilated moan, signaling my impending release. Our bodies tense together, and I feel Will collapse on top of me.

"I love you, Vivian," Will exhales as he tries to steady his breathing, "more than anything." I slowly open my eyes and take the sides of his face in my hands, using my thumbs to brush casually along his cheekbones. "I love you too, Will," I say, looking into his honey-colored eyes. I think about how he has made me see that love doesn't have to be perfect to be right. How he's shown me that life is not about perfection; it's about accepting the ride, and enjoying the people who want to take the trip with us. This man has helped to give me the most wonderful life. I love our life together, and it has everything to do with the imperfect love that we have together. But instead of telling him, I relax into his embrace and enjoy this man that has given me so much.

Will rises up on his elbow and sweeps a lock of loose hair away from my face. He then leans down to kiss my forehead; it's his way of telling me that he appreciates my declaration to him. The room is dark except for the small night lamp that is providing just enough light to see his amazingly bright smile.

"I need to ask you something, Viv," he says, allowing the smile to fade, and forcing a serious tone to hang in the air. I push up onto my elbows, and turn on my side to face him. "I've been thinking a lot lately about our life here. Well, more than that, I've been thinking about my job, your family, our friends in Denver...everything. I think it's time we actually follow through on what we've been talking about since we moved here."

I immediately think this is some kind of mid-life crisis or male menopause episode, and start to feel the anxiety of what that could mean. My already flush skin begins to burn from the fear seeping into my subconscious. I'm afraid that this new life doesn't include the family that we have made together, that he wants someone other than me. Will notices my worry; the man can read every one of my emotions like they are his own. He pulls me to him and tucks me into his arm. "I'm talking about changing our life together. We are a team; where I go, you go, love. It will always be us."

I relax into him as I let his words wash over me, and I nod into his chest, showing my approval. I wiggle away to hear the rest of what he has to say. Will doesn't let me get too far, hanging onto my hand and kissing the back of my knuckles.

"I don't think either of us thought that we would live here forever, but over time, we've become comfortable here. I know that one of the reasons you don't want to leave is because of my job. But, Viv, the more I've thought about it, I'm ready to be done being a cop."

I sit straight up in bed when he reveals this piece of information. "What are you talking about? You love being a cop, Will; it's who you are."

"No, babe, it's not who I am; it's what I do. You're right that I love the job, but I love my family more."

"We aren't going anywhere, Will. You can be a cop and still have a family," I say reassuringly, as I run my fingers down his chest. One of the reasons why Rob's wife left him was because of his job, and when it all happened, he worried that it would encourage me to leave as well. Yes, the hours are horrible; there are times when we only see each other for ten minutes in the morning when I'm leaving for school and he's coming home from a night shift. We are rarely able to go anywhere overnight, because he typically only has one full weekend off a month. His job is not conducive to family life, and as much as I would love for him to be home more, I would not ask him to quit, and I would never leave him because of it.

"I'm tired of what this job does to my family. I know you guys understand, and that's what helps me get through some of those tough shifts. But I don't want to miss out on our lives together anymore." Will sits up and tugs at his hair, and I scratch his back to show my support. "It's almost the end of the soccer season, and I've only been to two games. Tonight was the first date we've been on in probably three months, and then that invite for our college reunion came last week, the first thing you and I thought was it probably wouldn't happen because I wouldn't be able to get the time off," he rattles off in one long rant.

"So what are you thinking we should do?" I ask.

"I'm ready to quit the force and find something else, maybe parole or probation work. I've even looked into investigative consulting firms. We've talked about moving back to Denver tons of times. I know you miss your friends, and you can't tell me Jen doesn't try to convince you to move every time you talk to her on the phone. Besides, getting away from Charlotte and your mother would be enough of an incentive."

"You're really serious this time?" I ask. "We have a similar conversation every year, and we never follow through." If Will was finally ready to take this drastic step, I would follow, but I'm done with the indecisive back and forth we've been doing for the last few years.

"I'm ready, Viv," he says confidently. "I think we should finish out the school year for you and the kids, and make the move next summer. This has been a great home for us, but I'm ready to find a more family-friendly job, and I want to have our old friends in our lives. I want us to enjoy our life again, and your family here only makes us feel bad about how we're living it now."

"Okay." I couldn't think of any better response. If he was ready, I was ready. I knew I could find a job, and we could find plenty of smaller schools for the kids on the outskirts. Besides, I missed the girls, as well as my sister Amanda. What kept me here was Will's job, but if he really wanted to give it up, then I was ready to leave.

"Okay? Just like that?" he asks, not even hiding his shocked expression.

"Yeah, if you're ready for this change, then I'm on board. I'll give notice at the end of the year, and we can start preparing for the move."

A smile lights up his face, and he lets out a huge exhale of relief. He was obviously worried what my response would be. I lean into him, kissing him briskly on the lips, and then nestle myself into his arms. "Here's to our new city life," I say, giving him one last peck on his chest.

Will slides us down further onto the mattress, and rests his head on a pillow. He pulls the duvet over our now-chilled bodies, and squeezes me tightly. "Thank you for this, Vivian," he whispers in my ear as I feel myself fade into unconsciousness. "All I ever wanted was a life with you; it never mattered where, as long as you were there." I feel his lips against my temple as I allow the blackness of sleep to overtake me.

VIVIAN

The weekend was one of the best we have had in a long time. We enjoyed it as an entire family, which is rare for us. This morning when we left for work, there was a sense of relief radiating from both of us. We made the decision to leave, and I could feel Will's enthusiasm for that change when he kissed me goodbye this morning; he was rattling with it.

I'm certainly thrilled as well, but as I've gone from class to class today, or when I saw my kiddos in the hallway of our tiny little school going to breakfast this morning, I found myself somewhat sad about the things we would be leaving behind. I love the staff that I work with, and that there are preschoolers in the same building as high school kids. The dynamic creates a type of community that isn't easy to replicate, and I doubt I'll find it when we move. It's definitely something that I'll miss.

"How was your weekend?" Kerri James, our social studies teacher, asks as we sit down for lunch in the teachers' lounge.

"It was perfect," I tell her, pulling out my chair and quickly taking out my packed lunch. We only have a fifteen-minute break because of how our junior high and high school classes overlap. "Will was off, so we were able to go to Blake's soccer game together, and Char watched the kids so we could go to dinner afterwards. It was nice. Sunday we just stayed home; I had a ton of grading to do since I covered all of those classes last week." I don't tell her about our decision to move; that's something I plan to put off as long as possible. Kerri is one of the few people that I've grown close to here, and it will only make things tense for the remainder of the year. I know that she would be supportive; it's not that, but it would create this lingering cloud I'd like to avoid for a while.

"I hear ya; it always kills my weekend when I pick up a class. So, was Hot Rob involved in your weekend?" she asks, scooting her school lunch tray towards herself, and tossing her salad with her fork. I roll my eyes at the question. Kerri is one of the few single, attractive teachers at the school. She's tall, with bright blue eyes and long curly blonde hair, with the sweetest, most caring personality to match. How she's still single is beyond me. This town is not exactly the best place for single people; the sea full of fish that we all hear about is more like a dry creek bed of minnows. It's a great place for raising children, but it's horrible if you're looking for love.

It's no secret that she is infatuated with Rob. And if she actually went after him, instead of carrying on her passive aggressive high school approach towards him, they might actually hit it off. Kerri has always had a crush on him, even if she won't entirely admit it, and I know that when Rob found himself back on the market, she thought she won the lottery. Has she cashed in the ticket though? Hell no. Will she ever act on her own? Probably not. She'll just secretly hate every woman that he dates. If I thought Rob was ready, I would set them up, but right now I think it would be a train wreck in the making. He's still so damaged from the divorce, and now I'll be moving.

"No, we didn't see him, surprisingly." I laugh before tearing into my sandwich. "How about you; anything wild and crazy you need to share?"

She nearly chokes on her chocolate milk. "Have you forgotten where you live? The most exciting part of my weekend is usually the school football game, or an 80's chick flick marathon on TBS. I don't lead an overly-stimulating life; I haven't been on a date in over a year."

"Oh, come on; it's not that bad," I tell her, knowing full well that her dating life probably is as sad as the picture she's painting.

She drops her fork and tilts her head, looking at me like I'm insane. "I have an Adam and Eve rewards card, and when I call into the 1-800 number, the sales women know me by name. Which is not all that bad when you're placing an order to surprise your man, but mine are all for individual use."

"Okay," I giggle. "I'll help you find someone, at least to help you unpack your toy box."

"Hey, if you have connections with Hot Rob, he can pack and unpack whatever he'd like at my house."

"I don't think he's ready to date just yet, but when he is, I'll be sure to put you on the short list," I tell her, placing my leftovers back into my lunch sack.

"Short list!" she exclaims, glaring at me. "I better be the only woman on that list." We both laugh, but then she looks down at her watch and takes one last bite of her lunch. "We have to get going; the minions will be in my room any minute."

We push back from our chairs and head towards her classroom. Kerri and I try to combine English and social studies assignments as much as possible. Right now, we are in the middle of presentations with the eighth graders in a team teaching assignment. The students had to research the Virginia, New Jersey, and Connecticut plans, create a poster supporting one of the plans, and then present it to the class.

There is already a crowd of students waiting for us when we make it to her door. We squeeze through to unlock the door and the wave of sweaty 14-year-olds barrel through to grab their posters and find a seat. As soon as everyone is seated, Kerri addresses the class, reminding them of our expectations.

"You guys have done an excellent job on your projects so far; there are only a few people left that need to present. We should be finished with all the presentations today. Remember, Mrs. Matthews is grading your presentation skills and the arguments that you address within your poster, and I'll be grading the accuracy of the historical information that you share. Everyone, let's be good listeners. Now, is there anyone that would like to go first?"

I take a seat in the back of the room with my pile of rubric grading sheets, as a sea of hands fly into the air to be called upon. Kerri calls on someone, and she takes her seat next to me.

Halfway through the class hour, the number of volunteers has dwindled, and we start to randomly pick the remaining students left to present. I draw a name from the selection sticks from my class name jar, and Sarah's name is pulled. She is an above-average student, and I am surprised that she wasn't one of the first ones to volunteer.

Immediately, she freaks out and refuses to go to the front. "I can't present, Mrs. Matthews," she says.

"Is your poster complete?" Kerri intercepts.

"Yes, but I don't think I should share it."

Kerri and I look at each other, confused by the situation; Sarah isn't usually shy. "Honey, you do great work. I'm sure it's fine," I tell her. "If you're a little worried about being up there alone, just pick a friend to stand up there with you, and they can hold your poster while you talk to us."

She looks to her best friend Alison, who looks down at Sarah's poster and immediately starts to laugh. "I don't think she should present, Ms. James."

"Girls, what's going on?" Kerri asks.

Alison runs to the class marker basket and starts drawing on Sarah's poster. "I fixed it, I think. She can present."

The girls begin to make their way to the front, but I stop them, worried about what's on the poster. Concealing the poster, Alison speaks for Sarah, who is hiding her face in her hands with embarrassment. "There was a minor typo on the poster, Mrs. Matthews, but I fixed it. It should be okay now," she reassures me.

"Bring it here and let us see," Kerri tells them. By now, the class is struggling to hide their sneers and giggles. Information about what exactly is on this poster has not surprisingly made its way through the class, and they are all trying to hold themselves together.

Sarah stays planted where she's at, so Alison brings the poster to our desks in the back of the room. She turns it around and announces, "See? I think I did a pretty good job of fixing it."

I gasp, and Kerri tries to stifle a laugh, but when the class completely loses their composure, so do we. Sarah had apparently selected the Virginia Plan for her poster; however, she's misspelled the name of the state. In big, bold, pink and purple lettering across the top of the poster is 'The Vagina Plan.' Alison has attempted to make it look less like vagina and more like Virginia by squeezing a miniature 'r' between the 'a' and 'g,' but her attempt has failed miserably.

I dab the tears from my eyes and take a deep breath. "Sarah, it's okay; mistakes happen. Go ahead and sit down. You don't have to present in front of the class, just stay after class and you can present then."

"I thought I had fixed it just fine," I hear Alison mumble as they take their seats. The comment sends Kerri back into hysterics, and I smack her arm to get her to compose herself. We have to get the class back under control. I lean in and whisper to her, "I think I finally have the story that will beat all of Will's funny stories."

She nods vigorously, "That was seriously hilarious. I don't think I can ever look at that state the same way."

"Alright, everyone, let's pull ourselves together and finish our presentations," I announce. The class slowly smothers their laughter, and when a harsh knock on the door echoes through the room, the class goes silent.

Our principal, Mrs. Jacobs, pokes her head in the door. I internally groan; I've already been observed this semester, so her presence is more than likely to request that one of us covers a class. Our lack of substitutes is seriously ridiculous. It's not that it's Susan fault, but man, the lack of planning time is wearing us all out. We all love Susan; she is like everyone's adopted grandmother. She is short and plump, with a heart of gold. Make no mistake though; she is a principal for a reason. This woman can make a grown man cry. I've seen it; it's not pretty.

"Mrs. Matthews, I need you," she says before stepping back into the hallway. I look to Kerri, and her expression lets me know that she assumes the same thing; I'll be lacking a planning hour this afternoon.

I give Kerri all of my rubric papers so that they can continue without me, and I head out into the hallway. "Which class do I need to take today?" I ask as soon as the door closes behind me.

She grabs my hand, squeezing it when she takes a deep breath, "I don't need any classes covered today, Viv. I just need you to come with me."

I quickly trace my memory of anything I can think of that could have warranted being pulled out of class and taken to the principal's office. I come up with a big fat zero, so when she turns and heads in the direction of her office, I just follow.

Susan slows so that we walk shoulder-to-shoulder, but stays quiet as we walk. If I am in trouble, I'm not going to start a conversation in the hallway, so I remain quiet as well.

When we turn the corner down the last corridor towards the office, the situation becomes clearer. We are only fifty feet from the front desk, but when Rob in his uniform turns around, hearing our footsteps click on the tiled floor, I come to a standstill.

His red, puffy eyes and splotchy cheeks tell me everything that I need to know. My feet feel like they are in quicksand, and they refuse to move any farther to face what's waiting for me at the end of the hall. Susan continues on, not noticing at first that I've stopped moving. She turns around and steps towards me to encourage me to continue on, but I hold my hand up to stop her.

There are only two reasons why Rob would be here right now, and I lock eyes with him and attempt to reach into them with my soul to grasp how serious the news is. I hold my breath, waiting for him to tell me. When he shakes his head and looks down at the floor, I know Will is gone.

The hallway is empty, but I feel like I'm being crushed between the cinder block walls. My heart plummets to my stomach, and everything around me spins out of control. As the dizziness takes over, I fall to the floor, unable to breathe, unable to look up at Rob who I hear rushing towards me. My sweaty fingers claw into the tile, and I feel myself teetering on the brink of numbness—my emotional shelter. Rob hovers over me, his own tears landing on the back of neck. When his hand lands on my back, my grief bursts to the surface. I exhale the breath I have been holding and sob into the ground, letting the cold floor cool my warm tears.

Rob lifts me into his arms, and I weep into his shoulder. I hear mumbling as we continue down the hall towards the office, but my cries drown out the words around me. A door closes, and he places me in one of the chairs in Susan's office. Susan offers me a tissue and then leaves the room. They say an officer's wife should be prepared for something like this to happen, but right now, being suffocated by that situation, I can't think of anything that would have prepared me for this. Rob sits across from me and lets me cry; he offers no empty words of condolences, nor does he try to soothe me, and I'm so damn thankful for that.

I let myself feel every bit of my loss until my eyes have no more tears. I use Susan's tissue to wipe my nose and cheeks, and turn my shoulders toward Rob. I realize that he's hurting, too, but I need to know everything before I walk out that door. I need to be able to walk down that hall and face my children knowing the truth of what happened to my husband.

"I need to know what happened, Rob." My words are muffled and scratchy from my constricted throat, but I manage to squeeze them out.

"Viv, do you think now is the time? Why don't we worry about getting you home? I can have your mother get the kids; that way we can get you settled."

My sadness morphs into anger. I feel like I'm five-years-old all over again, and instead of my mother keeping the truth from me, it's now one of my closest friends. "I'm not going anywhere," I snap. "I will gather my children and take them home, only after I find out what happened to their father. I refuse to leave here until you tell me."

I grip onto the handles of the chair, readying myself for what he's going to tell me. He attempts to speak, and his voice cracks. He takes a second to gather his breath and clear his throat. "He was just south of town on a basic traffic stop for speeding. He had already cleared all of the information through dispatch, so we think he was out of the car talking to the driver, giving him all the information for the ticket. A semi-truck driver veered out of his lane onto the shoulder, and he hit both Will and the car that was pulled over."

"Did anyone survive?" I stutter.

Rob presses his hands together and keeps his head down, unable to look at me; he's struggling to keep himself together, but I offer him no reprieve. "The semi-driver made it, but everyone else died on impact. We took the driver to the hospital for minor injuries. All of his initial toxicology tests were clean; we interviewed him, and he said he fell asleep. We went through his log books and he was way over on hours." He says it all so quickly, I struggle to follow all of what he's saying. It's like he wants to hurry and spit it all out. Then he slows down and finally makes eye contact with me. "Viv, he shouldn't have been on the road," he sighs.

I sit silently, gradually letting the information settle. I know what arrangements need to be made, what needs to be done; I just need a minute to find the courage to stand up and take the first step towards that life—a life without Will. I feel like the longer I sit here, the easier it is to believe that it's not real. It won't feel real until I have to say the words aloud.

"Tell me what you need me to do, Viv," Rob says, moving to the edge of his chair, ready to act.

"I need you to notify my family," I quietly say, "but I want you to keep everyone away from my house. I need this time right now to be with the kids. I don't want it crawling with people, whether they mean well or not. I will let everyone know when we are ready for visitors."

"You got it, whatever you guys need," he says, sniffling.

I take in one last deep, ragged breath and stand on my wobbly legs. I begin to reach for the office doorknob, but turn toward Rob instead. He stands immediately, ready for whatever directive I need accomplished. I close the gap between us and rise up on my tiptoes to pull him into a hug. Realizing that he is probably hurting just as much as I am, I wrap my arms around him, giving him the moment he may need to mourn for the best friend he just lost.

Rob had held himself together exceptionally well, considering; I know that he is trying to be strong for me. But I know this man; he needs permission to breakdown, so I give it to him. He stands there with his hands at his sides, shocked by my sudden embrace. "We're both going to miss him, Rob," I tell him while I pat his back.

It is all the encouragement he needs to let his emotions breach the dam. He brings his arms around me, picking me up off the floor, squeezing so hard that I can hardly breathe. He buries his head in my shoulder and releases all of the pain he has been holding back for my sake. His body shakes with every sob, and I just hold on, letting him feel what he needs to. "I don't know what to do now, Viv," he cries. "He was my best friend, my brother; what am I supposed to do without him?"

"We just keep going, one day at a time. That's all we can do."

He nods into my neck and I massage his back, trying to soothe him, soothe us both.

When his cries subside, he gives me one last hard squeeze and places me back on the ground. "I'm sorry, Viv. I shouldn't have lost it like that. I should be here for you right now."

"Don't be sorry. Right now, we all need to be there for each other. I wasn't the only one who lost Will today; we all did."

He nods, but doesn't say anymore. I understand though. Will and Rob really were like brothers. His pain, I'm sure, feels just as deep as my own, and I wouldn't want to take anything away from him.

"The halls should be cleared out by now; I'm going to go get the kids and go home. Please keep everyone away," I say before turning toward the door.

I open it and walk through the threshold. The halls are desolate, as I expected. I have no intention of stopping into the main office to let them know I'm leaving. I'm sure word of the accident has spread, and I don't want to see or talk to anyone. My sole mission is to hug Blake and Emma and go home, so I head towards the direction of the preschool.

In a school the size of ours, it doesn't take long to get anywhere. Within a few minutes, I find myself standing outside the kids' classroom. There is a huge glass window next to the door, and I stand stationary, watching the kids play on the other side. I can't bring myself to open the door yet, knowing that when I do, their lives will forever change. I will smash the world that they know, and it will never be the same again. I wait, watching their laughter, hanging onto the final moments of their carefree childhood.

Their teachers begin to round up all of the students for naptime; my time to procrastinate has ended. As I enter, I'm immediately greeted by the preschool staff. My coworkers are friendly, but surprised to see me. They must not know.

"I need to pick up Blake and Emma," I tell them as I sign each child out and gather their backpacks.

"Is everything all right?" they ask. Thankfully, none of them are close enough to see the makeup streaked down my face. I figured that question was coming next; I never miss a day of school, and to be taking the kids as well is completely unorthodox. As much as I knew it was coming, I couldn't say the words out loud, so instead, I went with denial. "Just not feeling well, so I thought I would just take everyone home." I don't bother to elaborate that the reason I feel like my stomach is in my throat, or that my eyes burn with every blink, is because whatever bit of heart I had was put in a blender and pureed about an hour ago.

Both Blake and Emma run to me and attack my legs when they see me, which only makes the lump in my throat more difficult to swallow down. They grab their backpacks from me and ask nothing of the break in our routine until we pull away from the school.

"Where are we going, Momma?" Emma asks. I'm not about to talk about anything until we get home, so I generate the most generic answer I can that won't prompt more questions.

"Oh, we need to talk about something that couldn't wait until after school. Besides, I figured you guys wouldn't mind getting out of nap time," I say, looking in the rearview mirror. They ask me no more questions and quietly converse in the backseat until we pull down our dirt driveway.

I feel myself relax a bit when I see that there are no other cars parked in front of our house. It probably took Rob holding my mother at gunpoint to keep her away from our house; but whatever he did to accomplish the task that I asked, I'm so appreciative.

As soon as I park, the kids quickly unbuckle. I press the child lock so they can open the car doors on their own and go inside. "Please, go in and sit on Momma and Daddy's bed," I tell them, as they burst out of the car.

They rush into the house, but I remain in the car, holding onto the steering wheel, zoned in on the empty spot where Will usually parks his patrol car. I try to think of what to tell them, what the best way to go about telling a child that their father isn't coming home. I've been in their place before, and I don't know if there are any right words, but there sure as hell are bad ones. There are no do-overs with something like this, and I'm terrified that I'll screw it up.

Giving up, I open my door and slowly walk inside, where what's left of my world is waiting for me. I find them sitting patiently on my bed, both dangling their feet off the edge. I kneel down and take both of their shoes off, and then remove my own. I climb on to the bed and motion for them both to join me farther. We sit in a small circle, and I grab each of their tiny hands, rubbing my fingers along their knuckles.

"Guys, something happened today that we need to talk about."

"Did you quit your job like Aunt Charlotte and Grandma want you to? Is that why we are home early?" Blake asks which brings the first half-hearted smile to my face since I got the news.

"No, little man, I didn't quit," I answer, giving him a smirk that doesn't quite meet my eyes. "Your daddy was in a very bad accident today."

"Are we going to the hospital to see him? Did the doctor fix all his owies so he can come home?" Emma asks. The sweetness of her question makes the growing boulder in my throat painful. It becomes difficult to breathe, and my voice cracks when I try to speak. I have to look away from them to pull my emotions back under control.

"No, baby," I exhale through the tears. "The accident was too bad, and the doctors couldn't fix him. Daddy was just hurt too bad, and he went to Heaven."

Their little faces begin to scrunch as the tears hit their eyes and they comprehend that their father isn't coming back. When Emma's first tears hit my pillow, I allow my own tears to fall and wave them into my arms. Both quickly crawl into my lap and bury their faces in my chest.

"I'm so sorry. You know Momma loves you, and we will be okay. We just have to stick together," I tell them as I lean back against the headboard and begin stroking their hair.

Blake pulls away and looks up at me with tears running down his reddened cheeks. "But he said we were a team and that he was the captain; we would always be our own team. If he's not here, we won't be a team anymore." I see the panic pouring out of him at the idea of our family crumbling, and even though I need to ease that anxiety, I fear the exact same thing.

Cradling them in my arms, I ease down the bed to lay us all down. "Blake, our team is not going to fall apart. We may be changing the line-up, but we will always be a team; we will always be a family."

They snuggle in farther, and I just let them cry while I rub their backs. There are no words that will make this better. There is nothing I can do to make the hurt go away; it will just take time. We lay together, allowing each other to feel our loss. One by one, we cry ourselves to sleep in the safety of mine and Will's bed. The lingering smell of his cologne on his pillow surrounds us, and we breathe in the final pieces that we have left of him.

15

VIVIAN

It has almost been one year since my world crumbled beneath my feet. One year since my home was ripped away from me. Before Brooks and Will, I had never believed in love, but after them, I now not only believe in love, but I know how badly it can burn you. Brooks took my heart and handed it back to me completely shattered. But Will...he didn't just tape the pieces back together, he super-glued it, and when he died, he took my patched-up heart with him.

While I grew to love the town that I hated growing up, after Will, it became suffocating. That's how I referred to life these days, before and after Will. For the brief time that I had him, he made my life and my heart right. Now, my life could never be the same; there was a hole that would never be filled.

I tried going back to work in my same little school, but it became too difficult. My friends would give me their best looks of compassion, but I could tell they just didn't know what to say. And really, there wasn't anything they could say to make it better. It was never going to be better again. They treated me like I was a glass doll, and they were all waiting for me to break; too late though, I am already broken.

Life became my childhood all over again. I knew I was the hushed topic of conversation around town. Everyone wondered if I was okay, or what they could do to help the kids and me. For the life of me, I tried to appear all right, but God, I just couldn't face their sad looks of pity any longer. Every time someone would put their arm around me and ask how I was, it was like reliving that day all over again. I knew that they meant well, but I was tired of feeling the pain. I needed a new feeling, even if that meant I felt nothing.

Amanda was the only one to pull off the white gloves and call bullshit. She gave me a week in my jammies after the accident before she hauled my ass to the shower and forced me to get my shit together. My flake of a sister was the strongest I had ever seen her. She helped with funeral arrangements, made sure that Blake and Emma were fed and bathed, and made sure I was functioning. Yep, my little sister yanked the covers off my head and snapped me back to reality.

So when she showed up two weeks ago, I knew I was in for another Amanda intervention, but this time, instead of making sure my hair was combed and my shirt was not inside out, she was going to do a makeover on my entire life. She knew I needed to get on with things, if not for me, for the kids; she knew I needed to leave and start over. So after everything was settled with the courts and the insurance companies, Amanda offered that we move to Denver and find a place together. It was my chance to start fresh; to save Blake and Emma from the childhood that I had.

My days are now filled with my kids. Between all of the settlements and pension, I really don't need to work, and so I load my days with my kids' activities. When they are at school, I find it therapeutic to write. I write articles about children, being a single parent, education, book reviews, I blog about everything, and I have started submitting freelance articles to various magazines. Amanda would argue that I'm avoiding life, and that I'm hiding behind my computer. I would call it trying to survive each day when I can barely find enough air to breathe.

"Momma, what are you looking at?" Emma snaps me out of my daydream. I shake my head and take her hands into mine, wiping off some of the dirt she had gotten into on the playground.

"Nothing baby, I'm just thinking."

"Are you thinking about Daddy?" She asks this often, and I've tried to keep his presence in the house, letting them know that even though Will's not with us, he can still watch us from Heaven and be proud of us. It kills me though, every time I have to answer the question. Blake has been a little quieter about Will; Emma though, she's four and missed the memo about having a filter.

I lean down and swing her into the air; damn, she's getting to big too do that. I settle her on my hip and she lets out a little giggle. "Yes, baby, I was thinking about how excited your daddy would be that you are starting preschool at your new school. School starts in about a month; are you getting excited?"

Her eyebrows furrow slightly, and I brush the bits of hair that have fallen out of her braid away from her face. "What's wrong, baby girl?" I ask, trying to capture her attention.

She looks away from me and quietly responds, "What if I don't have any friends at my new school? I don't want to be the new kid."

I wrap her legs around my waist and sit down on the park bench that overlooks the playground equipment. I place my fingers under her chin to bring her eyes to mine. "Do you remember when we went to the carnival last year, and you were so scared to ride the carousel?"

Her bewildered expression almost has me laughing. "Yes, that horse was huge, and I'm small! If I fell off, I could have broken my arm like Blake did when he fell off the trampoline!" Her eyes are huge, and her hands fly around animatedly as she describes what could have been a tragic life moment for her.

"I remember, but you really wanted to go didn't you?"

"Yes. Blake told me that he would hold me up so I wouldn't fall, so I got brave and got in line."

"We couldn't get you off that white sparkly horse the rest of the day; what did you name him?

"Stormy. He had magic powers; he made me not afraid and I didn't even need Blake." By this point, her smile is huge, and even more of her blonde curls are falling down from her rambunctious story telling.

"You were brave, and you had so much fun that day. Well, baby, that's how preschool at the new school is going to be. Aunt Amanda went and saw it, and she told me that it looks so fun and the teachers are very nice. I think if you can be brave enough to start the day, you will love it by the end of it."

She gives me her best thinking-it-over look before exhaling a long sigh, "Ok, Momma, I'll be brave."

"Besides, you are one of the coolest chicks I know; all the kids will just love you!" I smile and tickle her as she lets out a loud screech.

Blake hears our laughter and comes running over from the swings. "Quick, Blake, get her! She needs more tickles!"

He hops onto the grass and joins in the fun, helping to playfully attack his little sister. Then I grab him and hold him to the ground to tickle him as well. When our stomachs and cheeks can't handle any more laughter, we lay back on the grass to catch our breath and look for shapes in the clouds.

It's moments like these that I really miss Will. My tears of sadness quickly replace my tears of joy. It's not fair that these great kids won't know their father, or that he won't get to share these small but wonderful moments with them. I just hope I can love Emma and Blake enough for both of us.

I pull them both into my arms, kiss their heads, and breathe in their strawberry kiddo shampoo. "I love you guys," I murmur into their hair. "I know this move is scary, but we are a team, and I know we can do anything if we stick together. I think this will be good for us."

They both curl into me, snuggling in tight. "Ok, Momma," Blake says.

"Ya, me too," Emma adds, "but I don't want to be on the team; I want to be the cheerleader."

"Deal," I chuckle. "Look out, Denver! Here we come."

VIVIAN

As I approach the old student union, my nerves are kicking into overdrive, revolting against my stomach to the point of making me dizzy. Tonight is big for me; not only am I about to see Will's college buddies, who I haven't seen since the funeral, it is very possible that Brooks will be making an appearance. Jen and Carly talked me into going to our college reunion. At this moment, I feel like I could seriously kill them; I really don't think I thought this entirely through. Campbell is out of town and couldn't come; I should have been more creative and come up with an excuse, as well.

Colorado has been having an unusually hot summer, but tonight, there is a slight warm breeze that gives a little relief. However, it did make it difficult to keep the beautiful but short dress Amanda had picked out for me from blowing up and revealing things I definitely do not want on any social media sites. "It will look gorgeous, Viv. Show all those guys that you still got it, and let Brooks suffer for what he lost," is what she told me. Yep, I'm adding her to the hit list, too.

I swing the front doors open, and I'm immediately greeted by Jen and Carly in the foyer. The entrance looks like somebody bought out the streamer section of Party America and *went to town*. If it weren't for the mixed variety of greens and yellows, and of course, the cardboard cutouts of ram heads, I would think the place had gotten toilet-papered.

"Holy crap, whoever was on the decorating committee needs to seriously reevaluate their design skills," I say as I trudge through the doors, desperately trying to adjust my dress and pat down my windblown hair.

"Hey! I worked hard on this; it took all afternoon!" Carly shouts. My eyes go wide at the realization that I just insulted one of my closest and oldest friends, but then both she and Jen double over in laughter.

I walk closer to them with a deep scowl on my face. "You bitch, that was not funny; I really thought I hurt your feelings."

Jen puts her arm around me and pulls me into her side, dabbing tears from her eyes. "Lighten up, Viv. That was fucking hilarious; you should have seen your face. I wish I had filmed it."

"Seriously, you've been so worried about tonight; I just thought we could start it off with a little laugh. We should be laughing and dancing all night, just like old times," Carly adds.

"God, this is stupid. I shouldn't be here; Amanda stuck me in this Queen Slut-o-rama dress, and I'm scared to face the guys. I'm just going to end up ruining your night; maybe I should just go home."

Jen covers my mouth with her hand before anything else can fly out of it. "Listen here, girlie. We wouldn't have talked you into coming if we thought it would be a bad idea. We are going to have a blast *because* you are here. The guys love you and will not make you feel uncomfortable, and the specific guy you are most worried about, well, if he's here, he can go fuck himself." Carly chuckles a little, but my eyes are bulging out of my head at this point; Jen has taken potty mouth to the extreme. "If he gives you trouble, Carly can hold him while I kick him in the balls; it will be a homecoming to remember."

At this, we all start laughing. Then Jen removes her hand from my mouth and begins fussing with my hair. "And by the way, sweetheart, this dress is smokin'! If I can just manage to tame the birds that have taken up residence in your hair, you will be one hot ticket tonight."

"I'm not quite sure if you were complimenting me or not, Jen, but right now, I'll take what I can get," I sigh as she finishes correcting my apparent mess of a hairstyle.

"There! You are officially a sexy momma. Watch out, CSU alums; we got a cougar on the prowl!"

I brush Jen off, quickly adjust my dress again, and dab some lip-gloss on. "Oh, good God, you did not just say that. I'm going to need some liquor tonight and pronto if this is what is to become of our evening," I laugh.

Jen leads our pack through the main entrance that opens into the ballroom. There is a dance floor in the center of the room, a bar off to the right, and tables scattered throughout the space. The tacky decorations have filtered in and have attacked every available flat surface available.

The music playing is reminiscent of ten years ago. *Damn, I feel old.* I told a student last year to check himself before he wrecked himself, and he looked at me like I had lost my mind. And now, here I am, getting ready to bust a move to *Crazy In Love.* There is no way Jen will allow me to sit on the sidelines tonight, so after a few shots, I will turn myself over to the twerking society, at least for a few hours.

I follow Jen to the bar and order what will be, I'm assuming, my first of many drinks for the night. "I'll have a margarita on the rocks, please, with extra salt. Jen wants a martini with extra olives and,–" Carly cuts in before I can tell the bartender her regular red wine order, "I'm just going to have water tonight."

In utter shock that Carly could think that it's okay that I be pushed into the social limelight while she sits this one out, I immediately call bullshit. "Uh, I'm sorry. I think I just heard you say, 'I'm glad you're being a good sport about tonight, but I'm going to stick to a pussy M.O. tonight.'" I turn to Jen. "Is that what you heard too, Jen?"

She just bobs her head in agreement, completely straight-faced; she's not going to let Carly off the hook either. Good.

After a long sigh, she finally responds. "Fine, but you know I don't handle my alcohol well, and if Jack has to hold my hair back tonight, he's going to be pissed," she resigns.

"We got you covered, girl. Amanda is keeping the kids all night for Viv, Jack can take care of Olivia in the morning, and we had planned on having coffee at A Scone's Throw in the morning anyway, so we can all just take a taxi and stay at my house tonight."

"Sounds like a plan," I say, letting the last bit hang in the air a little, encouraging Carly to loosen up and have a good time with us.

"Okay," she steps up to the bar, "I would like a Vodka Tonic with a twist of orange, and to get us started, we need three lemon drops, please."

She looks back to the two of us. "If we're going to do this, dammit, we're going to do it right, and that means loads of vodka."

That earns a huge smile from both of us. "Well, all right then, let's get this night rolling!" Jen shouts.

Over the next hour, several familiar faces have made their way to the bar. Some of Will's old friends stop to give hugs, but nothing awkward. Maybe it's the alcohol, but I was starting to feel all right with the evening.

Seth and Aaron showed up together and insist that we dance with them; neither is any more coordinated than they were ten years ago. Damn, I missed this crew. We are all grown-ups now, with careers, responsibilities, and some of us have kids and spouses, but we are all still friends. Nothing feels like it has changed. Well, that's not exactly true; our glue is gone. Will is gone. But I can't put myself back in that state of mind again. Our group just needs to reorganize and move forward; not forget him, but let go of him. That's what tonight is for us–realizing that we are all different; our group is different, but we are going to be okay.

I let the music take my body over, swaying to every beat that the speaker kicks out. I love the freeing feeling of the moment, but then I notice that Jen has stopped dancing all together. Her face has gone completely white, and her eyes are narrowed and zoned in on a target. My eyes follow her gaze and land on Brooks, making his way through the doors and to the bar.

He looks as handsome as I remember. Scratch that–he fucking looks *better*. He used to be tall and lean, but he has bulked up over the past decade. His dark hair is messy, but in a stylish, sexy way. At one time, I loved to pull my fingers through it; now I just hate him and every sexy little thing about him, including his fuck-me hair.

Wrapped around his side, sliding her polished hand up his suit jacket, is a statuesque beauty. Her long flowing blonde hair is tapered down to her shoulders, she looks like a model, and together they look like perfection. Typical. Of course Brooks had to bring arm candy, something shiny to show off.

I can only hope that she wants to partake in some dancing for the evening so I can trip her. *Yeah right.* I could never do that…but Jen would. "Watch out, Barbie," I mumble, laughing to myself at the thought.

Brooks catches me staring and gives me a slight smile. Well, fuck. There goes being cool and collected for the night. I nonchalantly nod and turn around to the girls. It's been ten damn years; surely I can be an adult in this situation.

Carly snaps me out of my moment of reverie. "Why don't we go sit at our table for a minute? I need to get something to drink." I agree. I need a second to cool off.

"Sure, I'm going to go the bathroom, and then I'll meet you at our table," I tell her.

"You want us to come with?" Jen asks.

I just laugh. "Thanks, but I think I can handle wiping myself. Check back in a few years and I might call in the offer."

"Ha ha, smartass, you know what I mean."

"I know. I'm good though, thanks," I say before heading off in the direction of the restrooms. The truth of the matter is that I needed a moment to pull myself together and freshen up without them. I am hoping to repair my weakened confidence. Seeing Brooks' date tonight has sent my emotions into a tailspin. It just confirms what I always thought—I was never good enough for him. While I wanted the safety that I found in Will, he wanted the shine, and that never would have been me. He needs glimmer, and the only thing sparkly about me is the body glitter lotion that Amanda insisted I wear.

I quickly do my thing in the restroom before Jen calls out the search party, and I head to the bar to buy another round of drinks for everyone. I'm not going to let Brooks' attendance ruin tonight.

There are very few people at the bar; most had found their way to their various cliques and are now socializing at tables. I take a seat on one of the stools and wait for my turn to order. The bartender is in the middle of blending a mixed drink, so I know it will be a few minutes before I can get his attention. I begin to mindlessly rip up a napkin in front me while I wait; it's a nervous habit I guess, but it's better than chewing on my nails like I used to.

I feel a warm body slide up next to mine, but then I hear the smooth, delicious voice that I have been dreading to hear.

"Hey, I'm glad to see you here tonight."

I tear my eyes away from the pile of paper I have accumulated and meet his stare. Bad choice on my part. Those cornflower eyes feel like they're searching my soul, and when he smiles, dammit if I don't just turn to mush right there. He could always do that with a single look, and I hate that I'm still so weak that I let him have that power over me.

Fuck the drinks. Without saying a word, I stand to leave—what feels like my only defense.

He quickly grabs my elbow to stop me. "Please, don't run; I just wanted to say hi, Red." He looks down to where he's touching me, no doubt feeling the current surging between us. "It's been a long time, and I was hoping that we could at least be civil."

I let out a heavy sigh, probably the same breath I have been holding since I first heard his voice. "You're right. It has been a long time, and we're both adults at a public function, so..." I move to shake his hand. "It was good to see you, too; I hope you enjoy your evening."

Holy shit, look at me! Not only do I have the big girl panties on, but I'm pretty sure if Jen just saw that extreme act of confidence, she would have pissed hers.

"Since we're being mature adults this evening, could I please have the next dance?" he asks and smiles brightly. I can tell he's trying to present himself with his usual cocky demeanor, but I can see some self-doubt in his eyes, fear that I'll reject him.

I turn my back, but he grabs my hand before I can take a step. "Please," he whispers. I drop my head, and for a moment, I think of all the pain this man caused. Then I push it away, if only for one dance. After giving him a small nod of my head, he leads me onto the dance floor.

Brooks wraps me up into his arms, arms that used to be the best place in the world, arms that eventually betrayed me. He pulls me close and breathes in my hair like he used to. My stomach begins to flutter, and I don't want to even think about the carnival ride in my panties. Damn you, vagina! You have betrayed me, too. Traitor.

We move together, perfectly matched to the music. Our bodies join in a cohesive movement, but I can't let my mind go there. He is the enemy; he shattered me, and given the chance, he would probably do it again.

"So your date looks nice. Girlfriend or plaything?" I ask him, regaining some of my hostility. I know that my comment is below the belt, but does he really think that a dance will change what he did to me? Does he think that ten years will wipe away the memory of his disloyalty?

He disappoints me by not playing into the grudge match I am hoping for. "She's just an acquaintance. I didn't want to come here alone, and she volunteered to be my date."

"I bet she did," I say with a huff. "I can only imagine the other things she would volunteer to do for you."

"Are you jealous, Red?"

I look up and narrow my eyes at him, trying not to waver. "Fuck no, I just feel sorry for her." He tilts his head to the side in his lack of understanding, and I have no problem clarifying for him. "You're a tornado, Brooks. You slam through women with little regard for what happens to them afterwards, and it's obvious that she has not been on the tail end of that destruction yet. But at some point, she'll feel exactly the same as I did once."

I hold his glare, hoping he feels every bit of what he did to me. Shame fills his eyes, and he lowers his forehead to mine. "I'm sorry for everything, Viv. All I ever wanted to do was keep you safe, even if it meant not being with me," he whispers.

"Keep me safe!" I shout, pulling away from him. "How does cheating on me keep me safe?"

His eyes go wide, and then he pulls me to him, tangling me in his arms. "I have nothing to say but I'm sorry; Will was the better man, *is* the better man. I didn't deserve you."

I sigh, "You're right; Will was the better man, and if he were alive, he would still be the better man, because no matter what the reason, he would never have hurt me the way you did."

Brooks stiffens and drops his arms from around me; he takes a step back, and I can see tears forming in his eyes. "What do you mean, *if he were alive?*"

I can barely hear him over the music; his eyes are searching mine, looking for comfort. I know that I'm about to crush him. No matter how it ended, Will was Brooks' friend in college. For him to not know, and not get the chance to attend the funeral, will hurt him. I lower my head and try to pull together my shaky ragged breaths.

I finally look up and nod. "He died last year in a car accident. We moved to Denver after everything was settled. I'm sorry I didn't contact you; I just couldn't, Brooks. You being there would have made it even harder to get through."

Brooks balls his fists, and I see he is trying desperately to hold together his emotions. "I understand," he says with a curt nod.

The tears that I had been holding back begin to slide down my cheeks. The last thing I wanted was for Brooks to see me cry, but talking about Will caught me off-guard. I take a deep cleansing breath to regain my poise.

Just when I think that I have my emotions under control, Brooks steps forward, runs his hands into my hair, and leans in cheek-to-cheek. I hear him breathing heavily into my ear, and for a moment, I let myself relax into his comfort. He is letting me collect myself, and I'm giving him the moment to grieve.

"Oh, Clover, I'm so sorry," he whispers. That one comment snaps me out of the warm abyss of our embrace. I place my hands on his chest and push him away.

"I'm not Clover anymore. I'm not your Clover anymore; you ruined that." My anguish that has twisted into anger is boiling. The sound of a name that represents my previous life with him has turned my veins to ice. "You don't ever get to call me that again; you shattered that girl, and I'll never be her again."

My hands are shaking with adrenalin, and my tears are now dried streaks on my face. I turn away from him before he can say another word, walk as quickly as I can to my group's table to collect my purse, and bolt towards the exit.

Thankfully, Brooks doesn't follow me. No one does. I climb into my car and sit in the driver's seat, desperately trying to steady my breathing. Pulling out my cell phone, I text Jen that I'm leaving.

> **Jen:** We're gathering our stuff. We can leave with u. Do Carly and I need to put into effect Operation Brooks' Balls Smash before we head out?
>
> **Me:** No, but thx. I'm ok. I just want to go home and go to bed. U guys just stay and have fun; I'll see u at the coffee shop in the morning.
>
> **Jen:** Ok, babe. If ur sure, see u in the am. <3 u!
>
> **Me:** <3 u 2.

After I text the final message to Jen, I throw my phone into my purse and hail a cab to go home. Everyone is asleep, and I'm able to easily escape to my room once I get home. I don't even bother changing clothes; I just slip off my shoes and collapse into bed, pulling the duvet over my head.

forgive us our Trespasses

My hope is that when I wake up, the past four hours will have never existed, and I will get a complete do-over–one that doesn't include Brooks Ryan.

VIVIAN

Amanda is planning to take the kids out for breakfast, so I am able to sleep in before getting ready for coffee with the girls. I shower, throw on some yoga pants and a sweatshirt, and toss my wet hair into a messy bun on top of my head. I'm in no mood to impress anyone this morning, and if my guess is correct, I will be the most dressed up of the three of us.

A Scone's Throw, our favorite little coffee shop, is just a five-minute walk from my house, so I slip into my sneakers, swipe on a little strawberry lip-gloss to complete the look, and start my walk toward what I assume will be a friendly inquisition.

The coffee house is packed to the brim with morning caffeine junkies in need of their espresso fix to function through their various Saturday activities. I wait in line for my white chocolate mocha and raspberry scone, and find that Jen and Carly are already sitting at our usual table in the back of the store.

The scene before me is quite pitiful, and I can only shake my head at the pair as I approach the table. Jen is rubbing her temples, and her eyes are closed like she is trying to meditate her hangover away. Carly, on the other hand, looks as though she has completely given in to hers. Her arms are folded on the tabletop, and her head is resting on her forearms, completely hiding her face from public judgment.

"Wow, I'm glad I left when I did," I say as I take a seat. "I think I saved myself from the pure hell that it looks like you two are experiencing right now."

"Shhh, not so loud," Jen mutters. "I would chop off my own head to save myself from this misery if I could."

"That bad, huh?" I laugh.

Jen finally opens her eyes, but continues to rub her head. "I'm not as bad as Carly; she threw up for an hour after we got home last night."

I look over to Carly, who still has not moved. She finally turns her head, remaining on her arms, and croaks out a defense. "True, and Jen wouldn't even hold my hair back. She just gave me a ponytail holder and bottle of water, and told me 'good luck with that.'"

"Hey, you both know I'm a sympathetic puker," Jen insists. "We all know that the caretaker role is your job, Viv. I did the best I could with what I had."

"Well, if we ever decide to revisit our youth again, I'll be sure to be available for hair holding and aspirin retrieval," I tease.

Jen takes a huge gulp of her venti cappuccino and then sits back in her chair, slouching her shoulders to settle in for what will be the inquiry of my life. Carly has since removed her arms from under her head, and has let her face settle on the tabletop, letting her breath fog over the Formica.

"Ok, chica, spill it."

"It was nothing, guys. Brooks showed up at the bar and asked me to dance. We agreed to disagree on the fact that he's an asshole, I told him about Will, I had a brief meltdown, and then I left."

Jen scowls at me, and I can tell that the short version of the story is not going to cut it for her. I sigh, feeling an emotional hangover coming on.

"I don't want to make a big deal out of it, okay? Besides, I'll probably never see him again. I said all the things that I needed to say ten years ago but never got the chance to, and now I'm over it. I refuse to let it bother me anymore."

Finally showing signs of life, Carly pops her head up and props her chin on her palm. "What did you say? Did the piece of shit even care what you had to say?"

"He just said that he was sorry, and that he was trying to protect me."

"What?" Carly exclaims. "Protect you from what, gonorrhea? Because I wouldn't doubt it if that slut Amber had some kind of STD."

"It's been a freaking decade; I shouldn't be conflicted by this anymore. I don't know what it is about him, but for some damn reason, whenever I'm near him, I let my guard down, and time and time again, he just slices me open and lets my heart spill out. The jerk called me *Clover;* can you believe the nerve?"

Carly and I turn our attention to Jen, who is staring out the window like she has completely zoned out of the conversation. "Really, you have nothing to say Jen? You were the kick-him-the-nuts-mission co-founder last night, and this morning you aren't going to chime in on this special edition of Brooks bashing?" Carly inquires.

Jen turns her head to looks at us. "Did he really call you Clover?" she quietly asks. Her sullen expression has my nerves on edge.

"Yes, why?" I rasp out slowly.

Jen looks down at the table, refusing to meet my eyes. Her uneasy behavior has me freaking out; my stomach is beginning to tie itself in knots. I slide to the edge of my chair and lean towards her. "What the hell is going on, Jen?" I demand.

She rubs her eyes with the heels of her hands and takes a deep breath. Fuck, I know this move; this is Jen gearing up to shake our world.

"I need to tell you something, but I need you to hear me out before you say anything."

"Okay, start talking."

"I've kept this secret for a long time. At first, I believed Brooks was protecting you; then when you married Will, I didn't think it mattered anymore. But things are different now. Will is gone and I know that Brooks loves you; he probably never stopped loving you."

"What are you talking about? He doesn't love me; people in love don't cheat. When you really want someone, you don't want someone else," I argue.

"He never cheated, Viv!" Jen shouts, cutting off my rant.

"Um, I'm sorry, did the lemon drops kill one too many brain cells last night? Jen, you were there; we all were. We all saw Amber walk out of his room." I feel my temper brewing below the surface, and I have to force myself to keep calm and lower my voice.

Giving me a second to recover, Carly begins a round of questioning. "You're going to have to explain why you think he didn't cheat, Jen; he never put up even a little bit of a fight."

Jen lets out a deep exhale, her eyes on me pleading for understanding. "After everything hit the fan, and Will had you settled in your room, I went back to Brooks' dorm to bitch him out, and possibly punch out a few teeth. When I barged through the door, I found him sitting on the couch crying...*crying*, Viv. I asked him how he could throw it all away, and he told me he lied. That he set the whole thing up to make it look like he cheated."

131

I can't believe what's coming out of her mouth; it doesn't make sense, and I'm starting to feel like my best friend got played.

"Oh, Jen, that sounds absolutely ridiculous. Why would anyone do something like that?" Apparently, Carly and I are on the same page.

"If he didn't love me and want to be with me, why not just tell me? Why go to all the trouble of breaking my heart? That's just fucking cruel."

"I know, Viv. I know. I didn't understand at first either."

"Okay, well, explain."

"He said if you found out who he really was, it would hurt worse than anything he did that night. He said he needed you to stay away from him in order to protect you. He knew that cheating was a deal-breaker for you, but he could never actually go through with being unfaithful to you. He said it was going to be bad enough that he would make you believe he did, and he would lose you. He thought he was keeping you safe from something; I don't know what he was hiding, but I figured it was bad if he was willing to go to the extent he did to keep it from you."

Tears are stinging my eyes; my throat begins to tighten, but the rest of my body is numb. I'm in disbelief that my best friend would keep this from me. She saw what he did to me, how long it took me to trust again, to love again. For months, I questioned what was wrong with me. I struggled with the thought that my past had damaged me so badly, that Brooks felt he had to run from me, and that he found me undeserving of his loyalty and love. How could she let me continue to believe that, when with a few words she could have restored my confidence?

"Why?" I struggle with the word, and it's all I'm able to say. My heart and head are raging a massive war with raw emotions of anger, betrayal, hurt, and, to some degree, relief, churning around me. I feel my face warming, and my stomach is unbearably twisting.

"I'm so sorry, Vivian," she says, shaking her head, panic written all over her face.

I turn my head away from her; I can't look at her. "Why?" I repeat.

"He begged me not to tell you the truth; he felt it was best that you stayed away from him. Whatever he was going through would have hurt you, and I believed him. Then once you and Will got together, I thought that you had moved on and it didn't really matter anymore. I didn't think that you would ever see him again, and he would just be some asshole ex-boyfriend we could add to the dickhead list."

"But you knew he would probably be there last night; didn't you think that that piece of information would have been useful for me to know? I treated him horribly; I said terrible things to him. It's pretty shitty to find out that I've hated him, and wasted this hurt and energy on a fucking lie."

"When you said that he called you Clover, I knew, Viv. This was never over for him, and he still loves you. I'm sorry; I just couldn't keep the secret anymore."

I push my chair back and stand, gathering my satchel and coffee. "I need to go. I'll text you later; I just can't talk to you about this right now."

"Please don't leave, Vivian. We can't leave it like this," Carly interjects. Jen sits quietly with her head down, and it's just as well; I don't want to hear anything else she has to say right now.

"I can't; I promise I'll call. I just need to be alone right now and process this fucking shit storm that I walked through this morning."

I fight my way through the remaining coffee crowd and escape through the front doors. Once outside, I let the sunlight hit my face and take in the crisp morning air, appreciating every bit of it as I take long breaths of it into my lungs.

Turning towards home, I slowly begin to make the trek. I let the words rattle around my head until they pound into my skull with every step. *He never cheated.* Step. *He was protecting you.* Step. *My best friend lied to me.* Step, step.

How can karma be this twisted? I must have been a major bitch in a past life; maybe I was an Amber, and this is my reincarnation punishment. *Instead of sending her back as a cockroach, nope, send her back as Vivian Matthews and fuck up her shit.*

I turn my five-minute walk into thirty, and Amanda's car is in the driveway by the time I get home. I scrub my hands over my face, clearing away any signs of the tears I shed throughout my excruciating morning. I may fool my munchkins, but my red swollen eyes and runny nose will surely give me away to Amanda, and it's August, so I can't exactly blame the weather.

I take a deep breath, clear my mind of the drama, and push open the large mahogany door that will lead me to the two bright stars I have in my cataclysmic mess of life.

"Momma, you're home!" they shout, running towards me.

I smile, and my world becomes right again, at least for the moment.

BROOKS

I'm sitting with my morning coffee on the back deck, letting the voices in my head invade my every thought. I live far enough away from town that I'm allotted a certain amount of solitude, and this morning I'm grateful for it. The sun has just come up over the horizon and the bright pinks of the morning light are a welcome sight to ease my melancholy mood. I don't usually wake up this early, not since my little girl started sleeping through the night, but my mind has been plagued with the regrets of my past, and it has negatively impacted my sleep.

It's been a week since I saw Vivian at the reunion, and I have felt every second of those 168 hours. I nearly had to cancel my phone service, or amputate my hands to keep from calling Jen to get her number. Because Jen knows the truth, she's the only one that wouldn't maim me for even asking for Vivian's information. I didn't expect to feel the way I did when I saw her. In a single moment, the pain I had been running from for all these years came slamming into me.

Vivian was my one, the only woman that I ever wanted to spend my life with. I may or may not have broken down and Facebook-stalked her for the last few days. I felt like I was spying on the life that I should have had with her. Hey, don't judge me.

I really figured that after this long, Jen would have told her what had really happened between Amber and me, which was absolutely nothing. Needless to say, I was shocked that she still thinks I cheated, and that she hates me.

I've spent the last decade trying to avoid the thought of her. I focused on my career, building a successful architectural firm. When it came to women, well, I spent my evenings fucking my way through the tri-state area, trying to let go of the one woman who I couldn't forget. I used women to dull the pain, numb the remaining shreds of my heart, but nothing worked.

It crushed me to let her go ten years ago, but I really thought I was letting the better man win. Will would never hurt her, and knowing who I was and where I came from was something I don't think she could have ever forgiven. Losing her only compounded my torment, but it was worth it to know that she was happy and her heart was safe.

But now Will is gone; Will is fucking dead.

"Daddy, can you come snuggle me?" Grace's sweet voice breaks through my self-deprecating thoughts. She is standing just inside the house, leaning on the doorframe to the deck, snuggled up in her pink fleece blanket, and gripping her favorite stuffed elephant. Her curly raven hair is standing on end; the back, I'm sure, is entirely frizzed, and my only hairstyle option for the day will be a ponytail.

"Sure, Lovebug, go warm up our spot on the couch, and I'll be there in just a second with Sleeping Beauty."

"No, Daddy, the mean dragon-lady is scary. I want Cinderella."

"You got it, baby. I'll be right there."

Satisfied with the plan for the morning, she turns and runs into the house to make our couch fort for the movie. No doubt, when I get in there, she will have a full zoo of stuffed animals propped all around the couch to view the family feature.

I slowly peel myself out of the lounge chair and stretch my arms above my head, trying to iron out the kinks in my neck and back. Gathering up my empty coffee cup, I walk back into the house to spend the day with my little girl.

"I have your spot all ready, Daddy," she says, pulling back the blanket on the couch. I put the DVD into the player and snuggle in next to her.

"Thank you, baby," I say, and kiss the top of her head as she settles into the crook of my arm. "Gracie, I was thinking that after the movie we could go shopping and get everything you're going to need for preschool this year. Does that sound like a plan?"

"Okay, Daddy, but you have to promise that I can pick out my own backpack. Last year you made me get that Care Bears bag, and they are not cool. I want a Hello Kitty backpack with sparkles."

"How do you know what's cool?"

"I'm four, and four is old enough to know cool, and Care Bears are not cool."

"Well, all right then. Hello Kitty it is." I laugh.

"I want a lunchbox, too."

"Don't push it, little girl."

She lets out a little sigh and then shakes her hands excitedly, shushing me when the opening credits come on. We have seen Cinderella more times than I can count, and yes, she makes me sing the songs. I may not sing on key, but I know every damn word, and I figure that's what counts.

She settles back against my chest, and we enjoy our father/daughter moment. I never thought I would have children unless it was with Vivian, but then I got the surprise of my life, little Grace. I was never with her mother—let me clarify that, I was never in a relationship with Grace's mom. She was a reoccurring one-night-stand that resulted in an unplanned pregnancy. She didn't want to have the baby, and well, I did.

I felt that a child could be my chance at redemption. I talked her into having the baby, promising to raise her on my own. She agreed to sign over her rights, but only after I paid her a hefty sum for what she called 'the destruction of her body.' I said I fucked quantity, and Grace's mother goes to show that I didn't exactly care about the level of quality.

"Grace, I don't think you need all of these school supplies for preschool. I'm pretty sure they have everything there for you; you just need to take a backpack," I say as Grace throws another package of glitter pens into the cart.

The child has gone insane in the school supply section of Target. My four-year-old is leading me around on what has become the biggest nerd-shopping spree known to man. I love her to death, but seriously, I was expecting a five-minute in-and-out trip to get her damn Hello Kitty backpack, and maybe splurge on the lunchbox, but I may have to whip out the platinum card for this haul.

Grace steps around the side of the cart, places her hands on her waist, and sticks out her hip in pure attitude mode. Good Lord, if she's like this now, Heaven help me when she's thirteen.

"Daddy, you never know what you might need, and what if my teacher gives me homework? I need things at home just in case. We should make me my own office like yours at home. Can we, Daddy? Pleeeease?"

Yeah, how do I argue with that? No matter what kind of a demanding dick I am at work, this little girl dissolves every bit of that hardness, and I'm putty in her hand. What's worse is I think that she knows it. *Dammit.*

"Okay, Lovebug, but we need to rein it in a little bit. We have enough markers in the cart to provide a stock pile for the entire school district."

"Hey, they are different sizes and colors; all of them are important, Daddy!" she exclaims. "How horrible would it be if I needed to draw a picture of the ocean for my teacher, and I didn't have light blue, only regular blue? You wouldn't be able to see any of the fish in my picture, and then my teacher would hate it and think that I didn't know that fish were in the ocean, and then she would hold me back. I wouldn't get to go to kindergarten! We need them all, Daddy!" Grace's arms are flailing about in the most animated fashion, and her voice has turned into a high-pitched squeal.

Yep, I totally lost that battle. "No one's flunking anything, Lovebug. The teacher will know that you know there are fish in the ocean, because I'm sure you'll tell her plenty of times."

I sigh, knowing I can't let her completely win. I refuse to have one of *those* kids at preschool; you know, the kind that thinks they can have anything. However, I also don't want to be one of those parents that have to carry his screaming and kicking four-year-old out of Target either, so a compromise is entirely necessary in this situation.

"You can have two boxes of markers, but that is it, Gracie Lou," I say, holding up two fingers for emphasis.

She huffs a little, and then exhales an extreme, "Fine. I'll go put them back."

She gathers up the other boxes and starts around the corner to the next aisle. "I'll be right behind you; put the markers back where they go, please." I figure that I can fall behind and clear out the cart a little while she's not with me. I can hopefully avoid another office supply confrontation.

I swear getting things away from this child is a planned event. I have to smuggle broken toys and crayons out of the house; it's like our own episode of Child Hoarders.

She ignores me, and as soon as she turns the corner, I begin to gather anything non-essential that I can fit in my arms, and throw the items on the shelves. No, I'm not concerned about how I return the objects, as long as they are out of my cart; desperate times call for desperate measures. I'll be sure to give an extra thank you to the check-out lady since I just made a mess of the school supply section.

As soon as I'm satisfied with the amount of space I cleared out in the cart, I make my way to the markers, only to find the aisle empty. I see where Grace has dropped off the discarded markers; her mess looks similar to mine. "Grace," I call out, trying not to panic. Grace is usually pretty good about not wandering off, so for her not to be here puts my stomach into knots.

I walk quickly down the aisle, my low tone turning into a holler, "Grace, where are you?" I stop suddenly in my tracks when I hear her little voice conversing with the only other voice that has been burned into my memory. I pause to listen to the conversation, enjoying the moment that I wish would have been my reality all along.

"So, Care Bears are not cool anymore, huh?" Vivian asks my little girl.

"No, I told my Daddy that I needed a Hello Kitty bag this year. He's going to buy me all kinds of stuff today for school." Good Lord, I never had a chance.

"Well, what a lucky little girl you are. Where are your mommy and daddy, sweetheart?"

"He was right behind me; he's probably trying to sneak some of my stuff out of the cart," she explains.

Well shit, how do I have a toddler that is one-step ahead of me? There's only one of me; that doesn't seem quite fair.

"Well, I think we should go find him so he's not worried."

I know that my opportunity for eavesdropping is over, so I turn the corner to see a sight that I only could have dreamed of. Grace is holding Vivian's hand, smiling up at her. Holding Grace's other hand is a little girl with adorable blonde tendrils that bounce as she moves, and on the opposite side of Vivian stands a little boy who looks just a little older than the girls. Fuck, I wish this was my life, that this was my family.

"Munchkin, you left me behind. You were supposed to be by the markers," I tell her. I strain not to smile at Vivian's incredulous expression. She is clearly surprised to not only see me, but I'm guessing that she was not expecting me to be a father. *Yeah, join the club.*

Grace looks to me, unsure of how to explain herself; she then looks to Vivian to help bail her out.

"Um, I'm sorry, we were just going to go look for you. She was telling me all about the backpack she's getting for school," Vivian clarifies.

"Thank you for taking care of her, Vivian," I tell her before turning my attention to Grace. "Looks like you found an ally, Lovebug. Don't run off like that again though; do you understand? That's not safe."

Grace nods her head and steps forward to give me a hug. I pat her back and mouth 'thank you' once again to Vivian. She whispers 'you're welcome' and smiles at me, the same smile that turned my world upside-down so many times in the past.

"We haven't finished picking out our backpacks; would you guys like to help us?" Vivian asks, and then introduces her crew. "Brooks, this is my daughter, Emma, and my son, Blake. Em is in preschool too, and Blake will be starting kindergarten this year."

"Well, guys, we would love some help picking something out; apparently I'm not up-to-date on what is hip." I wrap my arm around Grace, pulling her into my side to tickle her. "Grace here has informed me that I need assistance in the cool factor area."

I see Vivian's eyes widen when she hears the name of my daughter. I never told Grace who she was named after, just that it was for someone that I cared for. The shocked realization stretches all over Vivian's face, and the faint blush that is extending up her neck proves her unease with the situation.

"Grace, it's very nice to meet you; that is a very pretty name you have." The last bit is directed straight at me, and I can feel the heat of her glare.

"Thank you. My daddy named me after someone special, and he said that he wants me to grow up and be just as wonderful and beautiful as her one day."

Vivian's face softens, and the corners of her lips begin to curl up. When she bends down to meet Grace's eye level, I hear her whisper in her ear, "You already are beautiful and wonderful, Ms. Grace." When she pulls away, I can see the tears in her eyes.

When I gave Grace Vivian's middle name, I really had never thought they would ever meet. Seeing these two together now, the girl of my past and the little girl of my present, I realize that I need to do whatever it takes to have both of them in my future.

I smile at Vivian and reach for her hand, hoping that she doesn't pull away. I don't think I could handle her rejection. The things she said at the reunion last week stung like hell. Knowing that she still believes the lie I told her nearly a decade ago, I don't blame her for hating me, but dammit if I don't want to tell her the truth and make her love me again.

I can't help but hold my breath, waiting for her to deliberate on whether or not being near me is a good decision. Relief floods my system when she allows her hand to meet mine, and I weave our fingers together. This is where her hand should be, where it always should have been—wrapped in mine.

VIVIAN

We find the crucial items that apparently all four and six-year-olds need to start school, we load our children into our cars, and agree to meet at the playground nearby to let the kids play. However, I can't seem to put the car in drive.

As we walked up and down the aisles of the store hand-in-hand, I felt safe again. Every time he would let his thumb lightly feather across my knuckles, my stomach would flutter, making me want to let go of all my hesitations. I've had a week to settle myself with the grenade of information that Jen had thrown at me, and I'm still not sure if I want to run or tighten my grip.

Brooks had been the first one I ever let my walls down for. But once I let him into the fortress of my heart, not only did he invade it, but he burned it to the ground. I'm reluctant to believe that we can rise above the ashes and trust each other again. Even though I know he never cheated on me, he lied, and the betrayal feels the same. I just wish he had trusted me back then with the secret he was hiding. More than anything, I worry that if faced with similar circumstances, he would run again. How many lies would he tell before he would face the truth?

"Mom, they are going to beat us there; let's go!" Blake shouts from the backseat, snapping me out of my daydream.

"Sorry, sweetie, I was just thinking about how nice Brooks and Grace were to help us out today," I say, shifting the car into gear and sliding out of our parking space.

"I like Grace a lot; she was so funny. Can she maybe stay over?" Emma asks while she insistently zips and unzips her new backpack. Of course, Hello Kitty just like Grace's.

I think about that question for a minute, letting my mind wonder where it probably shouldn't in terms of adult sleepovers, before stumbling through an answer. "Um, baby, I'm not sure Brooks would be okay letting Grace spend the night; we just met her. But maybe once we get to know them a little better."

"I think Brooks likes you, Momma," Em says, completely changing the subject.

"Yeah, he kept holding your hand and smiling at you the way Dad used to," Blake adds.

His comment makes me pause again, but instead of thinking about alone-time with a very sexy man, I'm thinking about Will and what we lost, how having someone new in my life–whether it's Brooks or not–impacts my children, and how every man will always be compared to their father.

My throat tenses, and I struggle to take a deep breath to get myself under control before I answer them. "Oh, guys, Brooks and I used to be very good friends," I say, swallowing my grief. I pull the car over on a side street, and turn around to face them in the backseat.

"Brooks is my friend, and it's okay for you to be friends with both him and Grace, too. No matter who we let on the team, guys, no one will ever replace your daddy. He loved you, and you loved him; nothing will ever change that, all right?"

I grab both of their hands and give them a little reassuring squeeze. Both of them smile and nod; their acceptance and innocence astounds me.

I turn back around, and we make it to the park quickly. As they predicted, Brooks and Grace are already there. Grace is on the swings and when I park, both kids jump out and race over to her.

"Push us, please, Brooks?" Emma asks.

"Yeah, an underdog," Blake adds as they each climb onto a swing.

Obliging the trio, Brooks takes turns pushing them until they are flying high, all of them shrieking with excitement. "Okay, guys, give him a break. Go play while Brooks and I sit over on the bench and watch."

He leaves the whining children, agreeing to push them more after his rest. He follows me to the bench on the edge of the playground and sits next to me. After my conversation with Jen, I knew at some point I would have to really talk to Brooks. Now that the moment is here, though, I'm overwhelmed with a nervous feeling for where the conversation could lead.

"Before you say anything, Brooks, I have a few things I need to get off my chest," I say, fighting back the fear and deciding to dive right in. "I spoke with Jen after the reunion, and she told me everything."

Brooks' head snaps up, his eyes locking on mine. I see the fear settling in them. He starts to speak, but I cover his mouth with my fingertips. "No, let me finish; I need to say this."

He closes his eyes, his scowl deepening, and his worry showing through. He nods, and I begin to take my hand away, but he opens his eyes and catches my wrist, bringing my palm to his lips. Letting a soft kiss linger on my skin, I feel goose bumps pour across my body. He then entwines our fingers and lays them on his thigh.

I take a deep breath, attempting to compose myself. "Please, I need you to hear this."

"I'm listening, Viv. Even if what you have to say fucking guts me, I'm going to listen."

"Ten years ago, I loved you with everything that I was. I didn't think that I was capable of feeling that, but I felt it for you. When I thought that you cheated, I let myself believe that you didn't want me, that I wasn't good enough, and that my love wasn't enough for you. I was so angry for so long, and Will helped me fix the heart that you broke."

Brooks drops his head in defeat and crushes my hand between his, like he's gearing up for the fatal blow. I pull my hand out of his and cup his face, drawing his eyes back up to mine.

"I never thought that I would say this to you, but I'm sorry." Bewilderment overtakes him. "I'm sorry that you couldn't trust me with whatever you were running from back then, that you felt like your only option was to push me away to protect me. I now understand that that's what you were doing."

"The things I said to you at the reunion was me being angry at the idea of you choosing someone else over me. Even after knowing the truth, I still had the bitterness that I choke on every time I think about your lies. I know that I want you in my life–in what capacity–I don't know, but now that you're here, I can't let you just walk away again." I take a deep breath, releasing all the tension that had built within me. The heaviness in my shoulders finally begins to lessen.

"Is it my turn?" he asks with a smile. I can only answer with a nod.

"Anything that I ever did was to shelter you, even when I hurt you. I thought I was doing the best for you. What I was going through would have damaged you, and I couldn't let that happen, even if it meant that you had to hate me."

He grabs a piece of hair that has fallen across my face and tucks it behind my ear, then rubs his knuckles down my cheek. "Viv, my issue back then is no longer a part of my life, and I'm not in the same place that I was then. I'm not the same scared kid who runs; I'm a man who will stay put and stand by you."

"So what do we do now?" I ask.

"I'm not asking you to pretend like nothing ever happened. I know that I have to earn your trust and your love again, but fuck, Red, all I want is a chance to win you back. I don't mind if it takes every day for the rest of my life to make you believe in me, because after having a taste of what my family could be, I can't ever let you go again.

"Okay," I mutter.

Seeing that as a green light, Brooks runs his hands into my hair, whispering, "Thank God," before pulling me to him and crushing my lips to his. Electricity shoots through my body. Every bit of emotion that I once had for this man surges through me. I feel like I'm losing myself in him all over again.

Just as our kiss deepens, I hear laughter, followed by a collective, "Ewww, that's gross."

We pull away from each other, a Cheshire grin adorning Brooks' face, while I can feel the heat of embarrassment on mine. I quickly right myself to attend to our miniature audience.

"What do you guys say we go get ice cream together before we all have to go home and get dinner going?"

Cheers and shrieks fill the air, making me giggle.

"I think that's a yes," Brooks says as he stands, pulling me with him and tucking me into his side. "Come on, we can all ride together in my car, and I'll bring you guys back to get your car after."

"Sounds good," I agree.

Together we climb into Brooks' sleek SUV, settling into the comfortable surroundings. The easiness of the situation is not lost on me, and the feeling that our line-up just changed floods my thoughts.

VIVIAN

> **Jen:** R u talking 2 me yet?
>
> **Me:** Yes, please come over so we can talk about everything. I'm sorry that I stormed out.
>
> **Jen:** U better believe I was done with the silent treatment. I was coming over invited or not.
>
> **Me:** See u in a few…nab Carly 2. I need total girl pow-wow ASAP. Bring candy and coffee.
>
> **Jen:** Good Lord, woman. What has ur panties in a twist? I said I was sorry.
>
> **Me:** Not u…I kissed Brooks yesterday.
>
> **Jen:** WHAT! We'll be there in 5.

"So the kids just told me that you spent the day with Brooks and his daughter yesterday; care to fill me in, Sis?" Amanda asks, as she enters the kitchen and takes a seat on the barstool across from me.

I lay my cell phone on the counter and clasp my hands together, bracing for the impact of my sister's wrath. "Yes, we ran into each other a few times over the past week. I'll give you the whole story as soon as Jen and Carly get here; they are on their way."

"Hell no, Viv, cut the shit. Why in the fuck would you spend any time with that asshole after what he did?" Her face is entirely flushed, and I can tell she's trying to control herself.

"Wow, are you trying to meet some kind of curse-word count today?" I tease, trying to lighten her mood. Her perfectly-tweezed eyebrows pinch together, showing her obvious feelings for my humor.

"That's not even a little bit funny." She takes a deep breath before continuing, in an effort to maintain her temper. "I understand that you might be ready to move on with dating. I've encouraged you to date; I've even tried to set you up with some colleagues of mine. Instead, you choose the one man who has and will crush you. How many times will you let yourself be hurt by him?"

I open my clasped hands and rest my forehead into my palms. I understand where she's coming from. She saw what I was like after Brooks, and she put me back together after Will. I know what I'm telling her is not easy for her to hear.

Still looking down, I finally address her question. "Look, Manda, what happened in the past wasn't what I thought it was. He was never unfaithful; he was hiding something and made me believe that he cheated to push me away to protect me from whatever he was running from." I look up to see her stunned expression.

"Wait, he never cheated?" she asks.

"He didn't cheat; he lied, but didn't cheat."

"Okay, keep going."

"I know that Brooks Ryan is my biggest weakness, and that he has the power to shatter my soul all over again. I also realize that I'm a mom, and it's not just me I need to protect, but Emma and Blake's hearts as well."

Amanda's brow softens, and I can see the gears in her mind spinning. "So you promise that whatever it is, you guys will take it slow?"

"Yes."

"I'm not fully on-board, you know, and if he slips, I'm done with him," she clarifies.

"Thanks, Mom," I huff. "By the way, what colleagues were you going to set me up with that you haven't slept with? Your office is not that big."

"Ha ha, deflection is never an admirable quality, Viv," she says as she jumps off the stool. "I'm going upstairs to get dressed; holler when the girls get here, and I'll take the kids to the park."

I move around the kitchen island and pull Amanda into a big bear hug. It always makes her feel uncomfortable, so I smother her every chance I get. "Thank you, Manda," I say, stretching out the end of her name. Then I give her a big sloppy kiss on the cheek when she tries to pull away.

"Vivian! You know I hate that," she protests, struggling to get away from me.

I finally release her, and she hurries upstairs to get away from me. "You better run, chick-a-dee. I love me some Manda lovin'."

I can hear her laugh from upstairs, just as the doorbell rings. I rush to the front door, but don't get a chance to open it before Jen barges into the house.

"You know, you're in the city now; you should start locking this door," Jen says as she steps into the foyer with Carly right behind her.

"Well, hello to you, too. Why ring the bell if you're just going to walk right in?" I ask, taking one of the many sacks from Carly and a coffee from Jen.

"It's always imperative that I announce my arrival. How long have you known me? This shouldn't be a question after this long." Her reply drips with sarcasm.

We take the extreme amount of snack bags, and sprawl the buffet of junk food on the table. "Jesus, is there anything left in the candy aisle of Wal-Mart, you guys? This is ridiculous." I ask, surveying the piles of goodies.

Carly grabs a bag of Snickers off the table and holds it to her chest. "Hey now, you can never have too much chocolate available, and besides, we didn't know what kind of Brooks emergency we had on our hands," she says, sounding almost offended.

I just laugh at her dramatics, picking up a bag of licorice and tearing off a piece. "You know that this candy leaves with you, right? My kids will be on a sugar high for days from all this candy if they get into it."

Jen grabs a bag of Skittles and plops down on a barstool. "You are one stingy bitch, you know that? You probably sneak ice cream behind their backs just so you don't have to share."

Carly burst into giggles, and I feign insult. "That is not true! Besides, between your potty mouth and the sexual jokes that continuously fly out of your mouth, I can only imagine what your motherly skills will be like and the demon spawn that you will produce."

Jen throws a Skittle at me, and both Carly and I laugh.

"Oh, come on, Jen, you can't even keep plants alive," Carly adds, heading to the fridge to get a water. "You got that cat a few years back, and when you thought it would try to eat your face in your sleep because you kept forgetting to feed it, I ended up taking her. You still avoid Spunkin whenever you come over."

"At least I gave her a cool name before I handed her over," Jen defends.

"Are you kidding me? Do you know how wrong it is to hear my two-year-old try to say her name? Besides the fact that you named the cat after come, her little lisp makes it sound like fuckin'," she complains as she slams the fridge shut.

Jen chokes on her coffee, sputtering coffee all over my countertop. "That is so awesome," she stutters, cleaning up her mess with her sleeve.

"My point exactly," I say.

"Okay, enough, let's get down to business. I want all of the details," Jen interrupts, standing and leading us all into the living room.

I pause at the stairs and holler up to Emma and Blake, who have been watching a movie in the media room. "Hey guys, Aunt Amanda was going to go to the park; do you want to go?"

Both run out into the upstairs hallway, meeting Amanda at the top of the stairs. "Can we invite Grace?" Emma asks.

Amanda's eyes narrow on me. "Um, not today, sweetheart. We'll plan something with Brooks and Grace another day, but when you get back, why don't we go to lunch? You and Blake can pick the place," I say.

"Awesome!" they both shout, and barrel down the stairs and towards the garage.

"Hey! I think you both forgot something," I say, halting their descent. They turn around and run to me, wrapping their arms around my legs.

"Bye, Momma, love you," they each take turns saying.

"Love you too, guys. Have fun, and keep Aunt Amanda out of trouble."

"That's a hard job, Mom. I might need more allowance for that," Blake says.

"Good try; see you later, guys." Amanda then grabs their hands and takes them out the door leading to the garage. I then take my seat on the couch next to Carly and across from Jen, who's on the floor.

Breaking the silence, Carly jumps right in. "Okay, let me start by saying, um, what the hell? We all hated Brooks for ten years, taking turns comparing him to every piece of shit guy we came across over the years. I understand that he didn't do what we thought he did, but he lied to us all. Did he even tell you why he did what he did?"

"No, not really, he just said that the issues that he had back then are not issues anymore."

"And you're just all right with that?" Jen asks.

"I don't know," I say, tucking my feet under my butt and relaxing into the couch. "I know that it feels good to be with him again. I know that the connection we had ten years ago is still there. I know that I have to move slowly and protect myself and our kids this time around, but I don't want to run from it."

"So, sparks, huh?" Carly inquires, scooting closer to me.

"Remember back in college when we talked about love, and Pride and Prejudice?" I ask, and both my friends nod.

"Well, Will was my Bingley. He was flexible and pleasant. I loved him dearly, but it was a safe love. Brooks is my Mr. Darcy. The passion and electricity that sets your body on fire from a single stare kind of love. It's the unbending and unyielding sort of love that can just as easily burn you as it can heal you, but damn if it's not worth the risk."

"Okay."

I look at Jen, amazed that I'm not hearing her pretend to gag over my love description. "Okay?"

"Yeah, how can I argue with that? You know I don't want to see you hurt again, not after everything you've been through, so I ask that you please take things slowly."

We both look to Carly, trying to gauge her thoughts. She's chewing on the inside of her cheek and picking at the nonexistent lint on her pants.

"Just spit it out," I urge. "I know that you think this is a bad idea; you are picking a hole into your sweatpants, and I wouldn't be surprised if you've also bitten a hole into your cheek the way you've been grinding your teeth."

She just lets out a sigh. "All right, I'll be supportive, too. It's just that it wasn't a small lie that he told; it was a planned deception, and you have no idea what the issue was. Please don't be one of those women that we complain about that forgives so easily and we question their IQ level. If he does anything to make me question his loyalty or honesty, I will put Jen's balls-on-a-skewer plan back into effect. Got it, lady?"

Carly is usually so reserved. Jen is the opinionated one, so for her to speak so passionately about the issue with Brooks, I know she really has concerns, and that she has my best interest at heart. I move closer to her on the couch and grab her hand. "Deal," I say. "I will even provide the barbeque to make Rocky Mountain Oysters out of them."

She smiles, but pulls her hand back, "Now that is just gross."

"No, we could invite him over for a goodbye dinner and serve him his own balls. It would be priceless," Jen jokes. "Just add a little gravy and it will taste like chicken fried steak."

"All right, conversation is over; this has gone too far," I laugh as I stand from the loveseat. "Let's get the candy put away before the rug-rats get back."

They both stand and pull me into a sincere hug. "We love you, sweet pea," Carly says.

"I love you guys, too. Thank you for always being here for me."

"Anytime, babe," Jen says, patting my back. "Wait, scratch that! I revoke said friend status if any vajayjay checks for crabs are necessary; I draw the line there. So don't turn into a Missy McSlut Muffin, because then you're on your own."

We all pull away from each other, "Fuck, Jen, you know how to ruin a moment," I tell her as I walk towards the kitchen.

"What? Those things give me the hebegebees!" she explains, following behind me.

"Well that comment landed you clean-up duty," I say as I pick up my phone, noticing the blinking light alerting me of missed messages.

I sit down on the stool and pull open the screen to find a single message from Brooks.

> **Brooks:** I miss u, need 2 see u.
> Be ready at 7. I'm taking u 2
> dinner.

I smile, the flutter in my stomach returning at the thought of getting to see him again and getting another shot at the kiss we started at the park.

> **Me:** See u at 7... miss u 2.

I look up from my phone to see Jen and Carly both gawking at me.

"That good of a message, huh?" Carly asks.

"Looks like I need to call in one more favor," I answer.

"Crabs kill, girl. Crabs kill," Jen adds as she places the last bag of candy into the Wal-Mart sack.

I roll my eyes, "No, but thank you for that. I have a date tonight and I need help picking out an outfit. I want to look a little less like a throw- together mommy and more like a Slut McMuffin."

"It's McSlut Muffin; if you're going to use it, use it correctly," Jen demands.

"Whatever, I'd like to look a little less nice and a little more spice."

"We got you covered, babe; you're talking to the Queen Muffin here," Jen says, throwing her arm around me. Carly just shoots me a weak smile. Let the adventure begin.

BROOKS

When I texted Vivian and didn't hear back right away, I admit I went into freak-out panic mode pretty quickly. I thought she had changed her mind about me, and that this time she was going to push me away. To say I was excited when she finally texted me back would be an understatement. I actually picked up Grace and carried her out to the car as quickly as possible, leaving our lunch on the table at the McDonald's Playland. I had to hurry home to make plans for the evening. I needed this date to go well. I needed to show her I'm different, better, and that she is my priority.

I feel like I'm finally at a place where I can really prove my worth to her; I want to marry this woman and to create the family I always wanted with her. The issue of my past is not an issue anymore. I don't even refer to him by name; he has been reduced to being called my previous issue. I cut off all correspondence soon after it started, and I haven't heard from him since, and if ever put in the situation to choose again, I will choose Vivian.

I put in a call to Katie, my babysitter, and make reservations at a romantic Italian restaurant downtown that is just across from a piano bar that has dancing. On the way home, a very annoyed Grace and I stop at a flower shop. To redeem myself from the Playland fiasco, I let Grace choose the flowers.

Now I'm sitting outside her house, and fuck if I'm going to throw-up right in her driveway. I'm never scared, and I'm scared to death right now. In the business realm I'm calm and collected, the man that calls the shots and lets the others sweat it out. But at the moment, my nerves have a death grip on my gut, and I can feel my McNuggets from lunch rising up and burning my throat. I wipe my sweaty palms on my black suit pants, and take a few deep breaths to settle my stomach.

This woman has me turned inside out, and I can't get a handle on it. A banging on the window startles me out of my meltdown moment.

"Are you coming inside, or are you just going to sit in your car all night?" I hear Blake shout through the window. When I see him, I immediately begin to relax. The kid is the perfect mixture of Will and Vivian. He has Vivian's dark auburn hair and Will's whisky colored eyes. He's a thick little guy; I have no doubt he will be good at sports like his dad.

I'm slapped with a wave of jealousy as I think about how I wish that he was my son. I want to be the one that gets to show him how to throw a ball, how to be a gentleman and hold doors open for girls, and show him how to drive a car. He may not be mine, but I want to be the man he looks up to.

He taps on the window again. His impatience is obvious, and I'm sure he's beginning to wonder about my mental stability. I grab the lavender orchids that Grace chose and open the car door.

"Hey, buddy; sorry, you caught me daydreaming," I say, patting him on the back as we begin walking up the driveway to the front door.

"Yeah, you were kind of freaking me out; you looked like you were going to puke. I was getting ready to go get Mom."

Thank fuck he didn't, that would have put a damper on our first date; I'm going for *not* crazy tonight. I might as well have put on a name tag for the evening, *Hello, my name is Creeper.*

I begin to ring the doorbell, but Blake stops me. "I live here, Brooks. We can just go inside. Are you sure you're okay?"

Well, that's just great. "Yeah, I'm good, just nervous," I tell him, running my fingers through my hair and straightening my jacket. "Better?"

"Much better; you're not even all sweaty anymore. Don't be scared; Mom's been getting ready since we got back from lunch. She told Aunt Amanda that she put on double the deodorant; she must be all sweaty, too."

"Thanks, man, let's keep that last bit just between us though, deal?"

"Sure," he says with a shrug.

We pass through the entryway, and Blake leads me to the living room. The room is a complete reflection of Vivian's personality. With browns, golds, and oranges filling the space, the room has a rustic feel. It is warm and inviting, just like her. There are plants in every corner, something you would never find at my house. Mine is a place where plants come to die.

I'm browsing the pictures of Blake and Emma that line the walls when I hear someone clear their throat. I turn to see who I presume to be Amanda, walking down the stairs. Judging from the glower on her face, my reputation precedes me.

"Look, Vivian will be down in just a minute, so I'll just get to the point."

I watch her step down onto the landing and cross her arms across her chest. She's preparing for a confrontation, or at least put me in my place. Could I please catch a fucking break? Just one? I lay my flowers for Vivian on the coffee table and motion for her to continue, hoping to quickly get the reaming over with.

"I know everything that happened between you and Vivian, and I think that you were a total chicken shit. I'm trying to judge you by the man you are now, not who you were back then, and I'll try to be supportive. I promise not to make things difficult for you guys if you're really going to try and make this work."

She drops her hands down at her sides and begins to walk towards me. "However, I swear if you fuck this up again, I know men back home with thousands of open acreage, and it would be very easy to hide a body; do I make myself clear?" she adds, while her long polished index finger pokes into my chest.

I take her hand away from my chest, placing it into my grip and giving her my best handshake. "You must be Amanda; it's nice to finally meet you." Was it kind of dickish of me? Yeah, but I hate that she's judging me by my biggest mistakes, my biggest regrets.

I drop her hand and take a step back, knowing that I have invaded her personal space, and she just stares me down.

"I'm not the same man as when I was last with Vivian, and I'm sure that she's not the same either. The way things ended between us was the biggest blunder of my life, but what I did was only to protect her. I was a stupid kid who was too fucking scared of her rejection to let her really know me. Every day, I've wished I hadn't taken away that choice for her. I realize you don't owe me a damn thing here, but if you could give me a little leeway to prove myself to her, I would really appreciate it."

I hold my breath in anticipation of her response. She starts twirling a strand of her long blonde hair, and I realize that she has no problem letting me sweat it out.

Finally, she bobs her head in approval. "Okay, Brooks, but my threat still stands. One fuck-up and Jen, Carly, and I will be having a weenie roast."

"I'll bring the chocolate and marshmallows for dessert," I say, trying to lighten the heavy aura of the room. Her lips thin, but then they curl around her teeth as she desperately tries to stifle a laugh. "It's okay; you can laugh. I promise I'm not a total asshole."

"Well, if Vivian is giving you another shot, you must have some redeeming qualities," she says with a laugh, and then slugs me in the arm. "I'm supposed to be looking out for her; you're not supposed to be making me laugh, you jerk."

I hold my hands up in defense. "Sorry, I plan on being around for forever; I need to have someone on my side."

"Oh, Brooks, no matter how much you make me laugh, I will always be on her side; that's just how it goes."

I don't get a chance to respond though, because every bit of air is stolen from me when Vivian appears at the top of the stairs. I can't breathe. I can't blink. I'm entranced by the stunning sight before me. She is wearing a tight, mint green dress that hugs every perfect curve. Hanging off her shoulders and stopping just below her knees, it wraps around her like a second skin. All I can think is that there is no way there are undergarments underneath, and my dick twitches at the possibility of finding out. The heels that she's paired with it only make my discomfort even more unbearable; they are at least four inches. Undergarments or not, the heels will be staying on this evening.

She begins to move down the stairs, and I watch in amazement at the grace of her movements. Her auburn hair has been curled into large waves that cascade past her bare shoulders. It's long and looks so silky; I feel my hands tingling in anticipation of having my fingers in it. But then I notice the sway of her full hips and bounce of her generous chest, and I find it necessary to adjust myself before everyone in the room notices my approval.

"Good evening, Brooks. You look very handsome tonight," she says when she reaches the landing.

Still awestruck that this woman is real, and that I get a chance to make things right, I'm at a standstill and words escape me. Amanda walks next to me, placing her hand on my chin and closing my mouth. I give her a sideways glance and a tight smile.

"You kids have fun," Amanda laughs, taking the orchids and walking into the kitchen.

"Sorry, it's just...wow. I mean, you look exquisite." She smiles widely and I offer her my arm to lead her to my car.

"Thank you, you look great as well, and thank you for the flowers," she says, linking her arm with mine. I have to remind myself to breathe. She feels perfect next to me; it's where she should have always been, where I plan to always keep her.

VIVIAN

The car ride to the restaurant is relatively quiet with only the sound of the radio filling the car, but it's a comfortable silence. I keep catching Brooks looking at me; maybe I'm not what he remembers, or maybe I let damn Amanda put too much make-up on me.

The girls went all out fixing me up for tonight, but it might be a little much. I can barely breathe in Jen's dress, but I was outvoted, and from the look on Brook's face and the bulge in his pants, he admires their choice.

After Brooks parks the car, he slides around the front of the car and opens my door. He offers his hand and pulls me close to him, allowing me to feel his solid chest under his suit. He releases me, and we walk hand-in-hand into the restaurant.

We are greeted and taken to a cozy table in the back of the establishment. The atmosphere is warm and delicate, with deep maroon linens covering the tables, and candlelight providing a luminous glow. Brooks pulls out my chair and I ease into it, letting the scent of his cologne envelop me. I find myself taking a deep breath of the sandalwood and apple, trying to hang on to the delicious smell for as long as possible.

He places his hands on my shoulders and reaches down to sneak a light kiss on my exposed neck, making me shudder. I feel my disappointment when he takes his lips away to sit down. I've promised to take things slow, remembering the girl who, against her better judgment, trusted this man once and lost. I'm trying desperately to contain my lust for this man, but between his intoxicating smell and his perfect body, the task is proving futile.

I quickly take a sip of my water in an attempt to cool myself down.

"I'm glad that you agreed to tonight," he says, as I place the goblet back onto the table and begin twirling the stem. "I was afraid that you would have changed your mind, and I would have had to implement plan B."

"And what would that have entailed?" I ask.

"I didn't have all of the details worked out, but it involved at least a small mint in flowers and a whole lot of begging."

I softly laugh and look down at the water glass in front of me that I am sill holding. "We both know that you are not the begging kind."

Brooks takes my hand from the glass and surrounds it in both of his, causing me to look at him. "You're right; I'm not. I'm a man that always gets what he wants, and I never have to ask twice. But with you, Vivian, you are my weakness, my Achilles' heel."

My eyebrows pinch together. Brooks is a strong, proud man, and the idea of pulling him down unsettles me. I attempt to pull my hand away, but he tightens his grip and passes me a cocky smile.

"You are a weakness I would gladly beg to have, Red," he says as he takes my hand and kisses my palm, which forces me to smile. I feel myself melt into his intense stare as the weight of his words sink into me. Our eyes are locked until the waiter arrives at our table, interrupting our moment.

We pull ourselves apart long enough to order our drinks and entrees, but as soon as our server steps away, Brooks gathers my hand once again.

"This is pretty surreal, don't you think?" I ask him, rubbing my thumb along his knuckles. "Did you ever think in a million years that we would find ourselves here again?"

"In the back of my mind, I had hoped that this would have been in store for us someday, somehow. But then reality would wallop me across the face, and I would realize that you were happy in the life that you had without me, and I was fine with that because you were happy."

He rubs his lips along my wrist, feathering along my pulse line, and I find it difficult to focus on his words as the electricity of his touch causes butterflies to bounce around my stomach. He lands one tender kiss where I'm sure he can feel my heartbeat pulsing through my wrist and pulls away.

"Now that you're here, though, and I have the chance to be the one that makes you happy, I will do anything in my power to keep you. You always had my heart, every single fucking piece of it, and all I want to do is steal yours again."

I feel my heart slam into my chest, but I try to rein in the overwhelming feeling. I refuse to fall so easily for this man all over again. I want him—God, do I want him—but the fear of the unknown has me wanting to run; how can I risk coming up with the losing hand once again?

"You have to understand, Brooks, I'm scared. No matter what the reasons were, things ended badly between us. When Will stepped in, he made it safe to love again, to feel again, and yet, I ended up with nothing. Everything I love keeps slipping through my fingers, and I'm afraid to lose again."

"Let me be brave for both of us, Viv. We each have to take turns being the strong one, and now it's my turn. I will be the light for as long as it takes for you to step out of the darkness."

I look down at my wine glass that the waiter managed to bring without notice. I begin to twirl the stem, allowing my mind to digest this man's words. I silently watch the pink liquid swirl around the edge of the glass, threatening at any moment to spill over the lip.

"Viv, please say something."

"I need you to promise me something," I say before stealing my eyes away from the crystal glass and meeting his intense stare.

"Anything, Red. Everything I have, I would promise you."

"I know you said that you aren't going anywhere this time, but I need you to promise. No matter what, there's no more running. We both have been running long enough; it's time to be still, together."

"Vivian, I swear to you, and to anyone else that needs to hear this; I am yours, heart and soul. I have lived without my heart for ten years; I'm thankful to have it back, and I promise to never leave it behind again. Do you understand what I'm saying? I'm yours, and I plan with every bit of power that I possess that you will be mine. So no, I am not going anywhere."

Brooks suddenly pushes his chair back, and with a quick stride, stands in front of me. Grabbing the hand that still hasn't unleashed the glass, he pulls me from my chair, crushing me against his body. Although we garner the attention of the patrons around us, Brooks continues to hold me to him.

He slides his hand behind my neck and pulls me to him until I can hear his breath in my ear. The sensation sends shivers down my body, and I find my resolve melting away. I stand there waiting. Waiting for words, waiting for a kiss, I didn't know what.

But I know in that moment I would wait for as long as it took to have anything he would give me.

I feel his cheek against mine, his breathing harsh and labored like he's restraining himself. In a harsh whisper, he finally breaks the silence. "I think we need to get something clear right now, Vivian. I have loved you every second that I've known you. When I wasn't with you, I tried to force myself to not love you. I don't want to pretend anymore. Don't run from me, Red; don't run from us, because I'm not fucking going anywhere."

He kisses my forehead and sits down at his seat, just as quickly as he'd stood, leaving me standing stunned by our intense public moment. I slide back into my chair as the waiter arrives with our food, and I'm thankful that there is a distraction available.

His words tumble around in my mind, and as they sink in, I find myself believing his sincerity. He's not going anywhere; he will be different. He won't hurt me.

Our conversation lightens as the meal progresses, shifting the dialogue easily between topics. He tells me all about Grace and her mother, explaining his previous dating relationships, or lack thereof. He shares about his architectural firm, and I suggest Amanda's advertising agency when he mentions wanting to make a change in his marketing strategy. I share how I've moved away from teaching to pursue writing and to spend more time with Emma and Blake since Will died.

Time passes without notice, and soon we are the only ones left in the restaurant. My cheeks are aching and my stomach is sore from laughing at the stories we share about our children and my old students. Our waiter has since given up on us, and he is sitting at a back booth waiting for us to cash out our check.

"I think we've worn out our welcome; the servers are waiting on us to close the restaurant," I say, taking a final sip of my wine.

"You're right; we should probably get going. I just don't want tonight to end." Brooks takes out his wallet and throws a wad of cash onto the table. I'm sure he is severely over-tipping to make up for our late stay.

He takes my hand, easing me out of my chair, and then rests his palm at the small of my back to guide me out to the parking lot. The drive home is comfortable; all of the tension that started the date has dissipated, and it feels just like it always did with us. It feels natural; it feels right.

"Thank you for such a lovely evening, Brooks," I say as he pulls into my driveway.

He parks the car and laces our fingers together. "Thank you for agreeing to go," he mutters through a cocky grin before landing a soft kiss on my palm.

"School is going to be starting in a few weeks, so I had planned on taking Grace to the zoo. You know, one last trip before things get busy. Would you and Emma and Blake like to join us?"

I'm trying to focus on his words, but his touch is distracting, and I'm struggling to keep myself on my side of the car. I'm confident that my dress would probably split in two if I tried to propel across the middle console, though.

Brooks begins to laugh, pulling me from my sidetracked inner dialogue.

"Sorry, um, the zoo. Yeah, that sounds great. But do you think that it's alright to be a couple in front of the kids yet? Should we slow it down a little, at least when we're around them?"

"Why don't you ask Amanda if she'll come with us, and I'll invite my brother Lakin; we'll make it feel like a group outing instead of a family date. We can be somewhat slow if you need that."

"Thank you. I better go in before Amanda starts flickering the porch light."

He kisses my hand one more time and exits the car, running around to my side to open the passenger door. Pulling me into his side, we slowly walk up to the front door, trying to extend our time together until the last possible second.

As soon as we hit the bottom step, Brooks wraps his arms around me and pushes my back up against the exterior of the house. "I've waited all night to get my lips on yours, and I can't let you go into that house without getting a taste of what I've been missing."

I stiffen, shocked by his forward and swift advance. Placing his hands on either side of my head, he cages me in, his eyes darting from my eyes to my lips, begging for permission. When my body relaxes and I smile, he takes it as an open invitation, crushing his mouth to mine.

His hands move away from the wall and begin to explore my body, sliding down my ribs and resting on my hips, drawing me closer to him. Our kiss deepens; the fire between us ignites. I'm not sure at this point if the flame can be extinguished; the neighbors are no doubt getting a show.

"God, I've missed you," Brooks mutters as he drags his lips down my jaw.

"I forgot how good you feel," I say, tilting my head back to give him better access.

Hastily, he draws his head back, looking into my hooded eyes. "I'm going to spend every fucking day helping you remember, Viv. You're my Clover, and you always will be."

Expecting another passionate kiss, I brace myself for impact, but instead, Brooks slowly leans in and lightly touches his lips to mine. It's a feather-like peck that leaves my already-swollen lips tingling.

"Goodnight, Vivian," he says through a smile.

"Goodnight, Brooks," I breathlessly sigh.

I watch as he walks back to his car and opens the driver's side door. He turns to throw me one last grin over his shoulder before getting in and driving away. I'm left still pressed against the house, attempting to gather myself. I let my fingertips trace along my lips, feeling the lingering effects of his kiss. Finally, regaining my composure and adjusting my dress, I find my keys and enter the house. I don't even get my ankle-breaking shoes off before I hear my phone buzz.

> **Brooks:** *I can't wait to get lost in my green again. Sleep well, Clover.*

My stomach flip-flops at the sight of his nickname for me. I smile and grip my phone tightly to my chest. I silently make my way upstairs to my room. The house is quiet, still, just like my heart. Brooks has managed to stifle my fears and replace my missing heart. I just hope I can guard it better this time.

VIVIAN

"I don't know why you need me to go with you for this," Amanda complains, while putting her Audi into reverse and pulling out of the driveway.

I look at her, my eyes pleading with her to just get over it. "Because, Manda, he wanted to get the kids together, and he thought that if there were a few of us there, like a group family situation, there would be less pressure. His brother will be there, so I thought it would be good if you were there too."

She exhales deeply, and then looks straight ahead. I'm sure she's considering her options to pay me back for this. Amanda agreed to be supportive of my relationship with Brooks, but I know going with us, especially now that his brother will be there, too, is going to be a stretch for her.

"I think it will be fun, Aunt Amanda," Emma chimes in from the backseat. Blake is completely engaged in his Leap Pad story, and is the least bit interested in the current conversation.

Amanda looks at her through the rearview mirror, and a smile tugs at her lips. "You and me will definitely have a good time, baby girl. After we see the giraffes, I'll buy you a snow cone."

Emma's whole face lights up and she bounces in her seat, showing her agreement. "Okay, but Grace will want one, too," she adds.

"Deal. Now just sit back and relax; we will be at the zoo soon. Your momma and I need to have a little talk." She gives me a side glance, and I know she has a lot on her mind that she is going to freely unload on me. Thankfully, we only have a fifteen-minute car ride.

Emma sits back and looks out the window to watch the Saturday traffic buzz by on I-25. She loves to car watch. Since moving to the city, she loves to go on car rides just to zone into the hustle and bustle of the surroundings.

I look over to Amanda, and I see her hands gripping the steering wheel; I can tell her mind is working on overdrive. She begins to open her mouth, I'm sure to begin the lecture, but I butt in before she can get a word in.

"All right, first, before you say anything, remember that you have an audience in this car and they are sponges; anything you say can and will be used against you at some point, and more than likely in public, so keep it appropriate."

Amanda looks in the mirror again, and I turn my head around to peek into the backseat. "They are fine; they are totally zoned out," she says. "Besides, they have no idea what we are talking about. Just keep your voice down and I'll turn up the radio a little."

I sigh and look out the passenger window before looking back to my sister, who I know means well, but needs to loosen the leash a little. "Amanda, I understand that you said you would step back and let whatever this is between Brooks and me progress. However, you're my sister and I know you're worried that I will still end up hurt. Honestly, I'm scared of the same thing, and I'm kind of freaking out a little bit. But I'm willing to venture down that road anyway, and you know why?"

She gives me a side glance and just shakes her head, keeping quiet to let me finish.

"Win or lose, I'm willing to give him another chance, because I'm tired of being afraid. I haven't felt this happy and this content since Will. I haven't felt anything but numb for the last year, Amanda, and I may end up with a broken heart, but if Brooks can make me feel something again, if he can bring me back to life, then I think it's worth the heartache."

Amanda takes a deep, calming breath and I reach out to grab her hand. "I know you just want to protect me, Manda; thank you for that. The thing is if losing Will taught me anything, it was that there are no guarantees in life, and I don't want to regret a minute of it."

Amanda squeezes my hand and smiles through her teary eyes; I'm beginning to struggle to keep my own from spilling over. "Okay," she says.

She didn't need to say more; I know Amanda wouldn't be a silent spectator anymore, but would jump both feet in with me. If I stumble and face-plant, she will help me up and clean the dirt off me...then hunt Brooks down and drown him in the mud I fell in.

Pulling the visor down, Amanda checks her makeup in the mirror, wiping away any running mascara. She lets out a long sigh, and I know this particular topic is officially closed, thank goodness. "So tell me about the brother. If I'm going to spend the day with him, at least give me details."

"I've never met him; they are half-brothers, and his name is Lakin, but that is all I know about him."

"Lakin?" An obvious frown appears between her brows. "Brooks and Lakin...were his parents sailors or hippies, or something? What's with the water theme?"

"I never thought of that," I laugh. "Really, though, I know nothing about him. I'm assuming he's nice since Brooks is bringing him along; I don't even know what he looks like, but I would guess that he probably looks a lot like Brooks."

A devilish grin flashes across her face.

"Oh, no!" I warn. "Don't you even think about it; you go through men like bottles of water, and that will just make things awkward."

"I do not!" she protests. "Besides, if he looks anything like Brooks, I wouldn't mind taking a drink."

"Whatever, Amanda. You and I both know that you have the most–" I stop and turn to the back seat before whispering, "the most ravenous nether region known to man. You chew men up and spit them out. Keep your hands to yourself on this one."

She turns to me, noticeably trying to suppress a laugh, "Did you just say ravenous nether region?"

We both burst into laughter, drawing attention from our backseat audience just as we pull into the parking lot of the zoo. "We're there!" both children shout.

We quickly get our tickets and make our way to the spot we are meeting the rest of our group, by the giraffes; they are Emma's favorite. Brooks, Lakin, and Grace are already there waiting for us.

As we get closer, I give Lakin a once-over and yup, he's cute; he's nothing compared to Brooks, but he certainly can hold his own. I steal a glance at Amanda, and yeah, she likes what she sees. She's fluffing her hair and adjusting her sundress; she looks like she is about to go in for the kill. So much for the hands-off policy I was going for back in the car. Amanda is on a Defcon 5 manhunt. Poor Lakin doesn't have a chance.

Once Emma sees Grace, she grabs Blake's hand and they race over to her. They all point at the giraffes and begin an intense discussion about what animals they want to see.

As soon as I reach Brooks, he pulls me into his arms and gives me a chaste kiss on the mouth. Pulling away, he has a huge grin on his face. "Hi," he says.

I giggle—yes, I actually giggle. "Well, hi to you too."

Amanda clears her throat to get our attention. I'm a little surprised that my tiger of a sister is even waiting for an introduction. Brooks tucks me into his side, and I begin the formalities.

"Brooks, you remember my sister, Amanda," I say, and each gives a half-hearted smile and pathetic wave. The enthusiasm is just pouring from them. Maybe this was a bad idea.

Lakin smiles brightly at her, though, and grabs her hand to kiss her knuckles. "I'm Brooks' younger brother Lakin. It's lovely to meet you."

Amanda tucks her gorgeous blonde hair behind her ear and gives him her best flirtatious smile. "It's nice to meet you as well," she says. Oh, Jesus, shoot me now. I give it ten minutes before they wander off from the group to enjoy their own animal-like behavior.

Before it goes any further, all three children interrupt their googly eyes.

"Amanda! Amanda! It's time for snow cones!" Emma shouts as she starts tugging on Amanda's dress.

"I heard you promise snow cones, Aunt Amanda, and I want a blue one," Blake adds.

Amanda looks to me for help, clearly wanting to spend more time with Lakin and not her darling niece and nephew. I just raise my hand to her. "Hey, you did promise," I tell her, offering no help at all.

She looks to Lakin, and then to Emma. "I'm not very hungry, munchkin, and we just got here; let's check out some more animals and work up an appetite before we get snacks."

Emma frowns and places her hands on her hips, clearly thinking over her next move in the snow cone negotiation process. "But on the way here, Momma said that you were hungry."

"What? No she didn't, sweetheart."

"Oh yes, she did! You guys were talking about your Netherlands being hungry, and I think a snow cone will fix that." Clearly, our vehicle audience had better hearing than we thought.

Everyone looks to me to interpret the four-year-old lingo, and I try my best to mutter through my best PG explanation. "Um,

Manda, I clearly remember a conversation that included you being in need of something. I think our little sponge mixed up a few key pieces of information."

When Amanda's eyes go wide with her realization, I slowly nod at her. "I told you, no public filter, little sis."

Amanda grabs Emma's hand, her embarrassment showing all over her face. "Okay, kids, enough talking; it's snow cone time. Lakin, would you like to help?"

"I would love to," he tells her, and with that, the kids jump up and down and shout with excitement.

As they turn to walk towards the vendors, I hear Lakin tell her that he thinks it's awesome that she speaks Dutch, and I absolutely lose it. I laugh so hard that my eyes begin to water; Amanda hears me and looks at me over her shoulder to throw her nastiest of looks at me. It only makes me howl louder, barely able to catch my breath.

"Okay, fill me in; what in the world is so funny?" Brooks asks, noticeably confused at the inside joke.

I tell him the story of her all-consuming loins and by the time we are at the picnic tables by the vendors, he too is doubled over laughing. Amanda, understanding our amusement, is shooting daggers at us.

"Oh, come on, sis that was funny. I tried to warn you."

"Yeah, yeah. Thanks a bunch, Viv."

"Seriously, Amanda, don't worry about it. Grace does that kind of stuff to me all the time," Brooks tells her.

"Well, a change of topic would be much appreciated," she growls.

The kids finish their snow cones, and we continue our exploration of the zoo with just as much laughter, but with fewer embarrassing filter moments. Any time the kids have their heads turned, Brooks holds my hand or kisses my forehead or cheek. I swear my body is on fire by the time our zoo trip is over. My stomach quivers from the constant butterflies, and my cheeks hurt from smiling so much. This day has been perfect.

We still haven't told the kids that we are anything more than friends; it is less confusing for them, and we feel it's best to keep our relationship to ourselves for a while. To be honest, I'm scared at what their reaction will be. There are times when I feel like I'm betraying Will's memory by caring for Brooks, and my heart would break if Emma and Blake felt the same way. So for now, while we figure this out, our silence is golden.

Within a few hours, the kids are exhausted and our feet are sore from toting them around when their legs get tired.

I settle Blake and Emma into the car, and Lakin takes Grace to get buckled so that Brooks and I can say goodbye alone. "Thank you for today," I tell him.

He tangles our hands together and pulls me to him. "No, thank you, Viv. This has been the best day I've had in a long time. Any day that has you in it is perfect."

I smile up at him, and he leans down to kiss my forehead. "When can I see you again?"

I step back a little, but keep our hands connected. I desperately want to see him again, but I've been down this too-fast-too-soon road with Brooks before, and it got me shattered. I need to remember to keep myself guarded, because it's too easy to lose myself in him. "Um, I'm not sure what we have going on this week. Let me check the kids' schedules and I'll text you," I say, avoiding his gaze.

He releases one of my hands and lifts my chin, forcing me to meet his eyes. "Don't do that, Red."

"What?"

"You know what. You want to see me just as much as I want to see you, but you're scared. I get that, but you need to understand that I'm not the same kid that you met ten years ago who was afraid of who he was, and was embarrassed of his past. I'm a man who knows what he wants, and I'll spend every day for the rest of my life proving that you are what I want."

I exhale the breath that I am holding and nod. A million thoughts are racing through my mind, but I can't force any words to move past my lips.

"I'm not going anywhere; I'm not running this time. Please give me the chance to hang onto you."

I step forward and move onto my tiptoes to reach his lips. "Okay," I whisper against his lips. It's his turn to let out the sigh he was holding, waiting for my answer. "Call me tonight after Grace is in bed."

He smashes me to his chest and moves his hands to my hair. His lips meet mine, and he deepens the kiss, sending my dormant butterflies back into overdrive. He pulls back, smiling down at me with a mega-watt grin, showcasing his swoon-worthy dimples. "You bet your ass I'll call you, Clover," he says before he kisses my hand and walks away like he hadn't left me with swollen lips, weak knees, and soaking panties. Great, the car ride home will be just as uncomfortable as the ride here.

VIVIAN

Brooks follows through on his promise to call. He calls, texts, or stops by every day for the next week. Grace has been over to play a few times, and everyone is beginning to feel comfortable with each other. So when Blake suggests a group dinner and movie slumber party with Brooks and Grace, we see it as a great opportunity to introduce the kids to our relationship.

Jen and Carly, of course, see this as an opportunity for an adult slumber party. I had thrown out all of the lingerie that I owned after Will died. I know it seems silly, but it feels wrong to wear any of it for another man. Needless to say, Jen took me underwear shopping in preparation for our sleepover. I'm not sure my Visa will ever recover.

Armed with our overnight bags and enough movie options to last until the end of time, Emma, Blake, and I make the short trip to Brooks' for our weekend adventure. His house is somewhat secluded in the foothills of the Rockies, just a twenty-minute drive from our house in the suburbs of Denver.

We creep our way up the long, winding driveway, which is more like a gravel path. A luscious mixture of aspens and evergreens line the pathway on both sides, blocking our view of his actual home. The road begins to widen, exposing the largest, most beautiful log cabin, and I peer into the backseat to see both of my children's mouths hanging wide open. The house is not a simple family home; it should be showcased in the Parade of Homes or Architectural Digest. The two-story behemoth features a green roof with thick solid pine logs wrapping the exterior. It looks like Lincoln Logs on steroids.

I park the car in front of the entrance, and we all sit idly in wonder of the mansion before us. "Is this really Brooks' house?" Blake asks, his eyes still bulging out of his little head.

I slowly nod, still staring forward, "Yup, buddy, it is."

"Wow, it's like a wooden castle," Emma adds.

"All right, guys, it's just a house. We are going to have a ton of fun this weekend. Let's go find Brooks and Grace, and please remember to be polite. No fighting this weekend, okay?"

They both agree, and we all tumble out of the car and begin lugging our bags up the stone pathway to the front door. Before we even reach the porch steps, Brooks barrels through the front door and rushes down the stairs to grab our bags; his excitement is evident in his haste as he nearly trips on the flagstone.

I hear Blake laugh, but I turn around to shoot him my best mom-glare, and he suppresses his chuckle. Emma lightly punches him in the arm, emphasizing the tone of our silent family conversation. I turn the stare her way, and she throws her hands up in surrender just as Brooks reaches us.

"Hey, you guys. I'm glad you could make it," he says as he takes the bags out of my hands and kisses my cheek.

"Thank you for having us," Blake responds as he hands Brooks his bag.

Brooks reaches for Emma's bag as well, but she refuses to hand over her backpack; she hasn't let the thing out of her sight since we got it at Target. "Where's Grace?" she asks.

"She is with Katie, my babysitter. They were out running errands when I got home, but they should be here anytime," he answers as he throws everything over his shoulder. He leads us up the walkway. We enter the foyer and he immediately leads us upstairs to a long hallway with a string of doors on either side.

Brooks looks completely relaxed in his faded, scuffed-up blue jeans and soft cotton tee. Instead of the shrewd, polished architect, he is loosened up and carefree, just like I remember from college. His broad shoulders and toned muscles are at war with the thin, tight shirt he has selected. I can see every bit of his definition, and it's a gorgeous sight to behold. As the slapping of his sandals smack against the wood flooring, I begin to pull my eyes away from Brooks' body and take in our surroundings.

The décor throughout the house is very masculine; the color pallet a mixture of light greys and cobalt blue. It's certainly not what I would have expected in a log home, but it works and feels like Brooks. While there are pictures of Grace everywhere, the family pictures stop with her. There are none of his mother, or brother, or even friends—nothing, just him and Grace.

A lonely feeling settles within me at the thought of the two of them having only each other, and it makes me want to create more for them, build a family together. The thought hits me like a sledgehammer; it's not the typical Vivian line of thinking, and I can't explain my ease. In that moment, I'm not scared of the idea of creating a family with Brooks and our children, but I know that if I let my mind settle with the notion, guilt will no doubt creep in and squash my content.

We pass by Grace's room, which is completely decked out in hot pink and zebra print. It looks like Barbie and Joan Jett had a paint war. It melts my heart to see a girly room filled with dolls and Barbie cars in this masculine house. We then deposit each of the kids in their own guest room to let them get settled, allowing Brooks time to show me to my room. I'm a little surprised that he doesn't bring me to his room; I can't deny that I'm not a little disappointed.

Brooks lays my bag on the queen-sized bed and grabs me to sit on his lap on the edge of it. With one arm coiling around my waist, he uses the other to push my hair away from my neck. "You have the room across the hall from mine. I figured you might want your things in here for appearances for the kids, but I have no intention of letting you sleep in here," he whispers into my ear.

His breath tickles my neck and I giggle, attempting to turn away from his mouth. Scooting around to face him, I kiss his cheek, and then glide my tongue across his jaw to nibble on his earlobe. I feel him shiver under me. Brooks is not the type to relinquish control, and I certainly look forward to handing it over to him; in this moment, it is exciting to make this strong man squirm.

"That's good to hear," I mumble against his neck. "I may have brought some special pajamas I think you'll enjoy."

He throws his head back, and I take the opportunity to attack his neck, lathering it with soft kisses. "Fuck, Red, I'm not sure I can wait until tonight. Would it be bad to send all the kids to the movies with Katie, instead of staying here?"

"Yeah, I don't think that would fly," I answer, grinding into him and earning a muted groan.

"Can we maybe spike their juice with Benadryl to ensure they fall asleep early and stay out for the night?"

I pull away from his neck, "Did you just ask me to drug our children?" I laugh. "Yeah, I don't think that will work either."

"I'm kidding, but, Vivian, be prepared. I know you brought something special to wear tonight, but you have me so worked up that by the time I have you really alone, I don't think it will be on long enough to appreciate it."

"Noted, now let's go find everyone and get this show on the road," I say, giving him one last kiss before climbing off his lap.

"Why don't you get everyone unpacked, and I'll go get dinner going and wait for Grace." Brooks stands to leave, but slaps me on the ass as he passes. I yelp at the hard smack.

"See you downstairs, baby." He laughs as he exits the room.

Shaking my head at his lightheartedness, I immediately unzip my bag and hang my clothes that are prone to wrinkles. I work on unpacking my suitcase and let my mind reflect on the evening ahead of me, and the man that I can't help but think I'm betraying.

As I unfold the lingerie I bought, I think about my expectations for the evening. If I'm being honest with myself, I'm not sure what to expect from tonight or even if I truly want anything to happen. Either way, my nerves have reappeared full-force. I'm overwhelmed with the guilty feeling that I'm cheating on Will. I know he's gone, and I know that he would want me to move on, but I fear that things with Brooks are moving too fast. The heart that I finally found again feels like it is being torn in two. I want Brooks—with every breath I want him—but I feel like I'm being disloyal to Will for even considering it.

It hasn't even been a year since Will's accident, and I'm not sure any amount of time will completely take that hurt away. More than anything, though, I want Brooks to take that pain away. I'm desperately trying to ignore the guilt that consumes me every time I let myself think about Will. I wonder if he would be okay with Brooks and me being together, and letting him be a part of our children's lives. I can't help but feel like I'm disappointing him, but if I listen to my heart, I realize I don't want to let Brooks go again. Wrong or not, I want to fight for him, for us.

Closing the last drawer, I hear Blake's laughter down the hall. I take a cleansing breath, straighten my dark blue jeans, and smooth out the soft flowing pink shirt I have layered over a white tank top. I take one last look in the mirror, and then head in the direction of the other guestrooms.

forgive us our Trespasses

BROOKS

As soon as I close Vivian's door, I hustle down the stairs to get everything ready for everyone. I figure I would let the kids decide on dinner, but I want to lay out the options for them to pick. I want this evening to be perfect for her, and for the kids to be completely comfortable.

I don't think I would be able to wipe the grin off my face even if I tried. Vivian, my Clover, staying in my house–and by her own free will I might add–is a freaking miracle. I'm not sure how many karmic good deeds I need to do to show my thankfulness, but it would be worth the trouble.

Just as I reach the landing of the stairs, Katie and Grace come through the door. Katie is loaded down with grocery bags, and of course, Grace is toting her favorite stuffed elephant and her purse that she insists she carry everywhere. She races to me, crashing into my knees and wrapping her arms around them.

"Well, hello there, baby girl," I say before bending down to kiss her forehead. She looks up to greet me with a smile before she takes off past me and up the stairs.

I then rush to Katie and grab some of the bags she has begun dragging into the living room. "My God, Katie, I asked you to pick up a few groceries. I'm not stockpiling for the zombie apocalypse or anything."

She swings a bag at me in response to my verbal jab; preparing for the blow, it faintly collides with my stomach. "Very funny. Grace said you had a date tonight, so I picked up some extra things for her and me."

We make it into the kitchen, and she flings her bags onto the counter with an exaggerated huff and begins to put things away. "You know it would have been nice to know that I was babysitting tonight. What if I had plans?"

I try to interrupt, but she continues with her unnecessary rant. "I realize that I don't have much of a social life, but seriously, finding out from a four year-old that my Friday night has been

179

booked—that's not cool, Brooks. Besides, what is this new girl, flavor of the month, week, or just sprinkles for the evening?"

She slams the refrigerator shut and stands there, waiting for my response. Very few people would ever get away with talking to me the way Katie just did. She has been the closest thing to a female confidant that I've had since Grace was born, and I value her opinion. Not only is she a loyal employee, she is a friend, someone whom I can always trust to call me on my shit when others are afraid to stand up to me. So I look past her mini-tantrum.

"So, first of all, I do have a date tonight, but she and her children are here. I won't be going anywhere." Katie's hands that were resting on her hips slide down to her sides, and her mouth hangs open in disbelief. Yes, this is the first time I've ever had a woman over to my house, and she is very aware of that fact.

"Second, while I appreciate that you are willing to give up your Friday night for Grace and me, it would never be relayed through her; I think a whole hell of a lot more of you than that, Katie. And finally, Vivian is not just some flavor of the week; she is the whole damn sundae that I would feel lucky to have every day for the rest of my life."

Katie quickly steps to me and gives me a warm hug. "I always hoped this would happen for you; I was starting to think you were a lost cause." I pat her back, a little thrown off by her emotional outburst and drastic shift in moods.

"Um, thanks, I think," I tell her, moving away from her grasp.

"If she really is that great, though, please don't fuck it up. I would prefer we keep the Brooks brothel closed; I wouldn't be surprised if there is an "'I slept with Brooks Ryan'" support group out there somewhere," she laughs lightly, slugging me in the arm.

I pretend to be wounded, and feign insult, which she only laughs at. "Thanks a lot."

She and I both walk back to the front entrance where I open the door for her, and again thank her for bringing Grace home and running my errands.

"Anytime, Brooks, you know that." She exhales deeply and smiles once more before turning and walking down the front steps towards her car.

I close the door just as Vivian and all three children skip down the stairs, laughing about some giraffe joke Blake has shared. I turn and watch them giggle and bump into each other; Vivian's smile is bright, and when her eyes meet mine, it feels like I melt into them. This is my family. She is my family.

VIVIAN

Brooks is watching us move down the stairs, and every little butterfly that I thought I had gotten a grasp on has escaped from the net and is bouncing around my stomach. His look is one of admiration and desire, and if there were no children in the room with us, he would be taking our date night from PG to X-rated within seconds. I breathe through the anxiety and smile at him.

"Hey, guys," he says, returning my grin. "How about we go into the kitchen first and pick out dinner, and then we can narrow down the movie options."

He meets us at the bottom of the stairs and takes my hand to lead me to the kitchen. His thumb brushes along my knuckles, and the intimate touch calms my tension.

There are several dinner choices displayed on the counter top; the man has definitely prepared for the evening. "Okay, we have spaghetti, pot pie, chicken patties and potatoes, tacos, or Hamburger Helper," Brooks says as he travels down the line like Vanna White, offering up each kid-friendly option.

I scan the counter, eyeing my arch nemesis, hoping the kids don't select most kids' go-to dinner of choice. Hamburger Helper and my stomach don't get along well; I have actually banned the product from our house. I have an iron stomach, but when I even smell the little boxed wonder, my stomach revolts, and I experience the worst case of what I've come to call Momentary Irritable Bowel Syndrome.

Remembering my children's tendency towards unfiltered verbal diarrhea, I'm hoping to direct everyone's attention away from the demon noodles. Before I can get a word in though, my lovely daughter decides it's the perfect time to protect my stomach instead of my pride.

"We can NOT have Hamburger Helper," she loudly declares for the group.

"What? Why not? I love it." Grace asks.

"Mom says Hamburger Helper is the devil," Blake adds, trying to clarify, and everyone turns to me to explain further. I feel my hands begin to sweat as my face flushes with embarrassment and my eyes pin my son in place. He raises his hands in defense, as if my glare will physically harm him.

I grab the box off the counter, staring at the back label, trying desperately to avoid eye contact with Brooks. "I don't think that I have ever actually said that it is the devil." I quickly look to Blake again, daring him to contradict me. "I just said that I don't really like it, and since I'm the one that does the cooking, I choose not to make it." Seems like a plausible explanation, and I'm hoping the topic is dropped until I look at my second unfiltered child to see the wheels in her head grinding away.

"No, Mom, Blake is right! I remember. That one time we had it for dinner, you spent the whole night in the bathroom with a tummy ache, and the next day you said Hamburger Helper was never allowed in the house again because it gave you diarrpea."

Mayday! Mayday! I feel my eyes widen; I'm not sure what I could even say to save the moment. I am completely mortified, and when I hear Grace laughing, I know that our sexy evening has not only nose-dived, but has completely crashed and burned.

"It's not diarrpea, silly," Grace corrects through giggles.

"It is at our house. When Mom locked herself in the bathroom, it sounded like she was having a water gun fight in there. So now, we call it *dia-ppp-a*, because of the sounds she made," Blake explains. It clicks for Grace, and she bursts into even bigger hysterics. Yup, this is completely awesome; I now know why some animals eat their own young.

I see Brooks struggling to keep it together; his hand is balled up in front of his mouth, and I'm just waiting for the explosion of laughter. "Go ahead; I know you want to laugh. I'll put you out of your misery. Go ahead, ha ha, laugh it up," I say as I lightly punch him in the bicep.

He grabs my arm and pulls me into a bear hug of an embrace. "I'm sorry; I won't laugh, and we can take the devil food off the list of options for dinner. You have to admit, though; it's kind of funny."

I look up at him, his ear-to-ear grin shining down at me, and I can't help but laugh. "Yeah, okay, it's a little funny. But seriously, no Hamburger Helper, or the humor of this conversation will become tragically real."

"All right, deal," he says as he snuggles into my neck and kisses the skin below my ear. His attempt at calming my humiliation works and I relax into him, absorbing the moment. He then releases me and grabs the spaghetti noodles, tossing the closed package to Blake. "So, spaghetti it is!"

VIVIAN

After my dignity is restored and we make it through dinner, we all find spots in Brooks' media room to enjoy the movies. Of course, there is a buffet of junk food, and Brooks helps the kids make a massive fort to camp in during the films. By the second movie, all three have fallen asleep. We debated whether or not to just leave them, but in the end, we figure that Blake and Emma might get scared or lost if they wake up in the middle of night.

So, one-by-one Brooks carries them to their rooms. My heart melts watching each one lay their head on his shoulder and burrow into his neck.

Seeing Blake and Emma react so well to Brooks and Grace puts some of my fears to rest, but it has done nothing to ease the guilt. I am deep in thought when Brooks finally returns, and it isn't until he grabs my hand that my thoughts are entirely interrupted.

"Come on, sweetheart. Let's go upstairs; everyone is settled," he says, pulling me off the couch.

I wrap both of my arms around his and rest my head on his shoulder, allowing him to lead me up to his bedroom. I halt us in front of my door, though, and I insist that I need a few minutes to get ready for bed. He agrees to return to his own bedroom to wait for me, and when he turns to leave, for a split second I contemplate staying in my room for the night instead of going to him. But then he looks over his shoulder at me, his sapphire blue eyes calling to me, and his smile scorching me. "Don't be long, Red," he says as he slides past his doorframe and into his room.

I mop up the puddled mess of myself off the hallway floor, and enter my room with a new resolve; I must keep myself under control when in his swoon-worthy presence. I quickly slip out of my jeans and top and replace it with a simple tee shirt and boy shorts. I forgo the lingerie. I think that by wearing it, it ups the pressure, and I don't think I can handle anymore sexual tension between the two of us, or be strong enough to not be sucked into the heat of the moment.

I hurriedly wash my make-up off, brush my teeth, and take my hair out of the wild bun creation I had used to tame it during dinner. I tiptoe across the hallway and take a deep breath before knocking on Brooks' door.

It swings open within seconds, and Brooks' eyes stroll down the length of my body before eventually meeting my eyes. The corners of his mouth curl up, and a mischievous look takes hold, letting me know that he appreciates what he sees.

He looks completely edible in his blue flannel pajama pants and white tee shirt. I can smell the mint from his toothpaste and the apples and spice of his cologne.

I step through the door and quietly close it behind me, careful not to wake the sleeping children down the hall. Brooks pulls me into to his strong arms, and his cologne envelops me. I melt into him as the feeling of safety washes over me. He grasps my hips tightly, and I can hear him exhale deeply into my hair; he is allowing himself to relax into me as well.

"I still can't believe you're here. You have no idea how long I've wanted this; I just wouldn't let myself believe that it was possible," he whispers into my neck.

I rest my head against his chest, listening to the steady thump of his heart. "I never thought I would see you again. I think we both have tried to forget about one another, and what we had. I think we both know now that our love is unforgettable. When we aren't together, we are just pretending to be whole," I say softly. Brooks grips me tighter with every word, as if he's afraid that if he lets go my words will disappear.

I pry myself away from him, hoping that when I meet his eyes I will see my feelings reflected back at me. But I see more than yearning and love shining through–I see sadness, relief, even regret. Brooks cups my face and draws me to his lips.

"Thank you for letting me make this right, Red. I'll never disappoint you again," he murmurs before crashing down onto my eager lips.

His embrace and his kiss are firm, almost desperate. I match his enthusiasm as my own desires reach a fever pitch. We are clawing at each other's clothing, leaving a trail of garments as Brooks walks our tangled bodies from the door towards his massive bed. When the backs of my knees hit the mattress, he leans into me, causing me to lie flat on the bed. He quickly covers me with his own perfectly-sculpted body.

His kiss becomes more delicate as he hovers above me. I wrap my legs around him, pulling him closer, and I feel his excitement against me. Feeling empowered by him, I take control by deepening the kiss once more. I cannot get close enough to this man; with my body, I beg him to own me in every possible way.

As I edge closer to losing control, my heart begins to race, and the gravity of the situation slaps me in the face. We are both naked in his bed with our children just a few rooms away and I'm letting myself get too carried away too soon. My guilt takes hold as Will invades my thoughts, and I push Brooks away, tears beginning to swim in my eyes.

"What? Did I do something wrong?" Brooks asks; his look of confusion and hurt squeezes my already-bruised heart.

Unable to look at his wounded expression, I maintain a lowered gaze at his chest. I take notice of every inch, the firm defined muscles, the small patch of hair nestled between his pecs. "I'm so sorry, Brooks. We are just moving too fast. I'm not ready to move things forward yet." The fear of confessing my guilt is evident in the broken whisper of my voice.

He rolls off me, throwing his arms up to cover his face and I'm unsure of whether he's angry or hurt. I just lie still, struggling to steady my breathing and hold back the tears that threaten to spill over my lids. I wait for enough clues to understand his emotions, and enough time to control my own.

"Do you not want me because you don't trust me?" Brooks finally asks, not looking at me.

My confliction plays out across my face, and the dam holding back my tears crumbles. I hastily wipe away the drops of my pain, attempting to mask my emotions from Brooks. "I'm sorry, Brooks; it's not about that. I do trust you; I'm just not ready." My voice strains through the words.

Taking notice, Brooks lowers his arms and turns to face me. Slowly, he brings his thumb to my cheek to brush away my remaining tears. "Hey now," he whispers, his thumb sliding down to trace the lines of my lower lip. "I didn't mean to upset you. I'm not angry with you, Viv; I'm mad at myself for putting you in the position to question my sincerity. If that isn't the issue, please talk to me." He moves his hand to the back of my neck and rests his head on mine, closing his eyes. "Let me fix this," he exhales.

"I don't know if you can," I admit. "I want you; I want us. I just feel so guilty that I'm betraying Will by being with you. I want more than anything for that guilt to fade, and I'm so afraid that it never will."

His eyes slowly open as my confession sinks in and surrounds us. "Oh, babe, you aren't betraying him. I know that he hated me because of how I treated you, and I can never undo that. But at the time, I needed you to not want me; I needed you to fall in love with someone safe. Will was safe, and as much as it killed me that it wasn't me with you, I was so thankful that it was him in my place."

My breath trembles, and I feel my body quake as I listen to his explanation. "Why does that make it all right for us to be together now?" I ask as I lightly run my fingernails down the length of his back.

"Because, Clover, it's my turn to be the safe choice, and I will do anything and everything to prove that he would be thankful it's me in his place."

Relief washes over me, and I smile through my remaining tears. I lean forward and faintly caress his lips with mine, showing my appreciation for his words. "Thank you for that. Can we just hold each other tonight? I want to feel your arms around me."

"Of course, Viv, I wouldn't want you to be any other place. I'm not going anywhere; we can go as slow as you need."

I settle into his side and lay my head on his chest, listening to his easy breathing. The even rhythm calms me, and with his arms around me, peace shrouds me. Any bit of the guilt that had been crushing me is lifted.

We lay in a comfortable silence. Brooks occasionally places a tender kiss on my head, and I use my fingertips to trace the outline of the tattoo that covers his ribs. I hadn't really noticed it in our earlier frenzy, but now I pause to explore every colorful curve and solid line.

The script, 'Forgive Us Our Trespasses' is written in a beautifully intricate scroll. The words themselves are simple but familiar. I have never been religious, but the words are ones that have been imprinted in my mind since the death of my father. They carry a weight that I have struggled to live up to, break free from.

Each word flows freely down the length of his side in one long black line. The only color comes from the thorn-covered vines that weave through the lettering and the vibrant green clovers that pin down each side of the phrase.

I suspend my movement when I get to the clovers, but I disregard the possible meaning of their presence.

"What is it?" Brooks asks, feeling my hesitation.

"Nothing, it's just your tattoo. The quote you have is from the Lord's Prayer; I didn't know that you were religious," I say and then continue my skin perusal.

Brooks latches onto my hand, halting my inspection. "I'm not religious," he says, bringing my wrist to his lips and kissing my pulse line.

I stretch my neck to meet his gaze, and he smiles down at me. As quickly as his smile appears, it is replaced with a seriousness that heightens my anxiety level. "My tattoo represents many things, things that I don't want to ever forget. It's my reminder of the mistakes I've made, and my weaknesses that caused those mistakes, but it's not all bad. My dreams are there too, and my hopes for what I always wanted in my life."

I search his eyes for more understanding. He's telling me about his tattoo without really telling me, and the cryptic answers are doing nothing for my comprehension. He smiles, realizing my need for further clarification.

"You asked if my ink is religious, and the answer is no," he says before pausing to cup my cheek in his palm, capturing my full attention. "Vivian, this tattoo has nothing to do with wanting God's forgiveness; it's about seeking yours."

The symbolism of the art clicks into place, and I gasp at my realization. Placing my hand on the tattoo, I lean close to his ear. "You have it, Brooks; you've always had it," I sigh.

I'm swiftly pinned to the bed and Brooks hovers over me, his eyes shimmering with emotion, and the corners of his lips are arched in joy. "I have waited so long to hear that, thank you," he says before his lips collide with mine.

This time, I don't fight his advances. Instead, I encourage and invite every movement, every morsel of passion that develops between us. We match each other's fervor, both of us racing to our release. Our bodies and souls are entwined as tension builds until we finally reach a blissful explosion of pleasure.

As Brooks collapses, I stroke his back and let my tired legs fall around him. Together we stable our breathing, until Brooks rolls us so that my back is tucked into his front. Wrapping his arms around me, I feel his moist breath against my neck.

"I love you, Clover," Brooks sighs just as his body relaxes and gives itself over to sleep.

I kiss the forearm that he has coiled around me, and when I'm certain that he's asleep, I relax into him. "I love you too," I murmur before I allow myself to drift off as well.

VIVIAN

Since the weekend with Brooks and Grace, things, life, and our family have slowly found a routine. A routine with healed hearts and optimism for what our futures hold. School has started for the kids, and it really has felt odd not being a part of the preparation festivities this year. Usually I would have teacher in-services, spend countless hours decorating my classroom, planning lessons, matching standards with activities. But this year, I was able to stand back and just enjoy my kids' excitement for the new school year instead.

Brooks and Grace have found themselves woven into every fiber of our new lives. Although we said we would move gradually with our relationship, things have been anything but slow. Since I'm working from home now, I pick up all of the children after school each day, and Brooks then meets us at my house for dinner each night. During the week, Brooks and Grace go home after dinner, but over the weekends, we take turns hosting family sleepovers. Amanda has been out of town a great deal, so we try to work around her schedule, but there are plenty of evenings that she is a part of our crew. Life has become comfortable. Our life is content again.

Everyone is adjusting well. Our blended group actually doesn't feel blended at all; it feels natural, normal, like it always should have been. Even through the hard moments, Brooks stands by me, keeping his promise to stay put. The anniversary of Will's death is difficult, but we manage together without a meltdown. I still had Will's ashes from the funeral; I just could never decide what to do with them, or if by releasing them it would mean that I didn't love him anymore, so for the last year, I had held onto them.

After extinguishing my apprehension, Brooks comes up with the idea to have a memorial with just us and the kids to finally scatter his ashes. Blake and Emma are comfortable with the idea, and I finally feel at ease with the symbolic act of letting him go. I choose Bear Lake in Estes Park, one of Will's favorite spots. It is a special spot for many reasons: it was where we first took the kids to learn how to fish; in college, we camped there together several times each year; and it's where he proposed after we found out we were pregnant with Blake. The lake is beautiful and perfect, and will be a safe place to free my safe knight.

There are tears, there is laughter, and there is eventually liberation. I free myself of the guilt that was eating a hole through what remained of my heart. Blake and Emma find peace with saying goodbye in their own way. It is a moment that I never got as a child, and I'm so thankful that I'm able to give it to my children. I'm proud of them, of myself, and of Brooks for living up to his promise. So when Emma asks Brooks on the way home from the lake if he will call her Cricket, like her dad used to, I can't help but smile through the tears. In that moment, I know my family will be okay; we were going to be happy again.

Occasionally I still think about Bear Lake and Will. How they are such important pieces of my life, pieces that I will never forget, pieces that helped to make me who I am. I have moved past my worry about betraying Will. I feel as though I have honored him, his memory, and our previous life. Even though it's been a road filled with obstacles, I'm finally content with where I am and how I got there.

I gaze out the car window, these thoughts overpowering my mind, when I feel Brooks squeeze my hand, bringing me back to the present. I turn to face his concerned look, and I smile to ease his discomfort. We hold a silent conversation, speaking only with our eyes, and he knows where my thoughts have been. He gently nods, and he brings my wrist to his mouth, letting his lips trace along the delicate skin.

"I'm here, Viv," he says before taking a glance in the rearview mirror at our pint-sized passengers. This time it's my turn to nod.

We've been out to dinner at one of our favorite restaurants, Cheery Cricket. Set in the heart of upscale Cherry Creek, the diner sticks out in the posh neighborhood with its off-color menu and comfortable atmosphere. Brooks thinks that they have the best hamburger masterpieces in Denver, at least that's what Brooks calls them; and besides, Emma thinks that the place was named after her. Needless to say, we frequent the establishment often.

I peer into the backseat as well to see two children awake and looking stuffed to the brim from their burgers and fries, and Emma soundly sleeping. I'm a little surprised to see that any of them are awake, considering the amount of fun they had throwing darts at the burger toppings board, instead of ordering a pre-designed burger off the menu.

We always have a good time with the darts, and I find it hilarious watching Brooks hold each kid up in the air so that they can aim for the additions that they want for their order, hoping it doesn't land on something they will have to pick off later.

"Look, Mom, Aunt Charlotte's here!" Blake exclaims as we pull into the driveway of my house.

I turn back around in my seat to see the grey mini-van of my sister's parked in front of the house. Brooks looks to me, and I shrug in response. I have spoken only sporadically to my sister or mother since moving to Denver. They understood, but didn't necessarily agree with me uprooting the kids and moving away. They have let it be known, they thought it was doing more damage than good. Neither have been to the new house, so to see my sister here raises some red flags.

My mind immediately plays out all of the various horrible situations that could have brought her to my doorstep. Brooks sees my worry, and when he puts the SUV into park, he urges me out of the car.

"Go, Red, I'll get the kids in and settled," he says softly as I unbuckle and gather my purse. I mouth him a thank you, hastily open my door, and speed walk up the front steps. Unsure of what news I'll find on the other side of the door, I feel an overwhelming sense of dé-já-vu, and I find myself repeatedly muttering, "Please not again…please not again."

Stumbling through the door, I yell out for Charlotte and Amanda, the anxiety obvious in my voice. I hear them both in the kitchen, and I rush through the house towards their muffled conversation. As I approach, bits and pieces of the discussion are clearer, and I can feel the emotion radiating from the room.

"What happened? Is Mom okay?" I shout as I burst through the doorway. I'm met with grim expressions; Amanda's reddened cheeks are smeared with black mascara, and Charlotte's cool demeanor is one usually reserved for when she's angry.

Amanda wipes away her tears and dabs her nose with a tissue, but even surrounded by the sniffles next to her, Charlotte's strength doesn't falter as she pats the chair next to her. "Mom is fine, but something has happened; please sit so I can explain."

My stomach twists into knots, and I feel the dread of the atmosphere absorb into my pores. I slowly pull out the chair and sit down, my body rigid, preparing for the blow that is sure to come. I square my shoulders and face Charlotte, signaling my readiness for the impending bomb.

"Yesterday, Mom got a letter from the state parole board. It was notifying her that Raymond Michaels was being released," she states calmly, as the finality of the situation is out of her control. Amanda sobs, unable to bear hearing the words again.

"What do you mean released?" I demand. "When was the review; why wasn't I told? We have written letters to the board in the past; they can't just let him go without letting us speak to the parole board." My voice raises an octave with each word of my rant. I had a million possibilities of why Charlotte was here, but never did I think that Raymond Michaels' release would have been the reason.

"There was a review and we were notified, and both Mom and I wrote letters," she responds.

"What?" I say incredulously. "Why wouldn't Mom include us? Dad's death impacted all of us; it is not okay that you kept this from us."

Charlotte exhales loudly, and Amanda swiftly dries her remaining tears; she is also insulted by our sister and mother's secret.

"Guys, Mom thought that both of you had enough on your plate without worrying about this. Amanda, your job has you travelling all over the country and spread so thin. And Vivian, with you still healing from Will's accident, you know that this was an added stress that you didn't need."

"I appreciate the concern, but our involvement was something that we should have been able to decide for ourselves," Amanda snaps, the sarcasm dripping from each word.

"Look, I'm sorry that Mom didn't want to tell you, but we thought it was for the best. It was very likely that he was going to be released and we didn't want to worry you both until it was done."

My mind quickly computes the math, and when I realize that he hasn't even served the minimum of his 25 to life sentence, my blood rises and my face warms in rage. "What do you mean? It's only been 23 years; how could he even be up for parole if he hadn't served the minimum sentence? That doesn't make sense."

I begin taking out my aggression on the placemat in front of me, wringing the cloth between my white-knuckled grip. Amanda takes it from my hands and straightens the now-wrinkled placemat. "Easy there, tiger, these are my special harvest mats and Pottery Barn has discontinued them."

I smile and exhale the breath I had been holding, thankful for her slightest comic relief from our tense situation. "I'm sorry; it's all just a little overwhelming." My eyes slide to Charlotte, who has cast her glance down. "So tell us the rest; we won't interrupt, just explain. We want the whole story, everything, Char."

"Okay," she resigns. "When he was up for parole the last time, we knew that he had been making progress in prison. He hadn't had any behavior issues, and he was about to finish his Bachelor's degree. When he was transferred to a minimum security facility, and soon after became a leader in a mentor program for younger inmates, we both knew that his parole probably wouldn't be denied again." She looks back and forth between us, and we gesture her to continue.

"So when the state sent notification of the hearing, we sent the letters like we always did. But we knew that with the combination of his good behavior and the current overcrowding of the system, our efforts would prove futile, and he would be released early."

Footsteps interrupt her explanation, and all three of us look to the entryway to see Brooks standing there, his arms folded across his chest, emphasizing a threatening and daunting stance. He has been upstairs long enough to know that he has more than likely gotten all of the kids to sleep. I wish he had stayed up there as well, though; I don't want to scare him away with this conversation. The idea of my father's killer back on the streets scared him away once before, I can't risk that happening again.

"Where is he now?" he asks, his gruff voice causing me to slightly startle. I've never really seen Brooks angry, but his tone suggests that we should tread lightly. Once my nerves settle, I'm a little relieved to see him take such a huge interest in my safety.

"I'm sorry; who are you?" Charlotte asks, looking perturbed and her tone matching her attitude of disdain.

"Um, this is Brooks, my boyfriend." Her head twists around to face me so quickly that I wouldn't be surprised if she experiences symptoms of whiplash in the morning. Her look of utter disbelief matches her movement. She disapproves.

I give her my best please-be-nice glare, as I continue with introductions. "Brooks, this is my older sister, Charlotte."

Charlotte purses her lips, but since she was raised to be polite in all situations, she turns and reaches out to take Brooks' hand. "Good to meet you. I wish it could have been under better circumstances," she says.

"Nice to meet you as well and I agree, the circumstances could be much better," he reciprocates as he moves into the kitchen and shakes her hand. Instead of taking a seat at the table though, he continues to stand, his rigid demeanor unwavering. "Please continue. Where is he now? I want to make sure that he can never come in contact with Vivian."

"He was released to a half-way house in Greeley, where he will be on a strict probation for the next eighteen months. Then if he hasn't violated any of the stipulations of the probation, he will be officially released. He will still have to check in with his parole officer, and there will be rules surrounding that release over the next five years, but officially, he will be out and among us."

"This is so surreal," Amanda adds. "I could be walking down the street or standing in line for coffee and just bump into the man that killed our dad. It seems so twisted."

"I know; I mean I don't know what I would even say to him." I look to Brooks, whose eyes are burning a hole in the floor. His hands are now at his sides, but are balled into fists. I push my chair back, the wooden legs scraping against the tile flooring, and walk across the kitchen until I find myself standing toe-to-toe with a conflicted Brooks. I lace my fingers with his, drawing his attention from the floor.

There is a fire behind his eyes, causing my worry to no longer lie with the villain of my childhood, but with the man I love, who seems to be plagued by his own demons. "Hey, you," I whisper, rousing his eyes from their veil of fury. I stroke the backs of my fingers across his cheek, attempting to soothe his torment. "I'm okay, Brooks. We are going to be all right. He can't come anywhere near us, and the likelihood of running into him for any reason is slim to nothing. So don't worry about this; I'm not going to worry about it."

Brooks shakes his head. "How can you say that? That man is a monster; he killed your father, and now he is out like it never happened. How can you forgive and forget?"

"I have neither forgiven him nor forgotten what he did, but I can't let it run my life anymore. I had to move on from it, just like I had to move past Will's death. I couldn't let it consume me."

"Okay, but if he ever tries to contact you, you have to let me know right away. I will never let him near you; do you understand? This is not negotiable."

I take pause at his overwhelmingly-protective gesture, and then I slowly nod in agreement. I have no desire to ever see Raymond Michaels, and it feels nice that he's willing to intervene on my behalf, but the exchange feels odd and puts me on edge.

Pushing aside my unease, I rise up onto my tiptoes and kiss his cheek, taking in his unmistakable smell. The scent calms my nerves and I smile as I pull away.

"Come on, let's go to bed. There has been enough discussion for tonight," Brooks says as he kisses my palm. "The only place that I want to be is in bed, with you tucked tightly in my arms."

I turn to look at my sisters, who whirl around in their chairs and pretend to be in a deep discussion, like they weren't just spying on my intimate moment with Brooks. I just shake my head. "I'll talk to you guys more in the morning."

"Sure, sounds great," Amanda says.

"It was great to meet you, Brooks," Charlotte adds. Brooks nods in response, and we both give one last wave before heading through the doorway towards the stairs.

I stop before reaching the stairs, causing Brooks to yank backwards. "Give me a minute, I'll be right back.

I turn and walk back into the kitchen, gaining the attention of both of my sisters. Charlotte rises from her seat as I cross the distance between us, and I firmly pull her into a warm embrace. "Thank you for coming here. I know that this wasn't easy for you, and I know that it's a shock to see a man here with me. But please know, Char, I appreciate that you did this." I hang on tightly to her, and then give her an extra squeeze before pulling away. "Thank you for being my responsible big sister."

I give Amanda a wink and make my way back out of the kitchen to find Brooks. Waiting for me where I left him, he leads me upstairs to my room. Once we are behind closed doors, he pulls back the duvet and neither of us bothers with truly readying ourselves for bed. Instead, Brooks strips us both, and we crawl under the covers. Instead of making love, though, Brooks gathers me in his arms and buries his head into my hair. I can feel his warm breath against my neck as he plants soft kisses behind my ear.

"I will never let anything or anyone hurt you, Vivian. I promise you, you are my everything," he says, squeezing so tightly it becomes hard to breathe.

I wiggle out of his death grip and turn in his arms to look at his perplexed expression. I rub along the scowl lines that have entrenched themselves in his brow. "Shh," I murmur, "everything is fine; no one is going to hurt me, not even you."

He kisses my forehead, letting his lips linger. "Promise?" he asks his voice barely noticeable. He is looking for words of comfort.

I wrap my arms around him and let the darkness of the room and the warmth of Brooks' body possesses me.

BROOKS

Fear, an all-encompassing, suffocating, hide-in-the-dark kind of fear has consumed me. It has invaded my subconscious, and everything I find myself doing revolves around a name I thought I would never hear again, Raymond Michaels. I swore to myself and to Vivian I would keep her safe and that I would choose her. I intend to keep that vow, no matter the cost.

The weeks since Charlotte's arrival have been uneventful in regard to the man that haunts my past. He has been quiet, and went about his new life with little concern for those lives that he impacted 23 years ago. I have kept close tabs on his activity, hiring a private investigator to track his every movement. I refuse to risk the consequences of an accidental meeting. It could cost me everything, and I won't let him take it away, not again.

My hope has been that he'll make a dire mistake that will violate his strict parole terms. Him being sent back to a maximum-security facility is more than I could wish for though, so until he fucks it up, like he typically does, I stand back and watch from afar.

She's guarded. Vivian tries to act carefree and forgiving about the entire situation, but I can tell that it's a facade. She worries constantly. She's ventured into Mama Bear protector mode, but with a big giant smile and a sugary 'I'm fine.' I don't buy it for a second.

I have scanned through her computer history searches, and I know she is just as obsessed as I am. Although there wasn't anything specific to Raymond Michaels, there were plenty of Google searches about parolees contacting victims' families, and the location of the Greeley halfway house. She could probably get an A on the book report, or arrested for stalking…it can be such a fine line.

I've tried to set her mind at rest, but I'm extremely careful not to divulge too much. A detailed explanation would raise questions of history. She has never asked why I pushed her away ten years ago, and I have no intention of telling her. Her being in the dark about it keeps her safe. And, if she found out about the nightmare of my past, my biggest fear of losing her would more than likely become a reality.

There have only been a handful of times in my life when I wasn't sure what the outcome would be. I am a driven man who goes after what he wants. With my business, if I want things done a certain way, or I need to coerce investors to see a project my way, I win. I always win. When it comes to Vivian, though, she's a game-changer. She's the curve ball when you have a full count and are expecting the fastball. I can't predict how things will play out with her, and it drives me insane.

My auburn-haired beauty and her dusting of freckles bewitched me a decade ago, and I have spent the years since unsuccessfully attempting to expel her from my soul. In the short time since we have reconnected, she has found her way under my skin once more, but instead of trying to scratch her free, this time, I'm willing to use glue, staples, a wedding band, and any adhesive necessary to maintain our seamless bond. I cannot let her leave me.

Vivian is the only woman who I would ever consider marrying; all others have and would always be second-best. So, as I twirl the platinum and diamond ring between my fingers, my plan to make her mine grows. I've had the 1920s Pavé masterpiece for over a month. I found it through an antiques dealer that specializes in rare, high-end estate jewelry, and when I saw it, I knew it belonged on her delicate hand. I've had to contain myself from slipping it on her finger ever since, but I wanted to wait until Christmas. Since the news of Raymond Michaels hit our radars, though, I've had the constant nagging need to not only propose, but also marry her and make her officially, legally mine. I refuse to let her slip from my grasp again. She is mine, and I need it to be known, now more than ever.

My plan is to ask the kids this evening for permission, and then follow through with asking her over a trip to the mountains in two weeks. I know I'm gambling a lot on them not saying anything, but I feel like our kids need to be included in this. I've asked Katie to keep all of the kids, and I've let Amanda in on my intentions. She was actually supportive instead of serving me my balls–a favorite pastime she picked up from Jen. I reserved a cabin in Telluride for the weekend, and I have planned a romantic getaway for the occasion, which Vivian has no clue about.

When my phone buzzes, alerting me of an incoming message, I gently slide the miniature iceberg back into its box for safekeeping, and tuck it into my jacket pocket. Checking the screen, I see my lovely lady's name and picture appear, provoking a grin I can't even try to hide.

> **Vivian:** Be there in 20 minutes, packing overnight bags now.
>
> **Me:** Drive careful, but hurry. U should never leave my house, my love, and then I would never have to wait.
>
> **Vivian:** Lol. Good luck with that, my dear sir. I have to come up for air at some point. See you soon!
>
> **Brook:** Not soon enough, Clover.
>
> **Vivian:** ☺

I lay my phone on my dresser and call out to Grace. She has been in her room, doing the typical magical princess girl-shit that I pretend to not enjoy. If anyone ever caught me wearing the tiara and feather boa that she demands that I wear during our tea parties, I would never live it down. Lakin already thinks that I've become pussified since I started dating Vivian; I couldn't imagine the ration of shit that he would heap upon me for playing dress-up as well.

Decked out head-to-toe in Cinderella garb stands my three-foot-tall raven-haired beauty queen. Tapping her foot, she makes it obvious that I've interrupted something vitally important in the kingdom of Grace. I attempt to hide my amusement, which only serves to agitate my princess.

"What's so funny, Daddy? The prince was just about to rescue my Barbie."

I grab her and tickle her sides until her attitude melts into fits of laughter. "Really, is that right?" I say, continuing my attack.

She screams in between giggles, and I finally release her. Grace immediately straightens her gown, and I pick up the tiara that fell to the ground and place it on her head in a very majestic manner that I know she appreciates.

"There, perfect, Princess Grace," I add with an extra bow.

"You're so silly, Daddy. What's up? I really need to go help Barbie."

I sit down on my bed and pull her onto my lap. "I needed to talk to you about something important before everybody gets here. Besides, I'm sure Barbie can fend for herself. I saw her moves in Toy Story, and she can kick some butt."

That earns me a heart-melting grin that throws my train of thought off for a second. I'm nervous about her reaction. I need her approval, just as much as I need Blake and Emma's for my plan to move forward. This little girl is my absolute world. With all of the women that I have used as fillers, Grace has been my constant, and soon I will turn her world upside-down by almost tripling the size of our little family.

"Lovebug, how would you feel if Vivian, Blake, and Emma lived here with us?"

"Like our sleepovers?" she asks as she begins to twist my tie around her tiny fingers.

"Well, kind of, but instead of it being sometimes, they would be here all the time. Emma and Blake would be your new brother and sister."

Grace drops my tie and looks up at me, her eyes huge and tears building in them. "You mean, Vivian would be my mommy?"

"Would that be okay with you?"

"I've never had a mommy; I would love for Vivian to be my mommy," she says excitedly, but then her enthusiasm dwindles, and she begins to fiddle with my tie again.

I nudge her chin upward. "What's the matter, baby?"

"It's just, my own mommy didn't stay; do you think Vivian would really want me?" I see the quiver in her lip, and I realize just how much I've fallen short. No matter how hard I've tried, nothing can replace a mother, and my little girl has felt the consequences of those actions. It tears at my heart, and I want more than anything to make this right for her.

"Oh, Lovebug, the woman that had you is not a real mommy." I kiss her forehead and begin to stroke her silky hair as I try to ease her heartache. "Mommies do the things that Vivian does for Emma and Blake; they take care of their babies. The woman that had you isn't your mommy, sweetheart. She is the woman who agreed to give me the best gift I've ever received. You. But I promise, Grace, Vivian would love to be your mommy, because she wants to take care of you forever."

"You promise?" she asks; her voice is hopeful once more.

"Yes, baby. Vivian adores you, and she would love to be your mommy. But I don't want to ask them to be a part of our family unless you want them to be. It has to be okay with you."

"Are you gonna give her a pretty ring?" her eyes slide sideways, peering just over her lids like she is prepared to interrogate me. Her tiny little teeth reveal themselves past her cherry red lips, and I chuckle at her attempt to grill me.

"Yes, I bought her a ring." I pull it out of my jacket pocket and crack open the box; the light reflects off the stone, causing glimmers of white sparkles to bounce around the room. Grace inhales sharply and her eyes widen at the sight.

"It's so sparkly!" she squeals. "She is gonna love it."

"I hope so," I say as she runs her pointer finger across the solitaire and down the band, examining each stone.

"Oh yes, she will; it's so pretty. Will you buy me one, Daddy? My birthday is coming up, or maybe Santa could bring me one."

"No, honey, these rings are special. When you are old, like forty, you will fall in love with a boy, and if I like him, I'll let him buy you a ring like this."

Grace backs away scowling, her nose scrunches in disgust. "No way, boys are gross!" she insists. "They fart all the time and play with bugs. One boy in my class picks his nose and eats it. No, Daddy, I don't want to fall in love and get a ring from a boy."

I stand and pat her on the head, thankful for her epiphany about the opposite sex. "Just keep thinking boys are nasty and we will be just fine, kiddo." I laugh as I snap the box shut and place it back in its protective spot. "Come on, munchkin, they will be here soon; let's get everything ready. And not a word about our conversation; this is supposed to be a special surprise. You can't tell Blake or Emma, not even Katie, and especially not Vivian. Can you do that?"

"I pinky promise," she says as she holds out her petite pinky for me to seal the oath.

"Okay, pinky promise. Now let's get downstairs."

VIVIAN

The second we pile through his front door, I can tell that something is off about Brooks. He seems nervous and jittery, he's fumbling with his words, and he's constantly rubbing his hands on his pants. I've asked him several times if he was feeling sick, but he reassures me that he is fine. I would push him more if it wasn't for Grace, who has been glued to my side since our arrival. If she isn't upset, then I figure that whatever is bothering Brooks must not be that big of an issue.

I never imagined when I saw Brooks again that he would have a child, nor did I ever think that I could be someone's stepmother, but Grace is truly something special. She is sweet and funny, but has these feisty moments laced with attitude and spunk. She is the type of girl that forces a smile on your face no matter the situation. She is the most perfect little girl, and I have fallen in love with her, and if Brooks ever did ask me to marry him, I would be proud to call her my daughter. Blake and Emma both adore her, they and have taken her in as not only a friend, but like a sibling. Seeing the three of them together warms my heart and makes me hopeful about what our future could be like.

I can hear the three of them playing outside from the kitchen where I'm working on dinner. Their giggles filter into the house, creating a hum that's like soothing music to my ears. After the year that we've had, my children are truly happy, and it feels so good to have found that place. I slide the pan full of burritos I had been working on into the oven, when Brooks' footsteps break through the reverberating stream of laughter.

I turn around to see Brooks cross the kitchen, his usual confident demeanor slightly back into place; his illness or anxiety or whatever he had going on seems to be lessening. "Well hello, handsome, you look like you're feeling better."

He wipes his brow, but then smiles. "Yeah, I'm fine, really. Do you need any help in here with dinner?" he asks as he leans against the island worktop.

I hover over the opposite side of the island, reaching in until my lips find his. I give him a chaste but heartening kiss, one that signals my devotion, and that screams reassurance. I slowly move back to my side of the countertop and entangle my fingers with his, which are clawing into the granite. "I've got everything under control in here; why don't you relax? You seem wound tight tonight. Is everything going well at work?"

He tilts his head to the side incredulously. "Work?" he laughs. "Work is fine; we actually just closed a multi-million dollar deal this week, and I was thinking of asking Amanda to do some of the advertising and public relations with the project."

"She's been very busy, but I'm sure she would be interested." I pause for a moment, trying desperately to see into the eyes of the man before me. I attempt to read what's plaguing him.

Brooks steps around the corner and draws me to him, his firm arms winding around my waist. "I know I seem a little off, but I promise, there isn't anything wrong. I'm planning a surprise for you and the kids, and I'm just a little nervous that I won't be able to arrange everything, but I promise there is nothing wrong, all right?"

I let my eyes penetrate his crystal blue irises, looking for any ounce of deceit, but there is nothing evident. I relax into his arms and sigh. "Okay, but if something was wrong, you would tell me, right?"

"Of course, I don't want to ever keep things from you, if I can help it," he says as he bends down to kiss my lips. My tension releases and I melt into his arms. He finally pulls away, but I follow his lips, searching for more contact. He laughs and plants a soft kiss on my forehead before breaking away completely.

"I'm going to go outside with the kids; I need to talk to them about something. Holler out if you need me for anything." He grabs my waist once more and yanks me towards him, causing me to stumble into him. "I need a little more of you before I go," he whispers in my ear before crashing down on my lips.

The gentle, soft Brooks is gone, replaced with my urgent and greedy man. He took everything that I was willing to give and still searched for more. Chaste and overpowering, when he finally pulled away and walked out the backdoor like nothing had occurred, I was left fighting to catch my breath, my lips tingling and swollen, my stomach's butterflies in hyper speed. The man could make me go from zero to one hundred in a matter of seconds with only a look, and damn if I didn't love him for it.

I slowly make my way to the fridge, my wobbly legs struggling to aid in the task. Gathering the tomatoes and lettuce to garnish our Mexican feast, I take them to the sink to prep them, but my actions are halted when I see Brooks with the children outside. I watch out the window at my boys playing catch with a football, and the girls standing to the side cheering them on. I can't help but smile at the thought of how this really could be our life if we took the next steps forward.

I know I really love Brooks, and I can see a future with him but, there are still unanswered questions for me—questions that I have been too afraid to ask. I have never pried about what happened between us ten years ago. He's never told me why he not only led me to believe that he cheated, but then left school completely. At the end of the semester, I assumed he transferred, and I had heard that it was to the University of Northern Colorado, which was only a town away in Greeley, but those were only rumors.

Not discussing it and not revealing the old secrets has allowed my mind to run rampant as to why he would do it. Thoughts of a drug problem and Brooks checking into a rehab center were at the top of the list. However, when I really think back, I did not see any signs of drug use. He acted strange towards the end, but nothing that led me to believe he was doing drugs.

I desperately want to let it go, pretend that it does not matter. I know I have already forgiven him for his actions, and I know he was trying to protect me from whatever it was he was hiding. No matter how hard I try, though, the thoughts of what could have caused his extreme behavior nags at my brain like nails on a chalkboard. It's preventing me from completely wanting to take the next step. He says the issues of the past are gone, but what worries me more is that he's never taken it upon himself to explain what happened. Maybe I'm overreacting, and maybe I'm acting too much like an emotional girl, or maybe the foreboding feeling I have about the situation should push me to be strong enough to ask him. More than anything, I need him to tell me on his own accord. I don't want to have to ask; I want him to want to tell me.

I look out the window once more while I shake the vegetables dry from the thorough rinsing I had given them. My worries ease as

I glance out at the sight of Brooks huddled in a circle with all three kids. The way that he is with them tugs at my heart, he has stepped in to fill the hole that Will left behind. No matter what he's hiding, I'll still always be grateful for how he treats my children. He has taken them in like his own, loving them no different than Grace.

It is almost unbearably cold outside this afternoon. While the sun is still out providing slight warmth, a cold front has made its way through the state in preparation for a wintery Thanksgiving. The evergreens are the only trees with needles or leaves left on them, and other than the occasional deer you might see on Brooks' property, wildlife was pretty scarce. The chill is taking effect, and Brooks attempts to warm the girls by wrapping his arms around them both. They are all bundled in coats and hats, but Grace's wide grin can still be spotted from under the mountain of fleece.

All three are intently listening to whatever story Brooks is sharing with them, but Grace's smirk leads me to believe that she knows the tale already. I finally see Blake nod and Emma throw her arms around Brooks, knocking him back into the dead dry grass.

Feeling like I'm eavesdropping on a special moment, I turn from the window to begin chopping the vegetables on the cutting board laid out on the center island. Slicing my way through a tomato, I continue my assault on the lettuce, careful not to chop off a finger. I'm not exactly handy with a knife. The laughter from outside fills the atmosphere once more and I can't help but feel the warmth of the situation, even with the glitches that it contains.

Bringing my knife up to settle on the top of the head of lettuce, my blade stops when the sound of the doorbell reverberates through the house. I consider stepping outside to let Brooks know, but I decide not to interrupt the special time he's having. So instead, I set the butcher knife down carefully on the counter and head towards the front door.

I brush off any wayward food from my shirt, and wipe my hands on my jeans before reaching for the latches on the door. The solid oak door is heavy, and I have to use effort to even open it. Standing on the steps is Brooks, thirty years from now. The tall man before me is slim and has a haggard appearance, but the resemblance is undeniable; he without a doubt is related to Brooks. The dark hair that has sprinkles of white mixed throughout, and the same sapphire eyes that I love are peering back at me. I feel like

I should know who he is; he seems familiar to me, but I can't place him.

He looks nervous, shifting from one foot to the next, his hands deep in his pockets. "I'm sorry to bother you, miss," he says, almost stuttering the words.

"Oh, no worries at all, sir, what can I help you with?" I ask. I try to alleviate some of his apprehension.

"Um, I believe my son lives here, Brooks Ryan. I was hoping to speak with him."

Brooks has never shared much of his family dynamic with me, and this situation has caught me off guard. But I try to hide my confusion. I know that his mother and stepfather raised him, but I have never met either of them; Lakin is the only family member that I've ever met. I really have no idea whether this possible reunion will be a happy one or not. I haven't talked to Brooks about the situation surrounding his real father since college.

I swallow down the hesitation that is settling in my stomach like a pile of rocks. Giving the tired man before me one more once-over, I hold the door open further and ask him to come inside. "Please, let me take your jacket. Can I offer you anything to drink before I go get Brooks?" I ask closing the door.

"No thank you, I'm just hoping to speak with him," he says, handing over his dingy blue coat that's lined with wool; it's obviously warm, but has definitely seen better days. The rest of his clothes look relatively new, dark jeans and a green flannel button down shirt. I get the feeling that this is his version of dressy and he's gone to the trouble for just this occasion.

I hang his jacket on the coat hooks in the entry hallway and lead him into the living room. I look over my shoulder to ask if Brooks was expecting him.

"No, miss, I haven't seen him in many years, and I've tried contacting him recently, but I could never reach him. I thought my only chance would be to show up here. I don't want to cause any problems; I just wanted to see him." His voice tapers off at the end; his gait slouched in defeat. I don't know why they don't have a relationship, and it's not my place to meddle, but in this moment, I feel pity for both of them to have missed out on the bond that a son shares with his father.

I gesture for him to take a seat on the couch, and he obliges. I stay standing, ready to gather everyone from outside. Dinner has to be close to being ready, so I'll keep the kids in the kitchen with me while Brooks and his dad discuss whatever he came here for. I turn to leave, realizing that I hadn't even asked him his name. I face him once more.

"I'm sorry; I've completely lost my manners," I say, reaching for his hand. "My name is Vivian; I don't believe I caught yours."

He smiles at me and lets his hand meet mine. "Nice to meet you; my name is Raymond. Raymond Michaels."

As the name that has been embedded in my mind my entire life rolls off his tongue, I feel my body go completely rigid. Everything clicks into place as images of the mug shots, police line-up, and evidence photos flood my mind. He's older and rougher around the edges, but I can now see the man from those photos in the man sitting before me. Every bit of my air is knocked out of my lungs, and I can feel the color drain from my face. The knots in my stomach feel like boulders weighing me down, and I try to hold myself up, but my shaky legs give out and I stumble backwards, hitting the arm of the couch, gripping it to steady myself.

Over the last month, I had given a lot of thought to this moment. What would I do if I ever came in contact with this man? What would I have the courage to say? I would pride myself on keeping my emotions in check. But with the realization that the monster of my childhood is not only in Brooks' house, but is also his father, all of the bravery dissipates and I feel the overwhelming need to flee.

Raymond begins to stand, sensing my discomfort. "Vivian, are you all right; are you ill?" he asks, taking a step forward.

My knuckles are white, the upholstery straining under my vice-like grip. I try to compose myself by taking a deep breath. I move quickly before he can close any more of the distance between us. "I'm fine, just got a little dizzy. Let me go get Brooks for you."

"Thank you, dear, it really was nice to meet you. You seem lovely."

I simply nod; any words I have saved for this man fail to make it past my lips. I turn and rush into the kitchen. Without checking dinner, I shut off the oven and then open the backdoor.

"Brooks, you need to come inside; you have a visitor waiting for you. Kids, come on in; we need to go home." I try to yell, but my voice is strained by the tears I'm keeping at bay.

Everyone turns to look at me in confusion. "Who could possibly be here?" Brooks says as the kids groan. "Do we really have to leave? We haven't even gotten to eat dinner, and Brooks has a big surprise for you," Blake adds.

Brooks gives him a stern look that relays the message, 'say one more word and you'll regret opening your mouth.' I ignore them all, solely focusing on my objective of getting the hell out of this house and away from Brooks, who intentionally kept this information from me. I feel betrayed–again–and this time I'm not sure if I can forgive him.

"What's going on? Who's here, Viv; why do you guys need to leave?" Brooks implores, stepping in the direction of the house.

My emotions are hanging on by a thread, and when the final fiber breaks, my composure melts away. "Stop asking questions!" I shout. "Blake and Emma, get in this house; we need to leave *now*." The children startle at my outburst, but Brooks glides towards me. He captures the backs of my arms just as a sob breaks free, and I quickly cover it with the back of my hand. I feel his eyes roaming my face, looking for an explanation, but I refuse to let my eyes meet his.

"Please," he murmurs. "What's going on?" The pleading in his voice feels like sandpaper scraping against my skin. I push away from him, out of the arms that have made me feel safe; away from the man that I love that has once again broken my heart.

The children move past us and into the kitchen; once they are beyond earshot, I finally make eye contact with Brooks. "I think you know why I'm leaving." I try to be strong and confident with each word, but as the sentence tumbles from my lips, my voice sounds like a mere whisper.

His eyes widen when he realizes I've discovered his secret. He takes a step forward, trying in vain to reach for me once again. "No, please no!" he says as I move away from his grasp. "Please, let me explain; please don't go."

Swallowing down every bit of hesitation, I turn away from my defeated man. "I'll take Grace with me; she doesn't need to be here right now. I'll call Katie and have her pick her up in the morning."

I glance over my shoulder to see Brooks' head down, his beaten posture slouched. He slightly nods, but I don't move right away. I stand still, just looking at him for a moment, contemplating the gravity of the situation. I feel myself questioning my decision to leave him, to walk out the door. Can I really walk away? The reasons for his decade-long betrayal seep into my mind. Did he do it because of his love for me, or because of his fear of me not understanding?

Brooks brings his hands to his face, rubbing his palms harshly across his evening stubble. When he finally looks up to see me still standing there, my mind snaps back into the present. Finding my voice, steady and strong, I address him once last time. "When the lies run, Brooks, I hope the truth finally sets you free." Before he can speak, I turn on my heel, briskly leaving the kitchen.

Brooks doesn't follow me, and I don't bother going back into the living room to give my goodbyes. I meet the kids at the door where all three have congregated. I let Grace know she's staying at our house instead, and we all leave. It's not until I hear the click of the door behind me that I finally let my tears run down my cheeks. I walk away from the house, believing I'm walking away from love.

BROOKS

I hear the slam of the front door, leaving a silence throughout the house that blows a hole into my heart, exploding it into a million little pieces. I expected a desolate sadness, or even numbness to overtake my body; instead I feel a boiling anger flow through my veins, heating my skin and causing my heart to pound out of my chest.

I pace the kitchen, trying to calm down from the shaking tremors that are wracking my body. Realizing that nothing is easing my torment, I travel towards the living room where my demons await. I have been running from this exact situation since I found out about my true identity, and I know there isn't a damn thing that will change until I finally face the fact that this man is my father, and his sins have been what have kept me from the only woman that I've ever loved.

I walk through the threshold and see my same eyes peer back at me. My father looks worn, looks beaten, and I can't help but think that this could be me if I don't fix this. Alone, a pathetic existence that regrets every fucking moment of their life; I can't let that be me. As much as I want to feel bad for him, all I feel is disdain and rage. As much as I know that he and I are both to blame for Vivian leaving, I'm not ready to accept my role just yet.

"Did everyone leave on my account?" Raymond asks. I refuse to acknowledge that this man is my father.

"Yes," I snarl. "What the fuck are you doing here?" I haven't moved any closer to him, nor has he moved from his station on the couch, both of us unsure how to proceed. My hands are firmly stuffed into my pockets, but my eyes are narrowed directly at his. If he had any question whether I would warmly receive him into my house, he surely knows the answer by now.

"I'm sorry to interrupt your evening, son, I…" My hands fly out of my pockets, and before I realize that I'm even moving, I'm across the room and picking him up off the couch by the collar of his shirt. Slamming him into the nearest wall, I hear his head thud against the sheetrock. I hold him still, letting my forearm forcefully meet his throat. I feel his Adam's apple wobble under my grip. His eyes widen, and as he struggles for breath, his hands wrap around my arm to create a wedge. I don't loosen my grip; I slam him harder into the wall.

"I'm not your son. You haven't earned the title of Father. Everything you do turns to shit, and I don't want anything to do with you. I considered it ten years ago, and I lost everything because of that decision. I will not make the same mistake twice. Not when I'm so close to having everything I've ever wanted. And at no point were *you* ever part of that equation."

Raymond stops struggling against my hold, and I relax my arm. "I'm sorry to have come here; I will never bother you again." His voice is raspy and ragged; his eyes tell me he understands that I want nothing from him.

I let go of him, stumbling away, realizing that in this moment, I'm no better than he is. I feel my anger fade from my body, and remorse fills in the voids. After adjusting his rumpled clothing, he turns to leave, but I reach out, grabbing his elbow to stop him.

"Please, sit down, I need to you to understand this, understand me," I tell him without meeting his eyes. I hear him sigh, but he does what I ask and sits on the couch.

I find myself pacing in front of him. My mind is swirling with the words to tell him; everything is jumbled, and every coherent, intelligent thought has escaped me. So many times I have started to think about what I would tell him when this moment came, because I knew it would eventually; I just never counted on Vivian being in my life when he and I would meet again. Not only did I walk away from Vivian ten years ago, I left Raymond as well. I left him in that jail to rot, hoping that I could escape from this situation; it was naïve of me, and I'm even more stupid now for letting it play out the way it has. I should have been honest from the very beginning; I should have contacted him when he was released to talk with him, instead of waiting for this surprise appearance. I should have told Vivian so much sooner. But I was a fucking coward, and now I have a big shitty mess to clean up, and I don't care if it fucking kills me—I will clean it up.

"Look," I say as I sit across from him in the recliner, "I didn't mean to explode on you the way I did..."

"No, you don't need to apologize; I understand. I showed up unexpected after a lot of years of no contact at all. We didn't leave our relationship on good terms the last time we spoke, so I should have known better."

"Why, then? Why are you here?" I ask pinning him with the nastiest glare I can muster. I automatically assume my swindling father is once again in trouble and here for no other reason than money. I don't know a whole lot about this man, but from what little I do know, he was always after the quick buck, the next high, even if it was at the expense of those he cared about, including my mother and me. They never married, thank God, but he was also never in my life. No visits, Christmas cards, child support—I didn't even have his last name. It wasn't until I turned eighteen that the letters started, but even then I didn't realize what he had really done. Not until I went to the courthouse with Vivian to view the records. That's when I decided to see him for the first and last time.

Feeling the heat of my stare, he looks down at his hands, which are laced and roughly being rubbed together. "I know that I was a shit father, and that you don't consider me anything more than a sperm donor that left you and your mom to fend for yourselves."

"How much? Is that why you're here now? You know I have money and you want some start-up funds for your new grand scheme? Money to stay out of my life?" The sarcasm drips from every word, and when he finally looks at me, I see that I've wounded him.

"I don't want your money," he stutters in a hushed tone. "I wanted the chance to get to know you, see the man you've become. I know it's hard to believe, but I'm not the same person that I was; I'm trying to be better. I'm not proud of who I was, the things that I did, but I'm trying to be an honorable man for the first time in my life. I want to make something of the last half of my life, something you or I won't be ashamed of."

Fuck. I had waited my entire life to hear these golden fucking words from this man, and now that I know who he is, I wish he was still the big piece of shit that I remember so I could just walk away, just like I did ten years ago. I don't want to get warm and fuzzy sharing the holidays with this man, but I don't want to hate him anymore either.

I hop up and begin pacing in front of him, my hand violently gliding through my mangled hair. My options, what to tell him, and Vivian all twist in my mind. Things are spinning out of control, and I refuse to lose it all again like I did last time I found myself in this position. I swore that this time I would choose Vivian. Even though she left, I will find some way to get her back, and having lunches and friendly phone calls with Raymond Michaels is not the way back to the life that I could have, the one I've been waiting for.

"Dammit, you don't understand; by allowing you in my life, I will lose everything. When we talked at the prison, I told you that I was in love with Vivian Donavan. I told you that I wanted to marry her, but that I was afraid what would happen if she found out how she and I were really connected, and that you are my father. What did you tell me?"

"I told you that if you really loved her, to walk away. Her knowing would only hurt her, and it would cause her even more pain to have to choose between you and the memory of her father."

"Fuck if I didn't; I followed your advice because I loved her more than I could ever love anything or anyone. I walked away; I made her believe that I didn't love her and then disappeared. It was the biggest mistake I've made until now, and I've regretted it every day since. I should have told her; she had the right to make the choice for herself."

Looking slightly perplexed, Raymond rubs his brow. "So what does this have to do with you and me now?" he asks, which only enrages me.

"Who the fuck do you think you just met this evening?" I bark, stopping mid-step. "We ran into each other again a few months ago, and I've been lucky enough to have another chance to make things right. But I messed it up all over again."

"You never told her," he sighs. "Why? Don't you trust that she would pick you?"

"I was afraid of losing her. I wanted to tell her, but I couldn't risk losing her again." I allow my conquered body to fall onto the couch and slump into the side of the upholstered arm.

"Brooks?" he says, sliding toward the edge of his seat.

"Hmm?" My face is hidden in the crook of my arm, but I can hear him shuffle around.

"Vivian was the most polite, pleasant woman I've met in a long time. I could tell from the moment she spoke to me that she is forgiving and loving, and also, that she loves you. When she found out my name, she was surprised, but she never treated me any different. Her hurt didn't lie with my presence; it was in your deceit."

He stands from the couch, and I look up to meet his eyes. He was right; it wasn't him being here that really hurt her; it was me that hurt her all over again. It was me not being honest with her, not trusting that she would choose me.

"I know a lot about disappointing the ones you love; it's all I've ever been good at. I don't want that for you; it's a lonely existence. You need to figure out how to fix this, and if you think that my not being in the picture is a way to start..." Raymond strokes his grease stained fingers across his chin, letting the dusting of stubble rub the skin of his knuckles, and after a long pause, he finally finishes his speech. "Well, if you think it will help, then I will bow out. If you want me in your life, you can find me. I'll always be here if you're ready; if she's ready. But I won't pursue you anymore. I'm not letting you choose this time; I'm telling you to go get her."

I let out the breath I'd been holding, feeling the relief that his words bring me. "Thank you," is all I can muster.

"If she's what you really want, then you fight like hell for her, Brooks. My sins are not yours, and don't you think for one second that that beautiful girl doesn't know that."

He pats my knee as he passes by me, causing a smile to form on my face. The expression was a nice reprieve from the constant scowl I had been wearing for the last hour. "Good bye, Brooks."

"Bye, Ray."

I hear the door close behind him, and I'm left in solitude once again. This time though, instead of grieving over the woman I loved and lost, I devise a plan to win her back.

30

Friday Night

BROOKS

Her words play over and over again in my mind. She didn't want to see me, she didn't want to even look at me. All this time I had worried that it would be too much for her to handle, that she would refuse me, turn me away when she found out. That's exactly what happened. The thing that has my insides tangled though is that I'm not sure if it would have played out any differently had I told her the truth from the beginning.

I did the only thing I could think of to try to win her back. I tried to make her see that I was willing to put myself out there for her, and she didn't want anything to do with me. I hurt her so badly; who I am has hurt her, us, beyond repair.

Her words punctured my heart, and before I let myself bleed out all over the floor in front of her, I left as quickly as I could. As soon as I hit the door, though, my pace slowed, and for the last half hour I've been sitting in my car in the bar parking lot with the ignition running. I have no idea what to do or where to go next. Without Vivian in my life, I've lost all direction. Everything points toward her, toward our life together. The life I had before, filled with constant work and meaningless sex is not what I want anymore. But no matter how hard I try, I can't make her love me, make her want me, now that she knows who I am.

Picking up my cell, I call the only person I have in my life that would actually meet me at this hour, who would have no interest in lecturing me or fucking me. My list of friends is short, but Lakin is at the top of that list. He has always been there for me when I needed him, whether to listen, to kick my ass, or just get me drunk. Tonight called for the latter.

"Dude, what happened? I thought tonight was the big hoopla for Vivian?"

Niiiiice, not even a hello. Doesn't that give you a warm fuzzy feeling inside? "Yeah, it didn't go well; I'm still here, just in the parking lot."

"You know, if you sit there long enough, people will call the cops and tell them that there is a creepy stalker-like guy in the parking lot waiting to attack women. Man, I would hate to see you on the news."

I roll my eyes at his attempt to lighten the situation, but his humor does nothing for my mood. "Lakin, I need to let off steam, get drunk, wallow in my fucking misery right now—not joke about what a piece of shit I am. Are you in or out?"

"You know I'm in. Meet me at The Cruise Room in twenty minutes."

I really wasn't in the mood for Cruise, but if he was willing to hang out with my sorry ass, I would let him pick the place. The Cruise Room is a high-class martini bar styled in a 1930s art deco décor, even the waitresses wear 1930s attire. Its elegant crimson tapestries have earned the establishment the nickname The Red Room. It's a great place to enjoy a quiet drink with friends, and socialize—a.k.a. pick up professional women looking for an evening to release the tension of the stressful workday. It is not the place to get trashed and make a fool of yourself as pity swallows you alive, which is the situation I'm aiming for.

"You sure about Red Room tonight?" I ask. "I was thinking tequila, and a possible drunk and disorderly charge, not martinis and cougar prowls."

"Nice, smartass, you need a distraction. I'm pretty sure it doesn't matter what kind. See you in a few."

When I arrive at the bar inside the Oxford Hotel, Lakin is perched on a cream-colored leather barstool and is leaning on the black marble bar top. The red lighting provides an ambiance of elegance. It has a romantic tone of an era in the past, and stepping through the door is like transporting back to the time of prohibition. Lakin doesn't notice me as I approach. The bar is packed with men in their high-dollar Armani suits and women in their flashy designer dresses and heels. I feel the ladies' eyes on me as I pass by them, and a few months ago, I would have obliged their flirtations, but not anymore. I'm no longer interested in the easy one-night-stand fucks. All I want is Vivian.

I slide up next to my brother, taking in the row of liquor bottles lined up behind the bar, analyzing which one would get me to the state of numbness that I desire the fastest. When the bartender steps up to us, providing a slight head nod to ask what we would like to order, I begin to open my mouth to ask for a Johnny Walker Black, but Lakin speaks over me.

"He'll have a Jack and Coke, please." He glares at me from the corner of his eye, challenging me to change my order.

"Fine, but if you're going to order for me like an arrogant asshole, then you can pay for my drinks, too. Just remember, I'm not putting out, though," I tease.

"Well, I'm glad you haven't lost your sense of humor," he says, throwing down his credit card for the bartender.

I huff, and we wait in silence for my drink. I signal the bartender to wait a second while I down the drink, and then ask for another.

Lakin laughs, "You're a fucking mess, man. I was sure that your stunt tonight would have worked. You must have really screwed it up with her."

"You're a fuck-stick, Lakin, you know that?" I lightly punch him in the arm. He shields himself and laughs even harder.

"Okay, okay, well here then." He holds up his glass to toast. "Here's to the king bachelor, drinking himself into oblivion. Welcome back to the single life, buddy. What better place to start than The Red Room, brother?"

We clink our drinks together and take a gulp, but I say nothing about his comment. I have no intention of going down the same path of my previous single life. Looking back, it's not one that I'm proud of; I was the guy that I would want Grace to stay far away from.

We sit in silence for another few minutes before the thing that I was hoping to avoid happens. Two beautiful women surround Lakin and me at the bar. They are both gorgeous, and I'm fairly certain that with a little effort I could have my choice of either. A brunette takes a seat next to my brother, but the leggy blonde squeezes in between us, confidence and sex appeal oozing out of her. Her breasts are jacked up to the sky from Victoria's latest secret, and if she's not careful, everyone here will be able to see if

Spanx are keeping her ass from jiggling, or if a thong and lunges were the order of the day.

"Well hello, ladies, how are you this evening? Can we buy you a drink?" Lakin's eyes roam the body of the woman next to him; he's clearly interested in what could be in store for him this evening.

"We both would be up for a Screaming Orgasm, if you're offering," the blonde whispers in my ear as she begins to rub my forearm that's resting on the cool marble. Before Vivian, I would already have her spread out and under me in a room upstairs or pounding into her up against a bathroom stall. But now, I feel nothing. She doesn't smell like vanilla and jasmine, she doesn't feel like smooth rose petals, and her hair is not the fiery auburn that I love. No, she is everything Vivian isn't; this girl is in-your-face and overdone. She's the typical trophy wife material that would spend your money and then silence you with a blowjob. Exactly what I don't need or want.

Lakin orders the girls' drinks, and I attempt to slide my arm away from the talons of the blonde. She releases my arm, but then moves lower to my thigh. Her perusal up the inside of my leg towards my balls has me adjusting in my seat; uncomfortable with the situation is putting it lightly. I grab her hand and place it back onto the bar top.

She shoots me a look of displeasure. Yep, this one is not used to being rejected, and escaping the web she's weaving around me will not be easy. "Come on, let's go dance. You look like you need to loosen up," she coos.

"No, I'm good where I'm at, but thanks," I say, turning my attention back to my drink. I can see her turning to Lakin for help, and he indulges her by pushing me on my chair.

"Yeah, bro, you need to loosen up. It's not polite to refuse a lady when she requests a dance." His smirk slithers across his face. I need to remember to stay over at his apartment so I can smother him in his sleep; the shithead will pay for this.

I reluctantly shove off my stool and allow her to lead me out to an open area. There is no real dance floor, and the jukebox is meant to provide an ambiance, not dance music. As soon as she finds the spot she likes, she turns to me and wraps her arms around my neck, pulling me closer to her.

Her overwhelming scent of perfume and hair products almost make me gag, and her obviously fake boobs press into my chest, distracting me when she asks for my name.

"Feeling something you like?" she asks, weaving her fingers through my hair, snapping my attention back to her and the question she asked. "I said my name is Nicole, but my friends like to call me Nikki. What's yours, handsome?" She giggles.

"Sorry, it's been a long night; my name is Brooks." I move away from her a bit to give myself a little room to breathe.

Not taking the hint, Nikki moves in closer, rubbing her hands up my back under my suit jacket. I make a mental note to burn this suit when I get home. I don't care that it costs more than most people's paychecks; I would never get her smell out of it.

"Don't be so shy, Brooks. I won't bite," she breathes into my ear. "Well, unless you're into that kind of thing," she adds, and then licks the side of my neck.

I grab her arms and push her away as quickly as I can. This is heading out of the safe-zone, and I don't want anything to do with this girl. "Look, Nikki, you're an attractive girl, but I'm not interested. I'm here to have a drink and that's it. I'm not looking for any company."

Not giving up so easily, she throws me a curve by grabbing and massaging my dick. "Really?" she spits out. "I think your cock didn't get the message, because he clearly wants company."

I carefully remove her hand. My words, however, are not so delicate. She has crossed a line and I no longer care about her feelings. "Yes, maybe he does want company, but my cock never ventures into areas that will leave him with something extra that only a medical professional can get rid of…but thanks for the offer."

I hastily turn away from her stunned, disgruntled face and walk back to Lakin. He instantly notices my dismay and provides the similar perplexed look that I left behind on the dance floor. He leans around me, and I'm sure he sees one pissed off Nikki behind me.

"What the fuck, man?" he growls. "That chick was hot; what did you do? You asked for a distraction, and I'm trying to provide you with one."

I pat him on the shoulder in an attempt to cool his flaring temper. I know that by my rejection of Nikki, his evening with slutty brunette will now crash and burn. "I asked you to get me drunk, not laid, Lake. Besides, I've spent my entire adult life trying to avoid gonorrhea; I don't have any desire to have it now."

"Since when do you care if it's alcohol or pussy that brightens your night, Brooks?"

I throw a hundred dollar bill on the bar and adjust the sleeves on my jacket. "You're right; I never cared before. Now I care. I appreciate your effort, but I'm just not interested. Please stay, enjoy your evening, but I'm going to head home."

I don't let him try to talk me into staying or offer to come with me. I shuffle past Nikki, who has found her next target for the evening, and from the looks of it, the bloke she's selected will have no problem accepting her advances.

As quickly as I can, I drive home, aching to just collapse onto my bed. Everyone is sleeping, and I don't want to disturb anyone. I strip down to my boxer briefs and climb under the duvet. I stare at my phone, willing it to show a text or missed call from Vivian, but there's nothing. She has nothing that she wants to say to me. She wants nothing to do with me.

I bring up the keyboard and type the only words that I want her to remember, the only words that I have to say to her. My thumb hovers over the send button, but I stall, taking a deep breath, hesitating even more. Before I can change my mind, I hit send, turn off the lamp, and roll under my blankets, hoping that sleep will help to erase the heartache that has consumed me.

31

Friday Morning

VIVIAN

Nauseous. Every time I get my stomach under control, Brooks will call or text or the kids will ask if I'm getting excited for Brook's surprise, and the churning will return. The first snow of the season has finally moved in, and the backyard looks similar to how my heart feels–empty, blank, cold, and sad. For the last week, I've done well avoiding him, but it's been exhausting. I miss him. I don't know if that makes me weak, or stupid, or just in love, but after everything, I still just miss him.

I've tried diving into writing assignments to distract myself, but every article I try to write ends up turning into a soapbox about honesty, or about whether or not love is enough. Well, you get the idea, and needless to say, it had nothing to do with the product that I was supposed to be reviewing, and none of it would impress my editor.

I've made it to Friday, and I'm supposed to be having a girls' night out, but I'm not in the mood to drink and then cry in public, because I know that is what the night will turn into. Amanda has been home for a few days, but I haven't told her anything about Brooks, just that he and I were going to slow things down and spend a little time apart. I'm having a hard time admitting to myself, let alone anyone else, that it might be completely over.

The pulsing of my phone pulls me from my pit of misery. I slowly peek at the screen, hoping that it's not from Brooks, again. When I see Jen's name appear in the message box, I'm relieved but surprisingly disappointed too.

Jen: I hope u drank plenty of
water today. Us bitches are
going 2 tear it up tonight!!
Plus I have an extra surprise 4
u!

I let out a groan. Just as I suspected, a liquored-up evening of
embarrassing body bouncing that will ultimately end with me
sobbing about how Brooks has let me down again. If there's
enough tequila involved throughout the evening, it might even
include a cab ride to Brooks' house so Jen can skewer his balls. She
always follows through.

Me: I don't really feel like it
tonight, rain check.

Jen: Oh, hell no! Not
happening…I will be over at 5.
Get ur ass in the shower. I can
smell ur skank from here.

I scrunch my nose at the word skank as my eyes pass over it. I
love her to death, but damn if she isn't the most uncouth 28-year-
old professional woman I know.

Me: OMG, did you just really
call me skanky! I am a mom for
fuck's sake.

Jen: What can I say? I'm a
straight shooter lol. JK. Start
getting ready. I'll be over
soon. U R GOING!

Me: Grrrr

Jen: Shut it. I'll bring clothes
from the shoot today. Mom jeans
or yoga pants are not approved
attire for the evening. I'm
taking u somewhere fun tonight!

Me: Mom jeans? Really?

Jen: Well like u said, ur a mom
for fuck's sake. LMAO!

Me: Oh, sweet baby Jesus. Ttyl.

Jen: Bye muffin (without the
top) hehehe.

Letting out a giggle, I turn in my desk chair and toss my phone on my bed just as I hear the front door open. Amanda is home from picking up the kids from school, and their voices echo up the stairs. Raising my arms above my head, I stretch, letting my tired muscles burn. The stress of the situation is wearing on me. Maybe a girls' night would loosen the tension that's taking over my body.

After sliding on my slippers and adjusting my greasy–yes, I said greasy–ponytail, I adjust my sweatpants and tee shirt to go downstairs and greet the kids. Reflecting on my attire, maybe Jen had a point; I am one pathetic mess at the moment. She probably could smell me from the other side of the suburb. I smell my armpit, hoping for the scent of the deodorant that promised miracles. I pull away quickly from the detonation zone after catching the stench of my own wretched body odor. Yup, I'm an embarrassing disarray of a woman.

I spritz some body spray on, hoping to mask my obvious post-breakup meltdown, and then I head down the hall to find everyone. Just as I reach the top of the stairs, their conversation becomes clearer, forcing my body to halt. My feet refuse to take another step forward.

"So Brooks asked you guys for permission?" I hear Amanda ask.

"Yeah, he said he loves Mom and us, and wants us all to be a family. So he asked if it was okay if he married her," Blake answered.

I gasp, my hand flying to my mouth in disbelief. I knew we were serious; we both wanted to move forward. But after finding out the truth, I'm shocked that he would even consider making us a family without sharing his secret with me. It would have been a surprise, and I would struggle dealing with the ramifications, including what my family would say, but I would have never judged

227

him for it. I just wish he could have trusted me enough to know that.

"He showed us the ring and everything, Aunt Manda!" Emma squeals. "It's sooo pretty, and he said Grace and I will get to wear princess dresses and throw flowers at people."

"You mean you two get to be the flower girls," Amanda laughs.

"Yes!" she shouts. But then I hear Blake shush her.

"Quiet, it's a surprise, remember? Mom isn't supposed to find out. He's going to ask her next weekend when they go on a special trip. Then we can all talk about it. Okay, Em?"

"Okay, my lips are sealed." I picture her doing her special lip-zipper move and throwing away the key. She means well, but Emma has never been able to keep a secret. She is a blabbermouth in training. We can never tell her what anyone is getting for their birthday or Christmas because she always lets it slip.

Unable to hear any more of this gutting conversation, I try to make as much noise as possible as I march down the stairs so they'll quickly end their discussion.

True to her word, Jen shows up with her arms filled with dresses and accessories for our girls' night on the town. She pokes and prods, pins and fluffs until she feels I'm presentable. I feel like I'm doing an excellent job of masking my misery; hell, I'm used to it by now. For the last week, I would put on the 'everything is fine' show for Amanda and the kids, but as soon as they left, I would fall apart and spend the day soaking in my gloom.

However, as I sink onto the cool barstool at the bar she has dragged us all to, I see her glaring at me, and I know my façade has been discovered. I order a pink moscato, which surprisingly, Jen doesn't protest, but when she says nothing when Carly orders an ice water, I know some kind of inquisition is shooting my way.

Deflecting, I grab my drink and swing in my stool to look out to the sea of twenty-somethings chatting and laughing, letting off steam after what I imagine was a stressful work week. I only wish work was why I was tense.

"So, what is the surprise that you told me you just *had* to share with us, and was so important we all had to dress-up and come out for?" I ask as I click my four-inch, probably $400 heels together, which she brought over from her photo-shoot.

"You'll see soon, and by the way, I realize something is up with you, but you don't need to take it out on the shoes. Those are Manolo fucking Blahniks for Christ's sake; have some respect."

I stop my leg swinging and hold up my hands as a sign of surrender. "Sorry, I'm just anxious for your surprise," I lie.

"Seriously, what is going on, Jen? We've had this girls' night planned for a while, but I was thinking Sushi and a movie, maybe spice things up with a little Sake and some flirting with the Hibachi chef. I don't think anyone was thinking miniskirts, booze, and heels. So let us in on the big deal here."

Before she can answer, Jen lets out a bellowing screech that attracts the attention of all nearby patrons. I cover my ears, and then I watch as she sprints from our group toward the masses of people. People part as she approaches, until she finds her target, and is pulled into an embrace. I still can't see who is meant to be are fourth wheel for the evening, and Carly and I look to each other for the answer. We both come up blank until Jen pulls away from our mystery guest and begins walking back to us.

"Oh, my God, that is Campbell!" Carly shouts and runs towards Jen and our old roommate. She is bouncing up and down like a teenage girl who's just seen her favorite boy band member. Neither Jen nor Campbell joins in her bouncing; instead, they just grin and absorb her excitement.

I hop off my chair and follow her, happy to see my old friend, but nowhere near Carly's overabundance of enthusiasm. I haven't seen her since mine and Will's wedding, when the band that she was promoting played for the reception.

Cam's long black hair hits halfway down her back and her honey brown eyes make her pale skin even more pronounced. She is stunning; there is no other way to describe her. My Goth friend went and got all grown-up and gorgeous. She was always the girl that hung with the bands, wore torn, faded jeans, and the t-shirt of the band she was hanging with. Oddly enough, she never dated anyone in the bands, she just loved the music. And if she loved their sound, as she called it, then she promoted them like crazy. In college, she was constantly dragging us to shows and making us hand out show flyers around campus. Last time I heard, she was promoting and managing the publicity for several different bands.

I smile and start to say hello, but Campbell pulls me into her tightly and gives me a huge hug, which is very out of character for her. Growing up in foster care, Cam never had the affection most of us take for granted. She never shared stories with me about the different homes she had been in; but she did with Jen, and from what I came to understand was that things happened to her growing up, making her very uncomfortable with affection. So this hug is something to not take lightly.

"I'm sorry I couldn't be there for the funeral, Viv. I loved Will like a brother. He took care of all of us when we needed it." She whispers her sentiments low enough not to bring attention to the others, but her words sting my heart. I've moved on from the love that I lost, but the reminder still hurts, and it's not something I think I will ever fully get over.

"Thank you, Cam. We are doing okay. It took time, but I've been able to move on, and I can finally say that I'm all right. Thank you for that, though. Will was a good man, the best of men."

She pats my back, and we all turn to make our way back to our seats at the bar. We take our seats and immediately inundate Campbell with questions about what she has been doing, where she has been travelling, and what bands she's been with. She can barely keep up with our rapid fire.

"I can't believe you kept this a secret!" Carly shouts over the noise of the growing crowd, pointing at Jen like she might climb the bar.

"Cam's band is playing here, and I just found out like two days ago, so I thought it would be a fun surprise. Besides, it's not the only little-something in store for this evening."

"Well, I don't think anything can top Cam being here," I say, clinking my glass with Cam's.

"Surprise number two should be here anytime, so drink up ladies; this is going to be a group affair tonight!"

"Group affair?" Carly asks.

"Yeah, you didn't think you got dressed up for me, did you? I got you hot-to-trot for your men-folk. They should be here any minute. Amanda is watching everyone's children, even your little demonling, Carly. I'm getting my girls drunk and laid! Woohoo!" she yells.

My smile fades as her words sink in—Brooks has been invited out with us. I only hope that he has decided to stay away. The last thing I want is to see him tonight. I quickly plaster my fake smile into place, unwilling to call attention to my unease.

I glance over at Carly who is gleaming with anticipation. Apparently, this is one of the few date nights she and Jack have had in the two years since Olivia was born. I don't want to ruin her night, but I'm still angry at Brooks, and I don't think I could contain my anger like I did the last time I saw him. Her eyes light up and I follow her line of sight to see Jack come through the front doors. I feel myself holding my breath waiting to see Brooks just behind him, and relief washes over me when I see Jack is alone.

Just when I think I've caught my bearings, I hear the *tap, tap* on the microphone. Everyone in the bar directs their attention to the darkened stage, and my heart plummets into my stomach when I see the spotlights shine down on Brooks standing center stage, gripping onto the mic.

"I know you are all here to see Absolution, and they will be out in just a second to give you guys an awesome show, but they allowed me to steal the stage for a minute," Brooks announces, and the crowd greets him with groans and boos.

"There is someone special here tonight, and I've asked the band to sing a special song just for her." The drunken partygoers break into applause as I mumble curse words under my breath. I look to Jen, who is hardly able to contain her shit-eating grin, and then Carly, who has lost all focus and is making out with Jack like the sex-depraved parents I'm sure they are.

"You see, guys, I had the most amazing woman in the world, but I lost her. I lied to her, and hid something from her. I'm standing up here tonight to let her know I'm not running anymore. I'm not going anywhere this time. Vivian, I'm sorry for everything. You are my forever, and I meant every word of that. I only hope that you let me prove it."

Everyone erupts into cheers as he jumps off the stage and the band begins to play. The smooth guitar melody sweeps through the buzzing atmosphere. When the lead singer finally lets out the first notes of the hypnotic love song, the crowd screams and then sways with the rhythm of the music. I don't allow myself to be pulled into the soothing lyrics or overwhelming beats of the song. Instead, I focus on my embarrassment. Not only do my friends now know that something has happened between Brooks and me, he has presented our dirty laundry to every drunken patron of the bar. I'm sure every other girl in the world would be impressed and taken aback by the grand gesture. But as much as I love this man, I'm too hurt and pissed to care about this public announcement.

When the house lights darken, I lose Brooks in the crowd; I know he's headed my way, and my emotions are telling me to do so many different things, I feel like I'm being torn apart. The confusion on the faces of my friends does nothing to help my plagued psyche. All I know is I need to find Brooks before he finds me. I refuse to sit at a table for the duration of the evening with him pretending like his scene made everything better.

"What the fuck was that?" Jen asks as I hop off my barstool, scanning the crowd for Brooks.

Ignoring her question, I drain the last bit of my glass of wine and move away from the bar. "Stay here, I'll be back in a second."

I don't make it very far before I run into the strong, toned chest that I have spent many nights snuggled up against. He wraps his arms around me and kisses the crown of my head. I desperately want to melt into him, but I don't let myself. I have forever been that weak girl that didn't think she deserved this relationship, but I now know I deserve better than a relationship where honesty is not a priority. I can't just forget his betrayal and sweep this all under the rug.

I move out of his strong arms and step away. "Don't touch me."

"Vivian, give me a chance to explain everything. I pushed you away last time and it was such a huge mistake." I see the torment in his eyes pleading for forgiveness, but as much as I want to give it, I don't have the strength yet to overcome his betrayal.

"I can't right now, Brooks. This is not the time, nor the place for this conversation." I look around, noticing the crowd that was once focused on us has since gone back to their conversations; well, except for our friends, who are intently trying to listen to our confrontation. "I can't believe that you did this in front of everyone like this," I say in a loud, stern whisper as I duck my eyes away from our silent audience and back to Brooks. "I'm not ready to see you, Brooks, please just go."

A look of determination sweeps across his face, and I notice his hands ball into fists. "No. I'm not leaving. I realize that I hid from you; I know that I fucked things up not once, but twice." His voice begins to rise in decibel level with each word, and I feel the eyes around us begin to take notice of our situation. I feel my face heat up in both anger and embarrassment. Never have I ever had a public fight, and I feel that I am cornered into having one. I feel the tears stinging my eyes as I let them scan faces around the bar, the floor, the ceiling—any place other than Brooks' eyes.

"Look at me, Vivian," he shouts, bringing my attention to his sapphire orbs. "Every day I regret what I did to hurt you, but you are making the same mistake now. I can't be without you again. We belong together. Don't walk away from me, from us."

My blood boils with his insinuation that our separation is somehow my fault, and my temper rises to the surface. My hands shake, and my breathing hitches with words that are stuck in my constricting throat. When he reaches for me again, I unleash every emotion that I had been struggling to hold at bay.

"You fucking lied to me!" I scream, shoving him away from me. My face is streaked with tears, but this time I let them fall, the salty drops occasionally slipping into my mouth, the taste only serving as a reminder of the pain he has caused. "I let myself fall in love with you not once, but twice, and both times you proved to be disloyal." Finally gaining control of my voice, I step towards Brooks, jabbing my finger into his muscled chest. "You know what, Brooks? You're right. I did make a mistake in regard to you. My error is not in walking away from you now, it was with ever trusting you with my heart in the first place." Taking a deep breath, I close my eyes to avoid the hurt that I'm causing. I take a step back. "Please leave," I exhale.

I stand frozen, feet planted, eyes tightly shut. I feel Brooks kiss my forehead, and then nothing. I know before I open my eyes that I'm alone. My gut twists into knots when I open my eyes to see that Brooks did as I asked and left the bar.

I forcefully wipe the remainder of tears from my rosy cheeks and head to the bar. I bypass every questioning pair of eyes and head directly to the bartender, the only man here that I actually want to see. I knew this evening would end with liquor and tears; I just didn't figure on it happening so soon. The handsome young man behind the bar rushes to take my order, surprisingly remembering that I had ordered wine before.

"Another moscato, doll?" He pauses for a second, taking in my appearance and then shakes his head. "May I suggest something a little stronger?"

"Yes, please," I say, nodding while attempting to fix the smeared mascara that I'm sure is plastered and smudged under my eyes—waterproof, my ass.

The bartender turns to make my potent mystery concoction of future inebriated bliss, but pauses and turns back to the disheveled mess before him. "For what it's worth, he's obviously an ass," he says, leaning across the bar in my direction so that his words are only for me. "And let me add that you look like one hell of a woman, and any guy that has the balls to make you cry should have them removed."

I let out a half-snort half-laugh and pat his hand. "Thank you, I needed that. Remind me to introduce you to my friend Jen. I think you two would get along great. One of her favorite pastimes is to threaten to damage the jewels of every breathing man."

"Well, if it's warranted," he laughs before returning to my drink.

When he places the glass filled to the brim with electric green alcohol that looks like something out of Blake's Ninja Turtle movies in front of me, I chug it down without a word, letting the burn of it slide down my throat until the fire spreads through my chest. I cough and gasp for breath, and I fan myself, trying to ease the burn. I finally get myself under control and give him the signal for another.

"I think that should do the trick, love, but I figured you might want something else, so I made you something to chase it, but drink it slowly."

I grab the fruity-looking drink from the bar and take a sip. It is strong but delicious. I reach for my purse, but he reaches for my hand. "This was on me. I'll just call it my good deed for the day," he says with a smile.

"Thank you," I say, and when he nods and turns away from me, I slip a twenty across the bar and under his order book. I figure the kid brightened my dreary night; I can at least leave him a decent tip. I take one last guzzle of my frilly drink and head toward the firing squad waiting for me.

Deer in headlights...that is the best way to describe the expressions staring back at me. I throw myself down onto the empty chair and glance around the table at a sea of purely-dumbfounded gazes. To their credit, they remain silent, letting me down more of my liquid courage before having to address our overly curious group.

I see Jen's leg bouncing violently under the table, and I know my reprieve is quickly dissipating. Swallowing one last gulp, I neatly place my drink on the table, square my shoulders, and let the alcohol takeover.

"I found out his secret. I know now why he did everything he did in college." I throw it out there so matter-of-factly that the looks of confusion remain in place.

"Babe, we are going to need a little more than that," Jen coddles. I can tell she is barely able to contain herself though; her fingers are hastily tapping on the tabletop, a sign of her impatience.

I clear my throat and wiggle in my chair; the heat of the situation is causing me to sweat, and my comfort level is now at DEFCON 5. I wipe the moisture from my hands on a napkin on the table, and I begin to tear it into little shreds.

"You're killing us here; tell us the fucking story already!" We all turn to look at Carly, whose out-of-character outburst has taken us all by surprise. Her eyes widen, and her hand flies to her mouth to cover the verbal eruption. She slowly uncovers her lips and looks around the table, searching for forgiveness. "I just mean," she stutters, "I...we are dying to find out what this is all about. Please stop stalling, and tell us what happened. We thought you guys had moved past everything and the relationship was good. We were all putting bets in on when you guys were getting engaged."

"Well, you can hang on to your Benjamins, ladies; I think this relationship might just be O-V-E-R." I attempt to be nonchalant, but saying the words aloud slaps me in the face, and I feel the pain of its finality. As much as his dishonesty has injured me, I don't think I can really let him go.

Jen waves her hand, urging me to continue and clarify. I take another swig to numb my bruised heart, and inhale deeply to prepare for the next part of the story.

"You all know that my father was killed when I was a little girl, right?" Everyone nods, but Jen scowls; the lines between her brows deepen and her lips purse.

"Brooks' dad was the one that killed him. He's known since college, but never told me. Instead, he disappeared. This time, I guess he thought he could just keep it from me. But when his father showed up on his doorstep when I was there, his secret spilled out."

"That piece of shit!" Jen blurts out. "Get the supplies; it's ball-busting time!"

"Everyone, just calm down," I snip. "I don't think we need to go to that extreme."

"I don't understand why he wouldn't just tell you. I get that the situation sucked in every way, but why would he hide it? Especially if he wanted to marry you?"

"I have no idea. Maybe he thought I'm too stupid to figure it out on my own, or maybe he thought I would never cross paths with Raymond Michaels, so it would never come up. Really, who knows? To be honest, I'm not sure I want to know at this point."

All of the previous confusion fades and a mixture of emotions stares back at me. Jen is obviously angry and ready for blood. She would defend me until the day I die, whether I was in the right or not, and I'm so thankful for a friend like her. Carly just looks sad; you would think I ran over her dog or something. She looks as crushed as I feel, and the sympathy is pouring out of her.

Campbell, on the other hand, has been very silent. I'm sure that Jen caught her up on all of the drama while it played out in front of her, so there is no need to go through the back-story with her. She has always been the down-to-Earth, call-it-like-she-sees-it friend, who told you how it was, even if it meant that you were wrong or made you feel like shit. Love it or hate it about her, she always meant well. We are the only family she really has, and we love her like a sister. Her silence means she is overanalyzing the situation, and I'm probably not going to like her conclusion.

"Okay, Cam, give it to me," I sigh. "I know the gears in that head of yours are cranking, so give it to me."

She hesitates, which only makes me scoot farther towards the edge of my seat. She still hasn't said anything to me, only given me a half-hearted smile, which is Campbell code for, 'you don't want to hear what I'm going to say.'

"Oh, shit, that bad? Just spit it out already," Jen interrupts. I pin Jen with my eyes, silently scolding her for the interruption.

"Sorry," she mumbles and looks down at the table.

"Look, I'm not sure I know the whole story here. It's been a long time since there was ever a 'you and Brooks'. After you were over, you planned your forever with Will, so this is all a little overwhelming for me."

I'm taken off-guard by the direction of her speech, and all I can manage is a slight nod.

"No one ever would have thought that Will would die so young or that Brooks would enter your life again so soon after, but here you are widowed and in love with the man you—we all—swore to hate."

I adjust on the chair, ready to defend him, but she holds her hand up to stop my interjection. I'm not even sure what I would really say. What he's done is not something to defend, but I don't like the idea of people hating him, either. I certainly don't hate him, angry with him, yes. If I'm being honest with myself, I still love the prick. But that doesn't mean that I can pretend like he didn't lie to me.

"Viv, I've never shared a lot about my childhood with you guys. Jen probably knows the most, and even that is not a lot. Does that mean that I lied to you?"

"No, of course not. Those are your stories to share, and we would never make you feel like you had to tell us anything." I grab her hand, reassuring her of my feelings about her, and the horrible life she had bouncing around the foster care system.

"I had some great fosters, and some monsters for fosters, but the thing about it is, I could control none of those situations. Some of the children of those monsters were the very ones that protected me from being hurt worse. It was what I endured, and am I proud of some of the things that happened? No. Do I tell people everything that happened to me? No. That doesn't make me a liar; it makes me human."

"Of course, Cam, we love you. You're like a sister to us, and we would never think differently of you because of what happened when you were younger. If you didn't tell us, you had your reasons," I add.

"Campbell, hun, what does this have to do with Brooks?" Carly asks.

Campbell huffs with annoyance at our slow uptake. "Seriously, guys, you don't see where I'm going with this?"

We all shake our heads.

"Well, no fucking wonder you are in the position you're in," she sighs, which completely pisses me off. I knew I wasn't going to like this conversation, but damn.

"I knew it ten years ago, and I know it now. Brooks loves you, Vivian. That man would do anything in his power to protect you, even if it means hiding something from you in order to keep you from being hurt. Brooks didn't tell you about his biological father because he wanted to guard you from the pain of knowing the truth that he struggled with. Right or wrong, his biggest fear is that you would judge him for something that he has no control over. When you found out, you ran; you proved every one of those fears correct."

Well, shit. That just makes me feel like a big piece of judgmental crap. Will always told me how important it was to consider the perspective of the other person and sometimes a person needs to judge the intention and not the action to understand a situation. This is a prime example, and I utterly failed.

"Damn you, Campbell," I say, finishing off my drink. "It was easier to just be mad at him."

She laughs and finally picks up her neglected gin and tonic to take a small sip. It's a rarity to see Campbell drink; she usually orders a gin and tonic, but then nurses it all night long. It's her way of being with all of us without drinking, which is something that makes her a little uncomfortable. I've never seen her intoxicated.

"So you see, hun," she says, placing the full drink back on the table. "Brooks didn't tell you because he thought it would change how you feel about him. It's the same reason why I don't share my past with people. He wanted you two to have a happily ever after, and you knowing the truth could prevent that."

"Still, I think he should have told her," Carly adds. "How do you have a relationship without being completely honest with the other person? That doesn't seem fair."

Carly's thoughts were exactly where I was at before this conversation. Campbell was right. Brooks was just trying to protect both of our hearts. His tattoo is all about seeking forgiveness, and all this time I figured it was only about the faking-cheating-disappearing act he put together in college. Really, it's more than that. It's about me forgiving who he is; it's about me accepting him, even with the father that he has. This entire time he has been silently begging me to save him, but instead, I let him drown.

Well, fuck that. I'm done being the weak one. It's time for a grown-up Vivian; one that will eat alone at a restaurant, one that will finally confront the man that killed her father, and one that won't quietly let this relationship slip through her fingers. If Brooks needs a life preserver, I'm going to bring the whole damned Armada.

I feel my breathing pick up and my face flush. This determination thing is sending my heart rate into dangerous levels. Before anyone can answer Carly, I push back my chair and jump down from the stool. I grab Campbell and squeeze tightly, whispering a heartfelt thank you in her ear before pulling away.

"What are you doing? Where are you going?" Jen asks as I gather my purse.

"I have a lot to get done for what I plan on doing tomorrow. Don't worry, I'll call you." I blow them a kiss and turn to rush into the crowd, towards the door.

32

Saturday

VIVIAN

It took every bit of willpower not to text Brooks back last night after we both left the bar. I shoved my phone between my mattresses and then continued to toss and turn throughout the night with his words rolling around in my head. When I woke up this morning, it took an entire pot of coffee to revive myself from the dead. I busied myself with as many activities as possible throughout the morning; I made the kids chocolate chip pancakes, we went to an early movie, and Amanda even went with us out to lunch. Now I'm sitting outside a place I never thought I'd be, waiting for a person I never in a million years ever wanted to talk to.

It took over an hour to get to the United Postal Service distribution center in Commerce City. Raymond rides the RTD from the halfway house in Greeley to his job here each day. Apparently, the company is very selective when hiring prior felons, but because of the degree he earned and the mentoring work he did while incarcerated, he was hired, but with a longer work probationary period. The terms of his parole are extremely strict; missing the bus, missing work, having holes in his schedule that have not been cleared through his parole officer or half-way house supervisor will result in a violation of his parole, and would mean more prison time. So far, he has stayed in line.

I found out from a little internet research on the UPS website what the shift schedules are, and after pretending to be his daughter-in-law when I called the halfway house, I know Raymond will be getting off work at four in the afternoon, and will have to run to catch the bus home that leaves Commerce City by 4:15. So here I sit, in front of the huge warehouse in my freezing car waiting for the man of my childhood nightmares, Raymond Michaels.

My eyes bounce from my phone screen at Brooks' text, to the employee entrance. I'm not even sure why I keep looking at it; the words are burned into my memory. "I'm sorry for everything. I will never stop loving you." I suppose that seeing the words gives me the push I need to remain here waiting for Raymond; they keep me from chickening out.

Last night Campbell made me realize how in love with Brooks I am, and that our connection through our fathers has nothing to do with how we feel about each other. The second he found out the truth, he tried to protect me from knowing it, because he thought keeping me in the dark was the best way to protect me. He had taken on the guilt of his father's sins and hid it from me out of fear of rejection. Now it's my turn to fix this, make him see that I love him no matter who his father is.

The first step, though, is confronting Raymond, and finding out the actual truth about what happened between him and my father. I can't go to Brooks until I make peace with that situation for myself first. I know that I can't just show up to his residence without prior approval, and him riding in my car would also be against the rules, so I plan to follow him and sit next to him on the bus. That gives me at least an hour to talk to him. That's pretty much as far as I got in the planning process. I'm not sure what to do if he refuses to talk to me.

When Raymond walks out the doors, he looks tired and haggard, not only from a hard day's work, but I'm sure from a rough life in general. I can see his breath in the cool air, and he zips up his jacket, throwing the hood over his head to shield himself from the gusty frozen winds. He begins to walk towards the park and ride area, so I quickly grab my purse and tighten my scarf before jumping out of the car.

I shiver from the cold temperatures for a moment before the adrenaline takes over. I take off in the direction that Raymond is walking, making sure to stay at a safe distance. I don't want him to notice me before we get on the bus. If he has the chance to run from me, I'm afraid he will.

My pace quickens from the anticipation, and I have to remind myself to slow down. I struggle to catch my breath as I get in line to buy a bus pass. Note to self: work a little more cardio into the daily workout, because I look and feel pretty pitiful right now. I see Raymond board the bus, but I hang back with the crowd, slipping on through the back doors. I scan the mass of people, and when I find him sitting alone, I wait until the bus begins to move before I approach. He doesn't seem to notice me, nor does he pay me any attention when I sit down next to him as nonchalantly as possible.

I look straight ahead and focus on steadying my breathing. My stomach is doing flip-flops. I don't know how I ever found the courage to be here, doing this, but here I am. That's not true; I know exactly where this bravery is coming from: Brooks. My love for him is driving me to confront my past so that I can move forward with my future. If I want him, and I sincerely do, then I have to do this.

My mouth opens to speak several times, but I find no words; my lips are met with silence. I don't want this conversation to end before it even begins, or be escorted off the bus for some sort of public disturbance, so I have to choose my tactic carefully. I had everything mapped out in my mind, the conversation playing over and over in my head while I waited in the car. But now, I'm at a loss.

Giving myself more time, I twist off my scarf and pull off my gloves, tucking them all into my giant purse. My hands are shaking, and I try to hide the display of nerves by wringing my hands together in my lap. When I feel large warm hands cover mine, I startle, almost jumping completely out of my bus seat.

"Hello, Vivian. I have to say, I'm surprised to see you, especially here of all places. I'll assume that this is not a coincidence, considering you followed me from the distribution center." I gasp, and he responds by patting my hands and then returning them back to his jacket pockets.

"You don't make it around the block as many times as I have and not know when someone is tailing you," he chuckles. "So what do I owe the honor? Did Brooks not tell you that I swore to stay away from the two of you, and that I was bowing out?"

"I didn't give him the chance to tell me," I say, tilting my head down in embarrassment.

"Well, sounds to me like you're following the wrong person, little lady."

"No," I say adamantly, raising my eyes to meet his. "I'm exactly where I need to be. Brooks and I don't have a future—no matter where you fit into the equation—if I don't have this conversation with you first."

"Okay, then, my ride is plenty long to get whatever you need to off your chest. I'm all ears." Raymond takes his hands out of his pockets and crosses his arms across his chest, leaning back in his seat like he's getting comfortable to hear a massive ear-chewing.

"No, Raymond, I'm here to hear you talk. I want to know what happened that night with my father. I want to know what happened when Brooks went to visit you ten years ago. And you're right; you have over an hour to tell me, which is plenty of time."

He immediately sits up straighter, surprised at my demands. "There's nothing I can't tell you that you can't read in the police and trial records," he says, looking away from me out the window.

"That's bullshit and you know it. Brooks and I both read the records ten years ago, and there were plenty of holes. It's time you filled in the gaps for me."

The way he shifts in his seat, I can tell this trek down memory lane is extremely uncomfortable for him. Shit, it's uncomfortable for me too, but how I see it is that he owes me at least this.

He remains silent, and I quickly realize that I need to do or say something to save this conversation because it's going nowhere fast. "Look," I sigh, "I know enough to realize that my father was no saint. I understand that he was into something that got him into a situation that more than likely got him killed. But I don't know the details. I'm just looking for someone to fill in the gaps, and the only person who can do that is you."

Raymond finally looks at me, torment written all over his face, and then stares down at his hands he has begun to slowly rub together. "I'm not sure what you what to hear, Vivian. One of the reasons I took the plea bargain, the same reason your mother agreed to the plea bargain, was so you would never find out the negative things about your father. He was a good man that got wrapped up in the bullshit that I was always finding myself waist-deep in, but this time, we both got in way too deep."

I lean back in my seat, mimicking his earlier attitude. "Why don't you start at the beginning," I say, crossing my arms in front of my chest.

Raymond brings his hands to his face, rubbing his palms over his eyes. I can't tell if he's expecting me and this situation to disappear when he opens his eyes again or if he's trying to force the memories of his past to the surface. Either way, I feel no pity for this man, only disdain for his actions. Finally, he lowers his hands, looking straight ahead, and begins the story I've waited the last twenty years to hear.

"He gave me a job when no one else would. I had been in and out of trouble most of my life, but your dad took a chance on me and gave me a job. I was so thankful, so when he told me about his goal of wanting to open a second store, I thought I owed it to him to help."

"The police records said it was a burglary. This whole best friend picture you're painting doesn't make much sense," I say, my irritation in the direction of his story evident in my tone.

"The road to hell is paved with good intentions, little lady." His crystal blue glare pins me through the corner of his eye.

I nod and wave him on to continue.

"So like a said, I wanted to help. I knew some people from my younger days, suppliers that were making big money in the dope rings, and were venturing out into other arenas—guns, prostitution—the regular scores. I knew that by getting back into dealing I could make a huge chunk of change that could go to the new store. The way we worked it out, it was very palatable to your old man."

"How was everything supposed to operate?" I ask, shocked that my dad, the guy that promised cartoon Saturdays and fort-building sleepovers, would have anything to do with illegal drug and gun dealings.

"Your dad's store profit would be the bank roll. I would use the funds to buy from the suppliers and then hike up prices, deal it out to old contacts, pay off the suppliers, and then your dad would get his money back and then some. The plan was pretty perfect, and worked like a charm; your dad had his new store in half the time we thought it would take."

"Hold on," I say, scooting to the edge of my seat, facing him. "You want me to believe that you went back to the underbelly of society out of the goodness of your heart, just to help out my dad for giving you a job. That is the biggest joke I've ever heard. No one does crap like that."

"Believe whatever you want; I'm telling you how it was. Take it or leave it. Now, was I helping just out of the goodness of my heart? No. I was a different person back then. I saw an opportunity to help us both, and I took it. With the dough rolling in, I took a cut of the profit, and it was supporting some of my side businesses."

"So what went wrong?"

"I started using again. I was snorting and smoking more than I was selling, and I started getting behind paying back the suppliers. I always made sure that your dad had his money; he was my money source after all. But then when he was about to open the new store, he wanted out. The suppliers had given me a deadline and if I didn't have the money that I owed them, they were coming after me. These weren't the type of guys that would have stopped there, either; they would have gone after my family. They would have found out about you guys, and hurt you all to get their money back. Whatever it took; they didn't care."

"Come after us?"

"That's how it works, baby girl. Whatever it takes to get the message across."

"So what was the plan, get the last payment from my dad, pay off the people you owed, and just disappear?"

"Pretty much. I thought it would be better than people ending up hurt or dead."

"Except someone did die," I whisper, causing him to lower his head in shame. Silence ensues as he rubs his hand across his face, hiding his eyes from me.

"I never meant to hurt Greg; he was my friend," his voice cracks and stutters over my father's name. I try to keep my emotions in check, but the old wound is slowly ripping apart. "Vivian, you have to understand; I just got so scared, and I was high out of my mind. When he refused to give me any more money, I panicked."

"So what happened next?" I ask, already knowing the answer. I lived the answer. I know what the end result would be. I know that the final conclusion was that my father would not return home that night, but I needed to hear the words from him.

He sighs, stalling with the last piece of the story. The lump in my throat has become unbearable. My salty tears sting my cheeks, but I quickly wipe them away, refusing to let him see my hurt. He notices and reaches for my hands once again, but I pull away. "Finish the story, Raymond. I'm not here for your comfort; I'm here for the truth."

He hastily retreats and nods in understanding. When he begins his story once again, we both are looking forward, unable to look at each other. "We began to argue, and then it got physical. It escalated so fast; I couldn't control it. I just snapped. One minute we were wrestling on the ground, and then next I was squeezing his neck. When he stopped fighting, stopped moving, I knew I killed him."

"So you just left him there?" I ask as a sob breaks free.

My loss of control garners the attention of the passenger in front of us. The older gentleman, at least in his seventies, turns around, analyzing the situation. He glares at Raymond before turning compassionate eyes toward me. "Ma'am, is everything all right here? Is this man bothering you?"

I attempt a half-hearted smile and wave him off. "No sir," I say, slightly tilting my head in appreciation for his concern. "Thank you for asking, but we are fine." He looks back and forth between Raymond and me for a few more seconds before turning around and returning his attention to the newspaper that he had been reading. When I see that it's safe to continue, I nod to Raymond to go on.

He shifts in his seat, wiping his palms on his pant legs, and then begins the rest of his story. "I grabbed the money to pay the suppliers and left. As soon as the debt was paid, I skipped town. I knew all roads would lead to me, and it was only a matter of time before they figured out it was me so I ran. I didn't get far. With the drug habit I had, and the lack of connections, it was only three days before I got picked up, and well, you know the rest."

I take a few cleansing breaths to pull myself together. "So tell me about Brooks; where does he fit into all of this?" I ask when I can finally speak clearly, without the high-pitch squeal that usually takes over my voice when crying is involved.

"I wasn't a father, never wanted to be a father. The life I led wasn't cut out for a family. His mother and I had a brief fling, and when I found out she was pregnant, I took off, plain and simple. I heard through some people I knew that she met someone and got married and that he adopted Brooks and had more kids. So I left it alone."

"What, so he just never knew about you, or that you were in jail?"

"He eventually learned that his stepfather wasn't his real dad. When he was in middle school, I tried to contact him, you know, to get to know him. His mother, though, didn't want me anywhere near him, so she wrote to me and told me to stay away. Since I never heard from him, I assumed that she never gave him any of my letters."

"But he went to see you in prison? How did that come about?"

"Don't you think this is something that he should be telling you?" he asks his disapproving tone obvious. I'm stabbed with guilt, because I absolutely realize that this is something that I should have been brave enough to ask Brooks myself. I should have given him the opportunity to explain the situation the first time he pleaded with me, but instead, I turned my back and walked away.

I narrow my gaze at him, deflecting from the guilt that was seeping from my pores. "This from the man that kept his identity from his own son, I think I'll stay away from the dear-old-dad pep talk, but thanks, Ray."

"Touché," he chuckles, shooting me a slimy grin. "All right, fine. After he turned eighteen, I found out where he was going to college and was able to get an address for him in the dorms. I started to write to him, knowing that his mother couldn't keep me away anymore. I was shocked as shit when he wrote back, and we continued corresponding for a few months. I never told him why I was in jail; he asked but I avoided the question. Eventually, I asked if he would visit. He avoided that question as well. Until…"

"…until he went with me to research the case," I say, finishing his sentence.

"You got it. When he found out everything, he agreed to see me. It was not the father/son get-together I had envisioned. He was upset and angry with me, which I understood. More than anything, he didn't care about him and me; he was upset about you. He didn't know what to do, if he should tell you what he found out, or keep it a secret. I gave him the only fatherly advice I had, which wasn't saying much."

"You told him to run, like you had."

Raymond turns his attention to me, taking offense to my statement. "I told him that if you found out the truth, it would only hurt you," he snaps. "I told him that if he really loved you, he needed to let you go."

I look past Raymond, out the bus window. I stare at the wintery scenery that has changed from open fields to city lights as we approach Greeley. I let his words sink in; not only about the night my dad died, but about the advice he gave Brooks.

After several more minutes, Raymond's voice breaks through my thoughts. "Vivian, we are almost there, is there anything else you would like to ask me?"

I blink and shake my head, attempting to bring myself back to the present. "I'm sorry, what did you say?" I murmur.

"I asked if there was anything I could help you with?" he asks once more.

"Actually, yes, there is something I want you to do," I say, clearing my throat. "I have a proposition for you."

"I'm an ex-con on parole for murder, Vivian. I have absolutely no skills, no reputable connections, and I have done things to your family and mine that are unforgivable."

I gather as much courage as I can scrape together and look him straight in the eye. "That is exactly why you need to do what I'm going to ask of you. It's time I forgive, and it's time that you find redemption within yourself."

Squaring his shoulders to me like I was going to deliver some underworld job to him, I match his posture. "My husband died last year in an accident where the driver fell asleep," I begin. With that information, his shoulders slouch, deflating as my words hit him. "Every man that I've ever loved has been taken from me because of the mistakes of others."

"I don't understand, Vivian. How can I help here? I can't change the past."

"No, but you can help change the future of those that are on the same path you were on. I want to start a foundation to help at-risk teens get their lives on track. Help them go to college, get training, find a support system so that they don't end up where you and I are now."

"What would you need me to do?"

"Do what you did today; share your story. I want you to be a mentor for these kids, just like you were for the guys in prison. Help steer these kids onto the right path; they need to see how hard the wrong path can be. Only you can show them that."

"Why are you doing this? Most people wouldn't want anything to do with someone that's done the things I've done."

The brakes on the bus screech, and we all lurch forward from the sudden stop. When the bus driver announces our destination, I grab my purse, dig out my business card, and stand to let Raymond get off the bus. I know that he can't be late, so this conversation has to end.

Raymond stands when I enter the aisle to let him pass. "My family has endured a lot because of bad choices. It's only right that something positive be born from that misery," I say, placing my card in his hand. He only stares down at the card lying flat on his palm, not moving any further into the aisle. "If I can prevent one family from experiencing what mine has, then this was all worth it."

He closes his fingers around my card and begins to pass by me, but before he can get out of reach, I grab his elbow, forcing him to stop. "When you're ready to travel down the path of redemption, let me know."

His eyes finally reach mine, and I briefly hold his gaze until the doors of the bus begin to close. I pull down on the cord above our seats, alerting the driver that a passenger needs to get off the bus just as Raymond yells to the driver. Without looking at me again, he runs down the aisle of the bus and exits.

I sit back down and pull out my phone to put in motion the next step of my plan. I'm going to need the help of the entire crew. After I text everyone, I lean back and settle in for the ride home. I have more than an hour before I'll be back at my car. Hopefully, it's enough time to come up with how to explain everything to Amanda. I've left her pretty much in the dark, so the much-needed conversation won't exactly be pretty. To say I'm not looking forward to the argument headed my way is putting it lightly.

33

Wednesday

BROOKS

I about shit myself when I got the call Saturday evening from Jen, of all people. She didn't say much just that I needed to meet with her tonight, Wednesday, at Three Kings Tavern. Just the place I want to be, reliving one of the worst fucking days of my life. She didn't have to say what she wanted to talk about; I know what's on her agenda, and it probably includes some kind of humiliating public torture, followed by testicle removal. Considering I might lose an appendage, I guess tonight might get bumped up to *the* worst night of my life. Good thing we'll be at a bar. I'm going to need a lot of alcohol.

I told Lakin to show up in an hour to save me from the she-devil. Of course, being my brother and wanting forgiveness for his support system fuck-up Friday night, he not only agreed, but also promised to show up sooner and hang out in the wings.

I'm not surprised when I walk through the doors to see that the place is not all that busy. It's a Wednesday, after all. I came straight from work, so I'm still in my pristine charcoal suit and black dress shoes. Needless to say, I don't match the décor. I dressed up on Friday because I thought I was going to get my girl back and propose. Tonight, I just stick out like a sore thumb, and the looks that I'm getting as I pass the people enjoying their evening tells me that I'm right–I look like an out-of-place douche.

I squeeze through the small clusters of patrons in my hunt for Jen. Finally, I find her, sitting alone at a bar top that would seat a whole hell of a lot more people than just the two of us. The size of the table leads me to believe that I'm walking into an ambush. I look around, scanning the crowd for Amanda and Carly. If

Campbell is still in town, I'm sure she will be here, too. Damn my luck.

I saunter up to the table and give Jen my best 'hi, but what the fuck is going on?' look. Her response is a little-miss-innocent smile, but I know better than to ever really trust this firecracker. While I know that she held my secret for so long, I also know that she is passionately loyal to Vivian and would do anything to protect her, even if it's at the expense of my limbs. "Where is the rest of your posse?" I ask as I slide onto the barstool across from her.

"They are here somewhere. The band is playing again tonight, so Campbell is probably backstage, and knowing Carly, she's in the bathroom calling home to check on Olivia," she answers before tipping back her Coors Light beer to take a quick drink. She wipes her mouth and then calls a server over. "I wasn't sure what you would be in the mood for, or I would have ordered you something."

"Well, my order would kind of depend on what type of meeting this is. Do I need something to dull the pain, or am I here on friendly terms?"

She looks past me into the crowd, then up to the server, and then back to me, causing me to turn around in my chair in an attempt to follow her visual search. "He'll have a beer, as well, please," she says to the waitress without addressing me at all. I don't really appreciate her speaking over me. I should order something different just to piss her off, but if she's going to play nice, then, I suppose I will, too.

"Okay, Jen, what is this all about? You and I both know that I've lost Vivian for good, so I'm not quite sure why I'm here unless you're just looking for extra bitch points and want to rub it in my face. If that's the case, I don't plan on sticking around."

The server returns with my drink and I take a long pull, staring at her over the neck of the bottle. Her response is only to tap her fingers on the table like I'm boring her.

"Look, you know I want Vivian to be happy, and if that's with you, great. If not, well, I'm fine with that, too," she snarls once I place my drink back on the table.

"Don't sugar-coat anything on my account, Jen," I bark back. "What a great friend you are," I add, allowing my sarcasm to hang in the air.

"That's why I'm here, dickhead. I'm her best fucking friend, and she has been miserable since you guys crashed and burned."

"What? You're going to help me get her back?" I ask, leaning onto the table, now finding interest in this convoluted conversation.

"Sorry, my part's already done. I just had to get you here. Sit back, relax, and drink your beer; you have a lot in store for you tonight."

"What the fuck, Jen? I don't think this is very funny." I feel myself getting angry. I know Jen can be sneaky, but damn, this woman has taken her skills to a new level. I feel fucking stupid and gullible. I'm sitting here sharing a beer with someone that has nothing to say to me, and has no intention of helping me get Viv back. What a complete waste of time. "You need to tell me what's going on," I demand.

"You need to do as you're told," she says, picking up her beer and purse from the bar top. "Now if you'll excuse me, I need to use the ladies." She tips her beer to me in a goodbye, and leaves me alone at the table.

What the fuck just happened?

I start peeling the label off my beer waiting for what, I have no clue. I'm not even sure why I'm still here. I guess my curiosity is piqued enough to stick around for a little longer. I'm sure all of Vivian's girls will take their turns lecturing me on what a piece of shit I am, then I'll be let loose to crawl home alone and wallow in self-pity like I have for the last few days since Vivian told me she never wanted to see me again. I keep hoping that she'll change her mind and call or text, something. I still carry around her ring in my jacket pocket. I can't bring myself to return or sell it. Having it close to me makes me feel like I still have her, and I'm not ready to let her go. I've never been able to let that woman go.

I'm alone for only a few more minutes before my next girl-of-college-past appears and takes a seat at the table. At least this one is a little more benign. "Hello, Carly, good to see you. What do I owe the pleasure?"

"Cut the shit, Brooks. I'm not exactly thrilled to be here," she sneers.

Okay, maybe I was wrong. Mad Carly is something new, and I'm not sure I like it. I decide silence is my best means of protection, so I just raise my hands in surrender.

"I know everything that happened, and I don't like it, Brooks. Vivian is my friend. I love her like a sister, and that's why I'm here. I don't give a flying fuck about you or your happiness, but I do about hers. So I've come here to have a come-to-Jesus meeting with you."

Her fingers are laced together and folded on the table. She has no drink, and her eyes are severely narrowed on me. This is purely business, and in this moment, I feel horrible for the poor shmuck who married her, because Carly can be downright scary. I consider myself a very confident man's man, but this woman is forcing my balls to shrivel and die.

I push my beer away and lean back in my chair, waiting for the wrath to ensue. I gesture for her to continue, which is apparently the wrong move because I see her nostrils flare.

"In college, I thought you were a womanizing man-whore and other than your good looks, I never saw what Viv saw in you. Then when we all thought you cheated on her, I wasn't surprised. To see that your adult life hasn't ventured off that course, it only makes me think less of you. However, whatever you and she had behind closed doors has made her happy. You brought out the Vivian that no one else could. I understand that none of what appeared on the outside was the actual truth of the situation, but I still don't like it. I think Vivian deserves the world, and if you aren't prepared to give it to her, then I suggest you walk away, because even though I seem like the nice one, I promise I have the *best* Rocky Mountain Oyster recipe, and if need be, I know of plenty of places to hide a body. Are you catching my drift?"

Not wanting to poke the bear any more than I already have, I merely nod a response.

"Good. I'll keep an eye on you, Brooks," she says sternly, then like a light switch, she shifts gears and smears a smile on her face. "Enjoy the rest of your evening," she adds sweetly.

Good God that was the most frightening downshift known to man. Here, all this time, I thought Jen was who I needed to worry about, but wrong again. Carly can throw down like no one's business. I flag down the server to order something stronger. If I have to sit through any more lectures, I might drown myself in the alcohol behind the bar.

The waitress slides my Johnnie Walker Black across the table and I take a sip, allowing the burn to reach every centimeter of my throat. I take a second to let my mouth cool down, letting the ice clink in the glass. It provides a nice distraction from the clusterfuck that I just sat through. I bring the glass to my lips once more, and just as I let the amber liquid hit my tongue, I'm lurched forward, causing me to choke on my drink.

I look behind me for the asshole that bumped me, and I'm met with a beaming Lakin. I take a piece of ice from my glass and launch it at him. "You prick, what the hell?" I say through the hacking breaths and tears.

"That's not any way to greet the person who's here to save your sorry ass." He laughs as he takes a seat with his scotch. "Besides, I was just politely patting you on the back; I think you're just a little jumpy. Those women must have put you through the wringer tonight."

"You have no idea, Lakin. This was a waste of time. Let's just finish our drinks and head out. I should be home with Grace anyways; it's a school night."

"Just take it easy there, big brother. The night is still young; Grace is fine. Besides, I think if you stay around long enough, you might find that this evening will turn out better than you expected." The devilish grin that he isn't even attempting to hide does nothing to improve my mood.

"You're in on whatever this is, aren't you?" I say, slugging him in the arm. "You little shithead, you've known what's going on, that those women would corner me like that, and you didn't even give me a heads up. What happened to brotherly love?"

"Hey!" he whines. "You know I bruise like a peach," he adds, rubbing his bicep. I'm not buying the pussy show for a single second; Lakin has competed in mixed martial arts since we were kids. I guarantee that punch hurt me more than it did him.

"Suck it up, Nancy; you have some explaining to do."

He only laughs and takes another slow drink of his scotch. His eyes leave mine and track someone behind me. I turn around to see Campbell approaching the table. Fucking marvelous. The next girl-of-college-past is here for one last kick to the balls. Lakin is seriously going to pay for this. If the fucker didn't have his own money, I might have considered cutting him from my will.

She looks like some kind of 1950s pinup. Her ebony hair half pinned on top of her head and bright red lipstick match her red dress and black open-toe heels. For someone that never ventured far from her Hendrix tee, jeans, and Converse, she looks drastically different. Grown-up and sophisticated, her friendly demeanor is now mixed with a blend of confidence and sex appeal that Cam not only lacked, but avoided when I knew her before. I look to Lakin, and yes, he's taken notice. I give him a look that says 'put your tongue in your mouth and your eyes back in your head before I help you adjust your face.' He complies, and we both stand when she's within a few feet of the table. She holds a hand up and smiles, gesturing for us to sit back down. "There's no need, Brooks. I come in peace; take a load off." She laughs.

Her warm, easy smile melts into me, and I remember again why I liked Cam; she was never overly dramatic like Jen or emotional like Carly. She gave everyone a fair break, which was more than she ever got. I never really had friends that were girls, but Cam was that girl that I considered worthy of the label. She really cares for people, like Vivian does, and she has a quality that makes you want her to be taken care of. I wish I could have kept in contact with her, but considering how things ended with Vivian in college, having contact with anyone from that time wouldn't have been possible.

I stand up anyway, and reach out to give her hug. I always knew that she was the one that talked Viv into giving me a chance back in college, and even if she and I won't be together anymore, I'm grateful for the brief time I had with Vivian, and I owe that to Campbell. The least I could do is show my appreciation.

She taps my back, barely returning my embrace. I forgot how uncomfortable she is with physical affection, so I give her one more squeeze and take my seat. "It's good to see you, Cam," I say while Lakin pulls out a chair for her. Yeah, I can see the wheels in his head turning—*good luck with that, baby bro.* I would eat my own foot if Cam ever agreed to date my brother. She gives him a look of appreciation, which only encourages my brother even more. I take a drink and roll my eyes; this is definitely not why I'm here.

She finally directs her attention back to me when Lakin sits down, pushing his chair closer to Campbell. "Have you figured out why you're here yet, Brooks?" she asks, skipping over all introductory niceties.

"I don't know what to think, Cam. At first, I thought I was invited here to receive the royal ass-chewing of a lifetime, and then I thought maybe you guys were going to help me win Vivian back.

Now that even Lakin is in on this master plan, whatever it is, I have no fucking clue. But I would really like to be filled in; all of this is getting pretty damn old. Is Vivian here? Or did you girls plot to make me look like the prick that I already feel like I am?"

"She's here, Brooks." Those simple three words cause me to spring out of my chair, and I begin looking around for her. Vivian brought me here. Her girls were hurdles, and who the fuck knows if I passed, but if she brought me here, maybe that means she still wants me, could still love me. I feel myself begin to sweat and breathe heavily with anticipation and nervousness to see her. I'm so zoned-in on finding her that I completely tune out what Campbell is saying until I feel her grab my arm and pull me back to my chair.

"You won't find her. She's here, but I'm not quite ready for you to see her yet," she says, reclining into the back of her chair and crossing her legs. I turn around but remain standing; if Vivian is here, I want to see her. I'm done with the bullshit games these women have put me through tonight.

"What do you mean you're not ready for me to see her? Don't you think that this is between Vivian and me? I'm not sure why all three of you have stepped in tonight like middle men. We are fucking grown adults, who should be working things out like adults." I stand, shoulders squared and arms crossed, ready for the fight that I've been waiting for all night. I'm tired of playing nice; if Vivian is ready to talk to me, then she needs to get her ass out here and talk to me.

Campbell begins to laugh hysterically. She doubles over, placing her head on the table, and when she leans back up to gather air, she has to wipe tears from her eyes. I glance over to Lakin, and he looks as lost as I am. What the fuck is happening tonight? I have entered some kind of estrogen-induced twilight zone. Cam was my only chance of escaping and getting to Vivian, and now it looks as though she too has overdosed on the Kool-Aid.

"Sorry, Brooks," she says, trying to catch her breath. "It's just, you have absolutely no reason to get all worked up; in fact, you're about to get everything you ever wanted. I just need you to calm the fuck down and answer a few questions for me."

"Are you kidding me? You tell me Vivian is here, but you want me to play a round of twenty questions? This has to be a joke."

"Look, Brooks, I like you; I always have. I know good people and bad people, and you're good people. Jen and Carly don't see it, but Vivian and I do. I want to help, but I won't unless you answer a few questions first."

I plop down in my seat in a huff, cross my arms once again, and give her the nod to ask away.

Cam takes a napkin from the center condiment island and dabs her make-up, which ran during her hysterics, and takes a drink of the water that the server brought over soon after she arrived at the table. Cam has been here a lot with the current band she's promoting, and I'm sure the workers here are familiar with her dislike of alcohol.

She settles herself and begins to fire away. "When you set Vivian up to think that you cheated, was it to avoid telling her about your father?"

Well, we definitely aren't going to ease in with some simple ones, are we? I should have known they would have sent Campbell in for this type of inquisition. I lean in on the table, rubbing my face in my hands, contemplating my answer. I know that I can't lie to Campbell; besides, she would see right through me. "I wasn't trying to avoid anything, Cam," I sigh. "If I knew that she would have still loved me despite who my father is, I would have told her and let her decide. But I loved her too much to put her in that position. I knew that if I left, made her believe that I wasn't worth chasing after, then she would have found Will. He cared about her, always had. I thought he was the better man, and she deserved to be with someone like that."

"That's what I thought. So why didn't you tell her this time around?"

My back straightens at her tone. It feels like she's implying that I was maliciously trying to keep things from Vivian.

"I wanted to; I tried so many times. But I couldn't bring myself to do it. The more I thought about it, the more I thought about what it might change. I don't have contact with Raymond. He's never been a part of my life. Nothing would come from her knowing, other than hurting her, and I would do anything to keep from hurting her. But then he showed up, and my plan crumbled. I had to face it, but this time she ran."

"You know I, more than anyone, understand where you're coming from, Brooks, but not trusting her with the truth, protecting her or not, was a bit on the shady side," she calmly says as she rubs my forearm. Her attempt to comfort me throws me a bit; it is very out of character for her.

"One more question, I swear," she says, removing her hand and squaring her shoulders. "Do you promise to love that woman the way she deserves and never keep anything from her again, whether it's for her own good or not?"

I match her posture and meet her eyes, trying to convey every ounce of emotion I have into my final answer for her. "Campbell, I love Vivian more than I thought was ever even possible. Whether I'm with her or not, she is the only one that I could ever want. All I've ever wanted to do is give her what she deserved, even when I thought she deserved more than what I am. I would be honored just to have the chance to try and be that man for her."

She smiles, and I can see the tears beginning to build in her eyes. I try to hand her a napkin, but she shoos me away. "That's all I needed to know, Brooks. Hang tight. We will all be back soon."

"Vivian too?" I ask anxiously as we all stand up from the table.

"She smiles and pats my arm. "Vivian too." She turns to Lakin and offers her hand to shake but he immediately grabs her fingers and guides her hand to his lips. "It was lovely to meet you, Campbell," he says smoothly, and then kisses the back of her hand. She peers over to me, and I act like I'm going to throw up, which makes her laugh. Lakin backs away and shoots a death glare at me.

Cam turns on her heel and leaves us men alone once again. Lakin follows her with his eyes until she becomes lost in the crowd. Damn, this kid is clueless. He wouldn't have a shot in hell with Campbell. I slap his back, similar to how he did when he greeted me, and take my seat again, laughing.

"What?" he asks, offended.

"Don't even think about it; Cam is out of your league, and she's not the type to play. It's all or nothing with that girl."

"What, like I couldn't be serious?"

"That's exactly what I'm saying, Lakin. She's not the type that would go for you, let alone have anything to do with a guy like you."

"Well, fuck you, too, big brother."

"Oh now, don't take offense. She's just on a different wavelength; that's all."

"Whatever." He slouches back, completely pissed. He'll have to get over it; I wouldn't let him near Campbell any more than I

259

would have let him near Amanda when we went to the zoo. Those situations always collect collateral damage. No, thank you.

I laugh at his childish response and excuse myself to go to the restroom. I need a break from the emotional whirlpool that this table has become tonight. The bar is quickly filling up for the band that is supposed to take the stage soon. As soon as I step away, I already feel the weight of the previous conversations begin to lift. I'm hopeful that when I return, Vivian might be sitting there, and I can finally have the chance to explain things to her and not her friends. Her face is the only one I want to see.

Vivian

"Oh, my God, I think I'm going to throw up. Is he really out there? Do you think he'll leave when he sees me? There is a reason why men are supposed to do this; women are too emotional for this."

Amanda fluffs my hair for the hundredth time, and I smack her away. She's been quiet since I explained everything to her, but after I gave her a little time to digest it all, she was supportive. The calls home were not as pretty, but I wasn't expecting them to be. They will get over it; they always do. Even if my family is not entirely on board, I'm glad my friends are helping to pull this off. Even Katie stepped in to watch all the kids tonight, and agreed to keep it from Brooks.

Jen swoops in with a shot of vodka. "Here, hun, drink this; it will take the edge off." She places the glass in my hand and physically moves it to my mouth. I throw it back, feeling the familiar burn of the alcohol, and I shiver as it makes its way down my throat.

"Like a champ!" Jen whoops before slapping my ass. The sound of her hand on my ass cheek echoes loudly, matching my yelp. I'm wearing the same tight green number that I wore on my first date with Brooks, so I would bet there is a red hand print under the thin fabric of the dress that would match the hair on top of my head.

"Geez, Jen, settle down," I complain as I delicately rub my ass, trying to lessen the sting. Campbell joins us backstage, eyeing the situation before her. "Jen is a little amped up, and is having trouble keeping her hands to herself," I explain.

"Just as long as she keeps her hands off my band," Cam laughs. "Brooks is ready whenever you are. Jen and Carly got him wound pretty tight, but I think you guys are ready."

"Excuse me?" I scowl at Jen. "You were supposed to get him here, and then you guys were supposed to keep him entertained to *keep* him here, not interrogate him. What did you guys do?"

"Oh, settle down, Viv," Carly interrupts. "He's fine, no permanent damage done. Besides, we didn't say anything that didn't need to be said."

I look to Cam for reassurance, and am met with a supportive yet half-hearted smile. "He said everything that I needed to hear; I can honestly say that you deserve the man that's waiting for you out there."

I pull her into a tight hug, which surprisingly she returns. "Thank you," I whisper, and I feel her nod into my shoulder.

"Now, go get him," she says, backing away.

I take a deep breath and take a peek out at the swelling crowd mingling around the stage. The urge to throw up flares up once more, then I step away from the curtain to gain my bearings. I look back once more to my dearest friends, who are all silently encouraging me to get my ass out on the stage to take the leap that I've waited ten years to have the opportunity for. I close my eyes to take in the moment, letting my mind clear of all the pent-up anxiety, worries of loss and regret, and fears of rejection that I'm too late. My breath calms and I step out onto the stage, opening my eyes to see a faceless sea of bodies. The crew has turned off the stage lights, leaving a single spotlight directed at me. I can feel my body begin to move more and more towards the microphone, and I send out a silent prayer that I remember to keep my arms down at my sides so I don't flash everyone my ever-expanding pit stains that I can feel developing under my arms.

There was supposed to be a single table with a lamp on it to help me find Brooks in the crowd of people. I look out into the masses and locate the table, but I only see Lakin sitting there. My heart sinks into my stomach at the thought of Brooks leaving, and I look back to my friends for a little extra nudge. They saw and talked to Brooks; they would know if he left, and surely Lakin would have come behind stage to warn me, so I step up to the mic and let my heart spill out.

"Good evening, everyone. I have been given permission to steal the stage for a few minutes, so if you would all bear with me, that would be wonderful." I scan the audience for any dissension in the ranks, and I'm met with complete silence. Any chatter that had filled the void was now eaten up with my awkward address to the mob. In my mind, I keep replaying my mantra I've had since I crafted this plan, 'You're a superstar. You not only wear the big girl panties, you own the panty store.'

"Just a few nights ago, one of the most wonderful men I've had the pleasure of knowing stood up on this exact stage and put his heart out there for me. It was the sweetest gesture anyone has ever done for me, but instead of being forgiving and understanding of his flaws and working through our fears together, I rejected him. I trampled his heart and walked away so viciously, *I* now need to seek *his* forgiveness."

I notice movement towards the back of the crowd of motionless bodies. I don't need to see him to know that Brooks is on his way to me, and it gives me all the incentive I need to continue my speech.

"I need this man to know that I have forgiven his trespasses, and now I'm seeking the same redemption from him. He is my forever, and…"

BROOKS

As soon as I come out of the men's room, I see a crowd that has gathered around the stage. I bypass the route to my table and slowly head in that direction. When I hear Vivian's voice over the speaker system talking about me up on stage last weekend, my leisurely-pace transforms into a speed walk that would make the jazzercise lady proud.

I feel every one of her words absorb into my soul and cannot get to her fast enough. The sea of people before me is frozen in place listening to her plea for me, making it difficult to get to the front. I don't even bother saying excuse me as I bump into people trying to weave through the bodies. I earn a few dirty looks, but I don't give them a second thought, as my entire attention is on the gorgeous woman on stage that is saying everything I could have ever wanted to hear from her.

I come to a standstill when she references my tattoo. She now knows the entire meaning of it, that I've felt that my father's sins were my own, that it was only her who could release me from the debt of that turpitude, and if she accepted me knowing it all, I would give her eternity. I'm still at least fifty feet away from the stage, glued in place, mesmerized by her words like everyone else.

"He is my forever and…"

"Stop!" I shout over the heads in front of me. I know where the rest of that sentence is heading, and I refuse to let her steal the words that she deserves to be told. I have waited since the moment I woke up in her dorm room for the chance to ask her to marry me, and I'll be damned if she asks me first.

The attentive crowd turns to see the source of the disruption, and I begin to race as quickly as I can to the stage, to Vivian. As I pass, people begin to separate, allowing a path for me, and when I reach my destination, I hop onto the stage. Instead of rushing to Vivian right away, I fight that instinct and proceed towards her slowly, waiting for a green light from her. When she smiles at me, that all-consuming body tingling-smile, I storm forward. As soon as I'm within arm's reach, I cup her cheeks and pull her into me, crashing my lips to hers. I want her to feel my forgiveness, my gratitude for hers, and I want her to feel every ounce of love I have for her.

With a slow lingering kiss, I feel her smile against my mouth. "You're here," she whispers.

"My place is where you are, Clover; that is never going to change," I murmur back to her, sealing it with a kiss on her palm.

Looking into her inviting eyes, I see that this my moment to claim this woman as mine forever, and I plan to seize it. I always thought I would be nervous, that I would feel hesitation and stumble through the words, but instead, I'm overwhelmed with the light of this woman and the love she has for me. "Vivian, I have something I need to say," I tell her. She nods, but I can tell I've made her a little apprehensive. I maintain a serious expression, squeeze her hands, and begin my own speech for her.

"I have scars on my heart that you will never begin to understand, but make no mistake, they don't make me weak. They make me strong enough to love you. They make me want to love you more fiercely than anyone will ever be able to love you." I see emotions swirling in her eyes, threatening to pour over onto her rosy cheeks, but I continue. "For a long time, I didn't think I deserved someone as perfect as you, but Vivian, after all of these years, I've finally realized something."

"What's that?" she asks through the tears that have escaped.

"That we are perfect together, and because of that, we deserve each other. I want a forever with you, Red. Will you marry me, and live a forever with me?" I let go of Vivian, reach into my jacket pocket, and take out her ring, holding it out to her, hoping like hell that she'll take it. The spotlight shines on the center diamond, causing sparkles to refract off the ceiling of the club, earning gasps and awes from the entranced crowd.

Vivian's face has morphed into an ugly-cry expression that she tries to use her hands to hide. She manages to nod an answer, and I quickly take her left hand, sliding the ring into place. When I kiss her once again, slamming my body into hers, the audience erupts into applause. Even when the band fills in behind us, their roars don't soften. Within seconds, the girls surround us to yank us backstage, pulling Vivian and me into a group hug. The scene has left me floating. I've entered a bubble of bliss knowing that I now have everything I've ever wanted...my Clover.

The End

Look for Jen's story,

Lead Him Not into Temptation,

releasing
AUGUST 2014

About The Author

Colorado native M.L. Steinbrunn is new to the literary community, but has been in love with the world of fictional characters and plot twists since she was a child. Writing short stories and reading anything she could get her hands on, it could be argued that her hobby borders on an obsession.

She works full-time as a middle school and high school educator and coach in rural Colorado where she and her husband are raising their young children. Through education she has enjoyed guiding others on their paths and helping students build their stories. After countless evenings of discussing story ideas, it was her husband who encouraged her to follow her own path and publish her first novel.

In her free time M.L. enjoys travelling, Amazon one-clicking, watching movies, chauffeuring her children to their one and half million activities, and people watching.

She would like to add a big thank you to everyone that has been overwhelmingly supportive of this incredibly scary and exciting journey.

Where to follow her....

http://www.facebook.com/mlsteinbrunn

http://twitter.com/MSteinbrunn

http://www.goodreads.com/author/show/
7383392.M_L_Steinbrunn

Acknowledgements

There will be many people that know me and my own history that will attempt to piece together scenes of this book as autobiographical. However, I must stress that this story is entirely fictional. The characters and events are creations of my own imagination. While there are some slight similarities, those similarities are pure generalities.

With that said, I would like to thank the many people that helped me to take the first step on this journey...

My Family: The idea to write this book was not my own, my wonderful husband is responsible for this book ever seeing the light of day. After seeing my nose stuck in a Kindle, reading hundreds of books, he encouraged me to pursue writing something for myself. Every time I thought that the task was too large or that no one would want to read the book, he was there to push me forward. He read scenes, gave me input, and took care of the house in the evenings when I needed to reach my word count goal or meet an editing deadline. He and my children have been extremely understanding of this project. Thank you, you guys; Mom will finally cook some good meals and do the laundry.

My Hometown: The first two hundred people that liked my Facebook page, and who continuously commented on my updates were the people within my hometown community. Even knowing that this was a romance novel, my tiny, conservative community supported this endeavor and has encouraged me every step of the way. A few of you even proofread my synopsis, gave input on my cover, and were my behind the scenes cheerleaders.

Indie Author/Blogger Community: I have found this online literary community to be one of the most inspiring and compassionate groups. There have been so many authors and blogs that stepped up to help me, talk me off the ledge, donate, and share announcements. I appreciate every one of you. There are individuals that had a major hand in this project and deserve a special thank you. Becky, Kayla, and all of the betas at Hot Tree Editing: Debbie, Jacqueline, Kristin, Peggy, Sue, and Teri. This team took my ideas and made it a story worth reading. Ari with

Cover it Designs thank you for my gorgeous cover. Jovana at Unforeseen Editing did the formatting for this book, and she made it a work of art, not just words on a page. Tiffany at Chainsdesigns designed my wonderful swag and Lindsey with Daisy Dog Photography and Design created all of my awesome teasers. Nita at BookChick Blog Reviews made my fabulous trailer. All of the blog tours, review tours, and release blitz events were organized by Rachel at Dreams Come True Promotions and Kim with LipSmackin'GoodBooks. You ladies did a wonderful job, and I appreciate all of your hard work.

Readers and Fans: Thank you all so much for taking a chance on this newbie, no name author. This book and all future books in the series are possible because of you. None of my efforts would have mattered if I didn't have your support. Thank you so much for allowing me the opportunity to follow this dream.

Made in the USA
Charleston, SC
24 March 2014